DELIVER

TRICIA MINGERINK

DELIVER

THE BLADES OF ACKTAR

DELIVER

The Blades of Acktar Book Four

Copyright © 2017 by Tricia Mingerink

Published by Sword & Cross Publishing

Grand Rapids, MI

Cover Art by Jesus Da Silva on Fiverr

Typography by Get Covers and Sword & Cross Publishing

Map by Md Shah Alam on Fiverr

Edited by Nadine Brandes

This book is a work of fiction. All characters, events, and settings are the product of the author's overactive imagination. Any resemblance to any person, living or dead, events, or settings is purely coincidental or used fictitiously.

All Scripture quotes are taken from the King James Version of the Bible as found in the public domain.

To God, my King and Father. Soli Deo Gloria

2018 Realm Award - Reader's Choice Finalist

LCCN: 2019907320

ISBN: 978-1-943442-03-4

But we had the sentence of death in ourselves, that we should not trust in ourselves, but in God which raiseth the dead: Who delivered us from so great a death, and doth deliver: in whom we trust that he will yet deliver us.

\- II Cor. 1:9-10

Sheered Rock Hills
Kilm
Flayin Falls
Surgis
Sierra
ACK
Calloday
Nalgar Castle
Aven
Dently
Blathe
Penning
Hakon
Mackton
Glarbon
Keestone
Arroway
Lanson
Dyman
Ably
VERDEN

Eagle
Heights
Sparkling
Cave
The Waste
The Ramparts
N
W
E
S
Walden
Mountainwood
TAR
Ondieda River
Duelstone
Spires Canyon
Uster
Deadgrass
Stetterly
Resistance/Neutral
Towns who supported King Respen

1

To former Blade Martyn Hamish, victory sounded like the thud of an ax.

Martyn had managed not to flinch as the ax severed King Respen's head. He had even kept his composure while he'd been handed clemency for his actions in the Blades.

Now his former best friend Leith Torren was kissing Lady Rennelda Faythe, and Martyn grimaced.

He had to either grimace or punch something. King Respen had been dead for only a few minutes. This chamber, with its deep burgundy rugs and dark wood paneling, was the same room where King Respen had met with his First Blades.

Yet Leith didn't seem to care. After all their years in the Blades serving King Respen, he should've had some respect. Something.

Instead, Leith and Renna smiled and laughed and kissed.

Martyn dragged a hand through his hair and swore

under his breath. Not that anyone was paying enough attention to overhear. Leith and Renna's...distraction made sure everyone's eyes were fixed on them, from former Blade Ranson Harding huddled in the corner to Renna's sister Brandi perched on one of the chairs by the fireplace, smirking and whispering something to Jamie Cavendish, a former Blade trainee. Shadrach, Leith's new best friend, just shook his head and stared at the ceiling.

Prince Keevan's clenched jaw tightened the scar across his cheek and neck, the scar Leith had given him on the night Leith was supposed to kill the prince.

The night Martyn had killed his targets without hesitation. Without regret.

Shadrach Alistair bowed to Prince Keevan. "With your leave, I'd like to prepare the body for transport to Blathe as soon as possible."

King Respen's body. Martyn's stomach tightened. Thanks to Renna's intervention, King Respen would at least have a decent burial in Blathe next to his long-dead wife. But it would hardly be the funeral of a king. More a pauper's grave dug by his enemies.

Prince Keevan waved a hand, and when he spoke, his voice rasped like stone on steel. "Instruct General Stewart about the change of plans. He can organize a few men to bury a decoy coffin in the Sheered Rock Hills. Even the men must believe they're guarding Respen's body."

Because King Respen wouldn't even get the courtesy of a marked grave. No place for former followers to enshrine. If not for one choice there in the final battle, Martyn would've gotten the same sort of unmarked burial.

As Shadrach turned to leave, Martyn shoved away from the wall. "I'm going too."

Shadrach halted, his square jaw clenching. The brown eyes he turned Martyn's way burned. "Why?"

Martyn shrugged. He couldn't explain to Shadrach about duty or a lingering loyalty to King Respen. He wouldn't understand. "It'll take two men to transport the coffin, dig a grave, and bury it, and you can't ask anyone outside of this room to go on this mission with you. Leith is obviously too hurt and Ranson too young. That leaves me."

Shadrach glanced at Leith, but Martyn forced himself not to glance that way as well. Leith would guess Martyn's real reason for wanting to see King Respen properly buried. Did Leith harbor any of the same thoughts? Surely he did. King Respen hadn't been a father to his Blades, but he'd been the closest thing any of them had known for years.

Killer or not, King Respen should have at least one mourner at his graveside.

Shadrach's hand rested on his sword's hilt. "Fine. Come along, then."

Martyn followed Shadrach from the king's chambers, down the dark stairway, and into the passageway that connected the main cobblestone courtyard north of the Great Hall with the grassy Queen's Court on the southern end of Nalgar Castle.

At the edge of the cobblestone courtyard, Martyn paused in the patch of deep shadows. Many of the execution spectators remained in the courtyard, talking in groups or drifting toward the servants' wing. Guards wearing Prince Keevan's silver and green uniforms stood around a knot of well-dressed men, including the silver-haired Lord Beregern of Mountainwood and the tall, angular Lord Norton of Kilm.

Ducking his head, Martyn waited until a contingent of guards marched between him and the lords before he slipped into the courtyard, around the stables, and out of sight. Four and a half years ago, Lord Norton's and Lord Beregern's men had reinforced the soldiers from Blathe as they took Nalgar Castle for King Respen.

Best not to find out what sort of trouble Lord Norton could cause if he spotted Martyn wandering freely around Nalgar Castle, Prince Keevan's decree of clemency rustling in an inner pocket of his shirt. At the very least, Lord Norton could point out Martyn was a Blade to a crowd drunk with vengeance after seeing King Respen's blood spilled on the cobblestones.

Martyn caught up to Shadrach at the door to the section of rooms in the servants' wing that had been turned into a temporary morgue in the aftermath of the battle. General Stewart stood outside, hands clasped behind his back.

While Shadrach caught General Stewart's arm and whispered their two-pronged burial plan, Martyn shoved past them into the dim room. By this time, only a few bodies remained unclaimed. Most had been carted away to their towns or buried on the hill above the castle to reduce the flies and smell.

King Respen's body lay sprawled on a moldy blanket in the middle of the floor, his head unceremoniously tossed next to his arm. Blood still drained from his severed neck, staining the blanket a dark red. Death had reduced his figure to a pitiful, floppy rag of his former self. His eyes no longer burned; his voice no longer boomed.

Kneeling, Martyn gingerly placed King Respen's head in line with his body, tucked his arms along his sides, and wrapped the blanket around him as befitted a corpse.

As he finished, Shadrach and General Stewart entered the room. Shadrach scowled and crossed his arms. "You shouldn't have bothered. The martyrs of Stetterly weren't given the courtesy of proper coffins or shrouds. Respen doesn't deserve more than that."

Martyn bit back a curse and forced himself to take a deep, slow breath of air rancid with decaying body. Only a few minutes ago in the king's chamber, before all the kissing had started, Martyn had promised Leith he'd try to stick around. Even if it meant putting up with Leith's annoying new friends.

General Stewart rested a hand on Shadrach's shoulder. "Let it be. Best if we just get this matter over with as quickly as possible."

Together, Martyn, Shadrach, and General Stewart lifted King Respen's body into a coffin and nailed the lid shut. Shadrach scratched an *x* into the lid with a knife. If not for his promise to Leith, Martyn would've told Shadrach the *x* sort of looked like King Respen's crossed daggers symbol.

Setting the coffin in a corner next to other bodies to be returned to Blathe, they found the coffin containing the body of Seventh Blade Yees. After the battle, no one had known what to do with the body of a Blade.

But perhaps this was the most fitting burial possible for a Blade. Even in death, the Seventh Blade would perform one last duty for King Respen as the decoy body and coffin.

After nailing it shut, they placed the Seventh Blade's coffin in the center of the room. General Stewart called four soldiers into the room and ordered them to guard the coffin. The soldiers stood at attention, their hands grasping their swords' hilts while Shadrach and Martyn loaded a cart with the coffins meant for Blathe, including the nondescript one containing King Respen's remains.

Martyn shook his head. Nothing like guards and intense secrecy to get everyone talking. By nightfall when General Stewart and his four guards "sneaked" out the gate, everyone in the castle would know they were going to bury King Respen's body in the Sheered Rock Hills.

As expected, no one glanced twice as Shadrach and Martyn rode from Nalgar Castle, leading a mule pulling a cart heaped with coffins. It was a common sight in the days after the battle, and everyone was too busy gossiping about the coffin guarded in the morgue.

For the first hour, the rumble of the cart's wheels and the clump-thump of the horses' hooves were the only sounds interrupting their journey. The rolling prairie hills stretched into the distant horizon, most of the grass nipped short by cattle or bison. An occasional breeze stirred up the smell of dust and the stench of rotting body. Somewhere in the distance, a prairie dog chittered a warning to the rest of its clan and dove into a hole.

It would be so easy to turn his horse, kick it into a canter, and disappear into that distant horizon. With Prince Keevan's clemency, Martyn was free to go.

But then what? Where would he go? He had no friends. No family. No king.

And he'd promised Leith he'd try.

Why had he let himself get talked into that promise? What had he expected? That he could step into a new life with the ease of changing his shirt from black to brown? Leith was doing exactly that just fine.

Martyn couldn't. He should've died in the battle in the Tower or been executed along with Respen. His loyalties hadn't changed the way Leith's had. He wasn't a traitor. Or a hero.

He was someone neither side wanted.

Shadrach's tall, chestnut horse and his few extra inches of height gave him a great perch to look all lofty and condescending. "Why did you come?"

Martyn clenched his fingers against his thigh. His horse tossed his head and trotted a few steps. Martyn relaxed his muscles and his grip on the reins. What could he tell Shadrach? Not his loyalty to King Respen. That wouldn't go over well at all. "Maybe I want to know what made Leith choose your friendship over mine."

The words still hurt. He'd tried to forget about it. Tried to drown the sting with the guilt of what he caused Leith. But it didn't change anything. What made Shadrach's friendship more important than Martyn's? Why had it taken Leith only months to turn his back on a bond they'd built over six years together in the Blades?

Shadrach scowled. "I didn't chain him to a wall, whip him, and stand by while Respen tortured him."

"He betrayed me first." Martyn's horse hop-skipped below him, but he couldn't force his muscles to relax this time. "His betrayal nearly got me killed at Uster. He knew that, yet he did it anyway."

Shadrach yanked his horse around so quickly the horse twisted its head in protest. The mule pulling the cart skidded to avoid crashing into them. "You think it's an accident you survived that ambush? Leith asked us to tell Lord Segon not to kill you."

Was that the reason Martyn had survived? He'd slipped into Lord Segon's room, expecting no one besides the sleeping lord. Instead, he'd been confronted with a row of guardsmen. They could've filled him full of arrows then and there. Instead, they'd fought him. Driven him back until, wounded and exhausted, he'd finally had to admit defeat and return to Nalgar Castle.

Still, if Martyn had pressed harder...if he'd let anger override his good sense, he would've died that night.

And Leith had been willing to take that risk.

Martyn gripped the reins. His horse stomped but couldn't continue walking with Shad's horse still blocking their way. "He couldn't guarantee Lord Segon would spare me or even attempt to spare me."

"He had my father's word, and that was more than enough." Shadrach's finger jabbed him in the chest. "You keep your distance from Leith, got that? Leith might trust you, but I don't."

Martyn gritted his teeth and met Shadrach's hard, brown eyes. Of course Shad didn't trust Martyn. Not after what Martyn had done. "I wouldn't hurt Leith now."

That's all Martyn wanted from Shad. Not his trust. Not his friendship. Just his understanding that Martyn had done everything he could to prevent Leith's torture.

Leith was the one who'd so stubbornly headed for it anyway.

Shadrach's finger stabbed his chest again. "I barely managed to watch him cauterize his own wound once. You stood by while Respen had a red-hot poker pressed to his skin over and over again until even he couldn't help but cry out. Forgive me if I don't believe that is friendship."

Leith's screams still rang in Martyn's ears. Would he ever stop hearing their echoes?

He shoved Shadrach's hand away. "What was I supposed to do? Stand up to King Respen and get chained to the wall next to Leith? What's the sense in that? Without me helping where I could, he would be in far worse shape than he is."

Leith and Renna wouldn't have been fed half as well nor Leith have received any medical care had Martyn not been there. That reasoning had kept Martyn's mouth shut and his hands at his sides while King Respen had carried out torture after torture on Leith. If Martyn had stood up for him, he wouldn't have been able to help him.

It didn't make the memories any easier to swallow.

Shadrach's jaw muscles flexed. Of course he didn't understand. The perfect, flawless Shadrach would never do what Martyn had. "You shouldn't have stopped him when he tried to rescue Renna the first time. You should've trusted him enough to go with him."

"Trusted him? When he'd stopped trusting me months ago?"

"Based on the way things turned out, he was right not to." Shadrach wheeled his horse, his back straight, his voice hard. "We'd better keep going."

Martyn swore, kicked his horse, and cut Shadrach off. Shadrach didn't get to ride away thinking he was all self-righteous when it came to Leith's torture. "Not so fast. Don't pretend you're innocent in this. You're the one who let him walk into Nalgar, knowing he'd face torture. If you were so almighty concerned for him, you should've stopped him then."

"You don't think I wanted to?" Shadrach's fingers tightened on the reins as if he wanted to punch Martyn.

Let him try. Martyn would be more than happy to oblige him with a few punches of his own. "Why didn't you?"

"You don't know why he turned himself in, do you?" Shadrach's eyes took on a hard glint.

"He did it for Renna. That's pretty obvious." Martyn huffed. The whole kissing in front of everybody proved it.

"For being a Blade, you're rather blind." Shadrach blew out a breath and shook his head. "You were Respen's best tracker, yet instead of sending you after Leith or tracking me to Eagle Heights, he had you stay behind at Nalgar Castle guarding a girl with a broken leg. Why do you think that was?"

"I was his First Blade. He knew I was the only Blade left who could fight Leith one-on-one." Martyn swallowed. King Respen had expected him to fight Leith when he returned for Renna, just as Martyn had done in the North Tower dungeon the first time Leith had tried—and failed—to rescue Renna.

Shadrach snorted. "You still don't get it. Respen used you. He knew Leith wouldn't fight you like he'd fight someone else. Leith left Renna behind once because he refused to fight you. She might've been the bait, but you were the jaws of the trap. You prevented Leith from slipping in and sneaking Renna out quietly."

Martyn gripped his saddlehorn, his stomach hurting as if he'd taken a knife to the gut. Leith's torture hadn't been for Renna. It had been for him.

He should've seen it. He should've realized King Respen had needed more than Renna to make Leith surrender himself to torture. What had King Respen said when Martyn refused to kill Leith? *I expected such foolishness as friendship out of Torren.*

Shadrach's hand twitched as if he wanted to reach over his shoulder to the arrows and his bow slung across his back and finish Martyn off as he'd threatened. "Leith risked both his and Renna's lives for you. Honestly, I don't think it was worth it." Shadrach kicked his horse forward. The mule hauling the cart strained to keep up.

For a few moments, Martyn couldn't bring himself to nudge his horse. Leith had gone into that Tower trusting Martyn would come around.

He'd come very close to being wrong.

Martyn dug his hands into the wispy end of his horse's mane. All it would've taken was a hardening of his heart, a clearing of his mind, and he would've killed Leith. If not for Leith's murmured *I don't blame you*, Martyn would've done it.

Worst of all, Leith would've felt the tightening of Martyn's muscles, the pressure of the knife on his throat. So far, Leith hadn't said anything about it, but he had to know that up until that moment, Martyn had planned to kill him.

Friendships didn't recover from something like that. Not even Leith could pretend to be that forgiving.

THEY REACHED BLATHE BY LATE AFTERNOON. AFTER HIDING King Respen's coffin in a dry gully, they clopped into the town. Sullen, dirty faces peeked from broken windows and between the cracks of gray boards. The main road—once one of the few cobbled streets in Acktar and the pride of Blathe—wallowed in a layer of mud. Martyn steered his horse around the holes created by missing cobblestones. This place was even more decrepit than last time he'd been here.

On the left side of the street, Blathe's church remained nothing but blackened stones and rubble. Good riddance.

Shadrach halted his horse and the cart in the center of town next to the well. The neglected remains of Blathe Manor loomed in front of them. If Martyn were to slip inside, would he find the rooms where he and the other Blades had lived and trained before King Respen took the throne? Where he and Leith had once promised to be brothers?

Wraith-like figures drifted from the buildings and formed a mass of gray along the rotten boardwalks and mud-covered street. Gaunt bodies. Ragged clothing. As neglected as their town.

"In the name of Prince Keevan Eirdon, I've come to return the bodies of your soldiers that fell in the recent battle." Shadrach cast about at the faces, as if looking for someone in charge.

The staring people remained silent. Perhaps they distrusted any offering made by Prince Keevan, even an offering of their dead. The prince had little reason to show mercy to Blathe, the town that had spawned King Respen.

A thin man dressed in a stained tunic stepped from the crowd. "I'll speak for the town."

Shadrach tipped his chin at the man, and Martyn couldn't help but be reminded that Shadrach was the heir of

Walden. He certainly knew how to look the part. "Please organize a party of grave diggers."

The man nodded and shouted orders at some of the men and women surrounding them. Shadrach swung down from his horse, and Martyn followed. A shovel was thrust into his hand, and next thing he knew, he'd joined the party digging graves in the forlorn plot of land at the backside of Blathe Manor.

If only Shadrach would give Martyn more reason to hate him than simply being perfect. Perhaps if Shadrach acted like every other stuffed up hypocrite Martyn had met—if he treated the people of Blathe like scum, the way the self-righteous in this same town had treated Martyn when he'd been a part of this rejected, starving crowd—then Martyn could justify hating him.

But, no. Shadrach wandered through the crowd, lending a hand, issuing an order, listening to a woman ramble on about her husband or son whose body she had identified and now buried. Shadrach's infernal goodness made him take the time to see the people of Blathe with compassion instead of disgust.

Of course Martyn didn't get a scrap of that compassion. He apparently deserved less than a town of traitors.

As the evening waned, Shadrach paced the graveyard. Martyn rested his shovel on his shoulder and joined him as they meandered toward the section where wooden markers gave way to headstones.

Shadrach halted so quickly his boots scraped dust from the pebbles. Martyn peered around his shoulder at the wooden marker leaning to one side, the name still plainly legible: *Lena Torren.*

"Leith's mother is buried here." Shadrach blinked at the marker as if it hadn't occurred to him that he would see the gravesite of Leith's parents in Leith's former hometown. "Has Leith been here?"

Martyn shrugged. "Once. We didn't stay long. He had little reason to mourn." He pointed at a marker lying face-down on the ground a few yards away. "Leith's father is buried there."

Shadrach didn't ask what had knocked the marker over. Perhaps he could guess what had happened when thirteen-year-old Leith had seen his father given the honor of a marker and a grave so near his mother. Or maybe Shadrach didn't think to ask because he didn't know the rage that Leith had been capable of back then, especially toward his father.

Shadrach might know the new Leith, but Martyn knew the old one.

With dusk falling around them, they located the stones marking the graves of Clarisse Felix and the stillborn baby boy King Respen hadn't even bothered to name before bury-ing. Ignoring the blisters forming on his fingers, Martyn leaned his weight on his shovel and levered a hunk of sod from the ground. Beside him, Shadrach did the same.

By the time darkness fully cloaked the graveyard, they'd dug the grave to the necessary depth and length. They fetched King Respen's coffin from its hiding spot and lugged it around the town to the graveyard.

After they had lowered it into the hole, Martyn couldn't bring himself to reach for his shovel. It didn't seem right to just pile the dirt back in like they were burying a dead dog they'd found on the side of the road. But what sort of words could he say over King Respen's grave? Murderer of women and children. Destroyer of Acktar. King of his Blades. Few besides Martyn even mourned his death.

Shadrach grabbed his shovel and poured dirt onto the coffin. A steady thunk-thunk-thunk. "Let's get this done."

Martyn picked up his shovel. Was it possible he could bury the past with King Respen? Go on and start over the way Leith seemed so determined to do?

Probably not. The Blades were too much a part of him. Whoever he might have been had been abandoned long ago.

Before the moon had risen, Shadrach and Martyn had filled in the grave and replaced the layer of sod on top. In a few weeks, no one would even be able to tell a grave had been dug there.

King Respen was truly gone.

2

Being summoned to King Keevan's study the morning they were supposed to leave probably wasn't a good thing.

Martyn trudged through the dark passageway to the king's apartments behind a slip of a girl who'd flashed a smile, tossed her hair, and claimed she was the king's clerk. But at least he wasn't being escorted under guard. That boded somewhat well.

The early morning air pressed cool against his face, not even a breeze stirring the stillness yet. They passed no one, probably due to the earliness of the hour. After the late-night feasting following the coronation the night before, not many of the fancy pants nobles would roll out of bed before the sun rose. Except King Keevan, apparently.

At the base of the stairs, a broad-shouldered, brown-haired man halted them. He glared at Martyn. "You'll have to be searched for weapons."

Martyn sighed and held out his arms. If he'd wanted to

assassinate King Keevan, he would've slipped in during the night when he wouldn't be caught, not march in with everyone and their sister watching.

Once the guard patted him down enough to make sure Martyn didn't have a knife stuffed in his boots or hidden under his shirt, the guard waved a hand for the stairs. "You may proceed."

Yes, because Martyn needed this guard's permission to walk up a set of stairs.

When they reached the top of the stairs, the clerk flung the door open and flounced inside. "Martyn Hamish is here. Or should that be 'Martyn Hamish is here to see you'? That sounds more official."

King Keevan leaned back in his chair behind the desk placed in the far corner. Neat stacks of papers rose on either side of him while a candle burned off to one side to brighten the early dawn gray. "Either way is fine, Penelope. Could you take this stack of papers to the office wing?"

Martyn stepped off to the side as Penelope hurried across the room. Near the window overlooking the cobblestone courtyard, another guard eyed Martyn, his fingers drumming on his sword's hilt. Martyn crossed his arms and glared back. King Keevan had summoned him. The guards didn't have to act like he was a dangerous intruder.

Penelope hefted the stack of papers. "It'll be so nice when this is renovated to have the clerk's offices here. It'll save me so much walking."

Someone like Shadrach probably would've opened the door for her, but Martyn didn't bother. Penelope balanced the stack of papers in one hand and lifted the latch with the other. It wasn't like she needed help.

King Keevan tapped the papers in front of him to straighten them, glanced at Martyn, and gestured to the chair set in front of his desk. The candlelight traced the length of the long scar across his cheek and down his neck. "Sit down."

Martyn slid into the seat, all too aware of the guard moving into position a few feet behind him. Preventing him from escape?

King Keevan studied Martyn as if he expected Martyn to squirm if he stared long enough.

He was going to have to stare a whole lot longer if he wanted to get a squirm out of Martyn. Martyn slouched in his chair. "You wanted something?"

The lines around King Keevan's mouth deepened, but he didn't flinch from Martyn's gaze. "You and I both know you won't stay at Stetterly long. If you even make it there. Leith Torren may be ready to settle down in obscurity, but it's plain to see you aren't."

Blunt and to the point. Martyn could work with that. "What's it to you?"

King Keevan's blue eyes didn't waver. "I granted you clemency, but I don't trust you. Then again, you don't trust me."

Martyn straightened and forced himself to relax his crossed arms. King Keevan's honesty deserved the same back. "I promised Leith I'd try to stick around. I haven't thought much beyond that."

But King Keevan was right. Already, Martyn itched to leave. If not for his promise to Leith, he would've ridden off the moment he had King Keevan's clemency in his pocket.

King Keevan traced the ridged scar on his cheek with his thumb. "I have a proposition I would like you to consider."

Martyn didn't give in to the temptation to lean forward. That would be too eager. Like he was just waiting for the chance to toss his leash to the next master that came along. Which, of course, he wasn't. He just needed a mission that didn't involve farming or pretending he belonged where he didn't. "What would that be?"

"A week ago, my men escorted the rest of the Blades beyond Acktar's borders." King Keevan's thumb swiped back and forth on his scar. "While I have ordered patrols to watch the borders, I don't have the resources to keep up such a patrol indefinitely nor do I believe it'll hinder any of the Blades who might seek to return."

"Why didn't you just have them executed?" Martyn had to ask, even though the thought of watching his fellow Blades die as King Respen had done turned his stomach.

"Perhaps it would've been wiser. But once I start executing traitors, where would I stop? No, one execution was enough. I don't want Acktar to linger in the past but to move into the present." King Keevan hung his head and traced his scar again. "But the scars will remain. Healing doesn't happen overnight."

Martyn had only one friendship to heal. King Keevan had to heal an entire nation all while trying to forgive the Blade who had given him his scar and damaged his voice five years ago. A Blade who'd eventually be his family.

Martyn wouldn't want to take on that pair of boots for anything.

"I couldn't bring those Blades to a public trial or execution without risking Torren's or your name being brought up.

For Renna's and Brandi's sakes, I had to do what I could to protect Torren from that."

What would that protection cost? The Blades would return. It was the Blades' way. The code drilled into them with every whipcrack of King Respen's voice.

A Blade never failed, and a failed Blade must die.

Leith had failed. He'd betrayed King Respen and his fellow Blades, and in those final moments in the Tower, Ranson, Jamie, and Martyn had joined him in that failure. By the law of the Blades, they all must be hunted and killed.

The remaining five Blades wouldn't believe they had another choice. They would hunt, and they would kill. Leith. Ranson. Jamie. Martyn. Anyone that tried to stop them.

Would they look for another master? A Blade didn't know how to live without one. Martyn saw again Lord Norton standing straight, head high, moments after King Respen's death. If Martyn was one of those Blades, Lord Norton would be the first person he'd turn to.

Martyn forced himself to remain relaxed in his chair. What was King's Keevan's angle in all this? "What do you want from me?"

King Keevan leaned his elbows on the desktop, his voice lowering. "I'd like you to be my tracker. You know the Blades better than all but Torren. I'm not asking you to kill them. Merely help me hunt them should they return."

"They will." It was only a matter of time. Though, King Keevan's concern about that return probably had more to do with Renna, Brandi, and anyone else that might get in the way than actual worry about Leith or Martyn getting killed. "Why me? Why not ask Leith?"

King Keevan's jaw tightened as he rearranged the stacks

of paper on his desk. "I trust you more than I do him. Yes, you were loyal to Respen Felix, but you were unswerving in that loyalty. Once I have your loyalty, I can depend on you to turn on your fellow Blades for it."

Martyn hung his head. His loyalty. His honor and his downfall. He'd pursued his loyalty so far he'd nearly killed his best friend. But King Keevan was right. Martyn had given his loyalty to Leith, and through him to King Keevan.

"And you were the Sixth Blade at the time of my family's murder. My family's blood doesn't stain your hands the way my blood stains Torren's."

Martyn carried other blood. The murder of General Hannoran, Acktar's ranking general under King Leon, the night Leith had tried to kill King Keevan. But apparently King Keevan found that blood easier to forget.

Martyn swung to his feet and paced away from the desk, ignoring the guard who reached for his sword. Should Martyn take King Keevan's offer? It'd give him a purpose. A mission. He could protect Leith and Renna without being confined to watching their happiness play out.

He threaded his hand through his hair, the locks curling around his fingers. Could he go from Blade to Blade hunter? If he came across their tracks, could he turn them in to King Keevan? Wouldn't that be a betrayal like Leith had done to him?

He faced King Keevan. "Let me think about it."

This time when Martyn chose his loyalties, he wanted to do it without being forced.

King Keevan nodded. "Of course. I wouldn't expect you to rush into a decision." He shot a glance toward the window. "I believe they're gathering to depart."

If that wasn't a dismissal, Martyn was going to make it one. He bowed and hurried from the room and down the stairs.

Unlike before, the cobblestone courtyard teemed with soldiers, the flags of Sierra and Walden flying from poles and horses' bridles. Martyn ducked his head, hunched his shoulders, and ignored them. Hopefully they'd ignore him too. He strode into the stables, but the bustle flowed into there as well.

He shoved his way to the back where his horse munched on a mouthful of hay in a stall. A few stalls down, Shadrach eased a bit into his chestnut's mouth. Former Ninth Blade Harding tightened the saddle's girth on a horse in the stall next to Martyn's. Even that boy, Jamie, was there, saddling a horse.

Nothing he could do but ignore them. Martyn threw the blanket and saddle on his horse's back, tightened the girth, checked the other straps and buckles, and worked the bit between his horse's teeth. As soon as he strapped his gear behind the saddle, he led his horse from the stall.

"Where do you think you're going?"

Martyn sighed and faced Shadrach. "I'm riding out now. Might as well scout our route to make sure we don't run into any trouble."

"We'll be riding with a small army. No one's going to attack us." Shadrach crossed his arms. "You're the only trouble I'm worried about."

"Tough. I'm free to leave, so that's what I'm doing." Martyn shoved past Shadrach. "I'll meet up with your *small army* later this morning. I could hardly miss the dust cloud you'll be raising."

Martyn yanked his horse down the aisle, swung on, and kicked it into a canter. His horse's hooves clunked on the cobbles, through the main gate, and down the ramp leading to the castle.

The morning breeze whipped by his face, cool with last night's dew. Perhaps he should just keep riding. Maybe if he rode far and fast enough, he could outrun the ghosts of Leith's screams and the pain of betrayal.

3

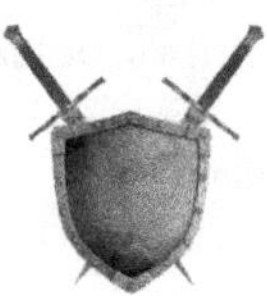

Renna gripped her saddlebags so tightly her arms quivered. She was finally leaving. After months of imprisonment in this castle, she was going to freely ride out of there. She stood next to the stable, trying to stay out of the way. Lady Lorraine stood in the center of the courtyard, directing the foot soldiers into a line on one side of the courtyard.

"I wish you didn't have to leave so soon."

Renna turned. Queen Adelaide—Addie as she'd insisted on being called when Renna met her a few days ago—lumbered from the passageway, leaning on Keevan's arm to steady her eight-months pregnant frame. Her hair puffed in a mass of brown curls around her head, striking against her deep green dress.

Renna smiled and hugged Addie, a difficult hug with Addie's giant belly. "I wish we could stay longer. But we've been gone from Stetterly long enough."

"You're welcome to visit any time." Addie straightened as

much as she could. "I know Keevan would enjoy having some of his family around instead of being stuck with only mine."

"You know I love your family." Despite his rasp grating through the words, Keevan smiled and wrapped his arm around Addie's waist as far as he could. The morning sunlight shone on the scar marring his cheek and neck. He stared past Renna, and his smile faded. He tightened his grip on Addie. "I suppose *he* will have to come with you."

Renna glanced over her shoulder. Leith limped toward them at an achingly slow pace, a cane in one hand for support. Ranson walked beside him, carrying both of their saddlebags. Leith's face tightened with the hint of a grimace at each step. Three weeks after the battle, the knife wound in his thigh and his broken ribs still pained him while the deep burns across his chest and the healing whiplashes across his back drained his strength. Not that Leith would admit any of that to her. He didn't have to. She was a healer, after all.

"Yes, he's sticking around." Renna raised her eyebrows. "Think of him like that one family member you love just because they're family, even if they're a pain. Every family has one."

Keevan had the decency to look away. Growing up, he'd been that family member. He'd pulled Renna's hair, stuffed snow down the back of her cloak, whacked her snowman to bits. Childish pranks, perhaps. But she didn't have any good memories of him from back then.

Addie covered her mouth, but a snort still escaped. "Some families have more than one." She glanced over her shoulder, and the shorter of the two bodyguards behind her and Keevan swiveled his gaze to the sky.

The muscle at the corner of Keevan's jaw knotted. "Torren isn't family."

"Yet. But he will be. Eventually." Once Leith got around to asking.

Keevan scowled.

Hooves rattled against the cobblestones as Shadrach stepped from the stable with two saddled horses. He bowed to Keevan, nodded at Renna, and turned to Ranson and Leith, who had finally hobbled into hearing range. Shadrach looped the horses' reins over rings in the stable wall and waved toward the stable. "Ranson, you'll have to saddle your own horse. The stablehands refuse to go near it."

Ranson glanced at Leith, as if making sure Leith wasn't going to fall over the moment Ranson left his side. Leith waved a hand and said something in a voice too low for Renna to hear.

Nodding, Ranson hurried into the stable, nearly running into Jamie and the two horses he was leading. Behind Jamie, Brandi tugged a limping Blizzard from the stable. Brandi's head remained wrapped in a bandage, and her short hair spiked in odd directions.

Renna walked over to Blizzard and ran her hand along the healing gash that marred his shoulder and chest. When she looked up, Brandi's eyes were wide, her mouth squinched as she waited for Renna's verdict.

"I'm not an expert on horse wounds, but Blizzard seems to be healing all right. No infection, at least, and the wound closed well." Renna patted Blizzard's neck.

Brandi's shoulders straightened, and a grin spread across her face. "That's good. Because I'm not leaving him behind again."

"Me either." The tapping of Leith's cane sounded behind Renna a moment before his hand joined hers stroking Blizzard's neck.

Renna glanced over her shoulder. Leith's face was inches from hers, and she was tempted to lean back and kiss him. But with the equivalent of an army gathered in the courtyard, this probably wasn't the time.

The corner of his mouth tipped up, as if he knew exactly what she was thinking.

Then he reached up and touched the side of his nose. "You got a smear of dirt. Right here."

Renna ducked her head and scrubbed at her nose. No, he hadn't known what she was thinking. He was just laughing at the dirt on her face. Probably just as well.

Keevan cleared his throat behind them. "Now that you're all here, there are a few things I need to do before you leave."

Renna turned back to Keevan. Shadrach stepped up behind him, gripping something in his hand.

Keevan straightened his shoulders and his face relaxed into a bland, impassive expression. "Lady Brandiline Faythe, please step forward."

Arms stiff at her sides, Brandi marched forward. Her short sword swung against her hip. She saluted Keevan, her mouth tipped upward. "Yes, sir?"

"For your bravery in the Alistair Riders and for nearly sacrificing your life to hold Nalgar's gates, I award you the King's Medal of Valor." Keevan waved to Shadrach.

Shadrach stepped forward. A silver medal unfurled at the end of a light green, silk ribbon. Brandi bowed, and Shadrach looped the ribbon over her head.

Renna drew in a deep breath. Brandi had been foolish.

Reckless. But she'd also been beyond brave. She deserved the recognition.

A tapping sound came from Renna's side. Leith's fingers slipped into hers.

"James Cavendish."

Jamie strode forward and bowed to Keevan.

"For your bravery in the Alistair Riders and for single-handedly clearing the way into the Tower for me and my men, I award you the King's Medal of Valor."

Shadrach looped a second medal and ribbon over Jamie's head.

Keevan shifted his stance. "I'm sorry I couldn't award you publicly after the coronation, Brandi. But to protect your reputation as a lady, it was decided it'd be better to have a private ceremony. Jamie requested to have his award presented at the same time as yours."

Brandi shot a grin at Jamie. Jamie grinned back.

Renna squeezed Leith's hand and leaned against his shoulder. Jamie had come a long way since Leith dragged him to Walden and introduced him to everyone at Brandi's birthday party.

The clatter of hooves behind them broke the moment. Ranson led a black horse from the stable and dodged a nip aimed at his shoulder.

Shadrach straightened. "We'd better head out if we're to reach Sierra by nightfall."

Leith limped over to one of the horses Jamie had led out of the stables. "Renna, you'll be riding Big Brown, and he's as docile and boring as his name suggests."

Renna walked to the horse's side. Its back stood taller than Blizzard's. Could Renna even get her foot high enough to pull herself into the saddle? After throwing her saddlebags over the horse's back and strapping them on, she eyed Leith. "Don't you dare try to boost me up."

His mouth quirked. "I thought about it."

While she'd appreciate a romantic gesture like that in a few months once Leith was fully healed, now wasn't the time. Leith needed to conserve his strength to make it through the ride ahead.

Ranson hurried to Renna's side, knelt, and cupped his hands. His light brown eyes peered up at her. "I'll do it, Lady Faythe."

"Thanks." She patted his shoulder, placed her foot in his hands, and grasped the saddle.

Ranson boosted her up high enough for her to swing her right leg over the horse. She settled into the saddle and gripped the reins when Ranson handed them to her. As Ranson strode toward another horse, Big Brown shifted beneath her, and Renna clung to the saddlehorn. Was the horse about to run off with her on its back?

Leith ran his hand down Big Brown's neck. "He isn't going to do anything unexpected."

"I'm not so sure about that." She winced as the horse swished its tail. If only she was as comfortable on a horse as Brandi. Brandi already perched on the back of a small, light brown mare, her body swaying with the horse's movements. Beside her, Jamie sat on his buckskin, the horse pawing at the cobblestones.

Ranson returned, leading a mouse-brown horse. Black markings covered its nose and legs. "First...uh, Daniel, you can ride this horse. It was...Blane's horse."

Blane Altin. Renna swallowed. Blane died fighting to

protect Ranson from the other Blades in the Battle of Nalgar Castle. He'd been so young. Too young to be killed before ever knowing freedom outside the Blades.

"Are you sure?" Leith ran his fingers along the horse's nose.

Ranson nodded. "Blane would like you to have him, I think."

"I'll borrow him for a while. When I get a new horse, you can have him back." Leith rested a hand on Ranson's shoulder. "Blane would want that."

While Ranson held the horse's head, Leith limped to the right side of the horse and grasped the saddle. Renna tensed. Leith should be the one getting helped into the saddle. Instead, he had that set to his jaw and glint in his green eyes she'd seen all too often over the past month, especially while in the Tower. He was either going to get into that saddle by himself or pass out trying. Nothing she said or did would make a difference.

Shadrach sidled closer to Leith, his arms loose at his sides as if he wasn't positioning himself to catch Leith if he passed out. Renna caught his gaze and mouthed thank you. Shadrach nodded.

Leith bounced on his good leg and heaved himself into the saddle. He hunched over the horse's neck, pressed an arm against his chest, and gasped for breath.

Renna clenched a fist in Big Brown's mane. Leith wasn't ready for this ride. All of them could see it. But Leith wouldn't admit it.

As if sensing her scrutiny, Leith straightened and steadied his breathing. Although his face remained pale, he managed a grin. "Did Blane ever name his horse?"

"No." Ranson handed the reins to Leith.

Leith raised an eyebrow. "Brandi?"

Brandi's face scrunched. "How about Valor?"

Renna caught a glimpse of Ranson's smile before he ducked his head. Leith gave one sharp nod. "Valor it is."

The rest of them swung onto their horses, and Renna waved to Keevan and Addie one last time. Leith turned Valor's head, and he and Shadrach led the way toward the gate. In the center of the cobblestone courtyard, Lady Lorraine, Jolene, and Lord Alistair joined them. The guards from both Sierra and Walden closed around them.

Renna held her breath as she rode through the dark tunnel of the main gates. She'd kept her promise to Respen. She hadn't escaped. Instead, she was riding out of Nalgar Castle in full daylight with an entire entourage to see her most of the way home.

Sunlight washed over her as she exited the castle's shadow. Before her, the prairie hills rolled into the distance, a smudge to the north marking the beginning of the Sheered Rock Hills. Nothing but sky and grass lay before her. No walls. No iron bars. No darkness.

She was free.

A week ago, she, Brandi, Jamie, and Keevan had left the castle for a short walk, so this wasn't the first time she'd left Nalgar since her capture. But this time, she was truly leaving. By the time she had to return for a visit, Keevan and Addie would've purged the castle of Respen's presence.

No matter what they did, the graves on the hill to the northwest of Nalgar Castle would remain. If she turned in the saddle, she could make out the rows of markers among the prairie grass. Somewhere in there stood the markers for

Blane Altin and Brandi's friend Ian McCrae. At the crest of the hill, the line of stones she and Brandi had hauled to mark the mass grave where Uncle Abel and Aunt Mara were buried blurred white and gray against the dust.

Memories flared. The flash of the ax. The blood flowing across the cobblestones. And the singing. That moment her aunt and uncle sang their way to death.

She drew in a deep breath and turned away, only to spot a horse, its saddle empty, trotting on a leadrope behind one of Walden's soldiers. An empty saddle. A life lost.

So many families broken and hurting. How would Acktar recover? This war was town fighting town, neighbor against neighbor.

How did a country move on from such betrayal within?

I predict Acktar will tear itself apart within a year. That's what Respen had told her. Was he right? Would this victory and peace last or was another battle, another war, burning beyond the horizon even now?

She shivered, and Big Brown gave some sort of hop-trot beneath her. Gasping, she gripped the saddlehorn and held her breath until the horse settled back into a walk.

Leith nudged Valor closer. "Are you all right?"

What would she have done without Leith? He was something solid for both her and Brandi to cling to. His faith strengthened hers.

Could she ever tell him how damaged she was? Her chest ached with the scars she'd gained in the last few months. Seeing Uncle Abel and Aunt Mara die. Hearing Leith's tortured screams. That broken, raw part of her that had almost cared for King Respen.

Would she ever be able to admit that secret to Leith?

He'd turned himself in to Respen and faced torture to save her. How could she admit even a momentary disloyalty? Even when she'd thought him dead? What was wrong with her that she considered choosing Respen even for a moment?

He was still waiting for her answer. She forced herself to smile. "Yes. I was just thinking about home."

Stetterly. Her town. It had a lot of rebuilding to do, and it would be different without Uncle Abel and Aunt Mara.

But it would be home.

4

Leith clung to the saddlehorn and gritted his teeth. Valor's strides jolted his cracked ribs and burned in the muscles of his wounded thigh. But he wasn't going to complain. Not when their pace already crawled to accommodate his wounds and Blizzard's limp.

The late summer sun warmed his face as it rose higher in the sky, filling the grass with a dry rustle and the air with the scent of baking earth. Sierra lay somewhere miles ahead, but for right now, only prairie met the far horizon.

He craned his neck as far as he could without twisting his ribs to glance at Blizzard. Blizzard's ears remained pricked, his head up, so the horse couldn't be in too much pain.

Blizzard's wound would probably fade until it was barely noticeable. While the muscle would never be strong enough to withstand the kind of arduous journeys Leith had put him through before, he might be able to be ridden again by a small rider.

But that was all right. Blizzard probably wouldn't mind being put out to pasture to grow fat and happy with all the attention Brandi would lavish on him.

Where did Leith fit into this peaceful future? What was God calling him to do now? In all his time wanting to leave the Blades, he'd barely considered...after. He'd been so focused on his goal to save Renna and help the Resistance, he'd never considered what would happen to him when the only skills he had were no longer needed.

Probably because he'd never expected to survive the final battle with Respen.

He let out a slow breath. He had to place the future in God's hands. He'd been able to do that when locked in the Tower facing Respen's torture. Why couldn't he do it now?

The torture he'd faced in the Tower had been predictable. He'd known he'd face it and exactly how long it would last.

But now? He wasn't a Blade. He hadn't been a Blade for months. But he wasn't anything besides a Blade either. He'd learned some about farming at Walden, but was that what he wanted to do for the rest of his life?

Leith gripped the saddlehorn. Perhaps it was his injuries or Valor's unfamiliar gait, but Leith couldn't seem to fall into a relaxed rhythm. Instead, Valor's strides jarred his bones as if he were no better rider than a two-year-old.

A new horse. A new life. And he couldn't find a rhythm with either of them.

There was also Renna to think about. How did he go about courting her properly? And—someday, eventually—when he married her, was there a role he was expected to take, a role he didn't even know existed?

What did he know about a peaceful life? About how towns or families or anything like that worked? He'd grown up in the back alleys of Blathe before being trained as a Blade. Shad and Renna and Brandi had all these things that they just knew, and Leith didn't.

Valor lurched over a clump of dead grass. Leith squeezed his eyes shut and sucked in a quick breath. Pain flared across his chest.

How far had they gone? He swayed. He shouldn't be this weak. It had been four weeks since the battle. But the burns and broken bones drained his strength, even if the bruises and whiplashes had faded.

"How're you holding up?"

Shad's voice dragged Leith from his pained stupor. He forced himself to straighten in his saddle. Sweat trickled between his shoulder blades. Was his forehead covered with sweat too? If he swiped at it, Shad would know he was trying to hide his pain. "I'll make it."

Shaking his head, Shad reined in his horse. "We'll take a break here."

All around them, horses huffed at the halt. Leather creaked as the soldiers stretched in their saddles.

"You don't have to call a break on my account." Leith gritted his teeth. He could keep going. He wasn't going to give in to the weakness lacing across his chest.

"The rest isn't just for you." Shad swung from the saddle and nodded toward Lord Alistair, who also didn't seem to be sitting straight in the saddle. He'd suffered wounds defending Walden, including a crushed elbow that paralyzed his left hand.

Leith gripped the saddlehorn. How was he going to get

off the horse? He'd barely managed getting on earlier this morning. The way his hands and legs shook, he would collapse the moment he tried to drop to the ground.

Shad strolled to Valor's side. Leith swung his left leg over the saddle. Thankfully, Valor was steady enough to stand still while Leith dismounted on the wrong side.

As soon as his left leg touched the ground, it buckled. Shad caught him, and he pulled his right foot from the stirrup. Pulling Leith's arm over his shoulder, Shad hauled him a few feet away where Renna had already spread a blanket on the ground. The tall grass beneath the blanket bent and cushioned Leith's ribs as he lay down.

He closed his eyes and concentrated on breathing. Shad was right. He'd needed a rest.

A soft touch grazed his forehead. "Is there anything I can get you?"

Her voice wrapped around him like a warm, summer breeze. Her fingers slipped into his hand and squeezed gently.

"A drink would be nice, but it can wait." Leith cracked one eye open and peered up at her. "How's Brandi?"

Brandi had suffered a head wound during the battle, but she seemed to be bouncing back with more energy than Leith. Not that Leith would complain. He'd take on any amount of pain if he never had to see Brandi so still and pale again.

"Fighting a headache. I'm brewing a pot of willow bark tea for both of you."

Leith grimaced, which only earned him a laugh and a pat on his hand from Renna.

"You can both grimace all you want, but you'll drink it."

After a moment, she looked away. "Is there anyone from Sierra who'll recognize you? What about those who were at Eagle's Heights? I should've realized earlier that someone here might realize you aren't just Daniel Grayce."

With her thumb stroking the back of his hand, his thoughts were going muddled. He swallowed and tried to draw in a deep breath past his aching ribs. "I entered Eagle's Heights as myself. Many in the Resistance saw me as a Blade. It's probably just as well that I spent most of my time at Eagle's Heights locked in a cave. It limited the number of people who got a good look at me."

Renna's face remained tight and drawn. "I know. But all I want is peace and happiness and no more danger, and I...if someone recognizes you..."

King Keevan's decision to execute only Respen left some in Acktar still longing for more vengeance, more blood. If they discovered Leith was a Blade? That King Keevan had pardoned rather than punished him? That Renna, King Keevan's cousin, intended to marry Leith? What sort of trouble would it spark? Would a mob try to kill Leith? Or would the nobles who had backed the Resistance, with the exceptions of Lady Lorraine and Lord Alistair, turn on King Keevan?

After the war, the balance of peace was so tenuous, no one knew what might upset it. And more killing was the last thing Leith wanted to cause.

No more danger. Like the Blades returning...

Leith couldn't think about them right now. He couldn't worry Renna.

Leith threaded his fingers through Renna's, shifting their clasped hands so they didn't rest on his broken rib. "The thing about being a Blade is that people rarely look at your face. They see the black clothes and the knives, and that's what they focus on. Dressed in clothes two sizes too big, limping, and lacking weapons, no one will give me a second glance."

For Renna's sake, that's what Leith had to hope. He didn't want his past—his marks or the remaining Blades—to get in the way of her happiness.

"Maybe you'll have to change your appearance even more. Grow your hair out. Maybe even tie it back in a queue like Lord Alistair does." She tapped their hands against his stomach. "I'm sure you'll fill out a little once you start eating regular meals."

"Never cut my hair and get fat." Leith adjusted his arm behind his head. "Anything else?"

"Keep smiling. No one will recognize you as a Blade if you're smiling."

She was smiling at him now. If Leith propped himself on his elbows, he'd close the few inches of space between them and kiss her.

But people were watching. And if he tried to move that much, his groans and grimacing would erase the smile from Renna's face.

She tugged her hand free and clambered to her feet. "I'd better check on the tea."

Leith missed the feel of her hand, but he couldn't prevent her from making tea for Brandi. Her head was probably pounding as painfully as his ribs.

He closed his eyes. The chatter of the others as they tended to their horses or stretched their legs washed over him. The grass rustled in a breeze that tasted of the first promise of autumn. Somewhere a few yards away, Shad's and Jolene's voices murmured words too low for him to hear.

Someone flopped onto the grass beside him. "War wounds are no fun."

Leith cracked an eye open. A bandage still wound around Brandi's head, short spikes of her red-blond hair sticking in all directions. But at least color had bloomed in her cheeks and the sparkle returned to her eyes. "Enjoy it. Your sister will be back to ordering you around before you know it."

Brandi smirked and laced her fingers behind her head. When Renna returned with a mug of tea for each of them, Brandi flapped her hand in the air. "Renna, I need a pillow. And a snack would be wonderful. And while you're at it…"

Renna held up Brandi's mug. "While I'm at it, I might dump this tea on your head. You could use a bath."

Brandi stuck her tongue out and accepted the mug. Leith pushed himself upright, wincing, and took his mug from Renna. He sniffed at the light brown liquid swirling in the ceramic mug. Smelled like boiled dirt. Blowing on it, he sipped, burning his lips and the tip of his tongue. Yep. Tasted like dirt too.

"Blegh." Brandi scowled at Renna. "Are you purposely making this taste awful? It gets worse every time."

Renna crossed her arms and glared. "You're drinking it whether you like it or not."

Leith held out his mug to Brandi. "Race you. First one to finish gets first choice at supper tonight."

"All right." Brandi clunked her mug against his. "Go." She set to slurping the tea so fast she must've burned her lips, tongue, and throat in the process.

He sipped at his. The hot liquid still scalded the roof of his mouth, causing a layer of skin to peel.

Brandi thrust her mug at Renna and swiped her arm across her mouth. "Done."

Renna peered into the mug. "You still have a mouthful swirling at the bottom."

"But that's…" Brandi sighed, gulped the dregs, and thrust the mug back at Renna with a grimace.

Leith still had half a mug to go. Not that he minded losing. Now that the tea had cooled, he finished his mug in three swallows and fought his gag reflex to keep the nasty flavor in his stomach where it belonged.

As Renna handed him a hard biscuit to wash the taste from his mouth, some of the soldiers at the far side of their temporary camp lunged to their feet and grabbed for their weapons. Leith reached for his knife but caught sight of Martyn dismounting and leading his horse through the crowd of soldiers.

Shad stepped in front of Martyn, and the two of them exchanged a few words. Martyn's jaw tightened, and the vein at Shad's temple pulsed. Leith shook his head. Too much anger. It seemed like the war would never truly die.

Renna stepped into Martyn's path and held out one of the biscuits. Martyn halted long enough to snatch the biscuit from her before he brushed around her. Reaching his horse, he swung back into the saddle and rode from the camp at a trot.

Leith eased back onto the blanket, his ribs aching with every breath. Next to him, Brandi gnawed on a second biscuit. "Brandi, could you do me a favor? A really, really big favor?"

She cocked her head, the bandage making the ends of her short hair stick up in all directions. "What?"

"If you get a chance, could you talk to Martyn? Tell him one of your Bible stories."

"Why?" Brandi wrinkled her nose and glared in the direction of Martyn's dust cloud. "He captured us, messed up our rescue, and tortured you."

"Please, Brandi. I've tried. Renna's tried. But you have a way of working past people's defenses. You might be the only person who can reach him." Leith forced himself onto one elbow, ignoring the bolts of pain shooting through his ribs. "I know he's done a lot of bad things. So have I. You forgave me for the things I did to your family."

"You asked for forgiveness." Brandi clenched her fists around handfuls of the tall grass. "He hasn't."

"He doesn't know how yet." Leith's arm shook from the effort of propping himself up, but he wasn't going to lie down until he had Brandi's cooperation. He'd given up on Martyn too quickly once. He wasn't going to do it again. "Please. For me."

"All right. I'll try." Brandi scowled.

Leith flopped back onto his blanket. "Think of it as a personal challenge. You're two for two on swaying Blades to your side. Why not make it three for three?"

"You and Jamie were easy. But Martyn's all kinds of stubborn." Brandi stretched out on her blanket again as well. "He would've made a great mule."

Leith huffed as much of a laugh as he could with his ribs aching and closed his eyes. Yep, Brandi was just the person to let loose on Martyn.

After half an hour, Shad gathered the party to get

moving again. He knelt by Leith. "Sorry. I hope that was enough rest."

Leith braced a hand on Shad's shoulder and levered himself upright. "It will be." His ribs and leg still ached, but Renna's tea had dulled the throbbing.

Brandi sprang to her feet and bounced to her horse, her headache apparently forgotten as the willow tea took effect. Jamie stood off to the side, rocking back and forth from his toes to his heels and eyeing Brandi as if he'd been waiting to help her.

Shad halted, and Leith followed his gaze to where Lord Alistair stood next to his horse, gripping the saddlehorn with his good hand. Leith managed to limp a step away from Shad's steadying grip. "Go on. I'm fine."

Shad raised his eyebrow.

Leith caught Jamie's eye and motioned to him. "Jamie can help me."

Shaking his head, Shad strolled toward Lord Alistair.

When Jamie reached his side, Leith leaned on his shoulder. "How are you holding up?"

Jamie huffed and shook his head. His shaggy brown hair flew across his eyes. "Of course I'm fine. I wasn't the one tortured."

No, but he'd fought in battles. He'd seen both Leith and Brandi struggle to recover from wounds. "I'm going to be fine, you know. We all are."

"I know." Jamie still stared straight ahead.

"No Blade has ever survived once Respen decreed their death. But here I am. Alive. I can't complain about a few cuts and bruises." Leith gritted his teeth and forced himself to limp a few more steps with Jamie's help. His injured thigh muscles ached, refusing to loosen after the morning's ride.

"The other Blades...they're going to hunt you, aren't they?" Jamie's free hand tightened over the sword at his side.

Yes, they would. And, if King Keevan's patrols didn't catch them first, Leith would have to face them.

But, for now, Leith didn't want Jamie or Renna or any of them to worry. Not yet. They should get a chance to enjoy their victory and peace.

"Maybe." Leith squeezed Jamie's shoulder as they reached Valor. "You did good. No one could've protected Brandi better than you did, and you saved my life by entering the Tower to fight the Blades."

Jamie straightened. "You think so?"

"Yes." Leith chose his next words carefully. They were the words he would've given anything to hear from his father. He wasn't Jamie's father, but someone had to say them. "I'm proud of you."

Jamie's grin stretched across his face and gleamed in his eyes. "Thanks."

Leith grasped the saddle, and this time he let Jamie give him a boost up. Still, he fell into the saddle, gasping and fighting a moan. So tired. Of weariness. Of pain. Of constantly fighting for his life.

He'd done what he'd set out to do when he'd joined the Resistance. He'd kept Renna and Brandi alive, even if he'd had to sacrifice blood and pain and friendship to do it.

So what now? What happened now that the battle was over and the war won?

He didn't know how to survive without something to fight.

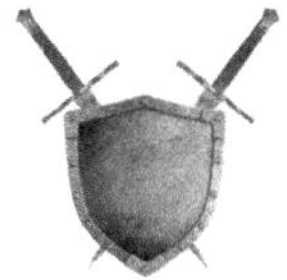

Martyn didn't belong here.

He lingered by the horses in front of the two-story brick Sierra Manor, the setting sun casting deep, long shadows. Behind him, wooden planks had been stretched across a ditch encircling the manor.

Leith limped at Renna's side as she talked with Jolene. Moments after they'd arrived, Martyn had overheard Shadrach ask Renna to distract Jolene, and, a few minutes later, Shadrach had slipped out the side of Sierra Manor with a bundle of candles and flowers in his arms. With Renna's grin and Shadrach's mushy-eyed expression, it didn't take half a brain to figure out what was going on.

Martyn swore under his breath. After tonight, this place would be filled with wedding planning and kissing and nonsensical rubbish.

And Martyn didn't fit with that. Not with Leith's faith and his perfect, do-gooder friends. Not with a life of farming and weddings and picturesque cabins on the prairie. Martyn had been abandoned. Again.

Perhaps it would've been better if Martyn had died in in the Tower. That's what former best friends like him did, wasn't it? Turn from their anger and save their best friends one last time before dying heroically. Martyn would've been something of a hero. The man who gave his life so Leith could have his.

Instead, Leith had a limp, and no one knew what to do with a man who should be dead. There wasn't a place for an ex-best friend that survived the final battle.

"I don't want to go in right now, either."

Martyn jumped and spun toward the voice. Renna's little sister Brandi bounced by his elbow, the leadrope for her horse in one hand and Leith's horse—the one that had been wounded—in the other.

She nodded toward Martyn's horse. "Let's help put the horses away. You can take Big Brown and your horse. Jamie's taking care of Valor. What's your horse's name?"

Martyn dragged his hand through his hair. "Big Brown? Name?" What was she talking about?

"Of course. You people don't name your horses." She rolled her eyes and jabbed a thumb at the horse Renna had been riding. "That's Big Brown."

Martyn glanced around. The servants seemed to be ignoring them, and Shadrach wasn't around to push Martyn away from Brandi. Why was she being nice to him? He'd captured her and her sister, forced Leith to rescue Brandi and leave Renna behind, and tortured Leith.

A few yards away, the former Blade trainee Jamie crossed his arms, his hands gripping the reins of his buckskin and the mouse-brown horse that used to belong to Blane Altin. When he noticed Martyn's stare, Jamie's eyes narrowed as if to say, *I'm watching you.*

So Martyn wasn't exactly free from surveillance. Still, Jamie didn't look like he was going to interfere. Martyn grabbed the lead of the horse Brandi called Big Brown. "All right. Lead the way."

She waltzed ahead, the two horses following her like puppies. Martyn trailed with his two horses while Jamie fell into line behind him.

As he stepped through the double-doors, the coolness of the long, low stable wrapped around him. Stalls lined either side of the stone building while a cupola on top provided light from a bank of small windows. At the far end of the stable, another set of double doors opened onto a paddock where several horses grazed.

A groom directed them to a series of empty stalls at the back of the stables. Brandi led her horses into two of them, and Martyn got his into the next two. Stablehands had already filled the feed and water troughs.

Martyn unsaddled the horses and set the saddlebags aside to carry to the manor. A few stalls away, Brandi did the same. Perhaps Martyn should've been chivalrous and offered to unsaddle the horses for her, but she seemed capable enough on her own.

Brandi somehow got her hands on a bucket of brushes, and she handed one to Martyn before she eased into the stall with Leith's wounded horse. "Blizzard really likes being brushed, especially when I scrub this itchy spot here. See? Look at the funny face he makes."

The horse was indeed craning its neck so far over its

head was sideways on its body. Drool globbed from the corner of its mouth and plopped onto the stone floor.

Martyn strode into his horse's stall and set to work brushing the dust and sweat from his horse's back. "Blizzard, huh?"

Months ago, Leith had mentioned that name but had brushed it aside when Martyn had questioned him about it. Martyn should've realized something was wrong. He should've...

What would he have done, really? He would've done exactly what he had done. Watched Leith closer. Tried to stop him from going down a path that led to torture.

It wouldn't have made any difference. Leith still would've mule-headedly kept on betraying Respen and lying to Martyn. Some brother he'd turned out to be.

"Yep. Leith let me name him when we first met in that big blizzard last winter." Brandi scrubbed the brush across another spot of Blizzard's spine.

Martyn concentrated on brushing each strand of his horse's hair. Leith had begun his betrayal of King Respen all the way back then.

"Your horse needs a name too." Brandi peered over the half wall at him.

He leaned against his horse's neck and breathed in the steadying scent of grass and dust. Why didn't she just leave him alone? Couldn't she tell he wasn't going to be charmed the way Leith had been? "Fine. Name him."

"Wanderer."

The name popped out too quickly. He eyed her over his horse's mane. A smirk tilted her mouth and eyebrows. "How long ago did you name my horse?"

"Back when you captured us, though you were too grumpy for me to say it back then."

Months. She'd named his horse months ago. A funny tightness spread across Martyn's stomach. He dropped his brush into the bucket. "Why are you being so nice to me? I captured you. Dragged you to Nalgar Castle. Let King Respen torment you. Forced Leith to leave your sister behind and tortured him when he returned for her."

Put that way, he didn't even want to be nice to himself. Why did he want her kindness or Shadrach's trust or Leith's friendship?

No, he didn't want it. Any of it. All he really wanted was to get away from it.

"You aren't going to make this easy, are you?" She placed her hands on her hips. "Now pick up your brush and get back to work. I'm going to tell you a story."

Martyn dutifully picked up his brush and applied it to his horse's fur once again. He had a suspicion he'd have to listen to this story whether he cooperated or not.

"Once there lived a king's son named Jonathan. He was a good man and a mighty warrior. He once defeated a big chunk of the enemy's army with just himself and his servant. But one day, a new warrior was brought to the palace, a shepherd and giant-slayer named David. Jonathan and David became best friends, so close they were almost brothers. At first, King Saul, Jonathan's father, was pleased with David. But after the people in the kingdom began praising David more than Saul, King Saul became jealous. One night, he threw his spear at David, and David had to flee for his life."

Great. A Bible story. Two friends. An angry king. Could she get any more obvious?

One big difference. David had done nothing to earn King Saul's anger besides doing his job a little too well. Leith had betrayed King Respen and deserved to be hunted. "And Jonathan turned on David, is that it? Stayed loyal to his father and broke his friendship."

"Nope." Brandi eased under Blizzard's neck and started brushing the horse's other side. "Jonathan intervened and pleaded David's case with his father. King Saul listened to Jonathan and let David return. A little bit later, David won another victory, and King Saul got jealous all over again. Again he threw his spear at David, and David had to run, this time even farther away."

"Now Jonathan chose his father over David."

"Nope. Jonathan tried again to intervene. This time, King Saul accused Jonathan of being more loyal to David than to him and threw a spear at his own son." Brandi wrinkled her nose. "Jonathan sneaked away and told David that King Saul wasn't going to calm down this time. The two friends promised they would always remain friends, and they would honor that friendship even to each other's children and grandchildren. Then, they parted, and only saw each other one other time."

Martyn's throat closed. When Leith had ridden away with Brandi, Martyn had hoped against hope he'd never see Leith again. That would've been better than having to face him across the wrong end of a knife. "What happened to them?"

"Jonathan and King Saul were killed, and David mourned his friend and became king. He remembered his promise to Jonathan and gave Jonathan's crippled son a place at the royal table, even though it would've been smarter to kill off King Saul's grandson."

Martyn rested his forehead against his horse's shoulder. Even Brandi thought he should be dead. Wasn't that the point of the story? He was the friend on the wrong side who needed to die and get out of his friend's way.

Besides, he and Leith were hardly Jonathan and David. Instead of remaining loyal, they'd nearly killed each other. Leith wasn't an innocent David, and Martyn not the loyal Jonathan.

Martyn didn't belong. Leith had a family here Martyn couldn't join. They might've once been brothers, but they weren't any more.

He'd tried, but trying wasn't enough.

It was time to face the facts and move on.

He dropped the brush and reached for his saddle blanket. "I can't stay. Thanks for making that obvious."

"What? But I...that wasn't what you were supposed to get from that story." Brandi tossed her brush into the bucket and glared. With her hair spiked like a porcupine, the look wasn't all that intimidating.

Martyn ignored her and hefted his saddle onto his horse's back. Best to leave now, quickly and quietly, before anyone tried to make a big hubbub about it.

Brandi sighed and hurried from the stables, pausing only long enough to whisper something to Jamie. Jamie remained at his horse's side in the stall across the way, eying Martyn.

One to distract him, and one to fetch Leith. How totally predictable. Martyn shook his head and reached for his horse's bridle. Leith could do all the pleading and arguing he wanted. Martyn couldn't stay.

He strapped his bedroll and saddlebags behind the saddle and led his horse from the stall.

"Leaving without saying goodbye?"

Right on time. Martyn bit back a groan.

Leith leaned against the wall next to the stable's outer doors, his arms crossed. Jamie had disappeared, leaving only the horses and Martyn and Leith.

Martyn planted his feet and gripped his horse's reins tighter. If Leith wanted Martyn to feel guilty about leaving, he was going to be disappointed. "Yes. It's for the best. This is your life, not mine."

A second of silence dragged into two, then three. Their friendship already frayed. Would this be the last tug that would tear it forever?

"All right. You'd better go then." Leith's stance relaxed. "Renna and I will be praying for you."

Martyn snorted. Prayers to an empty sky wouldn't do any good, but at least they'd be thinking about him. It was the parting of friends, not enemies.

Leith shoved himself away from the stall door, blocking the doorway. "I know I gave up on you too soon last time. I'm not going to make that mistake again."

Martyn eyed him. Was there enough space to lead his horse around Leith? "It wouldn't have made a difference. Perhaps I might've turned you in to King Respen sooner."

"What do you plan to do?"

That was the question, wasn't it? Leith seemed to have it all figured out with his hoity-toity new friends.

Martyn shrugged. "King Keevan has asked me to be

his…" What did he want to call it? "Tracker. He fears that bandits will overrun Acktar without the Blades to keep them in check."

"And he wants you to watch for the banished Blades?" Leith's gaze was too keen.

"Yes." Martyn fussed with his horse's bridle. "Not sure if I'll take that part of the job on. I don't want to…"

"Turn into me?" Leith's voice was flat.

Martyn swallowed down the bitter taste in his throat. Betrayer of his fellow Blades. No, Martyn didn't want to turn into that. Instead, he'd betrayed his former friend.

But someone had to guard against the Blades' return, and Leith was too distracted with Renna and his new family to watch properly. Maybe Martyn couldn't repair the torture he'd done or regain their friendship, but he could do this.

Leith extended a large book. "Will you at least take this?"

Martyn took it. He'd been a Blade long enough to recognize the once illegal book. "A Bible?"

Leith's mouth quirked at the corners. "I stole it from Lord Alistair's study months ago, and when I tried to return it, he gave it to me instead. I'd like you to have it now."

Martyn stuffed it in a saddlebag. He couldn't refuse, not with Leith looking at him like that. "I'll try reading it." Try. That was the most he'd promise.

Leading his horse from the stable, he swung on and nudged the horse's sides with his heels. When the horse didn't move, he kicked harder and slapped the reins against its neck. "Come on, horse."

The horse didn't budge. Martyn swore under his breath. What was wrong with the stupid horse?

"Brandi named your horse, didn't she?" Leith limped from the stable.

Martyn swore again. What had that girl said the name was? Something that started with a W. Winifred? Winter? Water?

Wanderer. That was it. Martyn slapped the reins again. "All right, Wanderer. Time to get moving."

The horse set out at a canter.

Martyn didn't look back.

6

Martyn halted Wanderer at the crest of the hill overlooking Nalgar Castle. It had once been home. The place he'd belonged.

Now? Now it was nothing but stone and memories.

King Respen lay buried in an unmarked grave in Blathe. Most of his fellow Blades had similar graves across Acktar, the Sheered Rock Hills, and the Waste. In a few years, no one would even remember most of them had lived, much less where they had died. The Blades that were left were either behind him at Sierra or somewhere out there, either sticking to the rules of their banishment or lurking at Acktar's corners until a new leader rallied them.

And he would have to hunt them. Could he? They'd once been almost his brothers. Then again, he'd once thought Leith was his brother and look how that had turned out.

The guards at the gate eyed Martyn as he entered, but he ducked his head and sagged his shoulders like a worn farmer. In his patched, brown clothes and most of his knives hidden in his bedroll, he no longer looked like someone they should worry about, much less like a Blade.

After passing Wanderer to a stablehand—a new man he didn't recognize and who thankfully didn't recognize him—Martyn strolled the familiar passageway from the stables to the dark stairwell leading into the rooms that had once been King Respen's, but now belonged to Renna's cousin King Keevan.

When Martyn was First Blade, the guards at the bottom of the stairs never dared question him. But now the guards at the bottom of the stairs barred his way. "Who are you and what's your business with the king?"

Martyn ran a hand through his curls, now gritty with dust. If only he could return to his room in the Tower and wash the trail dust from his body before he approached the king.

But he didn't have a room here. He didn't belong.

He forced himself to stand straighter. "I'd like to speak with the king about an offer of a job he made me."

"Name?"

Martyn clenched his jaw to stop his frown. He hadn't bothered coming up with a false name yet. Leith had been so eager to throw aside his past to become Daniel Grayce, but what would Martyn be without his past or name? He'd be starting all over again.

He'd done that once before.

Then again, why did he cling to his family name? It wasn't like it meant all that much to him. Why not abandon his name? It was far less than what his family had done to him.

"Well?" The guard angled his sword toward Martyn.

"Owen." Martyn barely stopped himself from swearing. Why had he said that name? Of all names he could've chosen, why that one? Too late now. He'd said it. "Owen Hill."

"Wait here." The talkative guard thumped up the stairs. The second guard remained, blinking and scowling as if he thought the expression made him look menacing.

Martyn could show *him* a thing or two about *menacing*.

A few minutes later, the other guard returned. After making Martyn go through the whole search-for-weapons hassle, the guard nodded. "Follow me."

The guard led the way up the stairs, his gaze focused on his feet as if he was still unused to the dark, narrow steps. Martyn gritted his teeth, not looking as *his* feet. How many times had he climbed these stairs in the past weeks and months as First Blade?

The guard opened the door and stepped inside.

Martyn halted in the doorway. In the two days since he'd been there, the king's chambers had been torn apart. All the furniture except for the two chairs and the desk in the corner had disappeared, along with all the rugs, tapestries, and curtains.

At the far wall beside the door to the bedchamber, several men pried the wainscoting off the wooden interior wall. An older man with black curls sketched something on a piece of paper.

King Keevan stood in the center of the room, his ever-present bodyguard a few yards behind him. King Keevan's hand pressed against Queen Adelaide's back where it arched to support the weight of the child growing within her. Martyn didn't know much about such things, but she didn't look like she could stand to get much bigger. Something else for Acktar to celebrate. A new king. A new queen. And a new prince or princess to distract them from the hurt still festering.

Queen Adelaide had her hand stuck in the air, her mass of brown curls puffing around her head. "...have to get someone to clean the cobwebs from the corners. My mother would never have let the king's apartment get into such a state. I'd climb on the desk to do it myself, but—"

"You're not going to be climbing on anything." The rasp in King Keevan's throat deepened into a growl. With all the rugs and tapestries gone, his voice echoed against the bare, stone floor.

Queen Adelaide bumped King Keevan with her elbow. "Of course not. I can't even see my feet right now, much less see what I'd climb on. But I'm not going to just sit around. I've been cleaning these rooms since I could walk, and I cleaned our cabin in Eagle's Heights. I'm not about to go soft and spoiled now."

Martyn raised his eyebrows. So this was the new queen. She wasn't quite the fine china he would've expected.

The guard coughed. "Your Majesties, Owen Hill to see you."

King Keevan turned and stiffened, his smile thinning and hardening. He took a half-step in front of Queen Adelaide, as if to shield her. "I need to speak with this man alone."

King Keevan's bodyguard darted a hand to his sword's hilt and stepped between Martyn and the king and queen.

The workmen looked up, then set their tools down and followed the guard down the stairs.

Queen Adelaide cocked her head, eyed Martyn for a moment, then kissed King Keevan on the cheek. "I was starting to feel a mite peckish anyway. Papa, could you help me down the stairs?"

As she held out her arm, the black-haired man joined her and matched her pace as she waddled from the room, leaving Martyn alone with King Keevan and his glaring bodyguard.

Martyn was getting really tired of being glared at. He crossed his arms and focused on the tall, brown-haired bodyguard. "Your king is the one who invited me back here. So unless you're questioning your king's judgment, I have as much right to be here as you."

The bodyguard tensed, and his fingers flexed on his sword's hilt.

King Keevan rested a hand on his arm, halting him. "Take it easy, Frank. I'm safe enough for the time being."

Safe enough. Martyn resisted the urge to snort. Safe enough wasn't the same thing as safe. Apparently King Keevan didn't trust him enough for that.

"Have a seat." King Keevan claimed his chair behind the desk while the bodyguard took his position near the window. From there, he could effectively glare holes in Martyn's back.

Martyn sank onto the chair. This time, it would probably be best if he waited for the king to speak first. He'd already pushed rather far into disrespectful territory.

King Keevan crossed his arms, his flattened mouth tugging at the jagged line of the scar across his cheek and neck. "You're back sooner than I expected. You've decided to scout for me?"

Martyn held back another snort. Why else would he be here? It wasn't to apply for a job as castle cook or stableboy. But this was polite conversation, and polite conversation usually consisted of a lot of inane questions.

Besides, he couldn't fault King Keevan for his surprise. Martyn should've agreed to King Keevan's offer the moment he'd made it rather than waste a trip to Sierra and back. He should've realized that trying to fit into a peaceful sort of life would last about as long as an ill-fitting pair of boots.

He drew in a deep breath, but for a moment, he couldn't make himself reply. Did he want to hunt his fellow Blades? Pledge himself to a new king? Once he gave his loyalty to King Keevan, he wouldn't ask for it back. Would King Keevan take advantage of that?

What choice did he have? He didn't know how to do anything besides track, fight, and follow orders. Like the banished Blades, he had no choice. They would find their new master, and he would find his.

"Yes." It was done.

King Keevan spread a map across the top of the desk, pinned the corners down with four, dust-colored rocks, and pointed at the northwest corner. "The remaining Blades were escorted out of Acktar here. They were last seen headed straight north. I want you to patrol the Sheered Rock Hills from Walden to Kilm. Watch for anything suspicious, Blades or otherwise."

"You sound like you're expecting trouble from more than just five former Blades."

King Keevan ran a finger along the scar on his neck. "After the Battle of Nalgar Castle, the remnants of Respen's army scattered. Some returned to their towns. Others had no families and no ties to any town. They're drifting, angry because they lost, and looking to cause trouble."

Acktar was a country divided. Hurt remained. Anger. King Keevan walked a dangerous line. Violence could erupt across the country if left unchecked, yet too much military rule would mirror Respen's actions.

"Do you think Ki—" Martyn cleared his throat, "Respen's soldiers will turn into Rovers?"

Back before King Respen took the throne, the bands of outlaws, known as Rovers, had terrorized Acktar, pillaging towns, kidnapping for ransom, and plundering trade wagons. The Blades had killed most of them, though a few Rovers had joined the Blades. And for the last two years, no Rovers had dared wander Acktar. It just wasn't healthy.

"Several already have. I've received several reports yesterday and today about Rover attacks." King Keevan tapped the map. "The Hills have always been the Rovers' main hiding place. That's why I need you there."

"What do you want me to do should I see anything suspicious?" Martyn forced himself to remain relaxed. This was the main question. Was King Keevan any different than King Respen? Was Martyn going to be his scout or his assassin?

"Report to Lord Alistair at Walden. He will be alerted to assist you." King Keevan rested his arms on the map. "But if you think you can encourage the troublemakers to leave without too much bloodshed, then by all means, handle it yourself. Then report to Lord Alistair."

Martyn nodded. He had a new master, and now he had a new leash.

"Any questions?"

"Nope." Martyn stood. Finally, he had a mission.

7

After a long day of riding south toward Stetterly, Leith sprawled on the grass, his ribs and thigh sore, but not throbbing like they had been a week ago. The time at Sierra and Walden had done him good, even if the busyness of Shad and Jolene's wedding hadn't left a lot of time for resting.

Dusk pooled below the hills and faded the horizon into black. A hush had settled across the prairie, the breeze and daytime sounds gone, and the nighttime crickets not yet awake.

A few feet away, Renna and Brandi tended the fire and whatever they were cooking for supper. Their peals of giggles didn't bode well for the end results. Ranson and Jamie sat on the other side of the fire, and even Ranson was smiling.

Martyn's absence stung worse than the lingering pain in Leith's ribs. What could Leith have done differently? If he'd made more of an effort, would Martyn still have left?

Perhaps not. Martyn needed to move on, and maybe this was his way of doing it.

Martyn might even have the right idea. What did either of them know about a normal life?

Nothing. Or almost nothing.

It was a mission he couldn't scout beforehand, but going in blind meant making mistakes. Failing.

He might not even need the revelation of his past as a Blade to ruin Renna's reputation and future happiness. He could do that simply with his own ignorance.

Until Shad and Lord Alistair had taken him aside, Leith hadn't known traveling like this, with only the five of them, would be considered improper, especially without a life or death situation to justify it. It wasn't like Leith and Renna were alone, not with Ranson, Jamie, and Brandi sleeping around the same, open campfire. And, once they reached Stetterly, there would be the surviving townsfolk of Stetterly to provide more than enough chaperones until Leith eventually asked Renna to marry him and one of the circuit riding ministers swung their way. Until then, Leith would bunk with Ranson and Jamie, and Renna with Brandi. All perfectly proper and practical.

But apparently not enough. It mattered that neither of them had parents or any guardians left besides Lord Alistair. It mattered that Renna was Lady Faythe and would outrank anyone at Stetterly who even tried to be a guardian.

Should they have agreed to guards, if just for propriety's sake? But that seemed like admitting he and Renna had done something wrong. And they hadn't. Wouldn't.

Leith touched his right shoulder where his thirty-seven marks still marred his skin. For years, he'd never failed

Respen. He'd apply that much determination and more to make sure he didn't fail God and Renna.

But if his self-control and determination failed? If he couldn't act as wise as he thought he was? His father had lacked self-control. Would Leith inherit the same failings?

He'd trusted God's strength in torture. Surely he could trust Him in peace too.

A low snort came from one of the horses. Blizzard raised his head, his ears pricked. His nostrils flared, testing the breeze. Jamie's and Ranson's horses also stopped grazing, staring at the dark, prairie hills rolling away from their campsite.

Leith scrambled to his feet, ignoring the ache shooting through his chest and down his left leg. He drew two of his knives and placed himself between the girls and the direction the horses were staring. "Someone's coming."

Ranson and Jamie both pulled their own knives and took up positions with their backs to the fire. Brandi drew her short sword and stepped into line with Leith. A hard look tightened her face, her short, spiky hair glowing in the firelight.

She'd fought battles. It crushed Leith's bones to see for himself. Her experienced stance. The way she'd left plenty of fighting room between them.

Hooves thundered. A vibration traveled through the ground beneath Leith's feet.

Six horsemen charged from the darkness. They circled, swords drawn. Underneath the dust covering them, the horses and saddles showed quality, as did the men's clothes and swords. Two wore helmets emblazoned with Respen's crossed daggers.

Some of Respen's scattered soldiers, now turned into Rovers.

A burly man halted his huge bay horse and leaned on his saddlehorn. His gaze swept across the horses, Leith, Ranson, Jamie, and Brandi, before resting on Renna. The corners of his mouth turned up a little.

Leith ground his teeth but didn't speak. Not yet.

"What do we have here? A pack of peasants returning to your farms?" The burly man's eyes scanned the horses again. "Though those horses are much too fine to belong to peasants. I believe we'll relieve you of them. Well, all except that maimed one. Not worth keeping around, that one."

Brandi's lips curled in a silent snarl, but she held her place in line. Thankfully her battle experience had given her the patience to wait for Leith's signal. Leith wasn't sure what he would've done had she rashly flung herself at the men.

Leith didn't move. Hobbled as he now was, he'd have only one chance at this. He didn't have his former speed or strength. Just surprise and cunning. They'd have to be enough.

If Brandi, Jamie, and Ranson each handled one of the men—and that was uncertain given that these men were trained soldiers—could Leith handle three on his own?

He forced away the churn in his stomach. He'd have to kill. Harsh and cold and quick. It was the only way he'd take out three of the men quickly enough.

"And you." The burly man's gaze fell on Leith. His sneer carved across his face. "You look like you aren't worth keeping around either. A bit maimed too, I see."

The other five men chuckled.

Leith felt Renna stiffen behind him. Before he could stop

her, she stepped next to him, still clutching a ladle filled with her and Brandi's supper concoction in one hand. Leith rested his free hand on her arm.

One of the men slapped his leg and grinned. "Looks like you've found us some easy pickings, Cap'n."

A captain? If he'd once been a captain in Respen's army, then would his men obey him as they would a superior officer? If so, then Leith wouldn't have to take out all of them. Just their leader. He might be able to get out of this without too much bloodshed after all.

"What do you see in a runt like that? He's a bit damaged, don't you think?" The burly captain ogled Renna. "Captain Loust, at your service. Why don't you come with me, and I'll show you what a real man is like."

If Martyn had been at Leith's side, he would've snorted.

Renna clenched her fists, her arm shaking beneath Leith's hand. "Not a chance. I'd scratch your eyes out first."

"Easy, Renna." Leith kept her in the corner of his eye. And he'd been worried about *Brandi* doing something rash?

Captain Loust snorted a laugh out his throat. "Stand aside, boy. You aren't man enough for a woman like that."

Leith met the captain's gaze and dredged up all the hard strength he'd had when he was King Respen's First Blade. He kept his tone flat, a statement of fact rather than a threat. "If you lay a hand on her, I will kill you."

Something slid across Captain Loust's eyes. He hesitated, his hand in the air wavering between retreat and signaling his men forward. His jaw tightened, and he nudged his horse. "Get them."

Leith ducked out of the horse's way and pivoted on his

right foot. As he did, Renna lifted the ladle and flung the contents into Captain Loust's face.

Captain Loust shrieked and clawed at his eyes. Leith grabbed the captain's arm and yanked him off his horse, using a knee to flip him as he fell. When he crashed to the dirt on his stomach, Leith twisted an arm behind his back and pressed a knee into his back. The tip of Leith's knife pricked Captain Loust's jaw above the big vein in his neck.

Leith risked a glance around. Renna had returned to the boiling pot, her ladle ready with another scoop to fling. Brandi had hold of a horse's bridle, her grip by the horse's head preventing the man from swinging at her. Jamie dodged one man's charge while Ranson stabbed another in the leg. The remaining two men worked at the horses' hobbles. Ranson's horse aimed a bite at a man's rear end.

"Call off your men." Leith applied a hint of pressure to his knife. "Unless you want to bleed to death right here."

Captain Loust squinted the one eye not pressed to the ground up at Leith. The skin on part of his face developed a red hue. He hesitated for a moment longer, his jaw set.

Leith pricked Captain Loust's skin. A rivulet of blood trickled from his neck and dripped onto the sand. Leith lowered his tone until it rang as cold as a mid-winter night. "How much wider do you think I can make this cut before you bleed out?"

The fight sagged from Captain Loust's body. "Hold up, men."

The scuffling and scraping metal ceased. Leith kept his focus on the captain. "Now all of you back up slowly and bring your horses around where I can see you."

When they were slow to comply, Leith pricked Captain

Loust again. The captain squirmed, sweat beading on his forehead. "Hurry it up, you fools!"

Moments later, the five men had gathered a few yards away from Leith, gripping their horses' bridles. Leith twisted the captain's arm higher onto his back until he cried out. "You all start riding. I'll set him free when I can no longer hear your hoofbeats. Now move."

They scrambled for their horses, wheeled them around, and kicked them into a gallop. Leith held his breath, listening, until the sounds faded into the dull whisper of shifting grass.

Easing to his feet, he stepped back. "Get up and get out."

Captain Loust rolled to his feet and slapped a hand to his neck. He glared at Leith, then Renna. "I won't forget this."

Leith held up his knife so the drops of blood on the end caught the firelight. "Neither will I."

Captain Loust grabbed his horse, swung on, and took off after his men. Leith waited until the hoofbeats had drummed into the distance before he pressed a hand to his stabbing ribs. "We need to get moving. Ranson, kick out the fire. Jamie, saddle the horses."

Brandi swiped her sword on the grass and jumped to help Jamie. Renna supported Leith's elbow. He leaned against her and eased the weight off his left leg. Her forehead puckered. "You're done in. Are you sure we can't take a few more minutes to rest and eat?"

He shook his head. "They're circling back even now."

She nodded, her expression taking on that determined sheen he'd seen so often when they'd been locked in the Blades' Tower. She didn't even protest when Ranson dumped the pot onto the fire to put it out.

Minutes later, they swung onto their horses and set out at a trot. The pace jarred Leith's ribs and strained his legs. A canter would've been smoother and faster, but in the dark they couldn't see prairie dog holes or variations in the ground that could cause a horse to stumble or even break a leg.

The cool air flowed around them, crisp with the hint of autumn. Leith strained his ears to pick up something behind the thumping of their own horses' hooves and the night insects buzzing and chirping.

After they'd been riding for half an hour, Leith motioned to Ranson. "Check our back trail."

Ranson nodded and turned his horse away from them. The horse's ears pressed to its skull, its teeth flashing, as it swiveled its head and bit at Ranson's leg. Ranson tugged on the reins and moved his foot out of the way. "Come on, Snapper. You already took a bite out of one person tonight."

Jamie nudged his horse into the lead as the rest of them kept going.

Leith snuck a side-long look at Brandi. "Snapper, huh?"

"It's a good name. I wish I could take credit for it." Brandi shrugged. "He actually named the horse himself."

Probably while cussing the horse out. But Ranson and Snapper seemed to have an understanding.

After fifteen minutes, Ranson caught up with them. "Didn't hear anything."

Leith peered into the darkness. His stomach knotted with hunger. His back ached with the effort to stay straight in the saddle. He could push them farther, yet what they gained in distance, they'd lose in strength.

If his bearings were right, then they were only a couple

of miles away from a path down into the Spires Canyon. There was a sheltered spot partway down where a small group like theirs could hole up. Set along the narrow path as it was, their pursuers couldn't come at them more than one at a time.

Leith checked Valor until he fell into step with Big Brown, Blizzard trotting on his leadrope. "There's a place up ahead where we can rest. Just a few more miles."

"Good." Renna sagged in her saddle, her mouth pressed into a line. Brandi had her eyes closed, a hand to her head.

After a few miles, the black line where the Spires Canyon sliced into the land appeared out of the gloom. It took a few minutes of scouting along the rim before Jamie found the faint rut leading down into the Canyon. Not a trail, exactly. Simply a less steep part of the cliff side where animals had worn it flat on their way to the river at the bottom.

Leith followed Jamie down the narrow track, Renna, then Brandi following him with Ranson guarding the rear.

The first part of the track curled downward along the slope before descending into a section of shale and gravel. Dismounting, Jamie braced himself and half-slid, half-walked down the shale to a narrow ledge. The rocks and gravel clattered and hissed, echoing in the still night air. If the Rovers were anywhere close, they'd hear it.

Once Jamie reached firm ground, Leith dismounted and stepped onto the shale, leading Blizzard and Valor. After two steps, his left leg buckled, the muscle in his thigh cramped. He fell to his knees and tore the skin of his palm when he braced himself to halt his forward momentum.

"Leith?" Renna's voice whispered through the dark.

"I'm all right." He gripped Valor's bridle and heaved

himself to his feet. The horse raised its head and backed up a step at Leith's weight. He kept his grip on Valor's bridle as he set out again.

This time, he made it two steps before his leg crumpled, but his grip on Valor kept him upright. Thankfully, both Blizzard and Valor kept their footing. If one of them had gone down, Leith wouldn't have been quick enough to get out of their way as they slid down the slope.

When he reached the stone at the bottom, he leaned against Valor and tried to stop his shaking. Still so weak.

He led his horses out of the way as Renna started down the slope. She wobbled a couple of times but reached the bottom without falling. When she was steady, Leith led Valor and Blizzard between a boulder and the cliff face. On the other side, the trail widened into a broad ledge, part of it tucked into a cave-like bowl at the back.

Jamie had already hobbled his horse on the far side. He tugged the saddle from its back. Leith led Valor and Blizzard over to him.

When he reached for Valor's saddle, Jamie stepped next to him. "I'll unsaddle him for you."

If Leith had been less tired, he would've argued. Or at least put up some protest. Instead, he limped a few feet away and lowered himself to the ground. Sticking his bad leg in front of him, he massaged the muscle.

After a few minutes, Renna led Big Brown into their camp, handed the horse's reins to Jamie, and knelt next to Leith. "Are you all right?"

"Yes." Leith leaned against the cliff face behind him. He needed to be strong. He had to push through this weakness.

Renna touched his shoulder. "I'll fetch your blanket and some dried meat. Then you need to rest."

As Renna spread out his blanket and Jamie placed his saddle at its head for a pillow, Brandi and Ranson led their horses around the boulder.

"Jamie and I can take watch tonight." Ranson set his saddle a few feet away from Leith. "You look done in."

Brandi's intake of breath indicated she'd opened her mouth to protest. Leith shook his head and turned to Ranson. "If we get attacked, you and Jamie are the strongest fighters we have at the moment. We need you both well-rested. Jamie can stand first watch, you second. Brandi and I will take the third watch. Between the two of us, we'll manage."

Leith spotted the flash of Brandi's teeth as she grinned.

Ranson's frown shadowed his face. Leith gave him a stern look. "And don't get any ideas about neglecting to wake us when your shift is over."

"Yes, sir." Ranson nodded, his right hand twitching like he'd nearly given Leith the Blade salute.

"I can take a watch, if it would help." Renna hugged her blanket to her chest.

Leith shook his head. "No, sorry. You could certainly watch and listen, but if trouble happens, you might not be able to handle it before you can wake us."

Renna nodded, as if she'd expected his answer.

Stifling his groan, Leith stretched out on his blanket. Weariness pressed into his eyes, and he collapsed into sleep despite the rock beneath him.

HE WOKE TO A HAND SHAKING HIS SHOULDER. HE REACHED FOR his knife but halted as Ranson's voice registered. "Your turn for watch."

Leith shoved himself into a sitting position. His hip and shoulder bones ached from the stone beneath him while his left leg had stiffened to the point he could barely move it.

"Are you sure you don't want me to stand watch for you?"

"No, I'm awake now. I'll be all right. Help me up."

Ranson hauled Leith to his feet. Leith kept his weight balanced on his right leg to keep Ranson from seeing how unsteady his left felt.

Ranson eyed him but headed for his own blanket and rolled himself into it. Within a few minutes, his steady breathing joined the others in chorus with the crickets and tree frogs near the stream below.

Brandi's snore warbled above the other night sounds. Should he wake her? She needed her sleep.

But she'd be beyond mad the next morning. And if trouble did come, it would take the two of them to handle it. With his leg as stiff as it was, Leith wouldn't be nimble enough to handle things on his own.

Picking up his blanket, he limped across the ledge, leaned over, and shook Brandi's shoulder. Her snores stuttered, then restarted louder than ever.

He shook her again. "Brandi."

Her eyes flew open, and she bolted upright so quickly her head nearly rammed Leith's chin. "Our turn for watch?"

"Yep. Grab your blanket. It's chilly tonight."

She scooped up her blanket and bounced next to him as he limped toward the boulder. Folding his blanket, he placed it at the base of the boulder and eased himself onto it. Brandi plopped next to him and spread the blanket over their legs.

After squirming a few minutes, she jumped back to her feet. "I'll be right back."

Leith leaned his head against the boulder and listened to the ebb and flow of the night sounds, memorizing the cadence so he'd notice if it changed. Sitting next to the boulder, he had a clear line of sight up the trail, though he and Brandi would be almost invisible in the boulder's shadow.

Brandi returned a moment later with both of their saddle blankets. "Let's sit on these and use your blanket for a back rest."

After they made the adjustments, Leith settled back against the boulder. "Standing watch isn't normally this comfortable."

Brandi pulled the blanket up to her chin. "But with two of us, we don't have to worry about falling asleep."

"Not with your chatter." Leith bumped her with his elbow.

Her grin flashed in the dark, but it faded after a moment. She plucked at the blanket.

Leith waited. Whatever Brandi had on her mind, she'd tell him eventually. She couldn't stand to remain silent for long.

"Does it ever go away?" She pulled up her knees and hugged them underneath the blanket. "The nightmares? The memories?"

Leith leaned his head against the boulder, his heart

aching in time with his muscles. "It fades somewhat. With time."

"But it never goes away completely, does it?"

If only he had something better to tell her. "Maybe it does, eventually." He rubbed his right shoulder as if he could feel the rows of scars marching down his arm. "Some are worse than others. Some are just a blur, and others I can still smell the blood and see..."

"And see them dying in front of you." Brandi rested her chin on her arms.

Leith clenched his fists. Bad enough that he had to fight memories of blood and death and the feel of his knife plunging through guts and muscle. But Brandi? She shouldn't have those kinds of memories. She should be care-free and innocent, as she had been when he'd met her over eight months ago.

But the war had taken its toll on her, and he couldn't hope to undo it.

He wiggled his arm from under the blanket and wrapped it around Brandi's shoulders. "I know it isn't easy to deal with. But if you ever need to talk or you can't sleep with bad dreams, I'm here for you, all right? You can wake me up any time. I don't mind."

She leaned her head against his shoulder. "Thanks, Leith."

"Of course." He squeezed her shoulder. The night's chilled breath brushed his cheek and shivered along his nose.

She quieted again, and Leith braced himself for what-ever else she had to ask. What other ghost of the war still clung to her?

"When you and Renna get married, where am I going to live? I mean, I know you're going to be starting your own house, and it'd probably be weird to have Renna's little sister hanging around and all that and..." She trailed off and stared at the darkness as if trying to see into the future.

That's what was bothering her? He cleared his throat, trying to get his brain to function after the *when you and Renna get married* part. Not that he was opposed to that at all. Just nervous. Scared he wouldn't be enough. Staggered that both of them were still alive. "You're our family, Brandi. We aren't just going to kick you out. Wherever we end up living, I'll build on your own room—a whole wing if I have to."

"Can it be a loft? I've always wanted a loft."

"A loft it is then."

Brandi grinned and pumped her fist. "Yes!"

"You do know I have no idea how to use a hammer, much less how to build anything. It's liable to collapse."

"Hit your fingers enough times, and you'll learn quick enough."

As he shared a grin with Brandi, he caught sight of her red-blond hair and oval face. He glanced over his shoulder. The eastern sky behind them veined pink and blue.

"Do you think—"

Blizzard's head shot up. His ears pricked, pointing up the trail they'd come down the night before.

Leith held up his hand. "Sssh."

Brandi froze. Leith held his breath.

A hoof clacked against stone. A distant voice murmured somewhere above them.

Leith eased the blanket off his legs. Brandi did the same

and reached for the short sword buckled at her side. Leith laid a hand on her arm.

She nodded, gripped her sword, but didn't draw it. Leith touched the hilts of his knives but also left them in their sheaths.

Pebbles danced down the path. A horse stomped on the cliff above. Voices rose and fell but didn't carry well enough for Leith to pick out words.

Would they notice their tracks? Or would they move on? Leith tensed. If the men started down the path, Leith would get into position and send Brandi to wake the others.

The hoofbeats continued along the cliff, headed south toward Stetterly.

As soon as the hoofbeats faded, Leith eased to his feet. "Wake the others. We need to pack our things and move out quietly."

With a nod, Brandi slid to her feet, her footsteps grinding on the stone. The bustle of noise increased behind Leith, but he kept his eyes and ears fixed on the cliff. Would the Rovers realize they'd missed their prey and circle back? Once full daylight came, the track down here would be too easy for them to spot.

Someone tapped Leith's shoulder. He turned, and Ranson handed him Valor's reins. Behind the horse, the others each lined up by their horses. Leith met Renna's gaze. Though her eyes were wide, her mouth was set.

Leith led the way down the trail. His muscles had stiffened during his watch, but they warmed with his movement. He gritted his teeth and ignored the ache flaring through his leg and chest. He couldn't slip now. If he fell, he'd cause too much noise and call their pursuers straight to them.

After a final bend around a tall pine tree, Leith reached the tufts of grass poking through the sandy wash at the bottom of the canyon. When the others gained the bottom, he gave himself a minute to lean against Valor and rest his leg.

A soft hand touched his arm. "Are you all right?"

He turned to Renna. Her blue eyes searched his face. Leith touched the pucker between her eyebrows. "I'm healing."

"I know." The pucker didn't go away.

He leaned his head against hers. "It's long and slow, but I'll heal. Now we need to get moving."

She straightened and her jaw tightened. A steel, hard as his knives, flashed in her eyes. She wasn't the quaking, spooked Renna she'd been when he'd met her. This Renna, while still scared, could handle the danger.

He motioned Jamie to take the lead. Jamie led his horse past Leith and set out along the cliff side, hugging the cliff face to stay out of sight.

Leith kept an eye on the cliff overhead but couldn't spot any sign of pursuit. Would the Rovers give up? Or would they continue to pursue them all the way to Stetterly?

And if Leith managed to guide them safely to Stetterly, how safe would they be there? From what Leith had heard, Stetterly had few men left to defend the remnants of the town.

Perhaps Leith was just leading this band of Rovers straight to Renna's home.

8

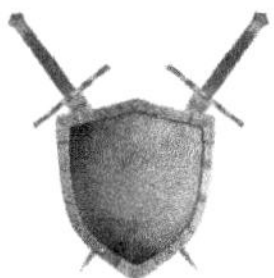

Martyn pointed Wanderer's nose northwest, deeper and deeper into the Sheered Rock Hills. Perhaps if they traveled far enough into the Hills, he could lose his past somewhere in the ragged cliffs and towering pines.

Would he ever be able to go far enough to outrun the guilt? Even now, away from Leith, Renna, and all reminders of what he'd done, Martyn still couldn't shake the weight of it. He flexed his fingers around the reins, reins that felt too much like the whip handle he'd once lifted to scourge his best friend's back.

His own back twinged with remembered pain. He'd given Leith no more pain than Leith had knowingly inflicted on him. Leith might not have held the whip himself, but he'd known the punishment Martyn would suffer the moment he'd taken Brandi from Nalgar Castle.

Should Martyn have gone with him? Helped him rescue Renna and joined the Resistance?

But wasn't Leith the one who had given up too easily? Given up on Martyn, on friendship, on the Blades, even on King Respen? Leith had tossed it all away without a second glance. Martyn had clung to loyalty. He hadn't given up.

Before him, the mountains dipped into a small valley, a lake pooling at one end. Since his horse seemed eager to head in that direction, he loosened the reins and let him pick the trail. When he stopped next to the lake, Martyn slipped from his back and dropped the reins to the ground. "Guess it's time to take a break."

Wanderer blew dust from his nose and extended his neck toward the water. Martyn loosened the saddle's girth and opened one of the saddlebags. After pulling out a wad of dried meat, his fingers hovered over the Bible Leith had given him.

Better keep at reading it. If he ever saw Leith again, he should at least be able to say he did that much.

Bible in one hand, meat in the other, Martyn found a spot against a tree, opened the book across his lap, and gnawed at the dried meat. The book fell open to one of the many little slips of paper marking sections of this book. Had Leith put those in there for his own benefit? Or had he already decided to give this book to Martyn and put them in for him?

Martyn tried to concentrate. Words. Just the same, insubstantial words he'd read growing up. Nothing to explain why they'd make Leith turn his back on everything he and Martyn had ever known. He slammed the book shut.

Martyn rested his elbows on his knees. "What's wrong with me, Wanderer? Why can't I see what Leith sees? Am I blind? Or is he delusional?"

Wanderer kept munching on the thick grass bordering the lake. Maybe Martyn was the delusional one. He was talking to his horse, after all.

"Guess it's time to move on, fella." Martyn pushed to his feet. His horse had wandered along the lake in its pursuit of grass. Dragging a hand through his hair, he trudged after the horse. "Wanderer, indeed."

As he reached for the reins trailing on the ground, he froze. There in the gravel lay a footprint. It wasn't a clear print, more an indent in the stone. Martyn padded a few steps further until he found a patch of sand. The footprints were a few days old, the edges crumbled inward and rounded.

Hoofprints layered with the footprints. Martyn ran his fingers over one, then another. From the shapes and sizes, about five horses. The footprints were too indistinct for him to count the number of people, but all the prints were large enough to be men.

Five horses for five Blades? Had he stumbled on their trail?

It could be anyone. These tracks didn't have to belong to the five banished Blades.

But any group of five men wandering through this part of the Sheered Rock Hills was bound to be trouble, even if they weren't the Blades circling back into Acktar. That meant they were Martyn's problem.

He led his horse along the tracks. After watering their horses, the men had ridden around the lake and headed west.

The town of Kilm lay to the west. Lord Norton had been an active supporter of King Respen. Or Surgis lay only a day south of Kilm. Lord Conree had also supported King Respen. Either of those could be a refuge for the five Blades.

If he was following the banished Blades and not someone else.

At least it was something. Better than drifting.

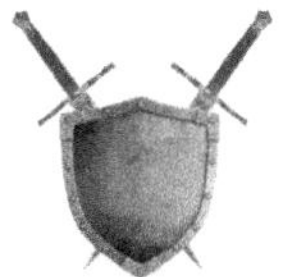

Renna braced herself as they climbed the trail out of the Spires Canyon, retracing the path she and Brandi had taken when they'd left Stetterly Manor all those months ago. Was she ready to see the destruction? Or return to a place that had once been home without Uncle Abel and Aunt Mara?

As they crested the ridge, four chimneys peeked above the horizon. Renna caught her breath. It was as if nothing had changed. As if she'd crest that ridge and see Stetterly Manor standing whole in the valley below.

But she couldn't let herself hope. Stetterly Manor had burned.

Leith led them across a stretch of prairie, into a small valley, then up another rise.

Below them, the prairie flattened around what was left of Stetterly Manor. Renna gripped her saddlehorn. The jagged remnants of fire-blackened walls jutted from the prairie.

Most of the walls had collapsed when the supporting girders inside burned away, leaving the four chimneys lonely pillars against the sky. Rubble piled in what had once been rooms.

A swathe of black ground surrounded the manor ruins. On the other side of a small ridge, blackened ground marked what had once been the town. Of all the wooden buildings along the single, dirt street, only charred logs and stone foundations remained. A few people moved among the rubble.

A horse stopped beside hers, so close their legs brushed. When she held out a hand, he clasped it but remained silent.

She swallowed and dragged her gaze back to the ruins of Stetterly Manor. "It's hard, seeing it like this. But perhaps it's best. It was hard enough to make it feel like home after Mother and Father died. It'd be impossible after losing Uncle Abel and Aunt Mara too."

Seeing Stetterly Manor in ashes nailed their deaths home in a way even their grave hadn't. Renna had pictured Stetterly Manor as she'd left it, Aunt Mara bustling around the kitchen, Uncle Abel at the table with his sermon notes. Even though she'd known they'd died, a small part of her still clung to that fantasy, as if she could somehow return to Stetterly Manor and everything would go back the way it had been.

But it couldn't. She couldn't.

In many ways, that wasn't a bad thing. Just different.

Brandi halted her horse on the other side of Renna. Below her short mop of hair, her face paled. Renna clasped her sister's hand as well. "We'll rebuild."

"I know." Brandi lifted her chin.

Renna turned to Leith and squeezed his hand. "Are you ready for this?"

It couldn't be easy for him. Stepping into this new life. Pretending to be less than what he was in a place where reminders of his past haunted the gravestones behind the remains of the manor.

"Yes."

She let herself be convinced and tugged her hands free. With a nudge, she sent her horse down the slope in the lead. She'd left this place as Renna, the daughter too scared to step into her role. Now, she returned as Lady Faythe. She could take charge. She had to.

At their approach, the people stopped what they were doing. Many reached for makeshift weapons stashed near them. A hammer. A plank of wood. A knife.

Renna halted her horse in what had once been the center of town beside the well. Long, hollow-eyed faces above forms clad in tattered homespun drifted into a circle around her, Leith, Brandi, Jamie, and Ranson.

A man stepped forward. Lines trenched across his face underneath a head of brown hair sprinkled with gray. "Lady Faythe."

Only his voice remained as Renna remembered. "Sheriff Allen. I'm glad to see you survived. Is your daughter all right?"

"Yes." He waved at the crowd gathered around them. "There's about three hundred of us, counting children, that have returned."

"I see." Renna swept her gaze across the town. At the far side, a few women tended cook fires. Behind them, a few tents flapped in the light breeze. Several ramshackle shelters leaned against wooden supports, closed on three sides but open to the elements on the fourth. It looked like most of the salvageable lumber had been used to build those huts.

Sheriff Allen stiffened and glared past Renna. She didn't have to turn around to know he was glaring at Leith. She couldn't let him speak or take out his hostility on Leith here. No time like the present to start acting like Lady Faythe.

"Sheriff Allen." She drew herself up straight and forced herself to wait until he turned his gaze back to her. "I'd like to discuss the state of the town and the efforts for rebuilding. Is there somewhere we can talk privately?"

He pointed toward the far end of town. "Over there will work."

Renna slid from her horse. "Jamie and Brandi, will you please see to the horses? Ranson, you can see about shelter for tonight. Daniel, if you'd come with us?"

She strode toward the far end of town and took several deep breaths to ease the knot in her stomach. This was actually going pretty well. She'd done a decent impression of Lady Lorraine's no-nonsense tone. Hopefully Renna could keep it up.

Near what had once been the blacksmith's shop, the anvil buried in a pile of charred boards, Renna halted and turned. Sheriff Allen scuffed to a stop in front of her. As Leith limped up to them, Sheriff Allen crossed his arms and scowled. "What's he doing here? I heard all the Blades were banished."

"Only the ones who ended the war on Respen's side." Renna spread her fingers flat along her skirts. She couldn't back down. If Leith was going to start a new life at Stetterly,

Sheriff Allen had to drop his anger. "Leith, and several other Blades, were pardoned for helping the Resistance."

Sheriff Allen's eyes drifted toward Ranson. His jaw tightened. "And you expect us to put up with Blades living here after what we've lived through? A Blade killed my wife. He might even be the Blade that did it."

Leith rested a hand on Renna's shoulder. "I'm sorry for your loss, and I'm sorry I wasn't able to prevent it that night. But I'm not the Blade who killed her. First Blade Harrison Vane took his anger out on the town when he couldn't find Renna and Brandi."

Renna clenched her fists. Because she hadn't died that night, someone else had.

Stepping away from Leith, she laid a hand on Sheriff Allen's arm. "Harrison Vane is dead. Shadrach Alistair killed him."

Sheriff Allen drew in a long breath. "There is some comfort in that." His eyes narrowed again. "That still doesn't take away the fact that this man is a Blade. He should be dancing on the end of a rope, not strutting around here like he owns the place."

Renna smoothed her skirts to hide her trembling fingers. Why did her trembling have to come back now? She was stronger than this. "Leith fought and nearly died for the Resistance, and King Keevan granted him a pardon. He has the same rights as any citizen of Acktar. As Lady Faythe, Stetterly is my town. He stays."

Leith slipped his hand into hers. His grip was strength and comfort, and it didn't matter that Sheriff Allen's face turned gray at the sight of it. The whole town would find out soon enough. Their courtship wasn't going to be a secret, even if Leith's past would be.

Sheriff Allen's shoulders slumped. "Lady Faythe, you're set on this?"

"Yes." Renna squeezed Leith's hand. He tipped his head toward her, and one corner of his mouth tilted upward. A flurry skittered through her chest. If he kept smiling at her like that, she'd turn into a dripping pile of March snow.

"Fine." Sheriff Allen's jaw worked. "But I'm keeping an eye on you. Any funny business will be promptly dealt with."

"You won't get any trouble from me." Leith pointed toward Ranson and Jamie. "Or them either. As far as anyone knows, we're peasant farmers who were uprooted in the war, and we've decided to settle in Stetterly. Ranson and Jamie are keeping their real names. They weren't Blades long enough for their names to be recognizable, but I'm going by the name Daniel Grayce."

Renna straightened her spine back into her Lady Faythe posture. Best to move things along. "Sheriff Allen, why don't you show us the progress you've made in the rebuilding efforts?"

Sheriff Allen coughed, straightened his jerkin, and strode to what had once been the center of Stetterly. "Right now, we're mostly scavenging what we can from the wreckage of the town and manor. We've been piling all the useful timber over here. There's still a lot to be done in salvaging the manor. Most of the stones can be reused for something, even if most of the woodwork didn't survive."

"Will we be able to build enough shelters for everyone before winter?" Renna studied the charred remains of what had once been her town. That pile of ash had once been the bakery. There the mercantile lay in a heap of black wood. The stench of smoke still clung to the air even after all this time, as if the town was a dead body still festering on the prairie.

"That's the real question." Sheriff Allen halted at the edge of town. The clusters of makeshift shelters dotted the grass in front of them. "We don't have enough wood to make houses for everyone. Even if we chop down every tree in the Canyon, the wood needs at least a year to dry before we could build cabins with it. Whatever dry wood we can find in the Canyon will be needed for firewood, not building."

Renna bit her lip. The wood provided by the Spires Canyon was too precious to waste all at once. They'd have to cut trees sparingly, as they'd always done, to preserve trees for the years to come. "So we're going to have to build sod dugouts then?"

"That's our only option. They'll be cozy enough this winter, if a little dark and dirty. Better than freezing." Sheriff Allen pointed toward a far valley. "We managed to round up some of the cattle herds, and most of the farm fields survived all right. That army didn't stick around here long enough to pick it clean like they did some towns."

Renna nodded. The townsfolk would've had a few lean months right after the army attacked, when all their food stores were confiscated or burned and the corn wasn't yet ripe. But now with fields ripe with corn meant for a town of over a thousand people instead of three hundred, they would have more than enough this winter, even if a few more people straggled in over the coming months. "Perhaps we can trade some of our excess corn to Walden for lumber and fabric. The fields around Walden were stripped bare from the long siege."

"Still won't be enough to build everyone cabins before winter, but we might be able to get in one trading trip before the snows lock us in." Sheriff Allen swept his gaze over the town. "But it would give us enough beams to reinforce the roofs of the dugouts and build proper doors. Most of what is left here is only good for firewood."

"What do you think, Leith?" Renna turned to him, but his eyes remained focused on the remains of Stetterly Manor. "I mean, Daniel?"

"We should build a church first." His gaze never wavered from the skeletal walls.

"While I understand the sentiment, shouldn't we work on more practical buildings?" Sheriff Allen frowned. "Stetterly's been without a church for five years. It can go a few more months."

"Perhaps. But it can double as a school building and a place for those who don't have homes to live through the winter if we don't get enough dugouts built in time."

"Where would we get enough wood for it?" Sheriff Allen shook his head. "It's a good idea, but not practical."

Leith's eyes glinted, and a smile tugged at his mouth. He pointed at the wreckage of Stetterly Manor. "We build it from stone."

Renna studied the tumbled stones. More than enough to build a large church, with extra stones to spare for foundations of the log cabins to be built next spring and summer.

And Stetterly Manor's stones would mean something. Would rise from the ashes as something new and better.

"That could work." This time, Sheriff Allen's gaze

appraised Leith. "We'll need a communal building during the winter. Something not damp and dirty to store the things that have to stay dry."

Leith waved toward the hill that currently separated the ruins of Stetterly and the manor. "We'll build it there. It'll have a good view of the approaches, and our sod huts can be spaced so barricades can be thrown up between them if needed."

Barricades? Renna turned to Leith. It didn't sound like he was designing a church. It sounded like… "You're designing a fort."

His eyes remained locked on the hill before them. "Tragedy has struck this town twice in the last five years. I'm going to do my best to make sure it doesn't happen again."

His voice was so warm, his tone low, Renna nearly leaned forward to kiss him. She might have, if Sheriff Allen hadn't been standing there. Leith didn't know this town. Didn't have any memories here besides those few weeks in a blizzard, yet he was protective of this town for her.

If she thought about it too long, she was going to lose all sense of her composure. She straightened her spine and locked the warmth into her heart to cherish it later. "Very well, we'll start work on the church along with the work on the sod dugouts. Daniel, you'll be in charge of the design. Sheriff Allen can assist you in figuring out the architectural part of it."

By the glance Sheriff Allen and Leith shot at each other, neither of them was entirely happy with this arrangement. But, it was the best they had.

As long as they didn't kill each other first.

Renna curled her fingers in her skirts. She mustn't worry

about that. She had to trust that Sheriff Allen and Leith would work it out themselves.

"Sheriff, if you could please put together a list of the division of jobs that must be done and who you think should be assigned to each job and crew? I'd like to get started first thing tomorrow morning."

He gave her a half bow. "Yes, milady." With a final glare at Leith, he turned and strode toward the cluster of tents.

Renna sagged. Even clutched in her skirts, her fingers shook. A tremor started at her knees and wobbled into her back. She closed her eyes. She'd managed to sound like the lady of Stetterly, but now the toll of keeping her composure together for so long poured through her muscles.

Warm hands closed around her fingers and tugged them free of her skirts. When she looked, up, Leith had both of her hands cradled in his.

He smiled, leaned forward, and kissed her forehead. "That's my Lady Faythe. Well done."

She rested her head on his shoulder. Her breath choked in her chest, a warmth curled in her stomach.

After a moment, he pulled back, his eyebrows tilted upward. "You do realize you just put me in charge of rebuilding the church I burned down almost five years ago?"

She tilted her head back and laughed. "There is a justice to it, isn't there? I did notice your design ideas are rather inflammable."

Leith grinned and leaned his forehead against hers.

She might just melt into his gaze. This is what she'd wanted all along. To return home. To rebuild Stetterly's church.

Respen had tried to use that against her. She tried to

shove back the memory. Respen didn't belong in this moment.

But he was all over it. In the ashes of the town his army had burned. In the graves behind what had once been Renna's home. In the past that shadowed all of them.

Leith's eyes narrowed, and he pulled away, his hand going to her jaw.

He was going to ask what was wrong. She couldn't have that. Not yet. How could she admit she'd thought of Respen moments ago when all she should've been thinking about was Leith?

She forced herself to smile as she had so often seen Brandi do, light and wide. She gripped Leith's hand. "Let's introduce you to the rest of the town."

And hopefully distract him.

Dawn broke warm and gray over Stetterly's graveyard. Leith dropped to the damp ground in front of a gravestone inscribed with *Laurence and Annita Faythe*.

What would it have been like to have met Renna's parents? Would her father have approved of him?

A year ago, no. But now? With his healing burns showing he was worthy to suffer for his faith? Renna seemed to think so. And Brandi. Even Lord Alistair, and he was the closest thing to a parent Renna and Brandi had left.

Leith rested his arms on his knees. What would it have been like to gain a father-in-law? A mother-in-law? Thanks to his own actions, he'd never know.

Was it wrong that he still ached for a father? He knew

God was his Father. Sort of. But how could he experience God as a father when he had no idea what that relationship felt like? Not the way it should feel, anyway. His relationship with his father was pounding fists and breaking bones.

The morning air wrapped around him with the promise of heat. Not even a breeze stirred his hair.

"I'm sorry."

Renna's parents were beyond hearing him now. But saying the words, asking their forgiveness, seemed like the right thing to do. If they were anything like Renna, they would've forgiven him if they'd had the chance.

Leith remained sitting by the graves for half an hour, long enough for the sun to peek through the trees of the Spires Canyon and a few people to venture from their tents and bedrolls in the makeshift town.

As Ranson strode toward him, Leith stood and dusted himself off.

Ranson glanced back over his shoulder at the town. "Any orders?"

"Orders? I'm not your First Blade anymore. You don't have to come to me for orders." Leith tried to meet Ranson's gaze, but he ducked his head before Leith could.

"I guess. I just...I don't know what to do."

"Me either." Leith gazed up the hill to the milling people. They seemed to know exactly where they should be and what was expected of them. Did Renna want Leith to organize them for the building of the church? Where did he even begin?

Jamie strolled down the hill toward him and Ranson, a similar look on his face. When he reached them, he shrugged. "Feels strange not to wake up to practice first thing in the morning."

"Yes." Ranson bobbed his head, as if Jamie had captured exactly what he'd been trying to say. "Like I'm trying to get on the horse on the wrong side or something."

Years of habit were hard to break. Leith fingered the hilt of his knife. He wore only one strapped to his waist along with a sword and two boot knives. He'd left his other three knives in his pack.

Was it a habit they should break? That group of Rovers was still out there somewhere, and not many citizens of Stetterly were fighters. If trouble came, Leith would have to deal with it. Along with Sheriff Allen probably.

Maybe he, Ranson, and Jamie would be wise to keep up their skills. Not as Blades, but as protectors.

Leith would have to talk to Sheriff Allen and Renna. The rest of the town should practice too. Sheriff Allen and a few of the other men knew a little of archery. Enough to put an arrow into Leith months ago. It wouldn't hurt to drill anyone who was willing to learn.

If Leith was going to build a fort, he would need people to defend it.

"Perhaps practice isn't a bad idea." Leith turned to Jamie. "Did you learn enough about swordplay at Walden that you could teach Ranson and me the basics? If we practice with swords as well as knives, no one will think we're former Blades."

Jamie rubbed the hilt of his sword. "I think so. I got a lot of practice in the army. Brandi would probably like to join us, if we can get her up this early."

Leith nodded. It wouldn't hurt for Brandi to hone her

skills. Not that Leith planned to let her near an army ever again. But she should have the skills to defend herself if the need came. "We'll practice without her this morning. Let her get her rest."

That's what they all needed. Rest, and a little practice at living a life other than that of a Blade.

10

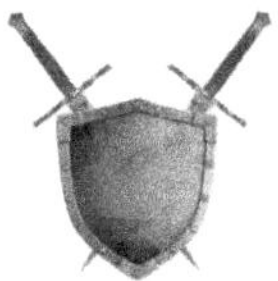

Martyn halted in a dense stand of pines, scanning the ground. The tracks he followed had wandered east nearly to Walden before they abruptly turned west once again. He couldn't even be sure he tracked the banished Blades. These could just be aimless travelers.

Except that so far, they hadn't gone into a town to look for work or a robbery target. They'd simply wandered, like men without a home.

Like Blades without a king.

In this part of the Sheered Rock Hills, the cliffs and rocks gave away to mountains covered in dense thickets of trees and interspersed with vast grassy meadows. Elk, bison, and wild horses roamed the Hills, along with packs of wolves, mountain lions, and the occasional bear.

Perhaps he should just give up and ride deeper and deeper until he lost his past and himself.

Wanderer pricked his ears and swiveled his head.

Martyn tensed and followed the horse's gaze. Animal or human? Friend or foe?

He drew his knife. Most likely foe.

He cocked his ear, listening to the wind sighing through the pine needles. There it came again. A cry of pain. Definitely human.

Just his luck. Someone in trouble. If only he could ignore the sound and go on his way. It wasn't his problem, after all.

But King Keevan would probably consider it Martyn's duty to stop and give aid. Help the helpless and all that nonsense.

Swearing under his breath, Martyn dropped Wanderer's reins on the ground and eased through the shadows under the trees. Whatever he found, he wanted to be the one doing the surprising.

He crept over a ridge. The thick pines prevented undergrowth and lower branches from growing. Despite the late summer sun pouring from the sky, the shadows under the trees remained dank and cool.

A figure, dressed in buckskin, sprawled on the ground a few yards down the slope near the roots of a fallen tree, chest heaving. A boy in his teens, slim, with short brown hair plastered to his forehead and around his ears.

The boy hauled himself upright, grasped something around his right leg and appeared to be pouring all his strength into yanking on it. A cry, both of pain and exertion, groaned from the boy's chest a moment before he flopped back to the ground.

Martyn scanned the area. No one in sight besides the boy. As Martyn drew closer, he spotted the jaws of a bear trap clamped around the boy's leg.

Well at least this should be simple. Rescue the boy, patch him up, return him to his family, and let them deal with the problem from there.

The boy's eyes popped open. He scrambled, pushed himself onto an elbow, and brandished a knife. "Don't come any closer."

Martyn halted. Something about the voice didn't seem right. And why would the boy fear a man stumbling on him? Wouldn't he beg for help first? Dressed in a brown shirt and trousers, Martyn didn't look like a Blade.

"I mean it." The boy tried to push himself straighter without moving his trapped leg. The movement stretched his shirt taut across his chest.

Not a boy. A girl.

This just turned into a whole new mountain of trouble.

Based on her boy's clothing and short-cropped hair, she'd probably joined the army like Renna's sister had. Which army, Martyn didn't know. Not that it mattered to him.

"Look, miss," Martyn ignored her intake of breath, "I have stuff I'd rather be doing, but you're obviously not getting out of that bear trap on your own. So unless you want to bleed to death or get eaten by the first wolf pack that comes along, I suggest you put that knife away."

Her jaw tightened into a decidedly mulish look. She stuck the knife into her belt, though her teeth remained gritted. "Fine. You can help me get it open."

Martyn knelt next to her leg. She gripped the jaws of the bear trap on one side, and Martyn grabbed the other. With a grunt, he pulled the two iron jaws apart. She yanked along with him, probably pretending to help to satisfy her pride.

Then she let go to maneuver her leg free, and the full force of the jaws strained against Martyn's hands. He grimaced. She'd been doing more than he'd thought.

She eased her leg free, blood staining the trap's iron teeth and blossoming on her trouser leg. As soon as her toes cleared the trap, Martyn let go and jerked his fingers out of the way. The iron jaws snapped shut with such force the whole trap bounced against the orange pine needles.

Martyn flexed his fingers. Pink grooves throbbed along his skin.

The girl gripped her leg, blood welling between her fingers. A gray cast washed over her face.

Martyn sighed. If only he could ride off and pretend she wasn't his problem. He wasn't a hero. Certainly not the self-sacrificing, ride up and save the day type Leith had turned out to be.

Why did Martyn always get stuck with the injured girls? He'd already dragged Renna, unable to walk due to a broken leg, through the Sheered Rock Hills. Now this girl, whoever she was.

Though, in Renna's case, she broke her leg trying to escape him. This girl's leg wasn't his fault. That made her even less Martyn's responsibility.

He dragged a hand through his hair. He couldn't abandon her. He didn't have any orders to justify the action. He'd just have to grit his teeth and get this dealt with as quickly as possible. Then he could return to his mind-numbing solitude.

Better get that bleeding stopped. Martyn drew a knife and yanked the ends of his shirt free of his belt and trousers. The girl flinched, releasing her grip on her leg to fumble for her own knife with trembling, bloodstained fingers.

Martyn huffed and sawed at the end of his shirt. "Relax. Just getting fabric to staunch the bleeding. Unless you'd rather use *your* shirt."

Her cheeks turned yet another shade of gray. "No. Your shirt's fine."

That's what he'd thought. If he'd been with one of his fellow Blades, he would've stripped off his shirt and not bothered with hacking a chunk off the bottom. But he couldn't take off his shirt in front of her, not without her seeing the marks on his shoulders.

When his knife parted the last thread, he tossed the fabric to her. "Try to staunch the bleeding while I fetch my horse."

He strode up the hill the way he'd come. Wanderer remained where he'd left him, cropping at pine needles. Snagging the horse's reins, Martyn led him down the embankment to where the girl huddled.

Since she seemed stable enough, if a bit pale and shaky, he set to work building a fire and filled his pot with water from his canteen. At least when he'd dragged Renna through the Hills, she'd taken care of her own leg. All he'd had to do was dose her with willow bark tea occasionally.

He remembered her soft touch on his back after his whipping almost two months ago. She talked then, and she'd kept talking a month later when she'd tended Leith during his torture. Her words and questions soothed and distracted.

Martyn couldn't manage the soothing part, but he supposed he could try the distraction. "What's your name?"

She hesitated, as if she wasn't sure what to tell him. Probably wondering if he'd buy whatever fake boy's name she'd been using. "Kayleigh." The name was barely legible past the girl's tightly clenched teeth. "Yours?"

What name should he give? His real name probably wouldn't cause a stir, but how much would she have heard? Best to stick with his fake name. "Owen."

She nodded, and her teeth made a chattering noise. He fetched his blanket from his bedroll. He nearly tossed it to her but stopped. She couldn't catch it with both hands pressed over her wounds.

Suppressing a sigh, he draped it around her shoulders and stepped back as quickly as possible. There. He'd at least made some effort to make her comfortable. Renna and Brandi would count it an improvement, right?

Kayleigh shivered harder, her face gray as an overcast sky.

He probably should give her some kind of painkiller. He dug into his saddlebag. Where had his medical supplies gotten to? "In case you pass out, where would you like me to take you? Do you have family nearby?"

Kayleigh eyed him, both hands still pressed to her wounded leg.

Telling her she might pass out and leave herself at the mercy of a male stranger probably wasn't the best way to go about reassuring her. How much more worried would she be if she knew the stranger tending her was a Blade?

"Fine. Don't tell me. I'll take you to the healer in Flayin Falls, how's that?" At least then she wouldn't have to tell him where her family lived, and Flayin Falls wasn't that far to the south.

"No, don't take me there." Kayleigh straightened and one

hand closed around the boot knife still strapped to her injured leg.

"Why not?" Surely her family would want to take her straight to the healer. Martyn would stitch the wound, of course, but they'd want a professional to look at the gash and restitch it into something neater.

"Just please don't take me to Flayin Falls. Please." She shivered harder, her eyes round and glassy.

"All right, I won't." Not unless it was necessary, anyways. Martyn found his medical supplies at the bottom of his saddlebag and dumped them out.

She rocked back and forth, shaking. "My...my family lives in the foothills north of Flayin Falls. There's a glade partway up a peak. They might be gone when you get there. Just leave me. They'll find me when they come back."

The directions weren't much to go on, but if worse came to worst, he could do his best to track her trail home. It'd slow him down since a girl on foot didn't leave much of a trail to find. But he'd manage, somehow.

"Just don't...not Flayin Falls...don't..." Her eyes rolled back in her head, and she slumped to the ground as if boneless.

He probably should've given her that painkiller. Oh well. Too late now.

At least she was out, and he could get to work. The sooner he tended her leg, hauled her through the Hills, and dumped her off at her family's cabin, the sooner he could return to tracking the five mysterious riders and pretending his life had a purpose.

He tugged off her boot and removed her boot knife and

sheath. He cut her trouser leg off at the knee and eased the soaked fabric off her wound.

Her boot knife had saved the bone from snapping, but the jaws of the bear trap still chewed up her leg badly. A nasty gash bit several inches into the muscle of her calf, the wound gaping like a red, oozing mouth.

Pouring some of the boiling water into a bowl, he washed his hands and cleaned the wound and the skin around it. Locating his bottle of alcohol, he dumped it over the wound.

Her leg jerked, and even in her sleep, she gave a tiny moan.

After cleaning a needle and thread with the alcohol, he did his best to sew the two lips of the gash closed. His stitches criss-crossed, both large and small, the thread slick and the needle tiny in his fingers. Renna would've been appalled by the job he'd done, but at least the stitches held. That was the main thing, right?

After he spread salve over the gash and the other, smaller scrapes and slashes on her calf, he wrapped her leg in a bandage. There. That was the best job he could do. At least she wouldn't bleed out on him. Digging a grave would be even more of a hassle than swinging miles out of the way to return her to her family.

He packed up his stuff, put out the fire, and buried the coals beneath a layer of dirt. After locating the rope holding the bear trap to a large log, he freed the trap and tied it to the back of his saddle with the rest of his things.

The trapper who set it should be tossed off a cliff. He should've left a marking nearby to give warning. Bad enough the girl stepped in it and got herself hurt. What if Martyn had ridden into it with his horse? It would've broken

Wanderer's leg, and he would've had to put the horse down and hike to Flayin Falls carrying all his gear.

Martyn wrapped the blanket tighter around the girl and picked her up, staggering under her weight. She wasn't a petite thing like Renna had been. If she'd been standing, she probably would've been nearly as tall as he was. Huffing, he heaved her onto the front of his saddle. She flopped like a dead body, but at least she'd remain limp, not stiffen up in a few hours. Stiff, dead bodies were annoying to lug on his saddle.

Climbing into the saddle, he rearranged her across his knees and pointed Wanderer south.

The underbrush and rocky terrain made for tough going. He had to constantly watch that he didn't bash her head or feet against trees. Thankfully, her short hair prevented it from getting caught in tree branches as they passed.

It took several hours to meander into the foothills above Flayin Falls and another hour to find her family's cabin. He stumbled across another cabin first, its door cracked open and signs of invading wildlife telling him it was abandoned. The next cabin he found had a faint wisp of smoke curling from the chimney.

He slung the girl over his shoulder and tromped to the front door. No answer greeted his knock, nor could he see any horses in the small paddock. When he tried the latch, the door swung open.

A dark, small room greeted him. He strode through it into one of the two bedrooms in the back. The bedroom had an empty bed, washstand, and men's clothes hanging from the pegs.

He tried the other room. A dress hung from the peg.

He dropped the unconscious girl onto the bed. Her arms flopped wide, and her body twisted. Sighing, he straightened her out into a somewhat natural-looking position. The short strands of her red-brown hair splayed across her pillow.

There. He'd done his duty. He'd tended her and got her home.

At least, he thought this was her home. What if he'd guessed wrong? What if this was some other trapper's cabin?

Surely the trapper would know this girl Kayleigh and help her get home.

Martyn shoved a hand through his hair. The tug on his scalp helped him focus past the storm heating his chest. He couldn't just dump her off and abandon her. He should at least stay until her family returned.

Especially since Kayleigh was still unconscious. Should she still be out? Or should she have woken up by now? He pressed a hand to her forehead. Did she feel a little warm, or was that normal?

If Renna was here, she'd have the girl fixed up in no time. Even Leith had more experience with wounds. He'd usually taken it upon himself to help the younger Blades when they got hurt. Martyn had always been happy to stay out of it and watch Leith's back instead.

Martyn could at least rekindle the fire. Maybe scrounge some food from the cupboards in case the girl was hungry when she woke up. His stomach growled. Surely her family wouldn't mind if he helped himself. After all, he'd skipped lunch because he was busy helping their daughter.

He coaxed the coals in the fireplace back to life, lit a lamp to brighten the room, and dug through the cupboards. Most of them were empty. Surprisingly empty for a family, especially with Flayin Falls so close. Maybe their cabin had been raided during the war and the army took all their supplies?

He took stock of the cabin for the first time. A few shingles on the roof needed repairing. A porcupine had gnawed on one part of the porch railing. On the inside, it was clean enough, though not the ultra-clean look he'd expect.

He trudged into the room with the man's clothing hanging from pegs. A fine layer of dust coated the clothes and the bed. This room hadn't been used in weeks, perhaps months.

A weight settled into Martyn's stomach. Kayleigh didn't have family. Of course she hadn't wanted to tell a stranger she lived alone. Instead, she'd ordered him to leave her to prevent him from discovering her lie. It explained why she was still dressed as a boy this many weeks after the war ended.

Now what should he do? He leaned against the doorjamb and tugged at his hair. He could leave. That's what she'd told him to do.

But what if she got worse? Or never woke up? Who would take her to the healer then? Who would even know? She'd be some long-dead corpse he'd stumble across next time he came through this area.

Did he really want her death on his conscience because he couldn't be bothered to stick around?

No. That wasn't the type of person he wanted to be. He didn't want to be like his parents.

As the evening lengthened, Martyn changed into his spare shirt, lit another lamp, and paced the cabin's tiny kitchen. Kayleigh didn't wake. When darkness fell, she began to toss, her skin hot and damp against his palm.

She needed a healer. She'd ordered him not to take her to Flayin Falls, but then again, what had following orders ever gotten Martyn? A cold stain of duty and a broken friendship.

Resaddling Wanderer, he wrapped Kayleigh in a blanket and slung her back over her saddle. The ride into Flayin Falls didn't take long. A few lamps burned in windows and on the lamppost to one side of the main square.

Martyn wandered down the main street until he spotted a pristine, white-painted signboard with *Healer* in black lettering, along with a man's name. Swinging down from Wanderer, he picked up Kayleigh. He nearly slung her over his shoulder again, but that might not be the image he wanted to project to the healer. Instead, he propped Kayleigh's head against his shoulder.

He pounded the healer's door with a foot. "Open up."

After a few minutes of pounding, the door creaked open. A tall man, a little plump around the middle, stood in the doorway, holding a lantern. "What can I do for you?"

"This girl is hurt." Martyn shrugged his shoulder. Kayleigh's head flopped to face the light.

The healer stiffened and backed away, his face contorted. "She isn't welcome here." He slammed the door.

Of all the...Martyn swore. What healer turned a hurt person away?

If his guess was correct about her fighting in an army, which army? Was it perhaps Respen's? It would explain some of the healer's reaction.

But not all. At Nalgar, Renna and the other healers had

tended the wounded of both sides. Then again, not everyone was as kind and forgiving as Renna.

Martyn kicked the door again. "What am I supposed to do with her?"

The door cracked open. The healer shoved a bundle of medical supplies on top of Kayleigh's unconscious body. "Take her back to her cabin, tend her, leave her to die, I don't care. Just don't take her back here." The door slammed in Martyn's face a second time.

Martyn glanced from the door to the medical supplies and swore. This was why he didn't rescue people. All too often, they became more trouble than they were worth.

He should storm in there and hold the healer at knife-point until the man tended her. All it would take would be a few jabs, a hint of the Blade he still was, and the healer would dissolve into stuttering and shaking.

But threatening healers probably wasn't what King Keevan had had in mind when he'd asked Martyn to scout for him, and Martyn couldn't lose this mission. It was all he had.

He marched back to his horse, juggled the girl while he stuffed the medical supplies in a saddlebag, and dumped her across his saddle once again.

Wanderer turned his head and sniffed at Kayleigh's head. Martyn patted the horse's neck. "Guess we're stuck with her a while longer. We're all she's got."

Somehow, knowing she was scorned by her town warmed a tiny corner of Martyn's chest. She was someone like him. Abandoned. Whatever she'd done to earn that scorn, it couldn't be worse than what he'd done.

He kept his head high as he rode from Flayin Falls. This

town had fought on the side of the Resistance, attacked by King Respen because most of them were Christians. Martyn should've expected the derision. Until Renna, he'd never met a Christian who actually lived like one.

But one person hardly made up for the hypocrisy of the rest. Only King Respen managed to be exactly who he said he was, and for that, Martyn had given his loyalty.

Martyn glanced at the girl flopped across his saddle. It had always been easier to live by duty. It was logical. Hard.

But at least no one could claim he was a hypocrite.

11

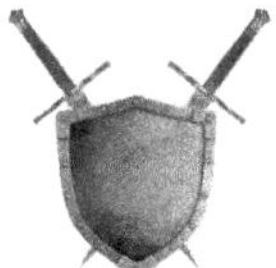

Martyn slumped in a chair next to Kayleigh's bed. Orange, dying sunlight winked through the tiny window. When he'd returned from Flayin Falls, he'd sorted through the supplies the healer had given him. Most of it was the same as the supplies he already had, but a few of the herbs were new, though he didn't know what they were for.

He'd remembered something about willow bark tea being good for fevers, so he'd brewed some of that and forced as much as he could down Kayleigh's throat. If it helped, he couldn't be sure.

He didn't dare sleep. What if she got worse? Or died while he slept? Somewhere in the past few hours, it had become his sole duty to keep her alive.

Shifting in the chair, he leaned his head against the back and stretched out his legs. What would King Respen think of him now? Playing nursemaid for a stranger.

It didn't matter what King Respen would think. He was dead. The Blades were dead or scattered.

Kayleigh moaned. Her eyes fluttered open and squinted. When she turned her head, she stiffened and gripped the blanket. "What are you still doing here?"

"You were unconscious. I couldn't just leave you." Martyn crossed his arms. He could've done that. Probably should've. Shouldn't he get some credit for doing the right thing once in a while? "Someone had to be here in case your leg had to be amputated."

She scowled and moved her foot beneath the blanket as if checking it was still attached. "Well, I'm fine now. Feel free to go."

Somehow, the more she tried to make him leave, the more Martyn planned to stay right where he was. It made no sense. Leaving all this hassle behind would've been the smart thing. She wasn't his problem.

If he was going to leave, he should've done it right away. Now, he had to see this through to the end.

"Not yet." He stood. "Go back to sleep."

She probably wouldn't sleep with him there. Fine by him. He was bored with sitting in the chair beside her bed anyway.

He strode into the next room, shutting the door behind him. He'd stay a few more hours. Long enough to make sure she woke up again and didn't fall back into a fever.

Just a few more hours.

With a lamp banishing the darkness to the corners, Martyn coaxed the fire back to life. He scavenged through the limited supplies in the cabin and his pack and set a pot to boiling with dried meat and a few assorted vegetables.

Noises came from Kayleigh's room. He straightened, but before he could move, her door creaked open. She tottered on her good leg and braced herself against the doorjamb.

At least she was up. That was a good sign. Maybe he wouldn't be stuck here much longer.

She limped forward, wincing as she put weight on her injured leg. When she reached the table, she gripped it with both hands, her face white. "Aren't you going to tell me I shouldn't be up? I should go back and rest?"

Martyn shrugged. "No. But if you pass out, don't expect me to catch you."

Grimacing, she slid onto the bench by the table.

He turned back to the pot. The smell of boiling meat wafted with the heat of the fire.

"What're you cooking?" Kayleigh's voice sounded like her nose was wrinkled.

"Boiled meat. A few vegetables." Martyn stirred the contents of the pot. She should be grateful he was even taking the time to cook something. He could've just fed her the dried beef and been done with it.

"Did you add any spices?" She sighed. The bench scraped against the wood floor. "Of course you didn't."

Her limping stride shuffled against the floor. She gave a tiny cry of pain.

Martyn shot to his feet and whirled. She swayed next to a cupboard, her face gray. He bounded two strides and gripped her upper arms as her knees buckled.

She blinked up at him, her teeth gritted. "I thought you weren't going to catch me."

"I decided I didn't want to patch up yet another gaping wound." That was mostly the truth. Actually, he hadn't thought before he'd acted. Rare that his instincts pushed him into something that could be misconstrued as heroic.

She straightened, braced herself against his arms, and reached into the cupboard. Pulling out a dried bundle of what looked like some kind of weed, she held it out to him. "Add a few leaves of this. And this one here." She shoved another bundle at him.

Martyn juggled the two bunches of suspicious-looking plants and Kayleigh. Somehow, he ended up with plants in each hand and her propped against his chest. Not what he'd intended. He juggled things again, got both bunches into one hand, and gripped her upper arm. He stepped back to put some space between them. "Got it. Sit."

After he steered her back to the table, he crumbled a few of the herbs into the pot. Was that enough? Probably not. He crumbled a few more.

Once he'd given the herbs time to simmer into the vegetables and meat, he retrieved two bowls and spoons from one of the cupboards. Kayleigh frowned. He probably could've been less obvious about the fact he'd rummaged through her house while she was unconscious. Though, why bother? It wasn't like he cared what she thought of him.

He scooped his improvised soup into the bowls, plunked one down in front of Kayleigh, and sat across the table from her.

How long had it been since he'd sat at a table in a cabin like this? Certainly not since...

He fisted his hands below the table. If he closed his eyes, he could see his mother placing a pot of stew on the table, his father already seated at the one end, his brother grinning across from him.

No. No memories. Not now.

He plunged his spoon into his bowl, blew, and popped the bite into his mouth. He was on his third bite by the time he realized Kayleigh was staring at him, eyes wide, as if she were scared. "What?"

"I..." She heaved a deep breath and straightened her shoulders. Without another glance in his direction, she folded her hands and bowed her head.

Martyn choked back a string of curses. Of all the low-down, flea-bitten, five-day-dead-body luck! He was stuck with *another* one. A Christian. Just like Renna and Leith and Shadrach Alistair and all their bunch. He'd ridden into the Sheered Rock Hills to get away from all that nonsense. But it seemed it had caught up with him anyway.

Kayleigh raised her head and peeked at him, a sheen covering her brown eyes in the lamplight. When she reached for her spoon, her fingers trembled. "I take it you don't... aren't..."

Martyn stirred the potatoes and beef around in his bowl. How much anger had shown on his face? No wonder she'd been scared. Not that long ago, she would've risked her life praying before a stranger when she didn't know what side he was on. As a Blade, he would've taken her straight to King Respen for execution.

Even now, she was alone and hurt, and she couldn't depend on anyone helping her if he turned out to be trouble. And he'd just made it abundantly clear where he stood.

Why shouldn't he? He wasn't going to hide his lack of faith any more than she hid her trust in it. "No, I'm not. Faith is an illogical trust in superstitions and myth."

She cocked her head and chewed a bite of meat. "Or perhaps it's a confidence in solid knowledge."

He shoved another bite into his mouth. He wasn't going to have this conversation. He'd already swallowed too much from Leith and Renna and Brandi over the past few months. "I'm surprised you think so, after how the supposedly good people of Flayin Falls treated you."

Her face whitened and the trembling returned to her fingers. "You went to Flayin Falls?"

"You had a fever and needed a healer. But the good healer tossed me out the moment he caught sight of you." Martyn eyed her. "Why does the healer hate you so much? What did you do?"

"I didn't do anything." She spat the words at her bowl.

"Is it because of..." He waved his spoon at her shorn hair, shirt, and trousers.

"No. They already hated me long before all this." She grimaced and stirred her soup first one way, then the other.

Martyn waited her out. He'd gone through all the trouble of helping her. The least he deserved was a few answers.

She sighed and glanced up at him. "I thought if I joined the Resistance army I could prove...it doesn't matter. It only made things worse. But you don't seem too shocked."

Renna's little sister had run off to join the war. Why not Kayleigh? If a girl wanted to fight, she didn't have any other option but to cut her hair and play a role. "You're not the first girl I've met who joined the army. You came out unscathed at least."

She scowled. "I got through the war all right, but then I blundered into a bear trap my first few weeks home. I should've realized Old Man Bendwick would've left a few traps out there when he died. Respen's army killed him when he refused to let them take his supplies."

"What happened to your family?" The question burst out before he could stop it. Did he really want to know? Then again, better she kept talking about herself and didn't ask too many questions about him.

She stilled, her spoon frozen part way through a stir. When she spoke, her voice was hard and flat, like all her emotions were walled away behind a layer of ice. "My mother died when I was born. My father was devastated, but he poured everything he had into raising me. He was killed a few months ago trying to defend Lord Westin from a Blade."

What would she think if she learned the man sitting across from her was a Blade? Not the Blade that killed her father, but she'd still throw him out.

Tempting. If she was the one who ordered him to leave, he could do it without guilt, right?

Something still held him back. He was here now. He wasn't the type to abandon someone. He knew how that felt all too well.

Besides, something in her story didn't add up. From all appearances, the townsfolk of Flayin Falls had no reason to scorn her. Her father had been a hero and had died defending his lord. She was a Christian, and she'd fought for the Resistance. She claimed she'd done nothing to cause their hatred.

So why did the townsfolk hate her so much that the healer would turn her away?

Kayleigh set down her spoon and shoved her bowl away. "Why did you stay? Who are you anyway? All you've told me is your name."

That was all he was going to tell her, at least where his past was concerned, and even that was a lie. But his current job? As far as he knew, it wasn't a huge secret.

"I'm scouting for King Keevan. Looking for Rovers." And Blades, but he'd rather keep that part to himself. The less she connected him with Blades, the better.

"And stopping to rescue helpless girls while you're at it. How heroic." She blew a lock of hair out of her face.

"You're a minor nuisance." Martyn shrugged. He wasn't going to tiptoe around the truth. "Besides, I could use a base of operations."

Until he'd said it, he hadn't put much thought into how he'd go about watching the Hills now that he'd lost the one trail he'd been following. Leith would've approached this with a plan in mind. He'd always been good like that, planning missions and leading others.

Of course, it was Leith's planning ability that made him such a good traitor.

"I'm not...wait, you mean to stay here?" Kayleigh gaped at him.

"Well, why not? You're obviously going to need help. You can't walk all the way to Flayin Falls on that leg, and you're not going to last another two days without more supplies." The more Martyn thought about it, the more he liked the idea. A place to restock. A base for his scouting missions.

"But you can't stay here! It isn't proper."

He snorted. "You care about proper? You're dressed in trousers."

"Trousers are more practical for hiking through the woods and checking traps." She clenched her fists and glared. "I'm in enough trouble with the townsfolk without having a strange man living in the same house."

"Who cares what they think? It's the most practical solution."

"But not wise. I don't know you, and you might...there are temptations..." Her face reddened in the orange glow of the lamp.

He swept his gaze from her shorn hair to her baggy shirt. "You think I'm tempted?" He snorted and grabbed the dishes. "Hobble back to bed. I'm not going anywhere at this time of night."

Dumping the dishes into the bucket on the countertop, he stalked into the second bedroom and closed the door.

He should just let her take care of herself. Why did he care if she tromped through the forest and tore all his stitches? She could get an infection and lose the leg for all he cared.

He didn't care. But he did. Somewhat. After all, it would be a waste of time if he'd gone through all the trouble of helping her and losing the trail only to have her die on him.

That was the only reason he was doing this.

12

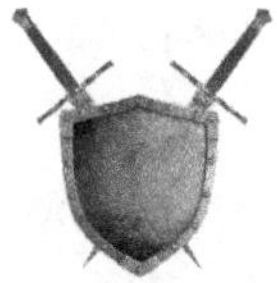

Leith yanked the ear of corn from the stalk, adding the twist at the end Brandi showed him after he'd struggled for several minutes to get the first ear off that morning. Adding the ear to the bushel basket, he straightened. His healing burns throbbed with the heat beating down on him. Sweat soaked through the front of his shirt, and probably his back as well.

To the west, the sun inched toward the horizon, slanting orange shafts between the rows of cornstalks. Every few rows, men and a few women filled their own bushel baskets, harvesting the long field of late-ripening sweet corn. Technically, the field belonged to Renna, as lady of Stetterly, and the townsfolk rented a portion of it by giving some of their produce to the manor. Renna still hadn't decided how much restructuring of the lands around Stetterly she planned to do.

Ranson stumbled down the row and claimed the basket. "Is that the last of it?"

Leith swiped his forehead against his shoulder. It only smeared the sweat around. "Think so. For today at least."

The men and women in the other rows began weaving their way through the field toward the town. Ranson heaved the basket to his shoulder, dirt from the bottom rubbing off on his shirt.

Leith checked that the rolled end of his right sleeve covered his marks. In the heat of the late summer day, most of the men had stripped off their shirts completely or wore only open vests. Even Jamie wore a sleeveless vest, his single mark passed off as a sword-scar from the war. Leith and Ranson were the only ones with sleeves to their elbows.

It wasn't a big deal. So he sweated through a shirt or two to hide his marks. But it was yet another reminder that Leith wasn't normal. He still had secrets.

When they reached the center of the encampment, Ranson set the bushel next to the pile of corn Leith, Ranson, Jamie, and Brandi had picked. Jamie and Brandi hunched over the firepit, discussing the best way to coax the fire into life.

Leith grimaced. The buffalo chip and cow pie fire had an unpleasant odor as it burned, like a grass fire mixed with something sour. But for the most part, they were saving their wood for winter when they'd rather have the smell of log instead of dung filling their dugouts.

The men clustered around the water trough, splashing water onto their chests and scrubbing away layers of dirt and sweat.

Leith headed for his lean-to. After digging out his spare shirt, he hiked down the path to the bottom of the Spires Canyon. The Ondieda River wound through the bottom, gurgling over rocks and churning around the bends in the canyon.

After hiking around the bend and checking that no one else was around, Leith peeled off his shirt. He splashed handfuls of water onto his chest and scrubbed away as much of the sweat and grime as he could. He dunked his head and scrubbed at his hair. When he straightened, rivulets of cold water trickled down his back.

Something crunched on gravel.

Blades.

Leith spun on his heel, rolled, and drew two of his knives.

One of the young men of Stetterly stood a few feet away, eyes wide, mouth open.

Leith tried to steady his breathing. Not Blades. Sheathing his knives, he yanked on his clean shirt.

Had he seen Leith's marks? Did he know what they meant?

Leith cleared his throat. "Did you need something?"

The young man held up a bucket. "My mama sent me for water, and I didn't want to wait in line at the well." He lowered the bucket, but his eyes remained focused on Leith. "You have a lot of scars."

The tight muscles in Leith's back relaxed. The young man hadn't seen his marks. Only the scars from his whipping and the almost healed burns across his chest. "Torture."

That was all Leith would tell him. Explaining anything more would get complicated.

The young man continued to stare. Leith shifted. Best to end this conversation as quickly as possible. He jerked a thumb over his shoulder. "You might want to head farther up stream to fetch your water."

The young man nodded and brushed past him. Once he was out of sight, Leith rinsed his soiled shirt, wrung it out, and hiked up the trail to the rim.

At the top, Leith hung his shirt outside his lean-to to dry. As he straightened, he spotted movement by the corral.

Brandi gripped a rope halter she'd slipped over Blizzard's head. She jogged next to him as she led him in circles around the paddock.

Leith leaned against one of the posts, watching Blizzard's stride. The horse still favored his injured leg, but it didn't hamper his stride like it had before. "He's looking good, Brandi. You're doing a good job with him."

She halted and led Blizzard over to him. Leith rubbed a hand over Blizzard's nose. When he stopped, the horse bumped him until he scratched his neck.

Brandi grinned and scratched the other side of Blizzard's neck. Her short hair frizzed around her head and mostly covered the scab along her scalp. "Won't be too much longer before he'll be galloping again."

"I'm sure." Leith waited while she slipped the halter off. "So what should I expect from this Festival?"

"You've never been to a Corn Festival before?" Brandi cocked her head. "No, of course not. Not the sort of thing someone like you attends."

Leith frowned. He had sort of attended one. Once. He'd used the Festival's distraction to kill his target. Not something he wanted to tell Brandi. Especially not in a place where someone might overhear. "No."

"Well, you shuck a lot of corn, then you eat a lot of corn."

Brandi's eyes wrinkled with her smirk. "If you find a red ear while you're shucking, you give it to the girl you'd like to kiss. If she accepts, you get to kiss her. Same thing if a girl finds a red ear of corn and gives it to a guy."

"So basically everyone shucks as many ears as possible looking for a red one?" Leith raised his eyebrows.

"Exactly, though only if you're over sixteen. I just get to have fun without that hassle." Brandi skipped ahead. "We'd better check if Renna needs any help."

By the time they reached what now was the town square, men were already busy setting up tables and dumping the corn they'd picked into piles in front of their spot. Leith helped Jamie set up a few more tables made of a few doors they'd scrounged from the burned houses and shops balanced on logs.

Ranson heaved a bushel basket onto the table. Leith poured out a second one while Jamie hauled a third basket onto the table.

Renna slipped into the space next to Leith. "You look a bit cleaner."

"Ready for your speech?"

She scowled and sighed. "No."

After a few more minutes, the last of the tables had been set up and the corn dumped onto them. The townsfolk quieted and stared toward Renna and Leith.

Renna sucked in a deep breath and stepped into the center of the tables. She held her shoulders back, her hair frizzing from its braid. "Welcome to this year's Corn Festival. There are a lot of missing faces. Fields we picked today were planted by family and friends we lost. It is all right to mourn, but tonight, we celebrate life. Stetterly might have been burned to the ground, but we still survive and we will rebuild. Starting now. Let the Festival begin."

A few cheers broke out. As the others dove into shucking their piles of corn, Renna leaned her forehead against Leith's shoulder. "I hate speeches."

He wrapped an arm around her. "I thought you did great."

"I'm getting better at faking it. I still fall apart afterwards." Her fingers shook as she slipped her hand into his.

Brandi rolled her eyes. "You won't get any corn shucked at that rate."

Leith reached for an ear. "Any tricks for shucking corn?"

Jamie leaned closer as Brandi demonstrated the best way to strip the husk from the cob. She tossed the husk into a pile and dumped the cob into a basket.

Leith set to work. The rough husk squeaked against the kernels. A green, sweet smell filled the air. The yellow silk of the tassel stuck to Leith's fingers.

At a table a few yards away, a man held up an ear of corn. Instead of pale yellow, this ear's kernels were tinged a deep burgundy. "Red ear!"

A few of the other men hooted. The hoots got louder as the man handed the ear to his wife, then kissed her soundly. When the kiss went a little too long, his wife pulled away and smacked his shoulder with her half-shucked ear of corn. That caused even more chuckles around the tables.

The sounds of creaking cobs and rustling husks filled the air once again, joined by the crackle of the fires. A few more red ears were found and exchanged.

Across the way, Sheriff Allen's daughter, the one that Ralph Chimb had kidnapped all those months ago, held up a red ear. She sashayed across the square, heading toward Leith's table.

Beside Leith, Renna tensed. Leith held his breath. He'd done his best to avoid Sheriff Allen's daughter, both because the sheriff would probably kill him if he got too close and because the girl might recognize him.

The girl held the corncob out to Ranson. His eyes widened, and he glanced at Leith as if asking permission.

Leith shrugged. It was up to Ranson.

Slowly, Ranson took the corncob and strode around the table. He tried to bend over and give her a quick peck, but she pulled him down for something longer. When Ranson straightened, his face was red, though his eyes had a glazed look.

Leith shook himself and redoubled his husking efforts. He was getting rather anxious to find one of those red corncobs himself before any of the other young men around the tables got any ideas about Renna. Not that she'd accept if they tried, but he'd rather head off any thoughts in that direction.

Brandi bumped his elbow. As he turned to her, she nudged an ear of corn under his hand. As it rolled, he caught a flash of red. He raised his eyebrows. She winked.

He winked back. At least he didn't have to worry about Brandi's opinion of his relationship with her sister.

He tore off the husk, revealing the red kernels.

Brandi raised her voice. "A red cob!"

As eyes turned their way, Leith scowled at Brandi. Of course she'd draw attention to them.

He drew in a deep breath and turned to Renna. He held out the red cob.

Renna smiled and took the cob. Leith tried to block out the sounds of the townsfolk hooting or calling out. His heart hammered in his ears. He cupped Renna's chin in his hand, leaned down, and kissed her.

She rested her hand against his chest and kissed him back.

He would've been more than happy to keep kissing her, but he pulled back before the kiss lasted too long.

Renna had an odd look on her face. Not a happy glint or an embarrassed blush like he'd expected. Her mouth drooped beneath her wavering smile.

Why was she sad? Had he done something wrong?

He didn't get a chance to ask her. Next thing he knew, everyone was hustling to their fires and dumping handfuls of their shucked corn into the pots of boiling water. The corn took only three minutes to cook. Then the ears were hoisted from the pot, slathered in butter, and sprinkled with a pinch of their precious store of salt.

Leith burned his fingers, then the roof of his mouth, as he bit into his first ear of corn. The kernels crunched, not too hard and not too mushy, and burst with the sugary taste of sunshine.

Beside him, Brandi already had butter and corn kernels smeared on her chin and cheeks.

Jamie held out his ear of corn and grinned at Ranson. "Think you can eat more than me?"

"Of course." Ranson reached for another ear and chomped into it.

The entire square sounded with the steady crunch-crunch-crunch of three hundred people gnawing on their corn like an entire forest full of hungry chipmunks.

Leith glanced at Renna. She bit at her ear of corn, still not smiling. He swiped at a kernel on her cheek. "What's wrong?"

"Nothing." She shook her head and stood. "I'd better put in more corn. Ranson and Jamie have eaten five each already."

Leith finished a second, third, and fourth ear of corn. When Renna still hadn't returned, he slid to his feet. Brandi glanced up at him, her cheeks chubby with corn. He patted her shoulder. "Stay here with Jamie and Ranson. Someone needs to make sure they don't eat themselves sick."

Considering they were on their eleventh, it was probably already too late for that.

Leith strode past the fire and its bubbling pot and headed into the darkness beyond. When he was far enough that he could hear the night sounds beyond the laughing and chomping behind him, he halted. For the first time all day, a breeze eased between the lean-tos and rustled the prairie grass.

A mewling sound drifted along with the crickets. Leith turned and followed the sound past the shelters to one of the half-burned buildings.

Renna hunched on the ground by the one standing wall, her arms wrapped around her knees and her face buried in her arms. Another shudder tore down her back.

Leith eased to the ground and pulled her to him. She melted into him and pressed her face against his shoulder, still sobbing.

"What's wrong?" Leith rubbed her back and hugged her tighter. Was it something he'd done?

She sobbed and sniffed. "I just...I can't...I can still hear your screams, and...and I nearly married Respen. Worse, I was prepared to try to love him, to try to give him my heart. When I had someone like you."

Leith sucked in a breath and tried to keep his muscles relaxed. "You thought I was dead."

"Yes. And I nearly married someone else a few weeks later. Nearly tried to move on." Another burst of sobs wracked her body. She curled tighter against him. "I can't believe I even thought about trying to love Respen. I thought I could change him. I didn't even know how wrong I was until I saw you, whipped and bleeding. For me."

Leith concentrated on breathing slowly, steadying the heat building in his chest. Who was he angry at? Not Renna. A part of her had broken at Nalgar. How could he blame her for being taken in by Respen when he'd willingly slaved for the man for nine years?

Leith shouldn't have left her so long at Nalgar. He should've done everything to get her out of Nalgar the first time. Before Respen had a chance to break her.

He prayed for wisdom. What did she need to hear right now? He pressed a kiss into her hair. "Did you ever tell him you loved him?"

Her fingers tightened in his shirt. "No."

"Kiss him?"

"Ugh, no!" She shuddered. "Though I might've, if Martyn hadn't told me you were alive right before the wedding."

Leith owed Martyn for that. "You refused to marry him as soon as you found out I was alive?"

She nodded, her hair brushing against his chin.

Something eased in his chest. He closed his eyes at the memories of those last few moments in the Tower. Respen raising his knife, the weakness flooding Leith's limbs, and Renna shielding him. Even now, Leith's stomach churned. He hadn't been strong enough. If Respen had thrown his knife, Renna would've died to save Leith.

And in that desperate moment, he'd never loved her more.

He needed to tell her that. He'd held back before, but now he had a future to promise her, as uncertain as it seemed. He'd already told her with every kiss, every sacrifice. But she still needed to hear it.

If he'd told her sooner, maybe she wouldn't be curled against him, crying.

Leith cupped her chin and tipped up her face. Her tears shone in the faint starlight. "You're kind. A healer. You couldn't help but care. It's one of the things I love about you."

"I know, but..." Her eyes widened, and her mouth hung open. "Did you just..."

A different sort of heat throbbed through his chest. The tempting sort of heat that could make a man lose his head if he wasn't careful.

If there were two things he'd learned as a Blade, they were self-control and self-denial when it came to temptations. The mission came first.

Now, God came first. Then Renna.

Leith planted his kiss on her forehead. Sometimes, it paid not to test his self-control too far. "Surely by now you know I love you."

"I just thought it'd take you a lot longer to say it, if you ever did." She rested her head on his shoulder once again.

Leith leaned his head against the wall behind him. In the

distance, the sounds of singing and clapping rang to the night sky. He probably should convince Renna to return to the Festival.

But right now, he couldn't help but savor these few minutes alone with her. That week in the Tower had some of his worst memories, but also some of his best. There, Renna didn't have to be Lady Faythe, and he wasn't a former Blade. They were simply Leith and Renna. No past. No future. Just that moment.

It had made them bold. Open. They'd talked more in that one week than they had in the months before that.

Now rebuilding Stetterly kept them busy from sunrise to sunset, and sometimes beyond that. Time had returned caution and uncertainty.

What kind of future did Renna want from him? Could he give it to her?

"Do you think about the future at all?" Leith swallowed and tried to put his thoughts into words.

Renna shifted and scrubbed at her face. "Sometimes. Well, a lot."

That answer didn't help him any. Couldn't she just come right out and say what she was thinking? "If you could do anything, what would it be? What would you like the future to look like?"

"I'd like to live in a cabin by the canyon. No responsibility except my family and my calling as a healer." Renna heaved a sigh. "But I'm the lady of Stetterly. I'm not even sure I can do that and remain Stetterly's healer. What if I was gone at the Gathering, and someone needed help? I can't be both. And I don't know if…"

Leith rested his chin on her head. She was waiting for

him. Of course she didn't know what her future held since her future rested on his. She couldn't plan on a home or a family until she knew if Leith planned to make good on his *someday, maybe* sort of promise he'd made her at Nalgar.

Of course he planned to ask her to marry him. Someday. Probably sooner than later. If he could figure out what it'd mean for her and for him.

When he married her, would he become lord of Stetterly? Did titles work that way? Or, maybe since he was a commoner, he couldn't inherit a title?

Perhaps it would've been better for Renna if she had fallen in love with someone like Shad. Someone who could've taken on the full responsibility of Lord of Stetterly and given Renna the life she used to have.

"What about you?" Renna peeked up at him.

A noise came from the darkness. Leith held his breath. Was that a horse? One of Stetterly's? Or an enemy?

Or worse yet, a Blade.

Her eyebrows scrunched. "What is it?"

The noise pounded closer. Horses, coming fast. Leith scrambled to his feet. He pulled Renna upright. "Might be trouble. Come on."

He gripped Renna's hand and sprinted as fast as he could for the square. As soon as they skidded to a halt in the center, Leith yanked out one of his knives. "Everyone, get behind the tables. Now."

Jamie drew his knife and grabbed Brandi's elbow. She shook him off as she drew her short sword. Ranson grabbed the door they were using as a tabletop and flipped it onto its side, heedless of the corncobs and utensils crashing to the ground.

No one else moved. The townsfolk stared.

He was a stranger. After only a week, they didn't yet trust him enough to react to the sound of his voice. Leith dropped Renna's hand. "Move!"

The hoofbeats drummed closer. Sheriff Allen stiffened and drew his sword. "Do as he says!"

Too late. Twelve riders—Rovers—thundered between the burned buildings, swinging weapons. Tables overturned. Men tried to drag the women and children out of the way. A girl screamed and flailed as one of the Rovers dragged her onto his horse in front of him.

A horse and rider charged at Leith. Leith stepped to the side, ducked the Rover's swinging sword, and pricked the horse's rump with his knife. He dove out of the way as the horse shot into the air, lashed out with its rear hooves, and bolted. The Rover kept his seat, but he could do nothing besides hang on.

Leith spun. Jamie and Brandi held back one Rover while Renna stood behind them, throwing corncobs. A few of the other women and children joined in, peppering the Rovers with a hail of corncobs. Ranson leapt in front of Sheriff Allen's daughter. Four Rovers held a cluster of townsfolk at swordpoint while another Rover was trying to plant a kiss on the girl he'd captured.

No time for a gentle rescue. Leith sprang to the Rover's horse, grabbed the man's shirt, and dragged him from the horse. The Rover and the girl he held tumbled to the ground. Before the Rover could catch his breath, Leith smashed the hilt of his knife into the man's temple. He slumped to the ground.

Leith leapt over him as one of the four Rovers menacing

the cluster of women and children turned to face Leith. Leith deflected the Rover's sword, stepped close, and plunged his knife into the man's shoulder.

A second Rover advanced, brandishing his sword. Leith grabbed his wrist and yanked him forward. While the man was still off-balance, Leith shoved the back of the man's neck and brought his knee up at the same time. The man's nose crunched, spurting blood onto Leith's trousers. The Rover dropped his sword and fell to his knees, both hands clamped over his gushing nose. Leith clubbed the back of his head with the pommel of his knife.

As the third and fourth Rovers whirled to face him, a hiss cut the air. One of the Rovers staggered, an arrow in his chest.

Leith glanced over his shoulder. Sheriff Allen nocked another arrow to his hunting bow. He drew back, aiming at the remaining Rover. "Drop it."

As the sword clattered to the ground, a cry pierced the night behind Leith. He whirled and drew another knife.

Captain Loust, the Rover who'd raided their campsite, held a knife to Renna's neck. Behind him, Jamie and Brandi picked themselves off the ground.

Captain Loust met Leith's gaze. "Drop your weapon, boy, before I slit her throat."

Leith glanced at Renna. Her eyes were wide, her body trembling, but her hand inched into her right pocket.

The knife he'd given her. She was still wearing it. Would she use it?

Leith dropped his knife. He still had one more in a boot sheath. If he'd been dressed as a Blade, he would've been wearing two more strapped across his chest. Perhaps he should've taken the risk in being recognized and remained fully armed, even here.

Renna eased the knife from her pocket, her hand hidden at her side. Behind Captain Loust, Jamie and Brandi both drew knives. Jamie's mouth moved, as if he were giving instructions to Brandi in a low tone.

Leith had to keep Captain Loust—and any of his Rovers who might be watching—distracted for a few more seconds. Leith stepped forward, his hands palms up. "What do you want? Stetterly was burned to the ground in the war. We have nothing valuable."

"A wagonload of corn fetches a good price these days. Aven, Walden, Uster, Duelstone, and more, they all had their crops destroyed in the war and will pay any price we demand." Captain Loust snorted and adjusted his grip on Renna's shoulder. His knife never wavered from her neck. "All we want is your cooperation. You load a few wagons full of corn, this little lady writes a letter certifying the corn came from Stetterly, and we ride away with no one getting hurt."

That wouldn't be the end of it. This Rover would be back. He'd demand more corn or Stetterly's herd. Perhaps he'd even take over the town. There were stories, back before the Blades wiped them out, that the Rovers had done just that to the town of Dyman. Did Captain Loust want to set himself up as the next great Rover leader?

Not at Stetterly, he wouldn't.

Renna gripped her knife, her eyes focused on Leith as if waiting for a signal. Both Jamie and Brandi also watched him. Leith met Jamie's gaze and slowly tapped his right arm.

Jamie nodded and leaned over to whisper instructions to Brandi.

Switching his gaze back to Renna, Leith gave her one, slow nod.

She drew in a deep breath, squeezed her eyes shut, and stabbed the knife into Captain Loust's thigh. Only the tip plunged into his leg, but it was still enough.

Even before Captain Loust howled at the pain, Leith swiped his knife from his boot and sprang forward. Jamie jumped to his feet and grabbed Captain Loust's right arm. Brandi joined him a heartbeat later. Their combined weight jerked Captain Loust's knife away from Renna's neck, and their knives stabbing into his arm caused him to drop his knife.

As Renna stumbled free, Leith darted between her and Captain Loust. A kick to the back of Captain Loust's legs brought him to his knees. Leith twisted his uninjured arm behind his back and pressed his knife to Captain Loust's throat.

Captain Loust peered up at him, his eyes widening.

The heat of battle coursed through Leith's body. At that moment, he wasn't Daniel Grayce, the meek role he'd been trying to play. He was Leith Torren, former First Blade.

Years ago, he might've killed Captain Loust right then and there. It was how the Blades had dealt with Rovers.

Now, Leith wasn't going to kill him, not when the man was on his knees and no longer armed. But Captain Loust didn't know that, and Leith didn't let any hint of softening touch his face or voice when he leaned closer so only Captain Loust could hear. "Leave this town. Tell any Rover you meet that Stetterly is mine."

Leith lifted his knife so the initials on the hilt were visible. Captain Loust's eyes followed his movement, and his throat bobbed. "You're a—"

Leith pressed the knife to Captain Loust's throat again, cutting off his words. "I'm a man you don't want to cross. Get out of my town."

He shoved the man away. Captain Loust scrambled to his feet, hobbling as he tried to press a hand to his injured leg and arm at the same time.

The other Rovers scrambled to their horses. Within minutes, none of the Rovers remained. Even the wounded lit out at a gallop, bent over the saddle, hands pressed to wounds.

Leith drew in a deep breath. An ache stiffened his left leg as the surge of battle wore off, but that was all.

Was it a mistake to let Captain Loust recognize Leith as a Blade? For now, it spared Stetterly. Once word got out that a former Blade had claimed Stetterly as his own, other Rovers would think twice before troubling the town. They all knew how Blades dealt out justice.

But if the word spread beyond Rovers?

Leith couldn't hide his identity forever. It would come out, eventually. But hopefully not anytime soon.

He sheathed his knife, stepped to Renna, and pulled her close.

She wrapped her arms around his neck and buried her face against his shoulder, trembling but not crying. "I stabbed him. I've never stabbed anyone before. I swiped at Vane once, but never stabbed anyone." Another shudder coursed down her back.

Leith rubbed her back and held her tighter. "You barely

scratched him. The knife only went in about an inch. Hardly life-threatening."

"I didn't want to hit the bone. Or the blood vessel. He would've bled out." Her cold fingers gripped his shirt collar and brushed the back of his neck.

He forced himself to concentrate on her rather than on the tingles running down his spine. "He won't even have a limp. Too bad you couldn't see his face. He was shocked you dared draw a knife on him."

"That makes two of us." Renna straightened and stepped back. "What a mess."

The doors and logs they had been using as tables lay overturned. Corncobs scattered over the ground. Spots of blood marred a few patches of earth.

Jamie and Brandi were already working to clean up their table while Ranson helped the sheriff's daughter. A few of the townsfolk began to bustle about to set things to right, but most stared at Leith.

The same young man who'd questioned him at the river earlier stepped forward. "Where did you learn to fight like that?"

Leith closed his eyes. Did he tell the whole truth now? Part of it?

"He spent a lot of the war at Walden." Renna's voice was firm, as if she hadn't been shaking a moment earlier.

Leith glanced at Sheriff Allen. The sheriff crossed his arms, his bow and arrow resting on a log next to him, but he didn't contradict Renna.

"I heard a Blade trained some of the guards there. Is that true?" The young man cocked his head.

"Yes." No need to tell him Leith had been the Blade doing the training.

Some of the townsfolk nodded, but others still eyed him, as if they realized Leith couldn't learn what he'd just done in a few weeks' time. With a few shrugs, they shuffled off to see to cleaning up.

Leith retrieved and cleaned his knives and the knife he'd given Renna. He handed it back to her. "Best keep this handy."

She slid it into her pocket, her arm disappearing past her wrist.

Leith motioned to Jamie and Ranson. They strode over, Brandi following. Leith focused on Renna. "I'm going to track the Rovers to make sure they get out of the area for good. I don't know how long I'll be gone."

With a deep breath, she nodded. "All right."

"Jamie, Ranson. Keep an eye on things here." He searched their faces until he saw their mouths tighten. Good. They understood that they'd have to watch for more than just Rovers. If the Blades were out there, they would most likely head south down the Spires Canyon since they'd been banished to the north of the Sheered Rock Hills. Leith would come across them first, if they were out there.

But Jamie and Ranson needed to be wary, just in case.

Brandi crossed her arms. The wild spikes of her hair matched her fierce scowl.

Leith managed a smile. "And you too, Brandi. Keep Blizzard close. He'll alert you of trouble."

"Of course. I'll take care of him." Brandi trotted forward and hugged him. "Take care of Valor."

"I will."

As Brandi stepped back, Jamie nudged her arm. "Let's saddle Valor." The two of them took off toward the corral.

"I'll gather your pack for you." Ranson slipped into the darkness after them.

When they were once again alone at the side of the town square, Leith gripped Renna's hands. "I'll try not to be gone too long."

"I understand." Renna squeezed his fingers. "If you get a chance, could you swing by Walden? I probably should send someone there to negotiate a trade of our corn for their timber, and I can't think of anyone I'd rather send."

"You do realize my only experience with negotiations involves threats and knives?" Leith leaned his forehead against hers.

"I think Lord Alistair can handle it." A smile lit Renna's face, though it didn't sparkle in her eyes. "Stay safe."

"Of course." Leith kissed her, turned, and strode away. He collected the rest of his knives from Ranson and strapped them across his chest.

Jamie led Valor over, Leith's saddlebags and bedroll already strapped behind the saddle. Leith checked the girth, patted Valor's neck, and swung into the saddle. With a wave at Ranson, Jamie, and Brandi, Leith pointed Valor's nose in the direction the Rovers had ridden and nudged him.

Valor jumped into a trot, tugging at the reins. He was a Blade's horse, no more used to staying cooped up in one place than Leith was.

The night breeze brushed Leith's face in a cool, familiar touch. He drew in a deep breath that smelled of sun-heated prairie grass cooling as night fell.

Why did that feel like the first decent breath he'd had in

weeks? The tension in his chest finally eased. He'd gotten exactly what he'd fought for. He was free of the Blades. Renna and Brandi were safe and home at Stetterly. King Respen was defeated.

So why wasn't it enough?

13

Was that meat frying? Martyn tried to scramble out of the bed, but his ankles tangled in the blanket. He fell, managing to roll and land on his back with a thump. Swearing, Martyn ripped his feet free and reached for his boots. Annoying fancy bed. Give him a bedroll on the ground or a simple cot like he'd had at Nalgar.

After straightening his clothes and buckling on the rest of his knives, Martyn stumbled from the room.

Kayleigh balanced on one leg by the table, dressed in a tan blouse and a divided skirt. Two plates rested on the table, and she dished onto them what looked like strips of his dried beef, now boiled and fried.

Martyn bit his tongue to stifle a curse. She'd rummaged through his pack while he'd slept. Not that there was anything personal for her to find.

He couldn't be angry at her when he'd done the same thing to her the night before. And she'd made breakfast. That made up for a lot.

As Martyn stepped farther into the kitchen, Kayleigh's head shot up. Her shoulders straightened, and she released a slow breath. "I realize last night didn't end so well. I should've kept a rein on my temper. Even if I do question your lack of...civil behavior, I realize I'm stuck with you."

Considering what she'd been through, he had been a touch prickly. Martyn eyed her white-knuckled grip on the frying pan's handle. Either she was thinking about using it on him or her leg hurt worse today. Probably a combination of the two. "Glad to see you came to your senses."

He started for the table, but she held up her hand and thrust the frying pan at him. "Wait. I'm not finished."

He crossed his arms. His stomach pinched against his ribs. He wasn't about to stand patiently through a lecture about propriety or some other nonsense. Propriety was just another name for stuffed up, self-righteous hypocrisy.

"Let me make one thing clear. You aren't staying here another night. Old Man Bendwick's cabin is empty and only a mile away. It's deeper into the Hills and would make a better base for your scouting excursions." She kept the frying pan leveled at his chest like a dagger. "In exchange for your help checking my snares and fetching supplies, I'd be willing to cook your meals and clean your cabin. Is that an acceptable deal?"

"Sounds reasonable enough." Martyn brushed past the frying pan, slid onto a bench, and dug into the beef on one of the plates.

Kayleigh set down the frying pan and took a seat across from him. After she did her whole praying thing, she cut into her breakfast. "Would you be willing to help me check my snares this morning? It would give you a chance to scout the Hills for whatever you're looking for, and this is the last of the food."

In other words, if he wanted lunch, he'd have to agree. Martyn swallowed and picked a sliver of meat from between his teeth. "Not a problem."

"Good. That'll take all morning, and we'll clean Old Man Bendwick's cabin in the afternoon." Kayleigh bobbed her head and jabbed at another bite.

She was getting all bossy again. Martyn squelched his retort. She'd made him breakfast. He could at least try to be civil, even if she didn't seem to think he could. "Fine. But I'm checking that leg before we go anywhere. Can't have you collapsing on me."

She sighed and nodded.

After they'd finished eating, Kayleigh rolled up on the leg of her divided skirt to her knee and swiveled in her seat so she could rest her injured leg on the bench. Martyn fetched the bandages and salve and knelt on the floor.

He began to unwrap the bandage, but she flinched and sucked in a breath.

Martyn sat back on his heels. He was being too cold, too efficient. She wasn't a fellow Blade who was supposed to tough out the pain. She was a young woman, alone, and, for some insane reason, trusting him. The least she deserved was some sort of gentleness on his part.

Except that Martyn didn't know how to be gentle.

He eased his grip on the bandages and tried to peel them away gently. His fingers were too thick. Too clumsy.

Finally, the last bandage tugged off her wounds. The wounds oozed wet and clear, the skin around them pink and warm with her body's efforts to heal. The deepest gash, the one in her calf, puckered around the jagged stitches he'd put in her leg.

His efforts to help her were pitiful. Raw wounds. Ugly stitches. Most likely, her muscles would heal in a deformed lump, her leg forever marred. A healer like Renna would've been able to minimize the damage. But Martyn didn't have that skill.

Kayleigh's scar was the price she'd pay for being turned away by Flayin Falls' healer. A heat filled Martyn's chest as he remembered that healer, so smug as he denied Kayleigh care. She could've died or lost her leg.

Was what she'd done or not done worth that?

He shook himself and met her gaze. She was staring back, as if trying to see past the mask he so carefully wore around everyone.

Something in her gaze crumbled a bit of that mask. Enough that he found himself saying, "I'm sorry I couldn't do better. It looks pretty rough."

She bit her lip and turned away, a glisten at the corner of her eyes. "You're helping me. That's more than anyone else has offered to do in a long time."

"Why?" Martyn reached for the jar of salve. He shouldn't ask. He shouldn't care. Caring just left scars worse than the ragged wound on Kayleigh's leg, and those wounds were a lot harder to stitch and heal.

She stiffened, and her face grew blank, a false smile painted across her mouth. "I'll only tell if you come clean about your own background. All I know about you is your first name and your job. For all I know, neither of those is correct."

Too close to the truth. The name he'd given her, Owen,

wasn't his, and scouting for King Keevan made it sound like he was someone loyal and trusted by the king. Not a former Blade.

"All right, don't tell me." Martyn slathered salve over her wounds and wrapped a new bandage around her leg.

While she cleaned the breakfast dishes, Martyn went outside and saddled Wanderer. By the time he finished, Kayleigh stood on the cabin's front step, balanced on her good leg.

Why did he always have to get stuck with temporarily crippled females? Martyn strode toward her, placed his hands on her waist, and slung her over his shoulder.

She shrieked and flailed. "What do you think you're doing?"

He balanced her on his shoulder as he scooped up her leather pack of supplies. "Carrying you to my horse."

"And you didn't think to bring the horse to me instead of carting me off like a sack of corn?"

Something dug into his back. It took him a few strides to figure out she'd propped herself up on the sharp points of her elbows. "I couldn't hold the horse still and help you mount. This way, Wanderer is still tied to the paddock fence."

"Or maybe I could've gotten on without your help." She huffed and squirmed. "Sometimes I really wonder where you learned your manners. Certainly not from your mother."

His mother. Not a topic he wanted to talk about. Besides, practicality trumped manners any day.

Somehow, he didn't think Kayleigh would agree with him.

He reached Wanderer and lifted her from his shoulder onto the horse's back behind the saddle. She swung her good leg over the saddle to sit astride.

Martyn tied her pack to one of the saddle rings and stepped into the stirrup. Kayleigh leaned backward as he swung his leg over, but he still managed to kick her in the stomach. He didn't apologize. She didn't ask him to. Perhaps they were getting somewhere.

He settled into the saddle. This was home. His horse. His saddle. The wild land of the Sheered Rock Hills rising above him farther than he could see.

Kayleigh's arms wormed around his waist and clasped in front of his stomach. He stiffened. "What are you doing?"

"Hanging on. Believe me, I'm no more pleased about it than you." Her voice was sharp against his ear, her breath whispering against the back of his neck.

He should've expected it. After all, it was the most practical option. But there was something about her arms around his waist. Like she trusted him.

She didn't. Not really. This was just a part of their deal, nothing more.

He should've listened to his gut and got out of here when he'd had a chance. Now he was stuck in this deal. He'd made a promise, and he kept his promises.

Even if Leith didn't. Even if his parents hadn't.

Martyn nudged Wanderer, and they set out north into the Hills. Kayleigh directed him to each of her snares. Most were empty, though she'd caught a small rabbit in one and a squirrel in another. The meat would barely last the two of them a day, but at least the snares weren't empty.

Sitting on Wanderer at the fifteenth snare they'd

checked, Martyn studied the way she reset each snare, the deft working of her fingers as she handled the rawhide laces, the careful placement. He had enough practice setting his own snares to know she was an expert.

"Who taught you?"

She cocked her head, her short, brown hair tumbling across her forehead and around her ears. "I thought we were going to leave prying, personal questions alone?"

He shrugged. "Just curious, since your skill with snares will in part be feeding me for the next few weeks."

She stood, brushed off her knees, and hop-limped toward Wanderer. After she'd placed her foot in the stirrup, Martyn reached down and tugged her up. As she settled in behind him, he wiggled his toes into the stirrup once more.

"The next one's that way." She pointed past his shoulder. One of her arms looped around his waist. "Old Man Bendwick taught me. I spent a lot of time with him the past five years when Papa was on duty. People tolerated Papa for Lord Westin's sake, but not me."

What was he missing? Martyn frowned and ducked a tree branch. Five years implied that the trouble had begun when Respen took over, yet her father was a loyal guard to Lord Westin and she claimed to be Christian. So why did the townsfolk of Flayin Falls seem to hate her so much when all the facts suggested they shouldn't?

"I've given you a bit of my background. It's only fair you say something about yourself."

"That wasn't a part of the deal."

"Which you broke first."

He gripped the reins tighter and stared at the slope ahead of them. What could he tell her? He was a Blade, like the one who'd killed her father. He was a man who'd tortured his best friend in the name of loyalty. He was a boy whose parents had chosen his brother over him.

She tightened her grip around his waist as they both leaned backward, shifting their weight on Wanderer's back to help him pick his way down the steep slope. "Start easy. What about your parents? Any family?"

Nothing about his past was easy.

But perhaps he could tell her some of it, enough that she'd stop asking. "My parents and brother are dead. They froze in a blizzard."

"And you survived. That must've been awful."

He didn't want her sympathy, especially not for his parents. "I wasn't there. They abandoned me at the church in Blathe. They chose to keep my brother and left me behind."

"That's horrible. Maybe they didn't mean to abandon you." Her arms remained tight around his waist even when they reached the gully at the bottom of the hill.

He gritted his teeth. Why was he telling her this? He'd known her less than two days. Not long enough to start having heart-to-heart conversations.

But she was *listening*. Why did it matter what he told her? Eventually, he'd leave and never see her again.

Maybe telling her would ease some of the ache in his chest. Enough that he could get in a decent breath past the pain and guilt and betrayal and years of blood filling him.

Martyn eyed the scraggly pine trees around them. Nothing but sky and mountains. No one to hear but her. "My father was...he was the type of man who couldn't get ahead no matter how he tried. If he bought his own field, his crop was wiped out with blight or drought. If he tried to open his own shop, it failed. We moved a lot, trying to find somewhere he could earn enough money to put food on the table. That winter was especially bad. One morning, after we'd gone hungry for three nights in a row and we'd barely begged a spot to sleep in the back room of Blathe's church, I woke up to find they'd left."

"I'm sorry." She leaned against his back, as if trying to comfort him.

He didn't want comfort. This was the past. It was hard. Done. No amount of sympathy could undo it. "Don't be. If I'd been with them, I would've died too."

Perhaps it would've been better if he had died. Was he any less of a failure than his father had been?

"So you were raised at the church in Blathe?"

He heard the skeptical lilt to her question. His reaction to her prayers didn't give the impression of a particularly religious person. He snorted. "No. The minister wasted no time in turning me out on the streets and telling me exactly what he thought of me and my vagabond family."

"I see."

Of course she did. Everything. Or, almost everything. Maybe she'd drop the subject now.

She drew in a deep breath. "You can't judge my faith based on the actions of one minister."

Nope, she wouldn't. Martyn sighed and pressed his palm against his thigh to stop himself from tugging on his hair. "If it was one man or even two, perhaps I could dismiss their actions as an exception. But I've found them to be the norm."

"I'm sorry you've been hurt by bad examples claiming the name Christian. But perhaps they go to prove that wickedness does exist and is a real danger even to those that know better."

"It's not the existence of evil I doubt. It's your claim that your faith changes you that I find suspect. I've seen very little evidence of that."

"I—"

Time to end this conversation. "Where's that next snare?"

MARTYN DIPPED HIS RAG IN A BUCKET, WRUNG IT OUT, AND slapped it back on the floor. How had he gotten talked into scrubbing the floor? Something about Kayleigh being in too much pain to get down on her hands and knees to do it.

Kayleigh balanced on one leg as she washed a window, musty curtains mounded at her feet. The other three windows in Old Man Bendwick's cabin already sparkled. She'd taken out the bed linens and restuffed the straw tick with straw they'd found in the shed behind the cabin.

Martyn shifted, his knees aching against the wooden planks of the floor. He was about ready to be done. They'd worked hard all morning checking the snares, skinning the rabbits and squirrel, and starting the tanning process on the skins. Now they'd spent all afternoon cleaning the cabin. More scrubbing and dusting than Martyn had done in years.

He crawled to a spot next to the fireplace and rubbed at a patch of dirt. His fingers slipped, and his knuckles scraped against the brick hearth.

Martyn swore and dropped the rag. Blood filled the tiny divots in his knuckles, flaps of skin sticking up. An ache speared his fingers. He swore again.

Kayleigh's walking stick, the one she'd insisted he fetch for her that morning, thumped on the wooden floor. "Your mother never washed your mouth out with soap, did she?"

"No." Martyn hadn't sworn a whole lot back then. It was a habit he'd picked up later. "You're going to get all bossy and tell me not to do it."

She crossed her arms and eyed him. "I bet you couldn't stop if you tried."

He couldn't rise to her bait. She wanted to trap him into a dare. "Doesn't matter to me what you think."

She huffed a lock of hair out of her eyes. "Fine. I'll make you a deal. If you swear in the next hour, you have to wash your mouth out with soap."

Martyn sat back on his heels. Should he accept the challenge or let it be? Why not? He could go a whole hour without swearing. A slow smile curled his lips. Perhaps he could get something out of this bargain. "Deal, on the condition that you'll wash your mouth out with soap if you can't refrain from dishing out orders."

"All right." She turned back to the window and stood on her tiptoes to scour the top corner.

No way would she survive an entire hour without giving him at least one order.

When he finished with the floor, he tossed the suspect-looking brown water outside. After refilling it, he strode back into the cabin and held up the bucket.

She didn't fall for his trap. Instead, she bit her lip, made a sound in the back of her throat, and drew in a deep breath. "Could you please set that down over there? And if you would like, could you please clean out the fireplace? Those are questions, not orders."

After setting the bucket next to the wall, he cleaned the ashes from the fireplace and hauled them outside. When the fireplace was mostly empty, he stuck his head inside and peered up the chimney to make sure it was free of buildup and animal nests. He could make out a patch of sky far above.

A gust of wind whined over the chimney opening, and cinders fell into his face. Something stung his eye. He yanked his head from the fireplace, clunking the back of his head on the bricks.

Pain scratched across his eye. Martyn forced himself to blink, but the speck wouldn't come out. He rubbed, but the speck clawed his eye into watering.

Through the blurring, Martyn could just make out Kayleigh standing in front of him. She held something out to him.

Soap.

"You've been swearing up a tornado for the past few minutes." She raised her eyebrows.

Since he'd already lost, Martyn allowed himself a few more choice swear words. She grimaced and waved the soap at him. He scowled back. "But I have ash in my eye."

She sighed and set down the soap. "Hold still and let me see."

He froze as she hobbled closer. She gripped his chin with one hand and tipped his face up.

The fingers of her hand grew large and fuzzy in his vision. It was all he could do to hold still as she held his eye open with one hand and touched his eyeball with a finger.

She swiped her finger from his eye and nodded. "There. Got it."

He blinked. His eye still watered, but the burning, scratching pain was gone. He blinked his vision clear, only to be confronted once again with the bar of soap thrust toward his face.

A deal was a deal. Martyn took the soap and grimaced at it. Brown-colored suds had dried in waves along its off-white surface. Dirt from the floor? The walls? Probably best if he didn't know. Flecks of some sort of plant imbedded in the bar.

Did he really have to put that thing in his mouth?

He drew in a deep breath, opened his mouth, and ran the bar of soap over his tongue. For a moment, he couldn't taste anything. Then, a floral something, tasting exactly as it smelled, coated his tongue followed by a bland, almost milky aftertaste.

He bolted to his feet, mouth watering. He prepared to spit.

Kayleigh pointed at the door. "Not on our nice clean floor. Spit outside."

He dashed for the door, found a convenient spot of dirt, and spit until his mouth was dry. When the floral, milky taste still wouldn't leave, he fetched water from the well and rinsed his mouth several times. The taste still wouldn't leave, pouring through his nose when he breathed out.

He nearly spit out a few curse words but managed to hold them in. Kayleigh would probably make him wash his mouth out again, and that would only make the taste worse.

Although...he marched back into the cabin. Kayleigh had finished scrubbing the window and was gathering up her cleaning supplies.

Martyn retrieved the bar of soap from the floor where he'd dropped it and held it out to her.

She eyed it, a wrinkle forming between her eyebrows. "What's this for?"

He grinned. "I believe you gave me two orders. I might even argue it was three."

"What?" Her eyes glazed as if she was running their conversation through her head. Her expression twisted. "Bother!"

"I held up my end of the deal." His grin widened until it hurt against his cheeks, as if his mouth wasn't used to stretching that far. "Your turn."

She scowled and took the soap. "Which side did you lick?"

He crossed his arms and leaned against the wall. Revenge was sweet. Or, in this case, an annoyingly floral taste that still clung to his tongue. "It's soap. I'm sure it's sanitary."

Opening her mouth, Kayleigh scrubbed the soap twice across her tongue. She clamped her mouth shut and hobbled for the door.

Martyn remained where he was. A silence filled the cabin, its windows and floor gleaming, the corners free of dust and spiderwebs. Smaller than Kayleigh's cabin, Old Man Bendwick's cabin had only two rooms, the kitchen where Martyn stood and the bedroom in back.

Not Old Man Bendwick's cabin. Martyn's cabin. Two whole rooms all to himself. With windows and everything.

Did he dare call this place home? For the first time since King Respen died, something loosened in his chest. He could see himself living here, gathering most of his food off the land, trading a few furs for the rest, having his meals made for him.

He slammed his thoughts away. No, he wasn't the daydreaming type. This was just a temporary arrangement. Nothing more.

Leaning on her cane, Kayleigh tromped back into the cabin, patches of her shirt wet as if she'd spilled water on herself in her haste to rinse out her mouth. "That wasn't as bad as I thought it would be, though the taste sticks with you, doesn't it?"

Martyn let the inner cold fill his chest. He couldn't get attached to this place. "Yes, now let's finish here and eat. I want to get an early start tomorrow."

The smile dropped from her face. "Where're you going?"

"We need supplies." And Martyn needed a bit of space, a measure of solitude, to get his logic back in place.

Her face whitened. "I know but..."

"I'm going to Walden. I need to report in. I'll be gone for three or four days."

Her body relaxed. "All right. Of course you need to report in. But you can't leave tomorrow. The rabbits and squirrel won't last three or four days, and I can't check my snares by myself, not with this leg."

Of course. He should've remembered. He had a responsibility to her. He couldn't just run off into the Sheered Rock Hills and disappear.

Was that really what he wanted?

He no longer knew.

14

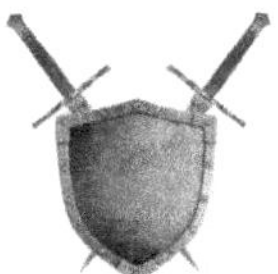

Renna stabbed her shovel into the ground and levered another scoop of dirt from the ground. She and Brandi stood knee-deep in a hole they were digging into the side of a hill. Jamie and Ranson dug a few yards away.

Behind them, scraping, grunting, and yelling came from the low walls of what would eventually be Stetterly's church. A greased timber ramp had been constructed from the ruins of Stetterly Manor up the side of the hill to the site of the church. Men strained against ropes and pulleys to haul each stone up the hill and into place on the slowly rising wall.

Brandi caught her gaze and jerked a thumb at the tan stones forming the church's outer wall. "Do you wish we were building a new manor with those stones?"

"No." Renna jabbed her shovel into the dirt again. She wasn't wishing for a fancy manor. Of course not. She sighed and swiped at a strand of damp hair. Sweat coated her forehead with a layer of gritty slime. "I just..."

She bit her lip. She wasn't going to complain. Not even about having to dig a hole to live in. Everyone else in Stetterly had the same living conditions.

"You don't want to live in a dugout with dirt walls and earthworms falling onto your head." Brandi flicked a wiggling earthworm to the side with her shovel.

Renna shuddered and gripped her shovel tighter. She could tough this out, couldn't she? "No, I don't. But I don't want to complain. No one else is."

She couldn't say a word of this, especially not to Leith. It would only make him feel guilty that he couldn't provide better for her. It would make him doubt, and he already struggled with that enough.

She carved into the hill again, attacking the hard-packed dirt. "I don't want to be weak. And helpless. And demanding. I'll handle it. Somehow."

"No one thinks you're weak." Brandi leaned against her shovel, the short strands of her hair plastered to her head with sweat. "You are Lady Faythe. You could demand a manor, yet you're planning on spending the winter in a dugout like everyone else. The reason you don't hear anyone else complaining is because they don't dare complain in front of you. If their lady is willing to live in a dugout, they can't complain about it either, can they?"

In other words, Renna was their example. "I'm not sure I can keep this up."

"You will." Brandi grinned. "It won't be forever. In the spring, Leith will build you the fanciest, best cabin ever—if he figures out how to use a hammer—and you'll get married —if he ever gets around to asking you, which he will, eventually—and this winter will seem like a short, slightly uncomfortable adventure."

Brandi made it sound so simple. But perhaps, it was. Leaving Stetterly had felt like she'd never see her town again, yet here she was, rebuilding. Captivity at Nalgar had seemed like forever, but now it was over. Living in a dirty dugout would only last a season.

"When did you get so wise?" Renna gripped her shovel once again.

Brandi smirked. "That sword must've clunked some sense into me."

"Nearly dying isn't something to joke about."

"Why not? I'm alive, so why mope about it? I'd rather laugh." Brandi's grin faded, and she kicked her shovel into the ground. "There are other, worse things that should be mourned."

That friend Brandi had lost in the war. Their parents. Uncle Abel and Aunt Mara. Renna swallowed and got back to shoveling.

"Lady Faythe?"

Renna turned. Michelle, Sheriff Allen's daughter stood at the edge of the hole. Dirt speckled the hem of her pink dress, its bodice well-fitted to her frame. Her hair lay in an artful twist and braid.

"Can we talk?" Michelle's blue eyes flicked to Renna's face before returning to the ground.

"Yes." Renna dropped her shovel, gripped her skirt, and climbed from the hole. She led Michelle a few yards away. "What did you need to speak with me about?"

Had Michelle recognized Leith? She'd seen him once as a Blade, but it'd been dark and she'd been terrified. Surely she hadn't gotten a good enough look at Leith to recognize him now.

Unless Sheriff Allen had told her. He still wasn't convinced Leith, Ranson, and Jamie were safe, and after Michelle had kissed Ranson at the Corn Festival, Sheriff Allen glared at Ranson with particular vehemence. It was possible he'd told Michelle to warn her away.

Michelle drew in a deep breath and faced Renna. "I'd like to learn healing."

Renna gaped. Michelle? A healer? She tried to imagine Michelle, the town flirt, as a patient, gentle healer. "You sure?"

Michelle nodded, her hair somehow remaining in place. "Yes."

Renna chewed on her lip. How to word her question gently? "Healing is a job for someone...steady. People have to see you as trustworthy. Wise."

"Not a flirtatious, wild girl who gets herself into bad situations. I know." Michelle wrapped her arms over her stomach. Her brow wrinkled, as if uncertain. "But I've changed. At least, I'm trying to change. Being taken by that Blade last winter, it made me rethink a few things. If Father hadn't come when he did, I might've...that Blade..."

Michelle shuddered and hugged her arms tighter across her stomach.

After all the time spent trying to show kindness to Respen and the Blades, Renna should've learned this lesson. She'd thought she'd learned to see the hurts and fractures that made people what they were.

Yet, here in her own town, she'd missed it.

"What that Blade did wasn't your fault. He's responsible

for his own actions. He could've just as easily taken you if you were walking to a neighbor's house to see if they needed help during that blizzard." Renna rested a hand on Michelle's shoulder. What did Michelle need to hear? Renna was barely a year and a half older. Could she claim to be all that much wiser?

"Yes, I know that. But I'm also responsible for my actions. I made it easy for him. I'm the sheriff's daughter. I know there are bad people in the world, and I didn't take wise precautions." Michelle shuddered and rubbed her arms.

Michelle was right. Wisdom meant taking precautions, the way Leith still wore his knives even when others felt safe.

But what was wise in this case? Train Michelle? Or look for someone else?

Renna released Michelle's shoulder. "Why do you want to be a healer?"

"When Respen's army attacked Stetterly, it took Mara Lachlan. The wounded had no healer, and some of us did the best we could." Michelle straightened and her arms dropped back to her sides. "For the first time in my life, I was useful. Not just a burden to my father or a young girl everyone believes doesn't have a thought in her head. I felt... confident for the first time in my life."

Different ways of expressing it, but the same doubts. Same feeling of uselessness. Renna let out a slow breath. Michelle had simply hidden it under her gleaming smile and fancy dresses.

Could Renna even train another healer? She hadn't even completed her own training with Aunt Mara.

She straightened her shoulders. Time to pull out an

answer she'd become rather good at giving. "Let me think about it. I'll let you know my answer soon."

Michelle's mouth drooped. "I see. Thank you for your time."

She turned and trudged off.

Renna nearly called after her, but she stopped herself. This was a part of leading. Sometimes she'd have to say no. Sometimes she'd have to make others wait to hear her answer.

She needed to talk with Leith. Surely he would have some advice.

Was he all right? What if he'd run into trouble tracking those bandits? He wasn't fully healed. Not as strong as he'd been a few months ago.

But he was Leith. A former First Blade. He could take care of himself.

LEITH SWUNG VALOR'S SADDLE ONTO THE HORSE'S BACK. Around him, the gray haze of dawn lay cool across the prairie. A hush wrapped around the grass as the night crickets silenced and the songbirds had yet to waken.

Such a familiar silence. An alone, yet not lonely, silence.

Did he dare admit how much he'd missed this?

He didn't miss the orders, the missions, the killing. But this, the long miles spreading before him. The steady companionship of a horse. And yes, even the thrill of being the hunter instead of the hunted. No wonder Martyn had taken off the first chance he'd had. He had even less to make him settle down than Leith.

Leith gathered his bedroll and strapped it behind the saddle. If the Rovers kept up their present course, they'd reach the Sheered Rock Hills in a few days, and Leith would be able to turn for Walden.

Leith tried not to think about the consequences of telling the Rovers a Blade guarded Stetterly. As long as the knowledge kept the Rovers away, Leith could deal with any other problems it had caused.

15

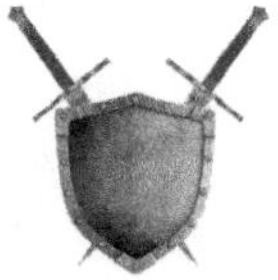

Martyn halted Wanderer near the top of a tall promontory. Several miles below, the town of Walden formed a black mass in the depression of several hills.

Just riding into Walden openly felt...wrong. Like the people down there were still the enemy. If not for one decision there in the Tower, they would be.

He should've been ready to face them. He'd had four days of making sure Kayleigh had enough food to last the days he'd be gone and packing a bundle of tanned hides onto the back of his horse, and another day and a half of riding to prepare himself.

It hadn't been enough. Perhaps because Martyn wasn't fully on their side. He hadn't joined the Resistance the way Leith and Jamie had. He hadn't stuck with Leith the way Ranson had. He was an oddity, straddled between sides.

Enough dawdling. The sooner he got down there and

made his report, the sooner he could grab supplies and return to Kayleigh. Well, the home-cooked meals, anyway.

Martyn turned Wanderer's head, and they headed down the Hills and across the prairie. Martyn skirted around one hill that was covered with stones and wooden plaques marking the graves of those who'd died in battle. The graves stretched toward the horizon, rolling down one hill and up the side of another.

Near Walden, the trampled remains of cornfields spread out in all directions. Circles of cleared ground and ashes marked the campsites of Respen's army while it'd held Walden under siege.

Walden itself showed damage. A band of bare earth marked the filled-in ditch encircling the manor house while the town rang with hammering as homes and business were rebuilt. A scaffold jutted next to one end of Walden Manor, and workmen bustled back and forth, reconstructing one section of wall.

By winter, all traces of war would be fixed, except for the graves decorating the hilltops.

Workmen halted and glanced up as Martyn rode past. A few gripped their hammers tighter, as if prepared to beat him senseless if he was a threat.

Four guards trotted their horses toward him. Martyn held still, one hand on his thigh, the other gripping the reins. Only four of his knives were visible, the rest hidden in the bundle of furs behind him.

One of the guards swept his gaze over Martyn, lingering on each of the knives. "Who are you and what's your business in Walden?"

"Owen Hill. I'm here to see Lord Alistair. The king's business." Martyn stared right back. He'd appear suspicious if he squirmed. Besides, he had nothing to squirm about. He had every right to be here. The paper hidden in a pocket of his shirt proved it.

"Don't remember seeing you before, and I thought I knew most of the king's messengers."

"I'm new." Martyn kept his voice even and a little cold.

The guard's expression soured further. He wheeled his horse. "Come with me."

The other three guards closed around Martyn, effectively keeping him and Wanderer caged as they rode the rest of the way to the manor.

As Martyn swung down, Jolene Lorraine—no, Alistair now—strode around the corner of the building, dusting off her hands. Her long, golden hair flowed around her shoulders and down the back of her light green shirt. Dust speckled her buckskin skirt. Her eyes flicked over Martyn, and a spark flared in their depths. She recognized him. Had she been told about Martyn's mission for King Keevan, or did she just remember him as the Blade who'd deserted them at Sierra?

"Lieutenant, thank you for escorting this man into Walden. My father-in-law was expecting him. I'll show him in."

He was expected? Lord Alistair must've told Shadrach and Jolene about Martyn's mission.

The lieutenant saluted and wheeled his horse. A stable-hand took Wanderer's reins from Martyn and led the horse toward the stable.

Jolene gestured from Martyn to the front door. "Come along."

Martyn followed her into the grand entry hall of Walden Manor. Wood paneling covered the lower half of the walls while a deep green rug lay across the polished floor. A grand, wooden staircase rose to the second floor.

Martyn cleared his throat as she headed down a hallway to their right. "You were expecting me?"

Jolene tilted her head but didn't slow her pace. "Shad and his father figured you'd swing by. Rovers are plaguing Uster and Duelstone, and some of the western towns are saying the same thing. It isn't too much of a stretch to guess you would've stumbled onto something worth reporting."

Thanks to Kayleigh, Martyn hadn't. He frowned. "Any word from Stetterly?"

Not that he was worried about Leith and Renna. Worry was too much like friendship.

"No." Her tone deepened, like *she* was worried. She halted in front of a door, knocked, and opened it. "There's—" She turned back to Martyn. "Which name do you want me to use?"

"Doesn't really matter." Martyn brushed past her into the room.

Lord Alistair perched behind the massive oak desk, the sunlight streaming through the windows casting sallow shadows beneath his eyes. He held a pen in his right hand, but his left hand drooped from the end of his sling. Shadrach leaned on the desk next to him. Both of them looked up as Martyn entered.

Shadrach's eyes darkened, and his face tightened. Lord Alistair's expression never changed.

Jolene shut the door behind Martyn. Locking him in?

Martyn drew in a deep breath and forced himself not to reach for a knife.

Shadrach straightened, crossed his arms, and leaned against the wall behind the desk. "We thought you'd show up around here soon, though we weren't sure if you'd come through the door or the window."

The words sounded like a joke, but Shadrach's mouth didn't even twitch into a smile. Actually, he looked like he'd rather punch Martyn than be polite.

The feeling was mutual.

Lord Alistair smiled and waved at the two chairs placed in front of his desk. "Please, have a seat."

Martyn strode toward the desk, planted his feet behind one of the chairs, and crossed his arms. "I'd rather stand."

Lord Alistair leaned back in his chair. "Very well. What do you have to report?"

This Martyn could handle. A report. Just like being a Blade, except that this time he could stand instead of kneel.

He focused on a spot a few inches above Lord Alistair's head. "About three weeks ago, I ran across five sets of tracks. I followed them for a week until I lost the trail near Flayin Falls. Last I saw, the tracks were headed west."

No need to tell Lord Alistair about Kayleigh. She was none of his business.

"Do you think it was banished Blades?"

"They moved like men who were wary of being seen. But without getting close enough to see them or being familiar with the horses they are riding, I can't confirm one way or the other." Martyn clenched his fingers. The rhythm and the tone of his voice all felt so familiar from his reports to King

Respen that he'd nearly saluted and called Lord Alistair "my king." Or at least, "my lord."

Did the five banished Blades feel the same way? Lost without a master, searching for someone to command them. Were all of them, Martyn included, like dogs too well-trained to do anything outside of a master's orders?

Even Leith, for all his claims of finding freedom, still served Lord Alistair and danced to his religion's demands.

Was there any such thing as freedom? Or was it all some sort of bondage with everyone seeking the master he or she wished to serve? No, even that made it sound like people had a choice. People were slaves to whims, bought and sold by desires. Was it worse to be the fools who deceived themselves into thinking they could escape or the cynics who knew they were trapped and did nothing but accept it?

"I see. Anything else?"

"No." Martyn kept his eyes focused on the map of Acktar behind Lord Alistair's desk, specifically on the dot marking Flayin Falls. Was Kayleigh all right? What if her leg became infected? Or she ran out of meat before he returned?

He shook himself. Why was he wasting time thinking about her? She had a knife. She had enough meat. She could take care of herself. Martyn cleared his throat. "I need more supplies."

"King Keevan authorized us to provision you as we would our own guards. I'm afraid we are a little short ourselves, but I believe we can scrape together enough. We received a shipment from Mountainwood a week ago."

Mountainwood? One of the towns that supported King Respen? Martyn dropped his gaze down to Lord Alistair.

Lord Alistair sighed and rubbed his beard with his good

hand. "Not my first choice, but that's the way of war. The Resistance may have won, but all the towns that supported them were devastated in the war. Respen's towns are prospering right now selling their supplies."

"At least Walden has timber to trade." Shadrach's scowl deepened lines around his mouth. "Other towns won't be so well off."

Martyn couldn't care less about the politics of trade. He needed to grab his supplies and leave. That was all.

The door cracked open again. Jolene stuck her head in once again, though this time she was smiling. "Daniel Grayce here to see you."

Daniel Grayce. The name sounded familiar. Did Martyn know someone—

Leith stood in the doorway.

Martyn stiffened and gripped the back of the chair. Of all times for Leith to show up, it had to be now. A few hours later, and Martyn could've been out of here without ever seeing him.

Leith went still, and his gaze caught on Martyn.

Shadrach cleared his throat. "Both of you remembered to use the door. You're almost becoming civilized."

Leith opened his mouth as if to reply with some retort, much the way he and Martyn used to.

Time to leave. Martyn straightened. "If that is all, I'd like to grab my supplies and get back on the trail."

Lord Alistair nodded, and that was all the dismissal that Martyn waited for. He strode to the door and tried to brush past Leith.

Leith caught his arm, but Martyn tore free. He had

nothing to say. They weren't friends or brothers. They weren't even enemies any more. They just were.

Martyn managed two strides before the study door shut. That was the annoying thing about Leith. He sometimes took it in his head to be stubborn. Martyn dragged a hand through his hair and spun on his heel.

Leith stood a few feet away, leaning his weight on his right leg, the one that hadn't been injured in the Tower. He'd filled out from the tortured skeleton he'd been when Martyn had left, but his eyes were still the same, piercing green.

A tight smile creased Leith's face. "You look...well."

"You too." What else was there to say? That he was glad Leith had recovered from the torture Martyn helped inflict?

A wrinkle formed between Leith's eyes. As if he was concerned about Martyn like the brother he'd once been.

Martyn probably should tell Leith about Kayleigh. Knowing Martyn had a base of operations and access to proper meals would reassure him.

But Martyn didn't. For once, he was keeping a secret from Leith. And that was a very satisfying feeling.

"I tracked twelve Rovers from Stetterly into the Sheered Rock Hills. Last I saw, they were headed west. You might want to stay alert." Leith lifted his hand, like he was about to clap Martyn on the shoulder. But his hand dropped back to his side.

West from Walden? Martyn's stomach tightened. Kayleigh. She was all alone and could barely walk. What if the Rovers stumbled across the cabin looking for supplies?

He shouldn't worry. He shouldn't care. Kayleigh wasn't anything to him but meals and a roof over his head.

But something hurt deep in his chest. If those Rovers hurt her...

"I need to go." He marched down the hallway and didn't look back.

LEITH WATCHED MARTYN STALK AWAY. HE'D TRIED. AT LEAST Martyn couldn't fault him for giving up this time.

The study door opened and closed behind him. Shad's footsteps paused next to him. "He's even more stubborn than you."

"He'll come around. Eventually." Leith had to believe that.

"You sure?"

"Yes. If he'd truly given up, he would've left Acktar behind and never looked back."

Shaking his head, Shad stepped past him. "We'll see. I'd better scrounge up supplies for him."

As Shad strolled down the hallway, Leith returned to the study. He sank into one of the leather chairs and rubbed at his thigh. While the wounds had healed, the weak muscles ached after the long ride.

When he looked up, Lord Alistair leaned back in his leather chair, his left hand dangling limply from the end of his sling. A reminder that Leith couldn't complain about his own sore muscles and bones. He, at least, retained the use of all his limbs, even if he limped.

"How are Renna and Brandi?" A smile broke through the deep lines on Lord Alistair's face.

"They're fine. We had some trouble with Rovers, but I

persuaded them to leave." Leith shrugged. No reason to mention how he'd done that. "I trailed them to the Sheered Rock Hills before I doubled back here. I don't think they'd attack a town as big as Walden, but it wouldn't hurt to stay wary."

Lord Alistair nodded, and the sunlight caught on the threads of silver in his hair. "A few Rovers have already tried. They quickly realized their mistake. Uster and Duelstone have also had problems. Even Mountainwood has experienced a few raids on their cattle herds."

Leith raised his eyebrows at that. "Mountainwood? I'd thought most of the Rovers were Respen's former soldiers? At least, the ones I ran into were."

"Soldiers of fortune could be found on both sides of the war, and that kind will prey on anybody they see as a target." Lord Alistair frowned. "King Keevan doesn't have the means to stop them. He could regather most of his army, but that would leave many towns vulnerable. And no one is sure how the country would react if he sent raiding parties of soldiers after the raiding parties of Rovers."

Leith shook his head. He didn't envy King Keevan's position. "What is he going to do?"

"Right now, track them and send small divisions to deal with the most problematic Rovers." After a moment, a smile broke through Lord Alistair's thick beard. "I'm not sure if the news has reached Stetterly yet, but King Keevan and Queen Adelaide's son Prince Duncan was born last week."

"I'll be sure to pass along the news to Renna." Leith flexed his fingers against his knees. Renna would want to visit, and Leith wouldn't let her make the trip alone, even if

King Keevan wouldn't want Leith anywhere near the newborn prince.

Shuffling in his pocket, Leith found the paper with the number of bushels—or was it wagonloads?—of corn Renna estimated Stetterly could comfortably trade with Walden. "Renna also sent me to ask about trading some of Stetterly's corn for timber from Walden. She gave me a list of what she thought Stetterly could spare."

Lord Alistair's right hand lifted, fingers splayed as if to steeple his fingers. He gave his left hand an annoyed look and let his right hand fall back to the desk. "You have no idea what a bushel of corn is worth, do you?"

Bushels, then. Leith shook his head. "Nope. Or timber either."

"I can see why Renna sent you here. She knows I won't take too much advantage of your ignorance." A slow grin creased Lord Alistair's face. He picked up the piece of paper Renna had given Leith and scanned what she'd written. "Here's my offer. Since Walden's repairs are almost complete, I'll send a group of my men with a load of timber down the Ondieda River to Stetterly. Some will stay and help with the rebuilding while others will provide an escort for Stetterly's corn to Walden. I'll also include another shipment of timber in the spring, as well as the four beams needed for Stetterly's church. In exchange, Walden will receive everything listed on this paper."

Was Lord Alistair giving him the better end of the deal? Timber couldn't be cheap, especially not the beams Stetterly needed for the new church building, not to mention the labor and the guards to transport the corn.

But Leith wasn't going to argue. "Done."

"Excellent. I was hoping Stetterly would have something to spare. It saves me having to trade exclusively with Mountainwood." Lord Alistair's hand twitched again, as if in a habit he was fighting to break.

Leith cleared his throat. It could be months before he had a chance to return to Walden. If he wanted to figure out how to court Renna properly—how to make good on his someday promise—he had to ask now. "I put a few things together at Shad's wedding. A groomsman takes on the responsibility of looking after the groom's family if something happens to him. You were one of Laurence Faythe's groomsmen. Renna and Brandi are in part your responsibility."

Lord Alistair leaned back in his chair. "Ah. You're asking why I didn't take Renna and Brandi to Walden immediately after Laurence and Annita's deaths. Why I left them in danger so long."

"I wondered that." Leith gripped the armrests of his chair. "But if you'd tried to bring them to Walden right away, Respen would've sent Blades to Walden to kill all of you. Your best chance was to pretend none of you were a threat."

Lord Alistair pressed his palm on the desk. "It killed me to leave Renna and Brandi unprotected, knowing that if trouble came, I was too far away to give aid."

"You did what you could. As soon as you received word First Blade Vane was after them, you left for Stetterly the next morning. Would've left that night if I hadn't delayed you."

A smile twitched Lord Alistair's mouth. "I was prepared to act sooner, as soon as I heard a Blade had been wounded and recovered at Stetterly, but Lachlan requested I wait. Even back then, he had faith in you."

Leith hung his head and stared at his hands. Lachlan had trusted him even then? How could he have done that, knowing Leith was his father's son? Had Lachlan believed Leith instead inherited his mother's courage?

Lachlan had trusted him. But enough that he would've given his blessing to Leith?

Leith swallowed. How could he even dare think it when he felt so inadequate? He didn't know how to be a good husband or a good father. His own father had killed Leith's mother in a drunken rage, and Respen hadn't been a better example.

What if Leith turned out like his father? If it was something born in him to turn violent to those around him? He was capable of violence. He had thirty-seven marks on his right arm to prove it. Was it possible that he could someday grow angry enough to lash out and hurt Renna?

No. Leith had something his father hadn't. Faith.

He touched his stomach as if he could feel the ridge of the burn scars through his shirt. He'd been worthy to suffer. Surely he was worthy to live out his faith in happiness too.

It was time to stop dragging his feet. Stop giving in to the doubts. Renna deserved someone who would actively build a relationship, not keep running away because he was too scared to reach for it.

When Leith raised his head, Lord Alistair was still watching him, waiting. Waiting for Leith to gather his courage and finally pursue a relationship with Renna as everyone from Shad to Brandi to Renna had been waiting for him to do.

Stop stalling. Leith drew in a deep breath, swiped his sweaty palms on his trousers, and met Lord Alistair's gaze. "Renna is eighteen, and doesn't legally need a guardian anymore. But you're the closest thing she and Brandi have to a guardian." He scrubbed his palms on his trousers again. Why was he so nervous? It wasn't like he was facing Respen and the threat of torture and death. "I want to ask her to marry me."

There. He'd said it. Out loud.

What would Lord Alistair say? What could he say to that? If he thought Leith wasn't ready or he didn't think Leith was a good fit for Renna after all, it would be worse torture than the fiery poker eating Leith's skin.

"Good." Warmth softened Lord Alistair's eyes.

Leith let out the breath he'd been holding in a whoosh. That hadn't been so bad.

"I'm honored to stand in Laurence's place for Renna, but did you consider that you might also need someone to be the father you never had?"

Lord Alistair's tone was so soft, almost vulnerable, that Leith couldn't hold his gaze any more. He wasn't sure he dared grasp what Lord Alistair was offering. If there was anyone who was an example of what being a husband and father should look like, it was Lord Alistair. "I...would appreciate it."

Lord Alistair leaned back in his chair. "In that case, I'm going to have the same discussion with you that I had with Shadrach before his wedding."

"You mean the how-to-be-a-good-Christian-husband lecture?" Shad's voice came from the doorway. Grinning, Shad closed the door behind him.

"Discussion." Lord Alistair raised his eyebrows.

"Lecture."

Lord Alistair waved at the chair next to Leith. "Since you seem to have a wealth of experience to add to this *discussion* after your three weeks of marriage, please have a seat."

Still grinning, Shad sprawled in the chair, his sword clacking against the armrest.

Leith glanced between the two of them, suppressing the urge to bolt.

16

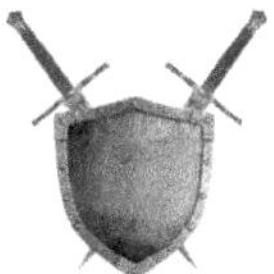

Martyn pushed Wanderer and the pack mule Shad Alistair had loaned him as hard as he dared. Would those Rovers pass Flayin Falls? If they stuck to the Hills, if they followed smoke to Kayleigh's cabin...

His chest tightened until he couldn't breathe the air whipping past his face. As a Blade, he'd seen what Rovers did when they raided.

He shouldn't care. He'd known Kayleigh only a week, and he'd spent most of that riding to Walden and back. But he was responsible if something happened to her. She was under his care, however inconvenient that was.

The Rovers couldn't be that far ahead of him. Martyn had pushed long after dark the night before and had risen before the sun. Surely he could arrive before the Rovers did too much damage.

A mile passed. Then another. Martyn's heart pounded in

his throat as he neared Kayleigh's cabin. He urged Wanderer into a canter around the final bend.

His heart stuttered. There, in the hollow in front of the cabin, stood twelve horses. The cabin door swung ajar.

Martyn kicked Wanderer into a gallop, releasing the pack mule's leadrope. They flew down the slope and skidded next to the other horses. Martyn threw himself from Wanderer's back, drawing two of his knives as he launched himself through the door.

Three of the Rovers were midway through smashing the door to Kayleigh's room with their shoulders. The door vibrated, its panels splintering, but held. Several men yanked open the cupboards, dumping everything onto the floor.

One man lounged on a bench by the table, a leg propped on the bench and a bandaged arm resting on the table top. Even beneath the dust, the captain's bars on his shoulder remained visible. He was slapping the table with his palm. "Put your backs into it. One girl can't be that much trouble."

Martyn didn't give them time to react. He stabbed one Rover in the back and slit another's throat before the captain's eyes even widened.

Ten on one still weren't the best odds, but Martyn charged forward anyway. His pulse pounded. His blood roared. And for the first time in months, he was truly alive.

The door splintered, sending two of the men tumbling to the floor. The third man cried out as a sword jabbed through the opening into his stomach.

Martyn grabbed a man's arm and smashed it so hard against the edge of the table he heard a crack. The man collapsed, moaning and clutching his arm. Martyn shoved him aside and whirled to face two Rovers charging him.

Martyn kicked one man's knee, sending him to the floor while grabbing the other man's arm and clubbing the back of his neck. The Rover tumbled over his fallen partner.

Amateurs. They wouldn't have lasted a day in the Blades.

Steel grated. Kayleigh balanced herself against the door-jamb to her room and blocked another strike. She was doing a surprisingly good job of holding her own.

Time to end this before the Rovers realized their numbers could overwhelm Martyn and Kayleigh even if their skills couldn't. Martyn shoved the table and toppled it onto the captain. Before the man could recover, Martyn vaulted over the upturned table, pinned the captain's unin-jured arm to the floor with the knee, and pressed a knife to the man's throat. "I have no qualms about killing you. Call off your men."

The captain's gaze traveled along Martyn's knife, and his eyes widened. He let loose with such a blistering string of curses that Martyn learned a few words. Since the soap was out of reach and it was only fair the captain got repri-manded, Martyn dug his knife harder against the captain's throat. "There's a lady present. If you're going to use such language, I'll cut your tongue out before I kill you."

The captain clamped his teeth shut, but his gaze remained locked on the initials on Martyn's knife.

Martyn couldn't care less if this inept Rover knew he was a former Blade. Who would he tell? Other Rovers? All the better if they were running scared.

Two of the other Rovers made as if to attack Martyn.

Martyn drew a second knife and prodded the captain, drawing a bead of blood.

"Don't move!" The captain waved his injured hand.

The other Rovers froze.

Martyn eased to his feet and placed his back to the kitchen counter. He put every ounce of cold conviction into his tone. "Leave. Before I kill you."

The remaining Rovers glanced between the men Martyn had stabbed in the back and slashed across the throat and the one Kayleigh had gutted. All three were dead. Three others lay moaning on the ground.

As one, they hustled to the door and dashed for their horses, their wounded leader outpacing them all in his haste to get away.

Martyn stepped to the door and watched them gallop up the slope and out of sight, making sure they left Wanderer and the pack mule behind.

That captain had known to look at Martyn's knife right away, and he'd cursed like he'd had a run-in with a former Blade. A *recent* run-in.

Had Leith revealed that he was a former Blade to drive the bandits from Stetterly? Martyn suppressed a satisfied smirk. Leith wasn't as changed and holy as he now claimed. When cornered, he was more than ready to claim his past.

Though in some ways, Leith had changed. Martyn's smirk faded. In the past, Leith would've trailed the Rovers to their camp and killed them in their sleep. There should've been no Rovers left for Martyn to face.

That's how the Blades had always dealt with Rovers. Kill them all, leaving only one or two to tremble at the arbitrary fate that left them alive to spread the word to the others. A mere two years after Respen had taken the throne, the Rovers had gone from a scourge to a memory.

Martyn bit his tongue to stop himself from swearing. He couldn't go after the Rovers and finish the job any more than Leith could. His current mission included defense and scouting, but not execution.

"They're gone. Once we clean up this mess, I'll scout the area to make sure they're gone for good." Martyn turned and stepped back into the cabin. He halted and raised his eyebrows.

Kayleigh leaned against the door frame and scrubbed her sword's blade clean. Blood soaked through the bandage on her leg. But what had set him to staring was the light green dress she wore, now spattered with blood.

"You're wearing a dress." Martyn blinked, but the light green dress was still there. It didn't fit against her short hair and bloodstained sword.

Kayleigh shoved her sword into its sheath and blinked up at him. "It's Sunday. I always wear my best, even if I can't go into town. But those Rovers came and..." She picked at one of the blood spots, her voice low. "This is the last dress I have. I had to sell the rest. And now it's ruined."

It wasn't the only thing ruined. Martyn dragged a hand through his hair. What a mess. Blood. Dead bodies. Wounds. And Kayleigh was in no shape to take care of it by herself.

He righted one of the benches and dragged one of the dead bodies out of her way. "Sit and let me look at that wound."

She hopped forward. Her mouth flattened into a tight, white line. After sinking onto the bench, she pressed both hands to her injured leg. "Could you drag the bodies outside first? I'd rather not stare at them any longer."

He started to protest but stopped. Her request made sense. Not the part about staring at them any longer. A dead body was a dead body. It wasn't that big of deal. But the longer they sat there, the more blood they would dump on the floor, making more work for him later.

He piled the three bodies in a heap outside, away from the cabin. The pack mule snorted and shied, but Wanderer merely twitched his ears and trotted a few steps away before returning to his grazing on the sparse patches of grass around the cabin.

When he returned to the cabin, Martyn set a pot of water to boil, righted the table and other bench, and hauled in a few buckets of sand, which he scattered over the floor to soak up the blood. By the time the water started boiling, he had gathered fresh bandages and a jar of salve, setting them on the table near Kayleigh.

After retrieving the pot and pouring some of the hot water into a bowl, he knelt next to the bench. Blood saturated the bandage on Kayleigh's leg from her calf to her ankle. "Looks like you messed up all my hard work."

"With twelve men trying to get me, my injured leg was the least of my worries." She gripped the edges of the wooden bench.

Martyn eased the layers of bandages off her leg. "Where did you learn to fight like that? You held your own pretty well."

Better than she could've if all her training came from a few weeks in the Resistance army.

"My father taught me. I was all he had, and as a guard

for Lord Westin, he was a little paranoid, especially since he spent long hours away from me." Kayleigh sucked in a breath as Martyn pulled away the final layer. The frayed and broken ends of the stitches stuck out from the puckered edges of the reopened wound. The muscles in her jaw flexed as she gritted her teeth. "I'll never be strong enough to defeat skilled men, but Father taught me to be good enough to either get away or hold my own until help arrived."

"Smart man." The surprise alone of a woman fighting back would buy her enough time to strike that first blow and run.

He dipped a rag in the hot water and dabbed at Kayleigh's wound. She made a sound in the back of her throat and flinched, but she didn't beg him to stop. After he cleaned the wound and pulled out the old stitches, he threaded a needle and began to stitch the wound closed once again.

She gripped her knee, her knuckles a blue-white. "Thank you for showing up when you did. It was pretty heroic."

Martyn scowled as he drew the thread through her skin. There he was again. Doing something almost heroic. What was wrong with him? Had he picked up some disease that was affecting his brain?

Even from several hundred miles away, Leith must still be a bad influence. Next thing Martyn knew, he'd get all self-sacrificial and saintly. He'd already started rescuing people, and he'd even stopped himself from swearing twice in the last few hours.

That had to stop now. No more heroics. They only got

people tortured or killed, usually due to an utter lack of self-preservation.

At least, he'd stop helping people right after he finished sewing up Kayleigh's leg. He had to complete what he'd started, after all.

She was still staring at him, waiting for his response. He grunted and tied off the last stitch. "Not all that heroic. I didn't want to lose my free meals."

"They aren't free. Most of the supplies are yours."

"I still don't have to cook them. You got a taste of my cooking the other night." He slathered salve over the wound. "Besides, it's my job to keep Rovers from troubling this area."

Yes. His job. Scare away Rovers. Keep an eye out in case they came back. Watch for Blades. That's what his life was. Kayleigh was just a means to an end. A way to get hot meals and a clean cabin all to himself.

He wrapped a bandage around her leg and stood. "I'll bury the bodies while you start cleaning this mess. I don't want to bring in the supplies until we have a place to put them."

We? Why had Martyn said *we*? It sounded too...he couldn't even think of a word to describe why he shouldn't have said it.

Running his hand through his hair, he wheeled and stalked from the cabin. Best to get out of there before Kayleigh noticed. She might get the wrong idea. Like he was going soft or nice or something.

Which wasn't the case. At all.

17

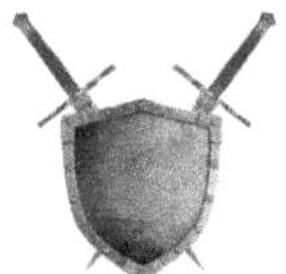

Renna studied the rising wall of Stetterly's new church. A line of men heaved on a rope strung through a pulley. A large block shifted on the ramp laid out on the hill from the manor's ruins to the construction site. In a square around the church, several of the holes for the dugouts were finished, and the women and children were hard at work cutting sod to build the walls and roofs. A few others continued to harvest the corn and hay in the fields.

Sheriff Allen strode to her and nodded his head toward the construction. "In a few more days, the walls will be high enough we'll have to build scaffolding."

Not everyone had been happy about using their limited supply of wood for scaffolding rather than building homes. But no one complained to Renna's face.

How had her father managed to stay sane? All the decisions, and no matter what she choose, someone wouldn't be happy about it. Some days—most days—she wanted to walk away from the whole dratted business and retreat into a cabin somewhere where no one could ever find her.

Instead, she straightened her shoulders and fell into step with Sheriff Allen. "Will we be able to finish by winter?"

"Don't think so. Not with the amount of labor we have available." Sheriff Allen's eyes swept across the line of men. "But a little snow won't hurt the half-finished walls, and if we get the beams from Walden, we'll be able to finish in the spring."

Renna leaned back so she could see past the sheriff's bulky shoulders. "Very well. Right now, preparing for winter is the priority. We must have the dugouts completed and enough food for ourselves and the animals stored in dry places."

That really sounded like a lady, didn't it? Like a leader. Renna straightened her spine. Even with Leith gone, she still held herself together.

By this time, Sheriff Allen's stride had led them a ways from the laboring men and around a corner of Stetterly Manor's collapsed wall. Sheriff Allen halted and cleared his throat. "Before that Blade returns, I had something I wanted to discuss with you."

This couldn't be good. Renna lifted her chin. "Yes?"

Sheriff Allen crossed his arms. "You plan to marry him, don't you?"

"Yes, someday." Trying to keep the daydreams from melting her spine, Renna crossed her own arms and forced herself not to take a step back to put more space between her and the sheriff. He stood a good foot taller than her, giving her an ache in the back of her neck as she tried to meet his gaze.

"Does he know that? He isn't just planning on using you?"

Leith's *someday, eventually* echoed in her ears. What kind of girl did Sheriff Allen think she was, if he could mistake her and Leith's courtship for anything other than what it was? "Yes, of course. If you're trying to accuse Leith of something, spit it out."

She bit her tongue. Daniel. She had to remember to call Leith by his new name. But when her knees melted around Leith or when her fingers heated and curled as they were now, his real name tended to slip out.

"I'm worried for you. Your parents and your aunt and uncle would expect me to watch out for you now that they can't." Sheriff Allen huffed out a breath. "Look. You saw how he took out those Rovers. He can still be violent. Vicious. Is that the kind of man you want to marry? To be the father of your children?"

Father of her children. A black-haired, blue-eyed boy reaching up with grubby fingers...a baby girl with Leith's green eyes...

Daydreams Renna had tucked close. Too close to let Sheriff Allen trample all over them when he knew nothing of Leith. Nothing of her. Nothing of what they'd been through together.

"He would *never* hurt me." The words rang all the way to her bones. If there was anything she was sure of besides her faith, that was it. "And he would never hurt a child."

"How can you be sure? He's killed. He's lashed out. He could do it again. He is a Blade, after all."

A heat hotter than the sunbeams slicking sweat down her back sizzled in her chest. "He *was* a Blade, but he isn't anymore. You don't know him. He was tortured and nearly died for me there in Nalgar Castle. His sacrifices defeated King Respen. If he fights now, it will be to defend me and his family. You've killed for that very reason. Leith is no different."

"Of course it's different. I killed the Blade who kidnapped my daughter." Sheriff Allen crossed his arms, his face reddening beneath his short-cropped hair. "And because I have a daughter, I know to be concerned about foolish mistakes."

Leith wasn't a foolish mistake, and if Sheriff Allen wasn't so busy meddling in Renna's life and trying to curtail Michelle's past mistakes, he'd see the ache in Michelle now.

Renna drew herself to her full height, though she still barely reached Sheriff Allen's chin, and glared with all the cold steel she could muster. "In case you have forgotten, I am the lady of Stetterly. My business is my own, and if I have need of a guardian's advice, that guardian would be Lord Alistair in Walden. *He* has expressed no such reservations. I thank you for your concern, but it is unfounded. Please return to the building site."

Sheriff Allen studied her a moment longer, searching her face. Renna clenched her fists and fought the urge to look away. She wouldn't back down now.

"Very well, my lady." Sheriff Allen gave her a half bow and marched off the way they had come.

As soon as the corner of the manor hid him from sight, Renna released a breath and sagged against the soot-stained wall. Her hands shook as her lady of Stetterly mask slipped.

How dare Sheriff Allen question Leith's motives. He didn't know Leith. He didn't even bother to listen when she tried to explain what Leith had done for her—the burns he'd taken, the way he'd offered to die to give her time to escape. Sheriff Allen refused to see beyond the Blade Leith had been to the man he was now.

A whisper of sound drew her gaze. Leith leaned against the wall a few yards away. Based on his tight expression, he'd heard everything.

Of course he had. With Leith's sense of timing, he would show up right during that conversation. She should've expected it.

The silence was stretching too long. He'd been gone for almost two weeks. Shouldn't she have run into his arms and hugged him by now? If not for Sheriff Allen's words ringing in her head, she probably would've. Instead, she shook and tried to think of something to say to stop those same words from ringing in Leith's head.

"You're back." Duh. Wasn't she done blurting out inane things when Leith was around? "Did you get a chance to talk to Lord Alistair?"

What was wrong with her? Why was she all business and clipped tone when she'd waited nearly two weeks to wrap her arms around his neck, bury her face in his shirt, and listen to the rumble of his voice beneath her ear?

But she couldn't make herself move. Not even to cross the space between them.

"Yes, I did." Leith's shoulders heaved with a deep breath, and he closed the distance. He gripped one of her hands and brushed his other hand along her cheek. "Did you really mean what you told Sheriff Allen? That you know I'd never hurt you?"

There. Now she was melting as she'd thought she would when he returned. "Of course I meant it. You wouldn't."

Leith traced a line under her chin, and it took a moment for her to remember that was where he'd drawn a thin line of blood with his knife months ago. "I did once."

"Only to protect me. To save me. I've hurt you far worse patching up your wounds." Leith was being ridiculous. If there was one thing her time with Respen had taught her, it was to tell the difference between a man who'd hurt her and a man who wouldn't. She met his gaze. "I know the look in a man's eyes when he's about to hit a woman and—"

Leith flinched and closed his eyes as if she'd stabbed him. "Renna, I'm sorry. I should've gotten you out sooner. I should've gotten you away from him."

She pressed her fingers over his mouth. Trust Leith to put the blame on himself and not on Respen where it belonged. "I'm not telling you this to make you feel guilty. But you have to know. I've seen the darkness in a man's eyes when he thinks it's acceptable to strike a woman, but I've *never* seen that look in you."

She couldn't undo the scars she had from Respen's fists— not scars on her person, but the scars from knowing what it was like to feel the back of a man's hand crash into her face. But, it helped show her the difference in Leith's gentle touch along her cheek.

Leith leaned his forehead against hers. "You sure? Absolutely sure? You know what my father was like. You don't fear that I inherited his violent streak? That I would...that our..."

Was he having the same sort of daydreams she was? If his forehead wasn't so furrowed, she might've closed her eyes and savored it. But she couldn't, not when the rest of his question lingered.

Would their children feel Leith's fist? Renna tried to imagine it.

She couldn't. She honestly couldn't. Not with Leith's eyes only inches above hers, green and pained with the memories of his childhood. No, not Leith. Not with the way he rested a hand on Jamie's shoulder to tell him *well done* or hugged Brandi when she celebrated Blizzard's progress. Or how he'd held Renna as she'd cried.

She cradled Leith's face in her hands. She needed him to look into her eyes and see her conviction. "The only thing I'm worried about is that our children will be utterly spoiled because you won't have the heart to say no."

"I can say no."

Renna raised her eyebrows. "How many times have you ever said no to Brandi?"

A slow smile softened the hard line of his jaw beneath her fingers. "Not many. If ever."

"Exactly."

If Renna closed her eyes, she could imagine it all too well. A dark-haired little girl, green eyes big and pleading. Asking for another cookie. A horse. One more story before bedtime.

Oh, yes. Their children were going to be horribly spoiled.

Leith drew back, putting space between them. "Hopefully you didn't have any plans for the rest of the day, but if you did, you're going to have to cancel them."

Maybe it was all her thoughts of marriage and future children, but her heart lurched. Was he about to...was this...

She didn't even dare think it. She had to be patient. "Is something wrong?"

Leith's smile grew into a grin. "Nothing's wrong. But you'll have to go tell Sheriff Allen that we won't be back until dark tonight, and in case he asks, Brandi, Jamie, and Ranson will be with us so we'll be well-chaperoned."

"I don't think they count. Brandi's hardly a reliable chaperone, and Jamie and Ranson would do anything you asked them to." Renna scrubbed her fingers along her skirt, trying to still her thumping pulse. Was Leith going to...

No, she couldn't get her hopes up.

"They're all we've got. If you tell Sheriff Allen, I'll round up Jamie and Ranson. Brandi's gathering a few things and getting Blizzard ready." Leith spun and strolled off. No, more like *sauntered* off, and he never sauntered.

Whatever Leith was planning, it had to be something good. A picnic. A horseback ride. A long walk with her hand tucked in his.

She gave herself a moment to savor the flutters in her stomach. She loved Leith Torren. Of that she was very, very certain.

LEITH TRIED TO KEEP HIS PACE STEADY AS HE LED BLIZZARD down the trail into the Spires Canyon. Blizzard's stride hitched, but his limp was much less noticeable than a few weeks ago. Leith's own stride had that same hesitation.

Brandi skipped ahead down the path, her grip on Jamie's arm dragging him along with her. Renna strode next to Leith when the path was wide enough. He squeezed her hand now. Could she feel his pulse hammering in his wrist and fingers?

He had to get this right. He had only one chance to give Renna the kind of day she deserved, especially after she'd shown such confidence in him that morning.

At the bottom of the canyon, Brandi turned and headed deeper into the canyon. Hopefully she knew where they were going. Leith hadn't had a chance to explore this section as well as he would've liked.

Renna's eyes widened. Had she figured it out already? So much for any sort of surprise.

Beside them, the Ondieda River gurgled and splashed around a bend in the canyon. Stands of grass lined the bank between the rocks and pebbles. The high walls rose in stark cliffs on either side of them, leaving a slice of light blue sky above them. The few cottonwoods and birches scattered through the pines gleamed with yellow among the green.

Brandi halted by a niche in the rock. As Leith drew closer, he spotted the dark line of a fissure. Was this the place?

Brandi glanced at Renna. "Is this all right?"

Renna stared at the crack before she nodded. "Even with what happened, I still love it."

Tension curled through Leith's body. What had happened? Brandi assured him Renna would love it here, wherever here was.

Brandi stepped forward and disappeared between the two jagged edges of rock. Jamie, then Renna followed her. Leith tugged Blizzard forward. Blizzard's stomach with the packs holding their picnic lunch barely squeezed through, but after a few yards the crack widened out. Blizzard's hooves clattered and echoed in the confined space. Behind them, Ranson's boots squeaked against the sandy ground.

The crevice opened into a stand of pines. Beyond them, a small clearing tucked against the canyon wall, an overhanging ledge protecting much of it from above. A small cabin, its porch sagging near the middle, hid beneath the ledge.

Renna waited underneath the interlocking pine branches. Leith passed Blizzard's reins to Ranson and drew Renna to the side. Somewhere, Brandi was chattering. A breeze murmured in the pine needles.

Leith slipped his hands into Renna's. She glanced at the pines around them and closed her eyes. "This is where Vane caught me when we tried to hide last spring. He promised he'd kill me."

Maybe this wasn't the perfect place. Leith swallowed and glanced around at the hidden clearing, piecing the past together. "This is where the Lachlans took you after your parents were killed."

"Yes." She drew in a deep breath and opened her eyes. "But it's more than that. Mother and Father would take us here when they wanted a few days with just us as a family. It has always been safe, full of picnics and laughter and some of my best memories of my parents."

Something eased in Leith's chest. But not enough that he could breathe properly. He'd planned this conversation on his ride from Walden. But now, facing Renna, the words stuck in the back of his throat.

His discussion with Lord Alistair rang in his head. Take initiative. Be a leader. Stop dragging his feet at every step and be the man she needed him to be.

Starting now.

He forced his jaws open and squeezed her hand. "Renna, I'm going to ask you to marry me."

Her eyes widened, and her mouth opened as if she were about to speak.

He placed a finger over her mouth. As much as he wanted that answer with every bone in his body, he couldn't let her say it yet. "No, not yet."

When he removed his hand, she arched her eyebrows. "Why not?"

"I need to tell you the truth of my past. All of it. Every mark. Every mission. Before you make any decision, you need to know exactly what I've done."

She sighed, almost like she was exasperated. "Your past is the past. You've been redeemed. I trust you."

"I know you do." It would be so easy to leave it at that. No, he didn't want to look into her eyes and confess everything he'd done as a Blade. It'd be hard for her to hear, and him to tell.

But it was the right thing to do. And for that reason, it had to be done.

He met her gaze. "If you marry me—"

"*When* I marry you." Renna speared him with a firm look. "No matter what you say, I'm going to say yes. Don't pretend otherwise."

Warmth flooded through his chest, and for a moment, all he could do was smile.

But he had to finish this before he lost his streak of courage. "Fine. *When* you marry me, you'll be taking my name, both Grayce and Torren. You deserve to know what that means. No more secrets. No more surprises."

All trace of humor left Renna's face, replaced by a line marring her forehead. She freed one of her hands and touched his cheek. He drew in shallow breaths, trying to concentrate on her eyes rather than her touch.

"All right."

The absolute trust there shook his resolve. "You sure? You're ready to hear all of it?"

She touched his right shoulder. "They aren't all killings."

"Most are." The words cut the back of his throat.

After a long moment, Renna's shoulders straightened. "It'll be hard to hear, but I already know the worst parts." She glanced over her shoulder to where Brandi and Jamie unpacked the picnic. "What about Brandi, Jamie, and Ranson?"

"They're family too. They deserve to know."

It would be that much harder, confessing years of marks to all of them, but perhaps it was best to get it done all at once.

Leith tugged her toward the others. He sat cross legged along one side of the blanket Brandi had laid out. Renna eased onto the blanket next to him, resting her head against his left shoulder.

Brandi's gaze flicked between him and Renna, her grin fading. Were Leith's nerves etched into his face?

Jamie and Ranson joined them, both silent.

Leith drew in a deep breath. He looked at each of them in turn. Ranson. Jamie. And, finally, Brandi. "You're my family. All of you. And because you're my family, you deserve to know my past. I don't want any of you to be surprised by it again."

Brandi tore her gaze away and picked at a strand of grass.

Leith swallowed, seeing again the pain and betrayal tearing across her eyes and face. Those days in the cave wondering if Brandi would ever speak to him again, much less forgive him, had been worse than Respen's torture.

He'd do anything to prevent that. Even this.

He rolled up his right sleeve. His thirty-seven marks marched down his arm. So much blood to confess. He tapped his finger against a barely visible line at the top of his shoulder. "I was thirteen when I got my first mark."

It took a good portion of the afternoon to go through each of his marks. As he'd known, it was hard. At times, he struggled to get the words out. These were the people he wanted to think the best of him, yet he had to tell the worst.

Renna never raised her head from his shoulder. A few times, she swiped tears from her cheeks. Brandi hugged her knees, but she too didn't walk away even while she flinched. As Renna had pointed out, they already knew the things that had affected them the most.

Jamie and Ranson didn't flinch. Ranson had heard first hand Leith's reports to Respen after many of the recent missions, and Jamie had lived in the world of the Blades long enough that nothing Leith said could surprise him.

Ranson took over once Leith finished, going through each of his own six marks.

It was healing. Restoration. A deliverance from the weight that had plagued all of them for so long.

By the time that afternoon ended, they'd moved on to other stories and laughter, and Renna's grip on Leith's hand had never faltered.

When he halted her on their walk back to Stetterly with the night breeze toying with her hair and the dancing stars reflected in her eyes, she smiled up at him. He cupped her chin and finally asked the question that had been on the tip of his tongue all day. "Will you marry me?"

"I already told you my answer." Renna huffed and rolled her eyes. "But, if you need an official answer, yes. Of course I'll marry you."

He couldn't be sure if he wanted to shout at those words or just sag to the ground in relief. He settled for pulling Renna in close and resting his cheek against her hair. Wherever else God led them now, he and Renna would face it together.

She raised her head. "When were you thinking for the wedding? I know you might not want to wait, but if we're going to invite Keevan, since he is my only other relative besides Brandi, and Lord Alistair and host people here, we might have to wait until spring because Stetterly doesn't have accommodations and the church isn't even finished and—"

"Spring is good." He'd had the whole ride from Walden to think this over, and he'd come to the same conclusion then, even if waiting would ache in his chest the entire long winter. "I'd rather wait until the church building is finished."

And he'd have time to build that cabin at the edge of the Spires Canyon like she wanted. Once he learned how to build a cabin, that was. Renna might not act like a noble lady all the time, but she still deserved to call something more than a dugout home.

Tension returned to his stomach, and he swallowed. "I have one last secret to confess."

Her forehead wrinkled. "What is it?"

"I can't be the lord of Stetterly." He couldn't meet her

gaze. How much would that decision hurt her? It meant she'd always have to bear the burden of ruling Stetterly, a burden she could've given to someone else had she chosen a different husband. Since she couldn't be both Stetterly's healer and its lady, she'd have to give up the one thing that had given her purpose for years.

If only he didn't have to ask. He'd sacrifice anything so she didn't have to give up her dreams.

But this was something that, thanks to his past, was out of his hands. "As the Third Blade, Respen sent me to Kilm and Mountainwood frequently to aid his two most important allies. I was asked to carry instructions to Deadgrass. Those lords would recognize me, and they would seize any opportunity to humiliate you, Lord Alistair, and King Keevan the moment they realized you and they were trying to pass off a Blade as a lord. The lords who fought for the Resistance would join the protest."

"It would tear the country apart, something we can't risk right now." Renna shook her head, glancing at the darkening canyon around them. "The citizens of Stetterly wouldn't react much better."

"I'm sorry." If only there was more he could say. But his past had consequences. Perhaps he and Renna would always live in its shadow.

"No, it's fine. I realized the same thing a while ago." Renna straightened her shoulders.

He leaned and kissed her forehead. "Besides, you're already a great lady of Stetterly."

She smiled, but it faded after a moment. "Where does that leave you? If you're not the lord of Stetterly, what will you be?"

"Steward maybe? Captain of the guard? Not sure yet." What place was there at Stetterly for a former Blade? Would he be content to farm a section of land? Or drill guards over and over again, day in and day out?

"Won't that get awkward once we're married? You'd be my husband and the head of the home, but also my employee and following my orders?"

"We'll work something out." He had to trust that. Surely God would show him where he was supposed to be now. God hadn't taken him out of the Blades and kept him alive through a war that should've killed him without a purpose for him. "What about your duties as healer?"

Renna bit her lip. "Michelle Allen asked me to train her, but I haven't decided if I will or not. She's...not the first person I would've picked."

Leith didn't know her that well, not besides the few minutes on a stormy night that had led to him being wounded. "Has anyone else volunteered?"

"No. And from what I gathered, Michelle did a good job of stepping into the role when Respen's army attacked Stetterly." Renna shifted and stared at the pebbles below their boots. "I'm not even sure if I should be the one to train anyone. I was still training with Aunt Mara myself. I don't know a lot of what she would've taught an official apprentice."

Not to mention, with her duties as lady of Stetterly, Renna didn't have time to devote to healing or training or anything. Leith barely saw her some days as it was.

But maybe, some of those problems could be solved. "With Sheriff Allen's permission, Michelle might be willing to travel to Walden and train with their healer."

Renna gasped and hugged Leith so tightly his ribs ached. "That's...that's brilliant. Lord and Lady Alistair would be more than willing to look after her, and Lydia would do her best to be a friend. I think it would do Michelle good to be away from Stetterly for a while."

With her lips pursed and her eyes shining, Leith leaned closer, tucking her against him. He'd asked her to marry him, and she'd said yes. Surely that deserved one kiss to...

"Renna? Leith?" Brandi hollered from farther up the path. "Did you guys get lost or something?"

Renna sighed and pulled away from Leith. "Trust Brandi to interrupt."

Leith gripped Renna's hand and set out once again up the path. He had a feeling he was going to regret promising Brandi a loft in their cabin.

When they reached the ruins of Stetterly, Sheriff Allen was sitting on a log in front of the lean-to where Renna and Brandi slept, his sword on his lap, a polishing cloth in his hand.

Leith ignored his glare. Might as well go through the whole process—stern guardian waiting up with a polished sword and all. He squeezed Renna's hands and resisted the urge to kiss her. "Goodnight."

She kissed his cheek, then brushed the blanket aside and entered.

Sheriff Allen scrubbed the polishing cloth rather slowly and emphatically along his sword's blade. Leith took the hint, spun on his heels, and headed toward his own lean-to. As he crawled inside, Jamie and Ranson both quieted and stilled.

Not a good sign. Leith raised his eyebrows. "What?"

Ranson shifted and glanced at Jamie. Jamie gripped his knees, rocked back and forth, and faced Leith. "What will happen to us? When you and Renna get married?"

Leith released a breath he hadn't realized he'd been holding. He should've expected this question. He glanced between Jamie and Ranson. "You two are my brothers. Just like I understand that Brandi comes with Renna, Renna understands you two come with me."

At least, that's what he hoped. He'd have to have that conversation with Renna first thing in the morning.

Jamie's shoulders relaxed, and a smile tilted Ranson's mouth.

"Of course, that does mean I'm going to need both of you to help build a really big cabin this spring since it'll have to fit all of us." Leith grinned.

Jamie grinned back. "Brothers, huh?"

"Yes, brothers." Leith lightly back-handed Jamie's shoulder. "And as the bossy older brother, I'm telling both of you to go to bed."

Ranson and Jamie both gave the expected groans and flopped onto their blankets.

18

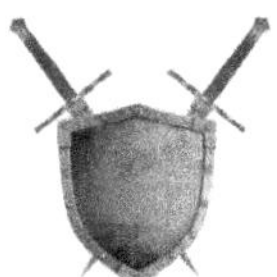

Martyn lay on his stomach on a rock outcropping in the shade of a spreading juniper. Below, the town of Kilm tucked into the foothills, the roads leading up to it curving up and over the first few ridges. Hawkpine Creek meandered down the hills behind the manor, paralleled the road for a while, before disappearing south into the prairie.

As far as towns went, Kilm wasn't much. Only a dirt track that dead-ended into the cliff side with a row of houses and shops. Kilm Manor rose off to one side, as if it wasn't sure it wanted to be associated with the small town.

And so blasted peaceful.

Four days ago, after coming across a set of fresh tracks, he'd grabbed supplies, let Kayleigh know he'd be gone for a few days or weeks, and set out after them.

Only to lose the tracks to rain and sleet that had only just let up. He'd gone on to Kilm as a hunch, but after a day and a half, even this was wasted time. Nothing unusual. No suspicious tracks around town, not that there would be any after all that rain. Not even soldiers training in the far fields. Only a few guards making their rounds, and there were less of them than Martyn might have expected, but that was probably due to losses in the war.

Movement by the manor caught Martyn's gaze. Two figures stepped from the manor. One turned and held out his hand. Two smaller figures dashed outside.

Martyn heaved a sigh. Just Lord Norton, his wife, and their two young children getting a breath of fresh air after the rain and sleet. With more dark clouds piling in the west, it might be the last somewhat sunny moment for a while.

And Martyn's opportunity for more snooping.

King Keevan wouldn't approve of his methods. There probably was a law against rifling through someone's house without permission, but Martyn had to find something to make this miserable trip worth it. Soon, the snow would come, and Martyn would have to wait until spring to go back to scouting.

He crept back from his position and circled into the foothills until he came out behind Kilm Manor. Not even a guard back here.

Too insultingly easy. Within minutes, Martyn slipped inside the manor, strolled down the hallway, and entered Lord Norton's study. Not much had changed since he'd been brought here once before when carrying orders from King Respen to Lord Norton. Same set of bookshelves in the corner. Same dark blue rugs. Same, dark cherry desk with spindly legs more ornate than sturdy.

A doll lay in the middle of the floor. Abandoned, perhaps, when Lord Norton's daughter convinced him to leave his study to go for a walk? Martyn avoided it and approached the desk.

Three stacks of papers lined up on the desk, pen and ink stiffly lined up at a corner. Martyn flipped through each stack, careful to tap the papers back into place once he was finished. Crop reports. Lists of those killed and injured during the war. Goods traded with other towns.

Nothing out of place. Nothing to indicate Lord Norton was harboring Blades or Rovers or doing anything else even mildly illegal.

It didn't sit right in the pit of his stomach. The Blades should be here. If they had at all stuck to their training as Blades, they should've returned by now, and they should've come here.

Was it possible the five Blades had truly left? Ridden off into the far west or north in the open, wild country? Maybe they were never coming back.

Martyn shook his head and checked over the desk, straightening one stack until it lined up as neatly as it had been. It didn't seem possible. Former Blade Offen had been a Rover before joining the Blades. He didn't know anything besides fighting and killing. Crossley and Tooley had always followed orders without question. Uldiney did whatever the older Blades told him. And Daas...Daas enjoyed seeing others suffer. Would any of them know how to ride away, even given the chance?

Martyn didn't know how, and he had Leith, Renna, and Shad pushing him in that direction. Kayleigh too, though she didn't know it.

The Blades might be taking their time about it—far longer than Martyn expected—but they would return.

Leaving the study, Martyn found what looked like a spare bedroom and squeezed under the bed until nightfall. Once the manor quieted for the night, he searched the place top to bottom. No sign of Blades. No extra weapons stashed in a storeroom. No one besides the servants, a few guards, Lord Norton and his wife, their son, and their daughter, her reclaimed doll clutched to her stomach as she slept.

Martyn would watch for a few more days to be sure, but as far as he could tell, the only one breaking the law at Kilm Manor was him.

MARTYN TUGGED HIS HOOD FARTHER OVER HIS HEAD AND tightened his cloak around his neck. Annoying rain and sleet. He gave vent to a few more curses, but the sleet didn't seem to care how much he swore or complained. It didn't stop.

At least he was almost back to his dry cabin, hot meals, and Kayleigh.

Why was he thinking about her? All he wanted was the hot meal, which she provided. And the dry cabin, which she would happen to be in when he got that hot meal.

It wasn't like he'd even thought about her while he'd been gone. Not to wonder if she was all right or if she'd caught enough meat or if she'd reinjured her mostly healed leg. Of course not.

Besides, he couldn't be blamed if his stomach was hoping she'd been more successful at snaring food than he had been at finding Blades.

He crested the ridge and let Wanderer trot down the

slope. Smoke wisped from the chimney and dissipated against the grey dome of clouds. The sleet muted the yellow leaves of the aspen and birch surrounding the cabin.

Martyn unsaddled Wanderer and turned him into the paddock. Strolling onto the porch, he stomped his feet to shake off clods of mud. Water squished between his toes from his boots' sodden leather.

After pushing open the door, Martyn stepped inside. A layer of warmth flushed against his cheeks and tingled into his hands. The fire at the far end of the room leapt and crackled as the open door changed the airflow in the room.

Kayleigh bowed her head over a book at the table in the kitchen, wearing the light green dress, its skirt now spattered with faint, brown stains she'd been unable to get out.

Martyn grimaced and swallowed back a curse. He'd forgotten what day it was. She was doing her whole praying, reading, worship church time.

As Martyn tromped across the room, Kayleigh looked up. "You're back. How'd it go?"

"The…annoying rain washed out all the tracks." Martyn strode to the fireplace and inspected the meat sizzling in a frying pan over the coals. Looked like rabbit, possibly, with a few thin slices of squirrel. Not that a person got much out of a squirrel besides a few mouthfuls of meat. "At least you fared better than I did."

"Much better. I caught an elk in one of the tree falls. I managed to drag it back here with the pack mule, but I'll need help with butchering and smoking."

An elk. Enough meat to provision them for several weeks. Grabbing a plate, Martyn speared several pieces of squirrel and rabbit meat with his knife and returned to the table.

Kayleigh hadn't moved, her Bible still before her on the table.

Martyn sighed as he dropped onto the bench across from her. "Why do you persist in your faith like that? It hasn't gotten you anything. It's not like the people in Flayin Falls are going to let you join back in due to a private show of piety."

Kayleigh fingered the ends of her shoulder-length, brown hair. "My faith is dependent on what God did, not on what people do. Not even on what I do."

Martyn dragged a hand through his hair. By all logic, her faith should be as imaginary as her imaginary God. So why did she keep insisting it wasn't? "Up until recently, I never met a Christian who actually lived like one. Most are self-righteous hypocrites."

He'd known when Renna didn't agree with his actions, yet she'd still been kind to him—annoyingly, disgustingly kind. It would've been easier all the way around if she'd either been a kindly pushover who'd condemned nothing or a shrew who had done all condemning without any kindness.

Kayleigh ran her fingers along the pages of the Bible she'd yet to close. "That's the struggle of being a Christian. We are called to walk the narrow path that balances condemning sin yet showing kindness. Often, we wander onto one side or the other."

"From what I've seen, people are rather happy to wander."

"Yes, they are." Kayleigh bowed her head and blinked.

If she started crying, Martyn was out of there. It wasn't fair to bring out tears in a discussion.

He cleared his throat. Time to tweak the subject a bit. "If it's so important for you to worship and stuff, why haven't you moved? Whatever you did is only known in Flayin Falls. You could always escape it in some other town."

Someday he was going to have to get her to admit what was so horrible that supposedly good people would be so quick to grab their swords when she was around.

"It's something I've thought about. I probably should do it, but..." Kayleigh glanced around the cabin until her gaze settled on the door to what had once been her father's room. "Things weren't so bad until a few months ago when Father died. And after that, I kept hoping I could prove myself and things would change. When I returned from the war and things only got worse, I realized I might have to move eventually. But it's hard to leave here. This cabin is all I have left of my father. I'm not sure I can leave it behind."

If only Martyn's parents had possessed a smidgen of her loyalty. She couldn't even leave the cabin her father built behind. His parents had been all right with abandoning their child.

"I'm sure this won't be for forever." Kayleigh traced the edge of her Bible again, her head bowed as if she couldn't face him. "Do you think I'm a hypocritical Christian?"

That was a question Martyn did *not* want to answer.

What did he think about her? She was kind. Not like Renna's ultra-sweet version of kindness. Kayleigh's kindness was harder. She hadn't thrown him out, after all, when he'd stomped all over propriety. She hadn't stopped talking to him the moment she'd learned he wasn't a Christian, though she was more than ready to match him argument for argument in their discussions. Thing was, Martyn *liked* matching wits and logic with her.

He'd rather have his tongue cut out than admit any of that to her. Swear words piled into his mouth, but he bit them back. Dragging a hand through his hair, he cleared his throat. "No, I don't."

Her shoulders relaxed, as if she cared about his answer. Had Kayleigh started caring about him? He couldn't let any sort of caring happen, even mild friendship. It would only make it worse for her.

Worse for her? Martyn suppressed a groan. That almost sounded like *he* cared, even a speck, for her. Bother and... and all the words he no longer could say out loud in front of her. He curled his fingers into fists. Perhaps he should make a dash for the door to spout the words outside?

Kayleigh fanned the pages of her Bible. "I want to make a deal with you, but I'm not sure what you'll want in return."

By the way she was toying with her Bible, he probably didn't want to take the deal, not with the way he tended to lose these deals around her. "Spit it out."

"I think you will be unable to read the whole Bible before the winter is over." For the first time in the past few minutes, she raised her head and met his gaze.

"And if I lose?" He had to force himself not to look away.

"Failing to read and understand would be enough of a loss in itself." A slight smile touched Kayleigh's face. "But if you lose, you have to clean out the whole horse shed by yourself."

Did he want to take that challenge? Martyn ground his teeth. He had attempted to read the Bible months ago, back when Leith had given it to him, but he'd given up. The only thing it'd stirred in him was memories of his parents.

What did he have to lose besides a little hard work and time? He cocked his head. "What would I have to gain if I won?"

She chewed on her bottom lip. "That's what I don't know. I'm afraid of what you'll ask."

This was his opening to ask why the townsfolk hated her so much. Except that she hadn't asked after his past. Annoying as it was, she believed she was pushing him into something good for him. He should answer this challenge in kind.

But what did he believe would be genuinely good for her?

Thinking about it meant caring about her. Worrying about her.

He should leave. Get out of her life before he caused damage. But he couldn't. Not when the townsfolk of Flayin Falls made it so difficult for her to get supplies. Not when winter was closing in, and she'd need those supplies to survive.

No, that wasn't why he was staying. He wanted a hot meal, and this was a convenient spot to get it. Nothing more.

He dragged a hand through his hair. She still stared at him, waiting.

This would be so much easier if he could dump her off on someone else.

Maybe he could.

He turned to her and met her gaze. "If I win, then you must consider leaving Flayin Falls. Move to Walden or Stetterly or somewhere besides here."

He snapped off his words before he said too much. Before he promised he'd help her. He couldn't promise. Not when he probably wouldn't stick around in the spring to even find out her decision. But if he could at least get her thinking about it, maybe he could send Shadrach or Leith this way. Heroic types that they were, they wouldn't refuse.

"Leave?" She blinked down at her Bible.

Would she agree? He was asking her to think about leaving her home, the place filled with memories of her father. But she couldn't stay. Whatever she had done or not done, surely there was somewhere in Acktar she could go that was better than here.

She straightened her spine. "All right. If you agree, then I agree."

"Fine. Deal." He could stand to read the whole Bible, couldn't he? He'd read most of it back in his childhood. He could forge through it again. How hard could it be?

Leith slapped Shad on the back. "We'll miss you."

"You'll miss all the extra hands, you mean." Shad waved past Leith.

Leith didn't have to turn around. Behind him, the walls of Stetterly's new church rose toward the horizon. The four large beams Shad had brought now spanned the upper part of the walls. The jagged ends of the stones still needed a few more feet of height and the pitch of the roof. None of that would be finished until spring, unless they caught a few breaks in the snow.

Surrounding the church, a square of snug, sod dugouts

would provide shelter throughout the winter. The rest of the crops had been gathered. The grass scythed and stored as fodder for the animals. Steers had been cut out, killed, and the meat smoked. All thanks to the added help of Shad and the men he'd brought with him.

A few yards away, Jolene hugged Renna one last time. "We'll be sure to distribute the invitations. Everyone will be so thrilled."

"Especially Father." Shad stepped closer to Jolene and rested his hand around her waist, tugging her closer.

Leith cleared his throat. "If you see Martyn…"

"I'll pass the word of the wedding along to him as well." Shad shook his head. "Not sure he'll show up."

Leith couldn't be sure either. Was Martyn even still alive? Or had he wandered off into the Sheered Rock Hills and gotten himself killed?

After the final goodbyes, Shad, Jolene, and their guard party mounted their horses. As they rode out of Stetterly, Renna leaned against Leith's shoulder. The chill in the air scurried along Leith's hands and face.

The first snowflake fell.

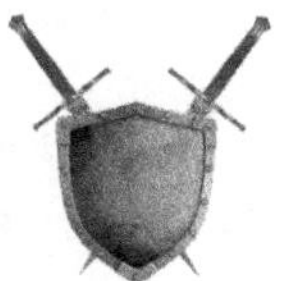

"You're sure this is his birthday? I'd hate to get it wrong." Renna whipped the butter, sugar, maple syrup, and other ingredients in a bowl. She couldn't mess this up. They had a limited amount of sugar to last the whole winter. She couldn't waste it.

"Yes, I'm sure. I triple-checked. Very secretly, of course." Brandi stoked the fire in the brick oven Leith and Sheriff Allen had built into one wall of their dugout. Brandi leaned over to blow on the coals, and her shoulder-length hair fell into her face. She huffed, dragged it out of her face with one hand, and kept blowing.

With Brandi's hair pulled back, the end of the pink scar along her scalp peeked through. Renna swallowed and turned back to the dough. Except for the occasional headache that now plagued Brandi during certain weather changes, she didn't seem to be affected by the injury. But it could've been so much worse.

Renna added the last of the ingredients into the bowl

and beat at the dough until her upper arm ached. When it was ready, she rolled the dough into balls and placed them a few inches apart on a metal tray.

Brandi knelt by the fireplace, a nook lined with rocks dug into the side of their hole in the ground. A shaft provided a chimney for both the fireplace and the brick oven. "Do you think the meat is almost ready?" She poked at the coals covering the lid of the metal pot where their dinner simmered.

"It probably has a little bit longer. I think." Renna eased the metal tray into the brick oven. Someday she'd master this cooking and baking thing. She was a lot better than she used to be. She no longer burned the eggs, and most of the time her stews turned out tasting all right. Her dishes didn't taste nearly as exquisite as Aunt Mara's used to, but Renna didn't have decades of practice either yet.

She leaned against the countertop behind her. It took up about a foot square of space near the oven and fireplace. A woodbox stood next to the door built into the side of the hill that was now their home while a rough table took up most of the floor space in the middle. At the back of the room, a curtain separated Brandi and Renna's pallets from the rest of the room. Along the opposite wall from the fireplace, a few shelves held dried vegetables and a few belongings.

But that was it. The rest was dirt. Hard-packed dirt floor. Dirt walls. Dirt roof. A few roots from the layer of grass above dangled from the ceiling. Occasionally, a trickle of dirt would cascade down onto Renna's hair.

It was just for the winter and into the spring. Renna fisted her hands in her skirt and drew in a deep breath that smelled of dry earth, smoke, and the hint of warm cookies.

At least it wasn't damp. The roaring fire dried out any trickles of water before they became too much of a nuisance. And there were fewer bugs than she expected. After the first week or two when earthworms would wiggle through the walls, the fire had dried the earth enough to discourage them.

Still, she couldn't help but count down the days until she could live in a snug cabin with real wooden walls and roof. She didn't care how small it was. She, Leith, Brandi, Jamie, and Ranson might all be piled on top of each other. At least there would be no more dirt.

What would her parents think of her now? She no longer flinched when she had to pick bugs out of her own hair when they fell down from the ceiling. Though, she let Brandi kill them.

A stomping sound came from outside, then a knock on their door. After a moment, the door eased open, and three bundles of cloaks, scarves, hats, and gloves tottered inside. Leith turned and shoved the door closed behind him.

After the first few days, when they'd realized the door and the walls muffled the sound of anyone yelling "come in" to someone outside, Renna had told Leith to knock as a warning, wait a few moments, then just come right in. It worked quite well, especially when there was a blizzard raging outside, and Renna didn't want to make Leith wait for her to open the door for him.

Leith, Jamie, and Ranson shrugged out of their snow-covered cloaks and gear, hanging them from pegs pounded into the dirt wall by the door.

Leith grinned and wrapped his arms around Renna's waist. "What's for dinner?"

She squirmed away from him. "Your hands are cold!"

"I've never heard of that kind of food before." Jamie hunched by the fireplace and extended his hands in front of him. Renna eyed his sleeves. How had they become too short on him? Again? Every time she turned around, he'd gained a couple more inches on her. Something Jamie seemed quite pleased about.

Ranson smiled and slipped onto one of the benches by the table. If Renna hadn't asked him to make sure he was here for this meal, he probably would've been over at Sheriff Allen's eating with him. Even though Michelle was spending the winter at Walden—or maybe because of that—Ranson had spent a lot of time with Sheriff Allen. It seemed to be working. Sheriff Allen no longer scowled at Ranson, and sometimes he even slapped him on the back when he thought no one else was looking.

"How is the arrow making and training coming?" Renna forced herself not to check the cookies yet again.

Leith joined Jamie by the fire and extended his hands. "Coming along. Most of them seem to be getting a feel for their larger bows, even if they haven't had a chance to practice any sort of distance yet."

With the snow so deep, they couldn't practice outside without losing too many arrows. At least the men and women who had volunteered to learn archery could shoot at the walls of their dugouts to build up their strength.

Leith cocked his head. "What's that smell?"

The cookies. Renna grabbed a thick towel and peered into the oven. The edges of the cookies were tanned, though the middle was still a touch gooey. Perfect. She pulled out the tray and set it on top of the counter to cool and let the cookies bake that last little bit on the pan, a trick Aunt Mara had once told her. "Your first surprise for today. Maple sugar cookies."

"I hope you like them. They're my favorite cookie, but since we didn't know what your favorite cookie is, we decided you had to try them." Brandi sat cross legged on the floor next to Jamie. "Since it is your birthday and all."

Leith gave her a lopsided grin. "I figured you were up to something when you tried to subtly ask when my birthday was."

Brandi scowled. "You weren't supposed to notice."

Renna shook her head and checked the cookies. Good enough. She peeled one off the tray and held it out to Leith. The heat from the cookie flared into her fingers, and she barely kept herself from dropping it.

He took it, flopping it between his hands to let it cool. He glanced between Renna and Brandi. "Should I be worried that this is poisoned? You're both staring at me like you expect me to fall over dead after one bite."

"It's a maple sugar cookie. The only thing that will happen is you'll pass out from the most amazing thing you have ever tasted." Brandi rested her elbows on her knees and leaned forward.

"Even better than cake?" Leith raised an eyebrow at her.

"Yes. Definitely."

"I'm not sure about that." Renna worked to peel a few more cookies from the tray. "I'm not as good at baking as Aunt Mara. She made the best cookies."

"But this is her recipe. We dug it out of the ashes of Stetterly Manor, so it has to be good." Brandi snatched the cookie from Renna the moment she held it out. "Now stop stalling, Leith, and eat it already."

Renna's stomach curled, strangely tense. She shouldn't really be so nervous about him eating one cookie, but what if it tasted awful? What if she'd messed this one up too?

Leith bit a small corner off one edge. He froze and swallowed. When he glanced at her, his expression was blank. "How large a batch did you make?"

"A pretty big one." Renna fisted her fingers in her skirt. How awful did they taste?

"And you made them for me, correct?" He only paused long enough for Renna to give a short nod. Then, a grin slowly spread across his face and danced in his green eyes. "Good. Because no one else can have any."

Brandi gripped her cookie tighter and half turned away from him as if worried he'd snatch her cookie away. A stricken look crossed Ranson's face, as if for a moment, he didn't realize Leith was joking.

Renna laughed. Leith liked them. That was a relief. "Now, now. You have to learn how to share, even on your birthday."

She handed each of them a second cookie before she finally bit into one herself. The cookie crumbled onto her tongue, the sugar melting into the purest bliss she could imagine. Maybe these cookies weren't quite as good as Aunt Mara's, but they were close.

A lump formed in Renna's throat. It tasted like one of Aunt Mara's hugs baked into a cookie. Renna would never have another of Aunt Mara's hugs and would never taste one of her cookies, but at least she and Brandi would still have this.

In another month, they'd celebrate again, this time to mark a year since Leith fell, wounded, into their kitchen at Stetterly Manor. That day would start a year of memories. A year since Harrison Vane died. A year since her and Brandi's capture. A year since Uncle Abel and Aunt Mara died.

And five years since their parents were killed.

Leith's arms wrapped around her, and she leaned her head against his shoulder. "Happy birthday, Leith."

He pulled her closer, and she had to hold her cookie out of the way before it got crushed between them. He kissed her forehead. "Thank you."

When he stepped back, he turned to Brandi. "You were right. Maple sugar cookies are the best food ever."

"Told you." Brandi shoved the rest of her cookie into her mouth. Her mouth still full, she reached for the metal coal shovel. "Think the food is ready, Renna?"

"Probably." Renna eased around Leith and Jamie, knelt, and helped Brandi uncover the cast iron pot. When she lifted the lid, a cloud of fragrant steam rose into the air. Saliva filled Renna's mouth, washing away the last taste of cookie.

Jamie and Ranson helped set the table, then they all gathered around for chunks of the beef roast, mushrooms, corn, and beans that had been baked together in a marinade of herbs and meat juice.

After they polished off the roast, ate a few more cookies, and cleaned up the dishes, Brandi grabbed a package wrapped in a scrap of fabric. "Time for presents."

"Presents? Wasn't that the cookies?" Leith slid onto the bench across from Brandi.

"They were part of it." Renna retrieved her own fabric-wrapped bundle from a shelf and perched on the bench next to Leith. She placed the bundle in front of Leith. "This is the second half."

Leith eased the fabric off, revealing Uncle Abel's Bible, the one Vane had stolen so long ago. A crease furrowed Leith's forehead. "You're giving this to me?"

Renna nodded and slid her hand into his. That lump clogged her throat again. "I know you gave Martyn your Bible, and I think Uncle Abel would've liked you to have it. Besides, we're getting married. It's not like you'll be taking it very far away."

"Thank you." Leith freed his hand from hers, wrapped his arm around her waist, and hugged her.

Brandi shoved her haphazard package across the table. "Mine next."

Leith unwrapped the fabric with one hand. A pair of black mittens and a scarf flopped free.

Brandi grinned. "I made them myself. My first try wasn't very good. There were huge holes, but these ones turned out all right. I hope they fit."

Leith tried them on, then held up his hands for Brandi to see. "Perfect. These will be much warmer than my gloves for shoveling snow. Thank you."

"You're welcome." Brandi hopped up. "They're also perfect for snow fights. Let's go. Renna, you too. You can't get out of it this time."

Renna sighed. The cold would filter through her mittens and soak through her clothes, but perhaps it would be worth it.

They all bundled up and tromped outside. By this time in the winter, several feet covered the ground, rolling away to the horizon in a dull white expanse. Clouds obscured the sky with the threat of more snow.

Somehow, the teams became Leith and Renna against Jamie, Brandi, and Ranson. And since the three of them seemed more intent on hitting Leith, Renna was spared the worst of it. Either that, or Jamie and Ranson were too nice to throw snowballs at her.

Renna stepped aside and watched Jamie and Ranson toss armloads of snow at Leith while Brandi sneaked behind him. A warmth filled her chest, despite her numb toes, fingers, and nose. This was her family. She could get used to many more winters of this.

Leith whirled and tackled Brandi. Brandi shrieked as she landed on her back in a snowdrift. She flung a handful of snow at Leith. Both of them collapsed on their backs in the snow, laughing and panting.

Renna smiled. Many, many years of this.

20

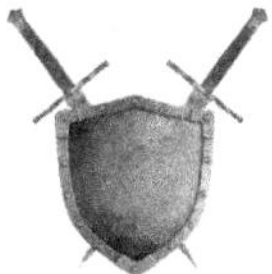

After three days of howling winds and driving snow, the crystal flakes finally lay silent and shimmering across the jagged cliffs and hollows of the Sheered Rock Hills. Martyn tucked his hood tighter around his ears as he ducked under a pine branch laden with several inches of the fresh snow.

Beneath him, Wanderer trudged through the drifted snow, sometimes plowing through patches that reached his chest. Even though the blizzard had obscured the trail Martyn had worn into the snow between his cabin and Kayleigh's, Wanderer automatically followed the same path.

Martyn breathed a little easier when he spotted the curl of smoke rising above the treetops as he neared Kayleigh's cabin. The blizzard had made it too dangerous to go any farther than the shed behind Old Man Bendwick's cabin where Wanderer and the pack mule stayed. Not that he'd really been worried that something would've happened to her. Of course not.

He and Wanderer crested a rise. Kayleigh's cabin tucked into the hollow in a nest of pine trees. After turning Wanderer into the corral to paw up what little grass he could still scavenge, Martyn trudged onto the porch and knocked.

After a moment, Kayleigh flung the door open. "You're all right! That blizzard was a nasty one, and I knew you were too smart to try to make it here, but I..." She trailed off and stepped aside. "Never mind. You'd better come in."

Martyn stepped into the bright warmth of her kitchen. Venison simmered in a pan, along with two small corn cakes. He grinned as he unwrapped his scarf, hung it on a peg, and unclasped his cloak. Just in time for breakfast. A hot breakfast. So much better than the dried meat and hard biscuits from his pack he'd lived on the past few days.

He grabbed the plates and utensils from the cupboard while Kayleigh brought the pan to the table. After he'd taken a seat, she folded her hands and prayed.

Martyn ignored her, set her plate and silverware in front of her, and helped himself to the food. When she opened her eyes, she claimed her corn cake and half of the venison sausage.

Martyn waved his fork at the cupboards behind her. "How are you set on supplies?"

She glared, furiously chewing on the bite she'd just popped into her mouth. The longer he stared, the redder her cheeks became. Martyn fought to hold back his grin.

She dipped her chin as she swallowed. "A little low on corn flour and other baking supplies. But I can stretch it if we have to. We have more than enough meat."

Martyn stabbed another bite. They could stretch it. Eat nothing besides venison stored in her smokehouse for the next month or two. But he'd gotten less than he'd hoped when he'd made his last trip to Walden in the fall. If this turned into a long winter, it'd be better if they had more supplies and to get them now before they were used up. "I was thinking I'd ride into town to see if I could get more."

Her forehead wrinkled. "I thought you said Walden would be too far of a ride once the snow came."

How much did Kayleigh trust him? Martyn met her gaze. "I wasn't planning on going to Walden."

"Oh." She stared at her plate, tapping her fork against what was left of her sausage as if she meant to torture it for answers. "I see."

Martyn waited. By the tone of her voice, she seemed convinced he'd learn the truth about her the moment he stepped into Flayin Falls. Did she really think it would make a difference to him?

Maybe she did. After all, Martyn had yet to tell her he was a Blade. He seemed to think the past would change things.

She straightened her back and met his gaze. Her brown eyes were strangely blank, her mouth a thin line. "If you think it's necessary, then you'd better go."

"I'll leave as soon as I finish eating." Best not to let her think about it too much. "I'll be taking the last of the furs to trade. I don't think the townsfolk know about my mission for the king."

She nodded and returned to stabbing her breakfast. Martyn took the hint and finished his breakfast in three large bites. He bundled in his cloak, gloves, and scarf and trudged out the door.

Wanderer flicked his ears and gave an annoyed snort as

Martyn led him from the corral. "Sorry, fella. You've been getting lazy in that stall of yours."

After strapping on the pile of furs behind his saddle, he set out for Flayin Falls. The ride stretched into several hours since he had to let Wanderer pick his way out of the Hills slowly to avoid drop offs hidden by several feet of snow. Occasionally, Martyn got off and walked to make sure it was safe for Wanderer.

He reached the main road through Flayin Falls at noon. Women bundled in cloaks and hoods chatted on the board-walks while men hustled back and forth on the ice-packed road. Most stopped and stared as Martyn rode by. He winced. Strangers weren't common, especially not in the middle of winter.

Martyn halted Wanderer in front of the general store, swung down, and untied the bundle of furs. A group of women edged away from him as he strode onto the board-walk. He suppressed a snort. If they'd known who he really was, they would've been running, not tiptoeing.

A bell chimed at a piercing pitch when he pushed open the door. Rows of shelves lined the room, though many of them stood empty. A few barrels sat beside the outer wall, and Martyn couldn't tell if they were filled with flour and sugar or not. Probably not. After the war, everyone was hurting this winter.

Footsteps sounded from behind one of the shelves, then a slim man wearing a neatly pressed shirt and trousers stepped into sight. He paused, eyed Martyn, then pasted on a smile. "Hello. What can I do for you?"

Another suppressed snort. This was the general store. Why else would Martyn be there except for supplies? The huge bundle of furs slung over his shoulder should be some indication.

But being sarcastic wasn't the way to avoid trouble. Martyn tossed the bundle of furs onto the counter, then set a torn scrap of paper next to it. "I need some supplies. I think these furs should be enough to trade for everything on this list."

The store's owner scanned the list, a small frown curling his mouth. "I'll have to see if we have everything. This time of winter, we tend to run a bit low."

Martyn made a noncommittal nod. Of course they ran low at this time of year. Next the man would spout some nonsense about the weather or some other useless chatter.

The man bustled behind one of the sets of shelves. "That was some blizzard we had, wasn't it?"

Martyn gritted his teeth. The quicker he got out of here, the better. "Yes."

"Haven't seen you around here before. Are you traveling through or planning on staying a while?" Something clattered as the man rummaged through his shelves. Based on where the man was standing, he currently had an unobstructed view of Wanderer through the store's window. Probably judging how far Martyn had ridden this morning.

Nosy shopkeeper. Full of gossip and nonsense, like every other general store in Acktar.

Just like the store Martyn's father had owned when Martyn was nine.

Martyn forced his stance to relax. He belonged here. He had nothing to hide. Far from it. "I'm scouting for King Keevan. Keeping an eye out for Rovers."

"Are you? Haven't seen any Rovers around these parts in

months." The shopkeeper peered over one of his empty shelves, his tone an accusation.

Suspicious as well as nosy. Not a good combination. Martyn leaned against the counter to hide his tense muscles. As curious as he was about Kayleigh, he didn't dare bring up the topic until after he had those supplies in his hands all traded for legally. Especially since the man seemed inclined to disbelieve anything he said. "Rovers don't move around much in the winter. I have a cabin up in the Hills. Doing a little trapping. Keep to myself, mostly."

"I see." The man returned to the counter and set down his armload. He ducked behind the counter and began filling a sack with corn meal from a barrel. "Where in the Hills?"

If this shopkeeper could mind his own business for five minutes...Martyn forced his hands to remain on the counter and not stray to the knife he'd hidden under his shirt. "North of here a ways."

"Hmmm." The man tied off the sack of corn and added it to the pile on the counter. "That's all I can spare. It won't quite make the amount for the furs. Anything else you'd like to add?"

Martyn scanned the shelves. Empty. Empty. A few spare saddles. Hoes and shovels for planting in the spring. A rack of hats. Nothing he or Kayleigh needed.

His gaze landed on the rack of cloth at the far end of the counter. The store had a few bolts of fabric, mostly cotton, in colors Kayleigh might call pretty. The thicker fabrics had probably sold out earlier in the winter.

Picking out fabric for her seemed too...nice. Like he cared about her. Or thought about how she'd look in a dress made of that deep green cloth instead of the bloodstained, faded thing she wore on Sundays.

He couldn't get attached to her. Not someone like him. He wasn't the settling down type like Leith, and it'd never work with Kayleigh anyway, not with her being a Christian and having standards.

But when would she be able to buy fabric to replace the dress the Rovers had ruined? Based on the state of her cupboards when he'd stumbled across her, this all-too-helpful store owner wasn't so helpful to her. If he deigned to do business with her, he probably overcharged her for the privilege.

Besides, if Martyn won their deal—and he was halfway through conquering Ezekiel—Kayleigh would need something nicer than her father's trousers and her worn dress to set her up in a new town.

It was just a thank you. No, not even that. It was just a practical purchase. Most of the work of trapping had been Kayleigh's, after all.

Martyn pointed at the bolt of dark green fabric the color of spring pine trees. "I'd like a few yards of that. However much it takes to make the trade even."

After pulling it from the rack, the store owner unrolled what looked like several yards. Up close, Martyn spotted a faint floral pattern to the fabric. He bit back a groan. He wouldn't be able to pass it off as a purchase for himself.

The man sliced off a chunk and folded it into a neat square. The same way Martyn had, years ago, while minding his father's store. The shopkeeper eyed him, not yet handing the fabric over. "You haven't come across a girl living up there, have you?"

Martyn stilled. He couldn't have the conversation. Not until that receipt was all tallied and in his hand. He tried to relax against the counter, nonchalant. Uncaring. "I've run into her a couple of times while trapping. And scouting for the king."

Some of the hard look in the shopkeeper's gaze faded at the emphasis Martyn placed on the word *king*. "Stay away from her, that's my advice. She's trouble."

"What did she do?" Martyn held his breath as the shopkeeper tallied the purchase and the furs on a slip of paper.

"It's not so much what she did, but who she is and what her uncle did." The store owner held out the receipt, glanced around the store as if to make sure they were alone, then leaned closer. "She's Respen's niece."

Martyn gaped. Respen's niece? His mind whirled. King Respen had never talked about a niece. Not that he would've shared that sort of thing with his Blades. "How did that happen?"

"Her mother and Respen's wife were sisters. A cursed family, they say. The older sister married John Ainsley, one of Lord Westin's guards. She died while having the girl. A few years later, the younger sister married Respen. She also died in childbirth. God's judgement on the lot of them, I say."

Martyn ground his teeth together. After spending so much time with Kayleigh and Renna, he'd forgotten what judgemental people most Christians were. They hated Kayleigh for this? She was Respen's niece. So what? She wasn't even related to him by blood. Only her aunt's marriage.

"The girl's poor father. He didn't know what he was

getting into when he married the girl's mother. Killed by his own brother-in-law's Blades. A shame a good man like that got mixed up in such a sorry family."

Martyn gathered his pile of supplies. He had to leave. Now. If he listened to another minute of this man's spouting, he'd put a knife in his chest. He wouldn't even feel sorry about it. Picking up the sack of corn, he spun on his heels and stalked from the store.

After loading the supplies into his saddlebags, Martyn nudged Wanderer into a canter. A few people had to dodge out of the way. Served them right. Served the whole confounded town right if the next blizzard caved in every house and store on top of their heads.

When he left the last few houses behind, he indulged in several minutes of swearing. Best to get it all out before he returned to Kayleigh.

It wasn't enough. His blood still pumped hot in his veins by the time he reached Kayleigh's cabin. He tore the saddlebags and the sack of corn from his saddle and stomped into the cabin.

Kayleigh glanced up, her eyes widening. "I know I should've explained. I'm sorry. I understand, really, if you want to cancel our deal."

What was she talking about? He dumped the saddlebags on the table. Wait, did she think he was mad at her?

She'd told the truth all along. She had done nothing to earn her town's scorn. "Those ridiculous, hateful, judgmental..." He couldn't think of a word mild enough to use in front of her. "They hate you because you're related to Respen? You had nothing to do with who your aunt married."

She relaxed against the counter behind her, her shoulders shuddering with a released breath. "You're not going to leave?"

"Why in Acktar would I leave over something as idiotic as that?" The words that came to mind were ones that were sure to earn him a soap scrubbing if he said them. "That town of rattlesnakes is the one to blame."

She sighed. "They aren't all that bad. They are sincere Christians, just blinded by their hurt."

"How can you defend them? After all they've done to you without reason?" Martyn dug his fingers into his hair. "Bad enough that there are men like..." he'd nearly said *like me*, but caught himself in time, "like the Blades running around. But worse are self-righteous hypocrites like that."

"They don't know they're acting like that. They sincerely believe they are living good, Christian lives. But people of faith can be blinded in some areas. Even David, a man after God's own heart, thought he could get away with arranging for a man's death to steal that man's wife. We all have things we can't see about ourselves." Kayleigh wrapped her arms around her stomach.

Martyn stiffened at the mention of David. He'd forged his way through that part of the Bible to keep his deal with Kayleigh, but it had been tough, especially with Brandi's voice ringing in his head during the stories about Jonathan. He crossed his arms. "I still don't see why that makes you defend them. You should be furious."

"I was angry. So angry I dressed in my father's clothes, walked to Walden, got a guide to Eagle Heights, and joined the Resistance army. You know the real reason I did all that? I wanted to kill Respen. My own uncle."

If she'd been in the Riders instead of the foot soldiers, she might've gone into the Tower with King Keevan. She would've seen Martyn among the Blades, and she would know his darkest secret as he now knew hers. Not a comfortable thought. "You're hardly the only person who plotted to kill Respen."

"No, but I was the closest thing he had to family. Of all people, I should've wanted to reach out to him. Instead, I wanted to kill him." She shuddered and swiped at her face.

Was she crying? She'd better not be. Martyn wasn't about to let her cry on his shoulder.

She sucked in a shaky breath. "At Eagle Heights, I was reminded what being a part of the community felt like, even if I was doing it under a false name and disguise. It made me hope I could return and be a part of them again."

But it hadn't happened. Instead they'd scorned her. Good thing he wasn't a Blade anymore, or he'd be highly tempted to march in there and show them what it truly meant to fear.

He fought to shove the heat deep into his chest. Nothing he could say would make things any better for Kayleigh. Perhaps he could reassure her that Respen hadn't died without someone trying to help him.

But telling Kayleigh that would mean admitting he had been a Blade. Did he dare tell her? Would she still trust him after that?

Somehow, her trust mattered. Maybe because he trusted her, trusted her even more now that he knew her secret.

Kayleigh sighed and shook her head. "I still struggle with anger. It's a good thing Respen is dead, or I might still want to kill him. And his Blades...I can't forget what they did to Papa. And sometimes, I think I don't have to forgive them since none of them are sorry for what they've done and would never ask for forgiveness."

Something curled in Martyn's chest, hardened, and died. He couldn't tell her the truth. When spring came, he would have to leave and never return. It would be best for both of them.

Why had he expected any different? Leith and Renna claimed they had forgiven him, but they probably didn't mean it deep down. How could they, after what Martyn did?

Especially when he still nursed that bitter rock deep in his gut when he thought of Leith's betrayal.

Kayleigh drew in a deep breath and straightened. "We probably should unpack. What did you manage to get?"

He snagged the saddlebags and pulled them from her reach. This wasn't how he imagined this going. Then again, he'd been too angry leaving Flayin Falls to really think through how he would go about giving her the fabric without her getting the wrong impression.

"Well, there was a slight problem. The general store was running low on supplies, so I got what I could." Martyn pointed at the sack of corn meal. "But there was a little left-over, so I..."

The saddlebags nearly slipped from his hands as he fumbled to open the one where he'd stuffed the fabric. Why were his fingers giving him so much trouble with this? It wasn't like he was nervous. Then again, maybe he was nervous, but not about her liking it. Of course not. He was just nervous she'd get the wrong impression. That was it.

"I, uh, got you this." He yanked out the fabric and shoved it at her.

She caught it. "Owen, it's...it's beautiful."

He forced himself not to wince at the fake name he'd given her. "They were your furs, and your dress got ruined because I wasn't quick enough to stop the Rovers. That's all. It's not much."

"It's *so* much." She hugged the fabric.

What was a person supposed to say to that? Martyn swiveled his gaze from the saddlebags to the window. Anywhere but her.

Kayleigh's footsteps whispered closer. He glanced up just as she wrapped one arm around his waist and hugged him.

Martyn held his breath. She was soft and warm. Like a sunbeam on a spring morning.

He jerked away. He wasn't made for sunbeams. He was the howling blizzard sweeping across the prairie and freezing everything it touched. Spinning on his heel, he stalked from the cabin.

21

Martyn stomped the mud from his boots on the front step. For the first time since the snow had melted, he'd found tracks, only hours old.

They might be nothing. The trail could turn north to Eagle Heights or south to Nalgar Castle. He couldn't tell from the tracks if they were Blades, Rovers, or innocent trappers.

But something in the pit of Martyn's stomach told him it wouldn't be that simple. These tracks were headed west—a group of ten people—and that couldn't be good. This time, he had to find something, even if he had to scour the entire Sheered Rock Hills to do it. If he was lucky, he might even have a good excuse to avoid Leith and Renna's wedding in three and a half weeks.

All he had to do was let Kayleigh know he'd be gone for a while, then he could leave.

He knocked and stepped inside. The kitchen was empty, but the doors to both bedrooms were closed. "Kayleigh?"

"Just a minute." The new, solid oak door to her bedroom muffled her voice.

Should he sit down to wait? He was losing daylight, and whoever had left those tracks gained more and more distance on him. He settled for standing, braced against the countertop.

Kayleigh's door opened. As she stepped from the room, Martyn's breath lodged in his chest. She wore a dress made of the dark green floral fabric he'd gotten her early in the winter. The bodice hugged her torso, not in a tight, revealing way. More a prim, proper way. The skirt flared from her hips and swirled around her ankles. Her shoulder-length brown hair gleamed with hints of red and gold.

"What do you think?" She twirled, and the skirt flared as it caught the air.

He wasn't about to say what he was thinking. Had he once told her so flippantly that he wasn't tempted by her?

Because he was. Very tempted.

Months ago, Martyn could've walked by her without a glance, even dressed as she was now. But now that he knew her heart—the kindness she gave, the struggles forced upon her by the prejudicial town—he truly saw her.

He shouldn't have stayed so long. He should've stuck to his original plan and gotten out of there as soon as Kayleigh's leg had healed enough for her to walk. He could've found somewhere else to spend the winter, made do with his own cooking, survived with only Wanderer's company.

Instead, he'd stayed. He'd let himself get attached. Let her think he cared.

"Well, aren't you going to say something?" She smoothed the skirt.

Martyn swallowed, but even that couldn't clear the hoarse gravel to his voice. "It looks...nice."

"I even have enough fabric left to make a blouse to wear with my divided skirt." Her smile glinted in her eyes. "Wait there. I have something for you."

He struggled to breathe as she swished back into her bedroom.

She returned a moment later, carrying what looked like a bundle of buckskin. She held it out to him. "I hope they fit."

He took the bundle and unrolled it into a pair of buckskin trousers and a matching vest of soft buckskin. What the...he stared at the clothes. When had she done this? And how?

Kayleigh rocked back and forth on her heels. "I measured your spare set of clothes one of the times I cleaned your cabin while you were out scouting. I hope you don't mind. Your clothes were getting a bit frayed, and we had a lot of buckskin and I thought that might be nice and sturdy for your long rides. Do you like them?"

Did he like them? Of course he did. How could he not when she was looking at him with such big, brown eyes and that low note to her voice?

But he couldn't tell her that. This was a big mistake. He shouldn't have let her care for him this much. He was a former Blade. He wasn't the type to settle down with a girl like her. He would abandon her, just like his parents had abandoned him.

He closed his eyes as pain plunged through his chest and bones. He had to leave. Now. And never return. Never even look back.

Worse, he had to crush her heart. He couldn't leave her

with any hope that he'd return. Hope would kill her slowly over the weeks and months when he didn't come back.

No, better to kill that hope quickly. She'd move on, looking back at this past winter with a shudder for the kind of man she'd been fool enough to befriend.

When he reported to Walden, he could ask Shadrach to check in on her. And he'd leave the pack mule here. But he could do nothing for her besides leave.

Forcing his eyes open and his heart to go cold as Acktar's winter, he faced her. "I have to tell you something. Something about my past."

She stilled, the smile dropping from her face. "All right. What's wrong?"

He shifted the buckskin trousers and vest to his right hand and braced himself. His muscles locked, as if trying to prevent him from doing this.

But he couldn't hesitate. Best to get this over with as quickly as possible. He grasped his right sleeve and pushed it all the way to his shoulder, revealing the rows of scars marching down his arm. His marks. All thirty-three of them.

She stared, as if she couldn't comprehend what she was seeing.

A strange tightness filled his throat. "Up until last summer, I was a King's Blade."

"I don't...but you're a scout. You fought for the Resistance." Kayleigh gaped at his marks, her face pale.

He could tell her King Keevan had granted him clemency. That in the Tower, Martyn had fought against King Respen. But he couldn't, not if he wanted to destroy her hope.

Martyn let go of his sleeve. "No, I didn't."

Red flooded into her cheeks. "You lied. This whole time, you were lying. Of course you didn't care that I'm Respen's niece. You worked for him. You *killed* for him."

Martyn clamped his mouth shut. This was what he wanted, right? Her hatred. Yet, it sliced him like Respen's whip had once slashed his back.

She grasped her sword, drew it, and pointed it at his chest. "Get out. How could you have pretended to help me? You might even be the Blade that killed my father."

No, he wasn't, but he couldn't lessen this blow. He couldn't even apologize. He backed toward the door.

"You used me. You pretended to help me. You listened while I told you about my father, yet you said nothing." She stepped forward and jabbed his chest with the sword's tip. A prick of pain formed above Martyn's sternum. "Get out. Now."

Martyn spun on his heels and strode from the cabin. Don't look back. Don't give in to the pain aching through his chest. Don't beg for her forgiveness. This was how it was supposed to be. How it was always supposed to be.

He stuffed the buckskin trousers and vest into a saddlebag, swung onto Wanderer, and nudged the horse into a trot. He didn't pause to look back. He didn't even turn Wanderer toward Old Man Bendwick's cabin.

He'd left nothing behind.

22

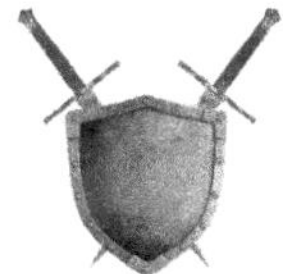

"I can't believe I got talked into this."

"Stetterly's lady should put in the last piece. It's only fitting." Leith balanced on the edge of the bell tower, its roof digging into his stomach. A rope wrapped around his waist and shoulders and disappeared into the tower where it looped over the iron bolt holding the church bell. Sheriff Allen gripped the other end. "I won't let you fall."

Renna balanced on the rim of the bell tower's windows next to him, a rope also tied around her waist. The wide legs of her divided skirt flapped around both of their ankles. She gripped the weather vane at the peak of the bell tower with one hand, and held a piece of slate tile with the other. Just below the peak stone, a gap in the slate tiles waited for her to insert the missing piece. "I know, but I can't stop thinking about slipping and falling in front of the whole town."

Leith glanced down. On the ground below, the townsfolk stood in a mass of figures staring up at them. "That would be a bit embarrassing. But it isn't going to happen. I have you, and Sheriff Allen has both of us in case we slip."

Renna sighed, stretched to reach the slot, and tried to ease the slate into place. It jammed against the other pieces around it. "I think I'm going to need two hands."

Leith adjusted his grip on the weather vane and wrapped his other arm around her waist. "I got you."

"You sure?" Renna's voice spiked higher. Her fingers remained white-knuckled on the weather vane below Leith's.

"Yes. You can let go." Leith braced himself to take her weight in case she slipped.

Renna pried her fingers from the weather vane, though every muscle remained tense beneath Leith's arm. She worked the tile into place and pressed it into the wet mortar the workmen had placed there a few minutes before they'd abandoned the roof to let their lady install the final piece. "There. Done."

"Now you'd better turn and wave to let everyone know."

Renna grimaced, twisted in Leith's grip, and waved at the townsfolk. They cheered, and some of the men threw their wide-brimmed hats into the air. Some of the women waved back, and the children hollered louder than anyone.

"Can we get down now?" Renna's fingers tightened into a claw-like grip on his arm.

"Are you sure you don't want to admire the view a while longer?" Behind them, the Spires Canyon furrowed into the ground, but beyond it and in every other direction, the trackless prairie rolled onward and onward, miles and miles of yellow and green waves, broken only by the patches of freshly tilled fields. The endless sky curved above them, merging into the prairie at the far off horizon.

Though, if she looked over his shoulder, she'd spot the walls of the cabin Leith was building, a cabin he'd so far kept a surprise.

"I can admire the view just as well from the tower." Renna's back was stiff. "Please help me down."

"All right. Hold on to me. That's it." Leith steadied her as she lowered herself into a sitting position on the edge of the bell tower. Hands from inside helped her the rest of the way to safety.

With a grip on the edge of the roof and a support post, Leith swung himself into the bell tower and landed on his feet. Ranson stepped out of the way, as if he'd been waiting to help Leith inside if he needed it.

After Leith and Renna untied the safety ropes, they followed Ranson and Sheriff Allen down the set of stairs that circled the outside of the bell tower all the way to the ground floor.

At the door to the church, Leith gave Renna a slight push. "Go on, Lady Faythe. Make your speech."

She scowled, but by the time she turned back to the crowd, she'd replaced the scowl with a serene expression. She stepped onto the front step, her back straight, her head high. "Five years ago, my parents were killed and Stetterly's church burned to the ground. But today we celebrate our rebuilding from the ashes."

Leith stayed in the shadows. This was her moment to truly be Lady Faythe, and he wasn't going to take any part of that away from her.

As she continued the speech he'd heard ten or eleven times already, he leaned against the wall and stared upward at the interior of the church. The vaulted ceiling rose several stories above him, slitted windows in the second story providing shafts of light. A parapet ran under the windows, spanning the ends of the four massive beams that had been rafted down the Ondieda River from Walden. Rough wooden benches filled the large room, but at the far end, a small dais provided just enough room for the minister to stand when he visited them as part of his circuit. Behind the dais, a doorway opened into the bell tower, which was flanked on either side by storage rooms. A cellar had been dug under one of the storage rooms, complete with a well.

In a little under three weeks, he and Renna would have their wedding in this church. He was ready. Of course he was.

So why did he still feel like he didn't have a place at Stetterly?

Sheriff Allen's heavy tread stopped near Leith. "That went well."

"Yes." Leith turned. "Now that the church is finished, you can have the men store the arrows in the far storage room."

Sheriff Allen folded his arms across his stomach. "You really think there's going to be trouble? We haven't seen any sign of Rovers since last fall."

"That's why I'm worried." Leith glanced at the open doorway, where Renna still stood finishing her speech. "Everyone from Arroway to Walden was having trouble with Rovers last fall. After spending a lean winter holed up in some hideaway, they should be out in droves once again. But we've seen nothing. Walden, Uster, and Duelstone haven't seen anything either."

"Maybe everyone decided to return home." Sheriff Allen

shrugged. "They lost the war. What else can they do at this point but try to build a new life like the rest of us?"

"Maybe some of them, surely not all of them. Not all at once." Leith shook his head. He couldn't explain the itchy, crawly feeling down his back. Something wasn't right in Acktar. "Especially not in the spring when farmers are alone and vulnerable while working their fields and the cattle herds have to be driven far from the towns to find green grass."

Sheriff Allen made a huffing sound, and Leith wasn't sure if it was in continued disbelief or beginning agreement.

He met Sheriff Allen's gaze. "This reminds me too much of the summer after the Blades drove the last of the Rovers out of Acktar. What has them running scared now?"

A frown curled Sheriff Allen's mouth, and his gaze sharpened. "King Keevan's armies were unable to do anything effective against the Rovers last fall. And no one else has done much against them, besides when you scared them away from here."

"Exactly."

Lord Alistair had written last fall that all the tracks Martyn had found in the Sheered Rock Hills went west. Were they going west because they were leaving...or because they were uniting?

He wasn't sure what he feared more, that something worse than Rovers had scared them out of Acktar or that someone had figured out a way to gather them once again into a lethal force.

"I see." Sheriff Allen nodded. "I'll have the arrows moved into here today, and I'll tell them to keep up the practice."

"We'd better move all the supplies that can be spared

into here as well." Leith gripped the hilt of the knife buckled to his belt. "If trouble comes, we have to be ready."

Sheriff Allen braced a hand along the thick, stone wall. "Then it's a good thing you designed this church to be a fortress."

And oddly fireproof, down to using slate tile instead of wooden shingles. But if anyone had noticed that detail, they hadn't asked.

Would it be enough? Leith also rested a hand on the cool stone. He had to trust God's will would be best. But that didn't guarantee safety. Didn't promise that Stetterly would survive to see the summer.

Trust. It didn't mean Leith shouldn't do everything in his power to protect and prevent the tragedy he feared was coming. Trust didn't mean making unwise choices.

Trust meant using the resources, skills, and knowledge God had provided, and trusting God with the outcome.

LEITH EASED THE BRICK INTO ITS SPOT ON THE FLOOR AND reached for the next one. The kitchen of the new cabin was coming together. Earlier that spring, the men had taken a break from building the church to raise the walls with logs floated down from Walden.

A knock sounded against the door post. Leith glanced up as Jamie stepped across the threshold. Leith waved at the stack of bricks he'd set to the side. "Here to help?"

Jamie nodded, picked up a brick, and tapped it down. The ends of his sleeves fell several inches short of his wrists. They'd have to find new clothes for him. Again.

They worked in silence for several minutes, but a furrow remained on Jamie's brow. Finally, Leith perched on his heels. "Something on your mind?"

Jamie sat back on the half-finished floor and rested his arms on his knees. "I've been thinking a lot. About the future."

"And?" Where was Jamie going with this? Jamie would be fifteen later that summer. If this was about noticing girls... Leith wasn't prepared for *that* conversation. At all.

Was it too late to send Jamie to Walden and have Lord Alistair take over?

"I..." Jamie swallowed, drew in a deep breath, and blurted out, "I want to be a minister."

Leith blew out a long breath. This he could handle.

He took a moment trying to form the right words. "If you've prayed about this, and you feel God is calling you in that direction, then you should pursue it."

Jamie remained stiff. "I have to start studying now, and I need to spend some time in Walden since we don't have the books I need here. And then there's the years of apprentice-ship with various ministers around Acktar."

"You've put a lot of thought into this." Leith sat back on his heels. Would he ever be that sure what God's calling was for him now?

"I wrote Jeremiah Alistair. He's planning to be a minister too. Since I'm a little behind, we'll probably end up training together." Jamie rocked and gripped his knees. "But I wasn't sure what you would think. Or Brandi. I'll be gone a lot. I might not even end up at Stetterly when I'm done."

"You'll still be family no matter where you are." Leith

rested a hand on Jamie's shoulder. "And we'll all be very proud of you."

Jamie nodded, but he still didn't relax. "Do you think I'll be able to be a minister? What if they don't let me be a minister because I used to be a Blade?"

Leith raised his eyebrow. "You were the Thirteenth Blade for all of a few hours. Yes, you have the training of a Blade. But you never killed anyone except during the war. I don't think it should be a problem."

Though, what did he know? Until last year, he'd never even stepped foot in a church except to burn it or kill the minister.

"But aren't ministers supposed to be peaceful and all that? And I'm not. Not totally."

That's what this was about. Leith rubbed a hand along the hilt of one of his knives. Always be prepared. It was ingrained into the fiber of their muscles and bones.

But how did that match with a God-fearing and blood-free life? When should someone defend himself and when should he peacefully surrender?

"There's a difference, I think, between being prepared and being a warrior. As a minister, you won't be called to be a warrior, not like you were in the war. But it's wise to be prepared." Leith rested his arms on his knees. "Rovers know ministers tend to be peaceful and unable to fight back, making them easy targets, especially now that they have to travel long distances, often alone, to visit all the towns. Last fall, two ministers were beaten and robbed while on their circuit."

Jamie hugged his knees, and kept staring at the floor.

Leith squeezed Jamie's shoulder. "Maybe someday

Acktar's prairie will be safe for travel, but right now it isn't. It's a good idea for everyone to know how to defend themselves and their families, including ministers."

Jamie lifted his head and finally grinned. "You think so?"

"Yes. Absolutely." Leith dropped his hand from Jamie's shoulder. Hopefully he'd never have to ask Jamie to walk into battle again. Jamie deserved to leave the fighting and bloodshed behind, even if Leith didn't know how to completely let it go himself.

Jamie's muscles relaxed. But only for a moment. He met Leith's gaze. "And what about trouble here? The Blades will be back."

"Yes." Leith released a breath. "I'm surprised they haven't returned already."

That was the heart of his edginess. The Blades should've come looking for Leith. But he hadn't seen any sign of them. Neither had Martyn.

Not knowing where they were was worse than being attacked. They were like rattlesnakes hidden in the grass, unseen, not even rattling. Just curled up, waiting, ready to strike.

23

Martyn gripped Wanderer's reins and forced himself to stroll long-legged and easy toward the campfire set into the hollow below. After catching up with the group of ten men the night before, he'd observed them during the day, spotting several wearing uniforms with King Respen's black, crossed daggers. He hadn't recognized any of them, so none of them should recognize him either, not with most of his knives tucked away.

If he was going to learn what was going on, he needed to get inside wherever these men were going. And to do that, it would be best if he joined these men and became one of them now. It would arouse less suspicion when he got where they were going.

As he approached the campfire, he stepped on sticks and clomped across patches of stone. When he was within earshot and the men around the campfire had stiffened, reaching for weapons, he cupped a hand around his mouth. "You there by the campfire. Permission to enter?"

The men relaxed, dropping their hands from their sword hilts at the standard greeting. One stirred the pot hanging over the fire. "Come on in, stranger. Food's hot."

That unspoken traveler's code. Approach as a friend; be welcomed as a friend.

Martyn plastered on a smile and strode into the campfire light, looping Wanderer's reins over a log next to the men's horses. After he dug out his plate and fork from his saddlebag, he sank onto one of the fallen logs the men had dragged into a circle around the campfire.

The man with the ladle scooped what looked like a thick beef and bean stew onto Martyn's plate. The rest of the men started into their own food once again, though now silent and staring.

Martyn blew on a bite and popped it in his mouth. Not too bad, though Kayleigh would've...

No, don't think about Kayleigh. Concentrate on the mission.

He tucked into the food, letting the silence linger. The questions would come, if he waited. They'd only get suspicious if he did the questioning.

The man with the ladle stopped stirring and dropped onto a seat. "Where are you bound?"

Martyn chewed a bite of beef slowly. He'd have to take a chance. "Kilm. My town ran me out last fall. Didn't like having one of King Respen's soldiers living there. Never mind my family has lived in Keestone for six generations."

Even if these men weren't headed for Kilm—but Martyn

was betting they were—the mention of Kilm and his made-up backstory should convince them he was on their side.

Several of the men nodded, their shoulders relaxing. Good. Exactly the response he'd been looking for.

"Hopefully Lord Norton can deliver on all his promises." One of the men stabbed a bite, muttering a few curse words. "We deserve something after all the fighting and dying we did."

Martyn grunted agreement. He'd been right. They were headed toward Kilm, and Lord Norton was neck-deep in whatever was going on.

"Got nothing but the clothes on my back out of the war." Another man picked at the tattered remains of his uniform.

"Not enough of my uniform left to salvage. I had to steal these." Martyn tugged at the buckskin trousers Kayleigh made him. They were too new and clean to match the wandering vagabond he was claiming to be otherwise.

That got him a few more nods and relaxed muscles. Just like that, he was one of them.

"It wasn't so bad in Hakon. I would've been all right, except for the Rovers attacks." A man across the campfire from Martyn shook his head. "King Respen at least managed to keep the Rovers under control."

Never mind that men like these were the problem, even as they complained about it. Martyn kept his expression as neutral as he could manage.

An older man in his forties snorted. "I won't serve another Eirdon king. I remember all too well how the last one messed up the country. Keevan was a shiftless boy, and he'll make a worse king than his father."

Martyn shoveled in another bite of the stew to hide his

stiffening muscles. Where did his loyalty stand? He'd given his loyalty to King Keevan out of a sense of duty to Leith all those months ago. But in the two times he'd met him, King Keevan's hard-eyed gaze and frank words merited some sort of respect.

These men around this campfire should've been Martyn's people. He should've shared their loyalties, their dissatisfaction with how the war ended.

Was it possible Martyn was more on King Keevan's side —on Leith's side—than he'd realized?

MARTYN TRIED NOT TO CHOKE ON THE HAY DUST IN THE SEMI-darkness in the barn at the edge of Kilm. Shafts of light speared through the cracks in the barn's siding, only visible above the layers of hay piled along the walls. One of the other men coughed, and a horse snorted to clear its nostrils before it went back to munching hay.

There were now twelve of them in this barn and their horses, crowded in a hollowed out section among stacks of bales and drifts of loose hay. Waiting. For what, Martyn would have to find out with the rest of them.

A sneeze built in Martyn's head. He pinched his nose, his nostrils tingling and burning, until the sensation passed.

Some scout he'd turned out to be. Why hadn't he done a more thorough search when he'd scouted Kilm before?

But he'd been so sure Lord Norton would keep the Blades and his scheme close to him. That's what King Respen had always done. And why would Martyn have thought to search a rundown barn—identical to every other rundown barn scattered along the edges of town—filled with innocent-looking hay?

Not that Martyn had stumbled across anything terribly illegal yet.

The barn door, out of sight behind mound of hay, creaked. Martyn straightened and sensed more than saw the other men stiffen as well.

A slim man with a small nose and squinty eyes rounded the hay bales and halted in a shaft of light and dustmotes. General Wentle, the man who had commanded King Respen's army. Even this long after the battle, his uniform remained crisp and clean.

Finally. Something good and suspicious.

Martyn stood with the others but hung back in the shadows. While Martyn knew General Wentle by sight, he hadn't personally worked with him on the battlefield the way most of the other Blades had. Odds were, General Wentle wouldn't recognize Martyn in broad daylight, much less in this partial light.

"Attention, men." General Wentle's high tenor cut through the dust-laden air. "You are here because you fought bravely for King Respen Felix, and now you have heeded Lord Norton's call to rally once again. Extend the same brave loyalty to him as you did King Respen, and he will right the wrongs that were done to you."

The men gave soft cheers, and Martyn joined them. What wrongs did Lord Norton plan to right? The scarcity of food in some towns? The anger simmering between towns that supported the Resistance and those that supported King Respen? More war would only make that worse.

Life was tough. Swaying to the promises of every man claiming he could make it better wouldn't help matters any.

But these men had taken the bait, and now General Wentle had them snared.

"Follow me in single file. No noise." General Wentle spun on his heels and marched out the barn door.

Martyn collected Wanderer and let most of the men fall into line ahead of him before he found a place near the back. Not the very back. That would've been almost as noticeable as the front of the line.

Outside, the setting sun cast uncertain shadows across the prairie. Lights shone in a few of the houses and businesses of Kilm, far enough down the road that no one from the town would be able to see what was happening at this barn clearly. To Martyn's left, two men rode around a small herd of cattle.

General Wentle swung onto a small, dark brown horse and set out north. Martyn mounted Wanderer, sticking to his place in line.

After only a few hundred yards, they reached the Hawkpine Creek. Their horses' footsteps clopped and splashed in the shallow water. In an hour or so, any sign that horses had come through here would be washed away.

At a sound behind him, Martyn turned in his saddle. The herd of cattle lowed as they ambled along the creek's bank and behind the barn, trampling whatever tracks Martyn and the other men might have left.

No wonder Martyn had never seen anything or found tracks. He would've had to be at Kilm the exact moment Lord Norton moved a new group of men, otherwise he'd never spot them. During all that rain and sleet last fall, Lord

Norton had probably moved them before Martyn even arrived.

General Wentle led them deeper into the Sheered Rock Hills, still riding in the Hawkpine Creek. The water grew deeper and faster, but still only came up to Wanderer's belly. Martyn lifted his toes to keep them dry.

After half an hour, they reached a section of a canyon where two rock walls buttressed the creek. General Wentle urged his horse forward. The horse snorted and lunged against the current, though even at its deepest, the water only reached the horse's chest.

Martyn directed Wanderer into the fast-flowing water when it was his turn. Wanderer blew a few deep breaths and forged against the current. Water splashed over the bottoms of Martyn's boots up to his knees.

As soon as they were clear of the rocks, the land opened into a broad valley, the sides bordered by cliffs and jagged mountains with a tall waterfall at the far end. The creek cut through the middle of the valley, and beside it, rows upon rows of tents, lean-tos, and small cabins dotted the valley.

This explained the lack of tracks this spring. The Rovers, King Respen's former soldiers...they were here. And there were a lot of them.

What was their target? And when? He couldn't send King Keevan's army off into the Hills on half-formed intelligence.

And he needed those answers soon. King Keevan and Lord Alistair would both leave for Stetterly within a week to get there in time for Leith and Renna's wedding two weeks from now. If Martyn wanted to report before they left, he'd have only a day or two here for gathering information.

A man dressed in a lieutenant's uniform directed Martyn

and the other men to a far end of the valley. "We don't have any spare tents for you, and you might want to construct a lean-to for tonight. But it won't be long. I've been told we'll be moving out soon."

How soon? And to where?

And maybe just as importantly, why? Gathering a secret army. Reinstating King Respen's army officers to their former positions. All for what?

If General Wentle and the lieutenants had regained their standing, had the Blades as well?

Martyn kept his head down as he unsaddled Wanderer and set about constructing a lean-to. The spring night would be freezing without proper shelter.

As he collected a bundle of pine branches, he glanced at one of the men a few feet away. "How soon do you think we'll move out?"

"Don't know." The man shrugged. "I heard Lord Norton was providing food and work for those who were hurt by the end of the war, and that's enough for me."

"What do you think his plan is?" Martyn grabbed another branch.

"Don't care. Anything Lord Norton does is bound to be better than wandering Acktar."

Martyn gritted his teeth. Did loyalty matter so little? What was Lord Norton going to accomplish? Another war?

For some reason, Martyn didn't want another war. He didn't want a return to a reign like King Respen's. King Keevan was king now, and Martyn would fight to keep it that way.

Starting now.

That night, Martyn rolled out of his lean-to and peered

into the darkness. Soft snores came from one of the nearby lean-tos while the fires simmered in low coals.

He eased to his feet and crept deeper into the massive camp. Somewhere in the center he should find General Wentle's cabin. Surely they had maps or sketches or something to indicate a target.

Deeper into the camp he reached the section of cabins. On one of the cabins, a flag stood silhouetted against the deep blue of the sky. Martyn couldn't see the colors, but if he were to guess, it would either be Lord Norton's emblem of a black mountain lion against dark green or King Respen's banner of dusky blue with black, crossed daggers.

Most likely, that was the command cabin. Martyn slid between the cabins and paused in a shadow.

Something moved.

Martyn froze. A man eased along the wall of the command cabin. He paused beside the door and glanced around. Something about his stance seemed familiar.

When the man turned, the light from one of the fires shone on his face. John Uldiney. He'd been the Seventh Blade. Was he Fifth Blade now?

If one Blade was here, they all were. Martyn wouldn't be able to sneak in tonight, especially since he didn't know where the other four Blades were.

Once Uldiney strolled around the corner of the command cabin, Martyn eased deeper into the shadows. He'd have to come up with some other way to find out what was going on. And soon. Acktar's future might depend on it.

Martyn halted in oiling his saddle as a commotion broke out at the far end of the valley near the creek entrance. A few of the other men around him also paused in their work. Would this be the opportunity for information that Martyn had been waiting for?

"Attention! Gather at the streambank!"

Martyn joined the other men from his area of camp as they strolled through the encampment. Near the creek, the cabins and lean-tos stopped, leaving a broad space.

Lord Norton rode past the ranks of men, his angular face tight. Though not a large man, his body exuded the confidence of someone comfortable with his own skills.

Martyn crossed his arms and leaned against the cabin behind him. This was about to get interesting.

The five Blades trailed Lord Norton, though they were dressed in brown rather than black. Martyn had to force himself not to duck out of sight. They wouldn't be able to pick out his face among the scores of men before them.

Lord Norton halted his horse, one hand resting on his thigh. His gaze swept over them, as if assessing their strengths and weaknesses with that one glance. "Gather your supplies, hone your weapons, and prepare to march at dawn. The time has come to overthrow this impostor calling himself king. We will take back our country and return it to the peace and prosperity we enjoyed under King Respen."

The men around Martyn cheered and stabbed their fists in the air. Some of them shouted insults about King Keevan. The noise echoed off the valley walls, turning the cheers into a roar.

Martyn jabbed his fist into the air to fit in, but a knot formed in his stomach. What was Lord Norton's plan? He had barely five hundred men, a far cry from the thousands both sides had gathered during the war.

What could he do with five hundred men? That wasn't nearly enough to take Nalgar Castle. Was he planning on gathering reinforcements from the other lords that once supported King Respen? Something like that would take time, and was bound to be noticed. Yet, everything Lord Norton had done so far hinted at secrecy. Was it possible that he had something else planned instead of a full-scale war?

If he wasn't going to attack Nalgar Castle, and he wasn't going to start another war, how did he plan to overthrow King Keevan?

Martyn stilled. King Keevan would leave for Leith and Renna's wedding soon. He and his men would be vulnerable out on the prairie. Would Lord Norton attack then? Or would he wait for King Keevan to leave and take Nalgar Castle while it was undermanned?

As Lord Norton forged his way through the men toward the command cabin, Martyn kept groups of men between him and the Blades. Surely Lord Norton would discuss some last-minute planning with General Wentle and the Blades.

Martyn followed them at a distance through the jostling bustle that had once been the camp. It seemed everyone now had somewhere to be and something to do right that minute and couldn't be bothered to get out of anyone's way while they were at it.

Lord Norton entered the command cabin, followed by General Wentle. Four of the Blades joined them, but the fifth —Former Fourth Blade Tooley—remained on the front porch. Martyn eyed him as he circled around the cabin in the crowd. Tooley seemed to be content to remain on the porch, glaring at anyone who stepped too close.

Martyn wound his way closer to the cabin. There, at the rear of the cabin, a stack of firewood piled beneath a window. Someone didn't want to walk all the way around the cabin to retrieve more firewood.

Martyn strolled up to the wood pile and knelt. He peeked through the window. A bed stood against the wall, pegs holding clothes beside it. Across from him, a partially open door led into the main room where a few figures hunched around a table.

After a glance around to make sure no one was paying attention to him, Martyn drew a knife and worked it between the window panes. After a few minutes, he lifted the latch and pulled the panes open a crack.

The voices were muffled, speaking in low tones that didn't carry. Martyn sheathed his knife and picked up a log from the stack of firewood. The best way to fit in was to look busy, even if that meant moving the stack of firewood over a few feet one log at a time.

"...avoid Sierra...ruin surprise...scout..."

Martyn gently picked up two logs and set them down on his new stack a few feet down the wall from the original stack.

"...Mountainwood...supplies...eight days march..."

Eight days march? Martyn stacked two more logs. What was eight days march from here? Pretty much anything. But also brought them past Mountainwood? That wasn't anywhere near Nalgar Castle or King Keevan's route to Stetterly.

"...wedding...Stetterly..."

Martyn froze, logs poised above his new stack. Wedding. Stetterly. Eight days march.

Lord Norton wasn't planning on attacking King Keevan directly. He planned to take the town of Stetterly first.

King Keevan's guards would be alert while the king and his family traveled. For most of the trip, they wouldn't be farther than a day from a Resistance town. If trouble happened, there was a good possibility King Keevan, his wife, and their child could ride to safety.

But Stetterly was three days from the nearest Resistance town. The guards would be relaxed, thinking they'd reached the end of the dangerous journey. Instead they would ride into a war. Leith, Renna, Brandi...they would fight. But they would die.

Martyn had to warn them. He stood and turned, joining the bustle of people in front of the command cabin. First, he'd get Wanderer. Then, he'd figure out a way to sneak out.

"Martyn!"

He froze. Why was someone calling his name? He didn't recognize the voice. He cast about but didn't see who was yelling.

"Martyn!" The shout grew louder.

People turned in Martyn's general direction, searching for the source of the shout. What was going on? He spun on his heels. If this yelling stranger got Martyn caught...

A hand grabbed his arm. "Martyn!"

Martyn whirled, reaching for his knife. A boy of about seventeen faced him, wavy blond hair cascading into his deep brown eyes. That was it? Just a random kid? "What?"

The better question would be how the boy knew

Martyn's name, but Martyn would get to that in a moment. If he could bite back the curses piling in his throat.

The boy crossed his arms. "I know you're all high and mighty now, but you could at least acknowledge your own brother."

24

Impossible. His brother was dead.

Martyn jerked out of the boy's grasp. He had to get out of here before the Blades investigated the shouting.

But...how did the boy know Martyn had once had a brother? Turning, Martyn studied the boy. He did have the Hamish blond hair and dark brown eyes. His chin wasn't as square as Martyn's, a softening of the features their mother had always claimed as her contribution in a pair of boys that so resembled their father.

Martyn gripped the boy's shoulders. He didn't dare believe it. Not without proof. "What was my brother's name?"

The boy sighed and shrugged out of Martyn's grip. "Seriously? You're going to pretend you don't recognize me? Give it a rest. Surely after eight years you aren't still going to be mad."

Eight years. That was the right time frame. But this couldn't...Martyn clenched his fists so tightly his arms shook. He didn't have time for this. He needed proof, and he needed to get out of here. "Your name."

"Owen Hamish. Same one I've always had." The boy crossed his arms. "Now that I've tracked you down, I won't let you ignore me like you have all these years."

Ignore him? But Owen was dead. Wasn't he?

Martyn shook his head and dragged his hands through his hair. This couldn't...he couldn't be. But how had this boy known his brother's name? As far as Martyn knew, none of the other Blades or Lord Norton or any of his enemies knew. None of them knew he was even here. Why would any of them go to all the trouble of faking this?

Besides, what proof did Martyn have that his brother had died? All he had was King Respen's word. No bodies. No graves.

How trustworthy did Martyn believe Respen to be anymore? He'd once trusted Respen's words wholeheartedly, but now, what was the truth?

If King Keevan—one of Leith's kills—could be alive, wasn't it possible that Martyn's brother, maybe even his whole family, could also be alive?

Martyn squeezed his eyes shut, reopened them, and blinked. The boy was still standing there, still looking so much like an older version of the nine-year-old brother Martyn had lost. He swallowed. "Owen?"

"Yes, it's me." Owen huffed and shook his head. "Why do you look so shocked? The war is over. It would be idiotic to keep avoiding me."

Avoid him? What was Owen talking about? Martyn opened his mouth, but movement caught his gaze.

The former Blade Quinten Daas stepped to the side of

the cabin, probably lured by all of Owen's shouting. As Martyn raised his head, their gazes locked. Daas' face hardened, and he gripped his knife.

Too many yards and people separated them. Martyn wouldn't be able to get out a knife and silence Daas before he raised the alarm.

Martyn grabbed Owen's arm. "We have to go. Now."

Daas whirled and dashed for the cabin door. Probably to gather the other four Blades. Martyn didn't have time to worry about that. He had to get himself and his brother out of this camp and out of this valley before the Blades caught them.

And, as soon as General Wentle heard Daas had spotted a spy in their midst, he would send the entire army of five hundred men after them.

"What are you doing? Let go." Owen dug in his heels.

"I don't have time to explain. We have to get out of here." Martyn yanked on his brother's arm. He didn't dare leave Owen behind. Daas had seen them together. He'd know Owen was somehow connected to Martyn, and he wouldn't be afraid to torture him to find out how. Daas had, after all, been the one to gleefully press red-hot pokers to Leith's skin in the Tower.

Owen must've sensed his urgency because he finally stopped resisting and matched Martyn's pace. Martyn increased his speed to a jog. Would it be better to sprint and hope for speed to save them? Or would they be better off trying to blend in? Somehow, they had to get to their horses, get out of here, and warn King Keevan.

Martyn glanced over his shoulder. The five Blades dashed into view. Daas pointed, and they broke into a run.

Martyn bit back a string of curses. So much for stealth. "Follow me."

He sprinted through a narrow gap between two cabins, Owen at his heels. With a quick right turn, Martyn led them into the bustling crowd of men loading the supply wagons.

After dodging through the chaos, Martyn slowed down on the other side once a row of lean-tos hid them from sight.

Owen leaned his hands on his knees, gasping for breath. "What was that all about?"

"The Blades are hunting me." That was about as simple as he could make it. Any more explanation would take too much time. "Where's your horse? We'll fetch it, then get mine. Please tell me you already started packing."

"Mostly. My horse is that way." Owen pointed, then fell into step as Martyn set out in that direction. His jaw was set, and his hand rested on his sword's hilt, as if Martyn's word that they had to leave was good enough for him.

Martyn darted glances at the men around them and kept their pace to a fast walk. No sign of the Blades. Yet.

Owen led him to a light brown horse standing next to a large lean-to constructed of logs and an interwoven mat of pine branches for a roof. Logs were piled along the front, turning the structure into a small cabin more than a lean-to.

After helping Owen saddle his horse and stuff the last of his possessions into his saddlebags, Martyn led the way to the outskirts of the camp where Wanderer cropped grass next to the makeshift shelter Martyn had constructed a day and a half ago.

Still no sign of the Blades. Had they managed to lose them? Martyn didn't dare hope.

It only took a moment to strap his things onto his saddle.

He grasped Wanderer's reins and studied the sides of the valley around them. They couldn't leave by the creek entrance. General Wentle would have it guarded.

The upstream end of Hawkpine Creek cascaded over a cliff and down into the valley in a roaring waterfall. No way to escape the valley in that direction.

The southern rim of mountains sloped in tree-covered ridges rather than the sharp cliffs to the north. It would be rough going, but it should be possible.

Should they leave now or try to hide until dark? Their chances of being spotted in the daylight were higher, but no one else would be moving at night, also making them noticeable. Leith would've known which was best. He'd outguess the Blades.

Martyn could only go with his instinct, and his instincts told him that darkness was always best.

Either way, they couldn't stay here. General Wentle would order the camp searched. Martyn would have to find a place to hide until darkness could conceal their movements as they crossed the creek and made their way up and over the mountain.

"We'll head in that direction." Martyn pointed toward the far end of the valley where dense stands of pine, birch, and willow crowded along the creek's banks so densely it was no longer visible. From here, they only had a short distance to cross until they reached cover. "Follow behind me exactly."

Owen nodded and gripped his horse's reins.

They set out in silence and crossed into the trees along the Hawkpine Creek. Martyn checked behind them, but he didn't see anyone following them.

A decent scout would be able to follow their trail. Did any of those Blades know how to track? With his own skills, Martyn had never relied on any of the other Blades for tracking. Leith would've known. He'd trained more of the younger Blades than Martyn had.

After nearly half an hour of trudging through the underbrush, the camp disappeared from view behind several bends in the creek. Martyn found a secluded section of willows and birches, surrounded by a stand of pines beyond that. It was the best he could do until nightfall. "We'll stop here until dark."

Owen loosened his horse's girth, sank onto a fallen log, and eyed Martyn. "Well, are you going to explain what's going on?"

Martyn shook his head and perched on a log a few feet away. Owen was the one who needed to do the explaining. "Are Mother and Father still alive too?"

Owen crossed his arms, his jaw jutting forward. "Mama and Papa. That's what you called them growing up. At least give them the courtesy of that."

Martyn swallowed, fisting his fingers. Mama and Papa. When had he stopped calling them that? Leith had called his parents *mother* and *father*, as if to distance himself, and Martyn picked up the habit. Mother and Father had abandoned him. Mother and Father had died. As if the Mama and Papa of his childhood no longer existed.

"Mama and Papa. Are they alive?" Martyn held his breath. Why was his heart beating, as if...as if in hope? Foolish, foolish hope.

Owen shook his head. "No. Papa died a few years ago, and Mama died last year."

A year. Martyn closed his eyes, aching deep in his chest. If he'd known, he could've seen her one last time. He could've asked her why they'd never returned, why they'd chosen to abandon him in the first place.

Mama. Martyn leaned his elbows on his knees, trying to breathe. What he wouldn't give to have one more minute with her. One moment to feel her hug, her touch in his hair.

"Wait, too? What do you mean, alive too?"

"Until today, I thought you were dead." Martyn swept his gaze over Owen. His *brother*. Alive and sitting across from him.

Owen cocked his head. "Who told you that? How did you think I died?"

Might as well start at the beginning. "You remember the night Mama and Papa abandoned me at the church in Blathe?"

"Yes. I woke in a wagon that morning, not knowing how I got there. Papa must've carried me out while I slept." Owen toyed with a stick as if unable to look at Martyn. "I was devastated when I couldn't find you. Papa explained you were being looked after and we'd be back for you when we could."

Martyn looked away. He'd always harbored such anger toward Owen for being the one their parents chose that he'd never considered what it was like for Owen to wake up without his brother. "That morning, the minister turned me out onto the streets. I spent nearly a year alone before Lord Respen Felix took me in. He told me he'd tried to track down my parents, but all of you froze to death in a blizzard during the winter."

"We came close, but, no, we didn't freeze. Or starve."

Owen cracked the stick. The snap resounded in the air between them. "It took Papa a year, but he got a job in Surgis working for Lord Conree. He paid off his debts and built a house. We returned to Blathe to find you, but the minister told us you'd died of a fever."

They'd come back for him. Martyn rested his head in his hands. All these years of hating his parents, and they'd come back for him.

Being abandoned had hurt. But Martyn had understood it, somewhat. It was the only way to survive. But as the days had stretched into weeks and months, he'd tried to cling to the hope they'd return. When they didn't, that hope had shriveled into something hard and dead.

He'd been loyal to Respen because he'd taken Martyn in when his parents had abandoned him. But that wasn't the truth. Not the whole truth, anyway. They hadn't abandoned him forever. They'd come back and would've brought him home.

Home. With his family. Mama. Papa. Owen.

Years of bloodshed and loyalty for Respen. It had been built on lies. Nothing Respen had told him was true. Leith had been right all along to turn his back on the Blades the first chance he got.

Martyn cleared his throat. "Respen was already training me to be a Blade by then. He had plans, and he couldn't let me return to you. He must've heard Papa and Mama were asking questions and ordered the minister to lie. He then told me you had died so I'd never go looking."

Why hadn't Respen just killed Martyn's parents? It would've been simpler. But if they'd come to Blathe under

Lord Conree's protection, Respen wouldn't have risked losing Lord Conree's support for his planned rebellion.

"It nearly killed Papa and Mama, you know." Owen's eyes glinted. "Something broke in them that day. We returned to Surgis, and Papa continued to work for Lord Conree, but his heart wasn't in it anymore. He expected me to work harder and act better than ever before. When he died shortly after Respen took over, Lord Conree was kind enough to take me into his service, young as I was. He was generous, and Mama and I were able to get by."

If he'd been there, Martyn could've protected them. He fisted both hands into his hair. What would it have been like to grow up as a family?

Respen had stolen that from him.

"I've known you were alive for years." Owen rested his elbows on his knees. "But I made sure Mama never found out."

"Why?" Martyn stared. Something stabbed deep in his chest.

"I'm sorry, but I decided it was best she didn't know. You were a Blade, and I thought you knew we were alive and were purposefully avoiding us." Owen scuffed his boot into the dirt. "Mama was already fragile after losing Papa. She'd built this picture of who you would've been had you lived. So strong and brave. A hard worker. A godly man. It would've broken her to learn you'd turned into a Blade ignoring his family."

Martyn gripped his right shoulder, the one covered with his marks. The blood on his hands had kept him from his family. "I'm sorry. I would've been there in a moment if I'd known. But Respen never sent me to Surgis. I truly thought you were all long dead."

"I realize that now." Owen scrubbed his thumb along his palm. "I resented you, you know. Papa and Mama were always telling me how great you would've been if you'd lived. I could never measure up to the image they built of you. Then I learned you were a Blade, and that only made it worse."

"I resented you too. You were the one Mama and Papa chose to keep, but they abandoned me." Martyn ran his fingers through his hair. "All they would've had to do was ask. I would've volunteered to stay behind. I would've..."

He wouldn't have given up hope. He would've run away from the Blades to get back to his family.

"I don't think they could." Owen shook his head. "What parents could look their child in the eye and admit they'd failed so badly they could no longer care for him?"

Instead, they'd slunk off into the night.

Martyn exhaled slowly. "I'm sorry. I'm sure a Blade is the last person you want for a brother."

Owen scrubbed the back of his neck. "Like I said, I've known for years. It's not a shock. And I fought in Respen's army. Lord Conree didn't agree with Respen on everything—he protected the Christians in Surgis, after all—but he fought on Respen's side, so I fought for him."

"You aren't going to hear any judgment from me." Something almost like a smile ached at the corners of Martyn's mouth.

"So why are the Blades hunting you? Aren't you one of them?"

"Not anymore." The words warmed Martyn's chest. He wasn't a Blade anymore. This side—King Keevan's side, Leith's side—was the side he should've been on all along. "In the Battle for Nalgar Castle, I turned on Respen to save Leith Torren, a fellow Blade who became a friend and brother. He'd betrayed Respen to the Resistance. I'm now scouting for King Keevan."

"I see." Owen's eyes narrowed as he nodded. "You were looking for the Blades in case they returned."

"Yes." Martyn checked the forest around them once again. He'd checked every several minutes this entire time, but he had yet to see or hear anything. "What are you doing here?"

"I didn't have anywhere to go last fall." Owen shrugged.

But there was something in his shrug, his words, that didn't add up. From what Owen had told him, he wasn't the type to turn into a Rover. So what was he doing here, really?

Martyn couldn't help a smile this time. "You were looking for me, weren't you?"

That's why Owen had been loitering near the command cabin, near the Blades, and why he'd recognized Martyn right away. He'd been scrutinizing every face that passed.

"Fine. Yes, I was searching for you. I assumed you had been banished with the other Blades. With Respen dead, I hoped...well, I hoped I could annoy you back to the straight and narrow if I had to. You're all I have left, even if you were a Blade." Owen's dark brown eyes, so like his own, focused on him. "You were abandoned once. I decided I wasn't going to abandon you again. It's time you came home."

Home. Did Martyn even know what that word meant anymore? "And where would that be?"

"Surgis, probably. The Resistance towns don't want one

of Respen's soldiers or a Blade there, and many of the towns that supported Respen are still antagonistic to Christians."

Martyn's stomach sank. "You're still a Christian? After everything that happened?"

"Yes. Of course." Owen cocked his head. "You aren't?"

How could he explain to Owen the years he'd spent under Respen, the way he'd lost all faith and replaced it with logic? And the fact that he still didn't think faith was real?

"No. I was a Blade, remember?" Martyn turned on his log. "We'd better get some sleep before nightfall. I'll take first watch."

Martyn didn't look to see if Owen followed his order. He needed time to think.

MARTYN WOKE TO THE CRISP NIGHT CARESSING HIS FACE. THE pine trees created a dense darkness. Owen's shape and that of the horses were barely discernible.

After getting to his feet, Martyn nudged Owen's shoulder. Owen jumped and whirled, but Martyn clapped a hand to his mouth. "It's only me. Time to get moving."

All they had to do was tighten girth straps, then they set out into the night, leading their horses. A chorus of frogs chirruped along the creek bank and in the trees surrounding them, masking any slight noises the horses made. The air was dead still, not even a whisper in the branches overhead.

At the edge of the creek, Martyn halted Wanderer and raised a hand to stop Owen. The moon had yet to rise, and the creek lay black before them, gurgling and rippling.

Martyn scanned the banks on both sides. Nothing moved. Not the grass. Not the trees. Not even the night breeze.

He stepped into the creek, feeling with his feet for holes or rocks that would cause the horses to stumble. Wanderer resisted for a moment before following him in. The horse's ears remained pricked, his nose flaring to pick up any lingering smells. Martyn gazed around them, never focusing in one spot for too long.

They reached the bank on the far side. Wanderer's hoof scuffed against a stone as he scrambled upward into the treeline.

Behind him, Owen let out an audible breath, but Martyn didn't relax. The trees crowded around them in blurred, black shapes.

They couldn't ride. Not in this darkness and this terrain. Once the moon rose, they would be able to move faster. They just had to get up and out of this valley before that happened.

Upward, ever upward. Martyn tried to peer through the branches, but he couldn't see enough of the sky to figure out the direction they traveled. It probably didn't matter. As long as they kept heading up the mountain, then down the other side, they wouldn't get lost. He could always halt them in a place to hide for the rest of the night if he didn't think he could safely navigate once they were free of this valley.

The forest opened in front of them next to a black mass that rose toward the sky. Martyn paused at the base of the cliff. It extended as far as he could see in either direction. Which way would lead to safety?

To the left, most likely. The ground seemed to continue to rise in that direction.

He turned left, and they trudged along the cliff. Martyn's calves burned. Behind him, Owen's ragged breathing rang through the forest.

Was it just him, or was the cliff face getting shorter? And was that a gap in the trees ahead with sky beyond? The way out, clear and open in front of them.

Wanderer snorted and shied. Martyn reached for his knife, but even as his hand closed around the hilt, a torch flared in the forest to his left.

More flames burst to life beside, behind, and in front of them. One torch moved, and a black shape sauntered between them and the valley's exit. "Really, First Blade, I expected more out of you. Did you think we wouldn't know all the routes out of this valley, and we wouldn't guess you'd try to take this way? It is the most logical escape route."

Martyn gritted his teeth at Quinten Daas' mocking tone. Even worse, he was right. Martyn should've guessed Daas and the other Blades would know every inch of the valley after spending the winter there. He should've known they would head him off rather than blindly chase him.

Leith would've known. But Martyn hadn't.

He glanced around at the five torches. None of these Blades could throw knives. If he and Owen moved quickly enough, could they mount their horses and gallop free before the Blades pounced?

He might be able to do it, but how fast was Owen? He had army training, but could he react fast enough once Martyn gave the signal?

Even if he did, chances were they'd ride off a cliff in this darkness.

"Drop your knife. Maybe you think you're good enough

to take us on, but does your friend here have the skills to fight off several Blades?"

Tension curled through Martyn's stomach and down into his toes. He glanced over his shoulder. The whites of Owen's eyes glinted in the faint starlight.

If it had been Leith at his back, Martyn would've taken these five Blades on, no question. But Owen? He wasn't trained to fight Blades. Especially not in the dark.

His chest ached. They couldn't win. He'd failed to warn Leith. He'd failed to keep Owen safe.

He released his grip on his knife. Nothing he could do but surrender.

25

Martyn's knees crashed into the plank floor of the command cabin. Daas' hand gripped the back of his neck.

General Wentle's polished black boots stopped a few feet away. "Good. You caught him."

"Wasn't that hard." Daas' fingers dug into the back of Martyn's neck.

Martyn gritted his teeth. If his hands weren't tied behind his back and former Blade Crossley didn't have a knife to Owen's throat, Martyn would show Daas just how hard capturing a former First Blade could be.

"It took you long enough to earn your keep." General Wentle snorted.

"The Blades did well. As I knew they would." A pair of boots strode into the room and halted next to General Wentle. Martyn craned his neck against the pressure of Daas' hand to glare at Lord Norton's slim face. The man's light blond hair fell in a straight, short cut above his piercing brown eyes. "Second Blade Crossley, please fetch Captain Loust."

"Yes, sir." The thud of a fist thumping into a chest accompanied Crossley's voice.

Martyn grimaced. He'd guessed right. Lord Norton was truly trying to return to Respen's reign. Giving the Blades ranks again. Using the Blade salute. It was as if nothing had even changed with Respen's death.

But it had. Everything had. Acktar was better off—would be better off—with Keevan as its king. The terror that the Blades had once been couldn't be allowed to return.

What could Martyn do? He'd led Owen right into a trap, and the two of them were no match for five Blades, as well as General Wentle, Lord Norton, and all the guards and men they could call up in a moment's notice.

"Sir, we also found this in Hamish's saddlebag." Uldiney stepped forward and held out a leather bound book.

Martyn groaned, barely biting a curse. The Bible Leith had given him. Of all things to get in trouble for. He hadn't even managed to read the whole wretched thing. He'd avoided having to admit to Kayleigh that he'd lost their deal. Not that it really mattered. Having to clean out the horse shed was a far cry better than where he was now.

Lord Norton took the book, examined it, then stared down his nose at Martyn. "I see you've been taken in by this foolishness."

Somehow, Martyn didn't want to admit that he hadn't, as if a shared lack of belief would make them similar.

Footsteps stomped on the porch and lumbered to a halt a few feet behind Martyn. "You wanted to see me?"

This time, Martyn gave vent to the torrent of curses. Of

course it would be that good-for-nothing slug of a Rover leader Martyn had chased out of Kayleigh's cabin last fall. The man couldn't have just gone off and died in some hole as worms like him should.

Lord Norton smirked and waved a hand in Martyn's direction. "Is this one of the Blades you had trouble with last fall?"

Captain Loust trudged into Martyn's peripheral vision. "Yep, that's the one I ran into near Flayin Falls."

"You may go, captain." Lord Norton crossed his arms and met Martyn's gaze. "It is as I guessed. You were the troublesome Blade in the Hills while Leith Torren is in Stetterly. I knew Lady Faythe, wilting flower that she is, wouldn't let her man stray too far from her grasp."

Martyn scowled. Lord Norton didn't know Renna. She'd thrown herself between Leith and Respen and challenged Respen to kill her. She'd brought about Respen's downfall. Wilting flower? Not a chance.

Heat flared down Martyn's arms and into his chest. Enough listening to Lord Norton's taunts and questions. "What do you think you'll accomplish? Respen's dead. The war's over."

"Is it?" Lord Norton stiffened. "How long will it be before Keevan quietly has me and the other lords who supported King Respen assassinated? I suspected he'd try something. He was too gracious at the end of the war. Then I learned he had you and Torren, two of Respen's best assassins, on his side. It would only be a matter of time before he used you. What am I supposed to do? Stand by and wait until my wife and children are killed in front of me?"

Martyn could try to defend himself. But Lord Norton

wouldn't believe him when the evidence pointed otherwise. Respen had lured his enemies into a false sense of security, then sent his Blades after them. Why would Lord Norton expect King Keevan to be any different? Of course he'd take measures to prevent Keevan assassinating him and his fellow lords. It was no more than what Lord Alistair and the Resistance had done.

How well did Martyn really know King Keevan? Would the king take revenge once the country had settled down into peace? Would he try to use Martyn and Leith as assassins once again?

No, Leith wouldn't stand for it, even if King Keevan tried. And, either way, it didn't matter. Martyn had to stop Lord Norton from killing Leith. Somehow.

"Thank you for saving me the trouble of tracking you down." Lord Norton waved at the Blades. "Take Hamish and his friend to the guardhouse and see that they are well tied and guarded."

Several pairs of hands grabbed Martyn and dragged him to his feet. Daas and former Blade Offen marched him out the cabin. Ahead, Crossley and Tooley gripped Owen.

They approached a squat cabin with iron bars across the window. Two beams and three latches locked the heavy door.

Uldiney was there already, gesturing as he gave the two guards standing at the door orders. After a few minutes, the guards unlocked the door and dragged three men outside, probably men who'd been caught stealing or otherwise causing trouble in the camp.

Daas and Offen hustled Martyn inside. Something smashed into the back of Martyn's knees, and his legs buckled. His knees struck the stone floor. Another kick crashed into Martyn's back, and he landed heavily on his shoulder. Pain stabbed down Martyn's arm. That would form a nice bruise before the night was over.

Daas knelt and dug a knee into the small of Martyn's back. He tied Martyn's ankles, then ran a length of rope between Martyn's bound hands and feet, tightening it until Martyn couldn't straighten his legs.

Martyn gritted his teeth and forced himself to remain still. Lashing out and kicking Daas' face was a rather appealing thought, but the Blades would retaliate against both Martyn and Owen.

Daas stood and swung a kick into Martyn's stomach. Martyn gasped and doubled over as much as the rope binding his hands and feet would allow.

After another kick, Daas whirled and followed the other Blades from the jail. The bars, bolts, and other locks shoved into place.

Once it was quiet, Martyn twisted and managed to roll over. The interior of the cabin remained black except for the faint glow around the one, barred window next to the door. "Owen? Are you all right?"

A shuffling sound came from the darkness a few feet away. "I'm fine, except that my fingers are already numb."

Martyn wiggled and rolled until his feet connected with something solid, yet giving.

Owen grunted. "That's my stomach you're kicking."

"Sorry." Martyn used his shoulders and feet to inch down until he faced Owen. Even this close, all he could make out was his brother's vague form. "And I'm sorry I got you into this mess."

Not that it was entirely his fault. If Owen hadn't bellowed his name loud enough to draw Daas' attention, they both would've been better off. Nothing either of them could do about that now.

"You can stop apologizing and start getting us out of this mess." Owen wiggled, his bootheels scraping against the stone floor. "You're a Blade. Pull out a knife or something and cut us loose."

Martyn heaved a sigh. If only it were that simple. If he'd been facing another opponent, maybe. But these were his fellow Blades. They knew all his tricks. "They took my knives when they searched me."

"Maybe we can untie each other?"

"We can try." Martyn rolled over so that his back faced Owen. He scooted closer as he heard Owen roll over and shuffle around. Martyn's fingers brushed Owen's hand, then the rough rope binding him.

With his own hands bound, Martyn struggled to move his fingers enough to explore the knot and find where to loosen it. He couldn't picture the rope and how it had been knotted. It just felt like a jumble to him.

He tugged. Rope slivers clawed under his fingernails. Even if he could find the knot, he couldn't get a good enough grip to pry it apart. "This isn't going to work."

"Let me try." Owen's fingers patted across Martyn's hand until reaching the rope. Martyn held still, hardly daring to breath, as the rope around his wrists was tugged and pulled and yanked.

Owen growled out a breath and slumped. "It isn't budging."

It had been a false hope all along. The Blades knew better than to leave captives with faulty knots.

Martyn rested his head against the stone. He wasn't going to escape. He just had to accept that.

Leith would die, never knowing that Martyn had even tried to save him this time. Owen, the brother he'd finally regained, would join them in death for no other reason than that he'd been seen with Martyn. And Kayleigh. She'd go on thinking the stranger called Owen Hill had been a heartless Blade who'd done nothing but use her generosity for the winter.

Martyn might as well have abandoned them in a blizzard for all the good he'd managed to do. It would've been better if he'd died during the Battle for Nalgar Castle. At least then Owen and Kayleigh wouldn't have been hurt.

"We'll have to wait until morning and hope we have a chance to escape once they take us out of here." Martyn sagged onto the floor.

Did Owen believe it? Martyn couldn't convince himself. The Blades wouldn't let Martyn out of their sight.

He was well and truly trapped.

Owen heaved a sigh, and his clothes scraped against the stone as he rolled. He drew in a deep breath and held it like he was preparing to ask a question.

Martyn braced himself. What question would he ask? Something about Martyn's past? His life as a Blade? How many men he'd killed?

"Why aren't you a Christian anymore?"

Martyn rolled. In the darkness, all he could make out was Owen's black shape. "Of all the questions you could've asked, that's the one you went with?"

"It's the most important one." Owen moved, in a shrug perhaps. "I know you were a Blade, and I already told you what happened to me. There's nothing else to tell."

Martyn itched to drag his fingers through his hair. That pretty much summed it up, but he'd rather confess what he'd done as a Blade than discuss this topic. "Look, I told you what that minister in Blathe did. Then I became a Blade. Do you really need more of an explanation than that?"

"Yes. Because I don't believe faith can die that easily."

Martyn gritted his teeth, fighting the heat pulsing in his chest. Then again, why fight it? Why hold back? "I never bought into it. Not even when we were kids. Is that the answer you want?"

"No, and I don't believe it either. I can't believe the brother who told me Bible stories and made me say my prayers before bed even when Mama and Papa forgot doesn't exist. That part of you is still there. I have to believe it."

Blind, illogical faith. Martyn clenched his fists against the ropes binding his wrists. "The brother you remember never existed. Even then, I thought Mama and Papa were foolish for dragging us to church on the occasions when they did. I decided it couldn't be real because Mama and Papa never took a stand for anything, not even their own beliefs."

Martyn bit his tongue. He'd already said too much. How could he possibly explain the emptiness he'd felt as a child watching Papa waffle between opinions and drift in and out of churches and towns as if truth was as solid as prairie dust on the breeze? He'd struggled to understand how the Bible could say one thing when the people in church lived either like self-righteous prats or waffling fools who didn't know what they believed. The only thing that made sense was that it wasn't real.

"Mama and Papa changed after they thought you died. Yes, it broke them. But it also made them more firm in their faith than before."

Martyn couldn't suppress a snort. Clinging to a useless faith even more tightly after a tragedy. How typical.

"After I learned you were still alive in the Blades, I asked around. That minister you were left with? He'd only been there about a year after the previous minister was kicked out under mysterious circumstances. Respen put his own lackey in place instead."

Guess that figured. It would explain why he was so ready to lie. But it didn't change anything. Not really. "He was hardly the only hypocrite I've met."

"I don't doubt that. But surely you've met some Christians you feel are actually living their faith?"

Renna. Brandi. Kayleigh. Even Leith, there at the end when Martyn had pressed his dagger to his throat and all Leith had said was I don't blame you. Even Shadrach Alistair, for all his insufferable perfectness. "A few."

"And it will always be a few. Personally, I think Christians are the worst bunch of people imaginable. We know the truth, but often we don't follow it. The thing is, Christians have more opportunities to sin because we know better and still sin anyway." Owen's voice dropped. "That's what makes salvation so amazing. God loves His people, awful as they are, and sent His Son to die for them."

"I know. I have read the Bible." Well, most of it. Martyn yanked against the ropes binding his hands. If he yelled loud enough, could he convince Daas to lock him up somewhere away from Owen?

"You just don't trust that it's real."

"No."

Owen snorted. "Do you trust anybody?"

Martyn opened his mouth. Did he trust anybody? He'd trusted Leith, until Leith betrayed him.

But how much had Martyn ever trusted Leith? If their roles had been reversed and Martyn had been the one to have doubts about the Blades, would Leith have listened?

He probably would've. He was annoying that way.

Martyn snapped his mouth shut. He couldn't bring himself to say the word *no*. How could he ever trust anyone when everyone always failed, betrayed, or abandoned him?

"Of course you don't trust anybody. You can't. Not when you don't trust God, the only One who will never break that trust."

Martyn sighed. Of course, it would get back to that. Did his brother have to be this irritating?

Owen's voice rose and hardened. "You know what I think? You're just as guilty of hypocrisy as everyone you're accusing. You're self-righteous about your lack of faith, and you're plenty quick to condemn others. Now I'm going to get some sleep. I'm done talking."

Owen rolled over and wiggled, putting more distance between them.

Martyn stared at his brother's back. Was he being the hypocritical one? Was he doing exactly what he always accused others of doing?

26

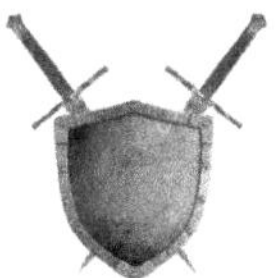

A branch slapped Martyn's face. Squinting into the rising sun, he tried to duck the next one, but the ropes tying him to his saddle and binding his hands behind his back restricted his movements.

His tongue stuck to the roof of his mouth. The Blades hadn't given him or Owen much in the way of water and nothing for food since their capture two nights ago.

He craned his neck to peer over his shoulder. Owen swayed and his head lolled in time with his horse's stride.

This was too much for him. He didn't have the kind of training and discipline Martyn had.

The command to halt worked its way down the column of men. Daas drew his horse to a stop, and Wanderer, attached by a lead to Daas' saddle, paused too.

Lord Norton cantered his horse along the line and skidded to a halt. "Offen, Daas, Crossley, and Tooley, you'll come with me. Uldiney, you'll remain with the men and report to General Wentle until I return. And, Daas, gag our prisoners."

Martyn didn't resist as Daas shoved a rag into his mouth, then tied another rag over his mouth. Martyn coughed. The fabric clung to his already dry tongue.

What was Lord Norton doing? Martyn's stomach twisted. They weren't far from Flayin Falls or Kayleigh's cabin. Surely Lord Norton wouldn't target Kayleigh, would he?

Five soldiers dropped out of line and joined them, including that Rover Captain Loust. Martyn yanked on the ropes holding him to the saddle. At a signal from General Wentle, the army began moving again. It would probably circle around Flayin Falls before striking south for Stetterly.

Martyn could do nothing but uselessly twist and jerk against the ropes binding him tightly to the saddle. He chewed on the gag, but the wad of fabric in his mouth prevented him from digging his teeth into the fabric without choking himself.

As Lord Norton set out headed directly south toward Flayin Falls, they passed close to the familiar rise over-looking Kayleigh's cabin.

If they made enough noise, would Kayleigh hear? If she spotted them, would she think to warn someone?

Martyn had to do something. He couldn't make more than a muffled croak against the gag. He couldn't move more than his upper body and his heels.

It had to be enough. He dug his heels into Wanderer's ribs harder than he ever had before. Wanderer jumped and snorted loudly.

Lord Norton swiveled in the saddle. "Keep that horse quiet."

Daas turned in his saddle, trying to shush the horse.

Martyn kicked Wanderer again. The horse reared, and Martyn leaned forward to keep himself and the horse balanced. If Wanderer toppled over backward, Martyn had no way to get free before being crushed.

Daas's eyes widened as he was dragged from his saddle by his grip on Wanderer's leadrope. His own horse snorted and shied away, freeing Daas to dangle from the end of the leadrope.

Wanderer crashed to the ground, his front hooves missing Daas' leg by inches, and trumpeted a whinny.

Crossley and Tooley scrambled from their horses and grabbed Wanderer's bridle on either side of his head. Daas leapt to his feet, groaned, and clutched his left shoulder. "I think that horse pulled my arm from its socket."

Lord Norton turned and glared at all of them. Daas stopped moaning but continued to grip his shoulder.

Dallen Offen, now Lord Norton's First Blade, sighed, swung down from his horse, and marched to Daas. "Hold still." He gripped Daas's arm and shoulder, twisted to hold the arm straight, and shoved.

Daas cried out and collapsed to his knees, moaning again.

A few yards away, Owen stared at Daas, a wrinkle forming between his eyes as if in pity. Martyn shook his head. Daas didn't deserve pity. Not after all the torture he'd inflicted so willingly on others.

Was Martyn's commotion enough to warn Kayleigh of trouble? Martyn would have no way of knowing.

Lord Norton wheeled his horse and stopped beside

Martyn, his face impassive. Martyn met his gaze. This was the moment Respen's fist would've lashed out.

But Lord Norton remained cold and calm on his horse. "You may think you accomplished something with that prank, but you will pay dearly for it."

Martyn didn't look away, gritting his teeth against the gag and the words he couldn't say. If Leith could handle Respen's torture, then surely Martyn could hold up under whatever punishment Lord Norton had planned.

A smile touched the corners of Lord Norton's mouth as if the man laughed at Martyn's show of defiance. "I'm not going to lay a finger on you. Nor will the Blades." Lord Norton nudged his horse, and the Blades rushed to remount.

What did that mean? Martyn glanced over his shoulder at Owen as Daas once again tugged Wanderer into line. A knot formed in Martyn's chest, snagged his breath. Was Lord Norton planning on torturing Owen to punish Martyn?

But to what end? He didn't have to punish Martyn to keep the Blades in line, like Respen had to. As far as Martyn could figure, Lord Norton didn't know Owen was Martyn's brother, just that they'd been trying to escape the camp together.

Why was Martyn still alive? Lord Norton would've been smart to kill Martyn right away rather than risk him escaping to warn King Keevan.

The knot in Martyn's chest tightened when Lord Norton turned, not in the direction of his army, but toward Flayin Falls. Flayin Falls hated Respen and everybody and anybody connected even remotely to him. As Respen's biggest supporter, Lord Norton would hardly make their favorite person list.

Apparently, Lord Norton didn't care. He rode straight down the main street. People darted out of his way, peeking between doors and shuttered windows. Ahead, one young man took off toward Flayin Falls Manor at the far end.

Lord Norton halted in the main square and waited, one hand resting lightly on his thigh as if he hadn't marched into the middle of a town that was liable to kill him. For a few minutes, the square remained empty except for Lord Norton and the single iron lamppost rising off to one side.

Men poured from Flayin Falls Manor, racing toward the stables. More men began appearing on the boardwalk and porches with swords, axes, and pitchforks in their hands. The healer was there, glaring at Martyn, as was the shopkeeper, who crossed his arms and frowned.

Martyn tugged at his hands, trying to loosen the ropes. What was Lord Norton planning? If a fight broke out, he didn't have nearly enough men to stave it off, and, defenseless as they were, Martyn and Owen could be killed in the crossfire.

His gaze snagged on a figure huddled in the shadows in the alley beside the general store. Her brown hair was tied back from her face, and her dark green blouse stood out against the dusty brown of her divided, buckskin skirt.

Kayleigh. She hadn't been in her cabin. She was here.

Their gazes locked, and her mouth gaped. Martyn shook his head and turned away. Whatever was about to happen, he didn't want to draw attention to her.

A group of riders set out from the manor and cantered down the main street, the hilts of their swords glinting in the morning sunlight. At the far end of the main square, they halted. The man in the center walked his horse another few yards into the square before he too stopped, facing Lord Norton.

Based on his quality silk shirt and his air of authority, this had to be the late Lord Westin's younger brother, the one put in charge until Lord Westin's son Kurt grew old enough to take over. If Martyn remembered right, the young lord was being raised by his mother's brother and his wife to prevent this younger Westin brother from getting any ideas of dispatching of the boy and taking the lordship of Flayin Falls for himself permanently.

Westin eyed Lord Norton, one hand fisted at his side and the other clamped on the reins. His horse pawed and flicked its tail. "What do you want, Norton? The king will not take kindly to any intrusion here."

"I come here as a peaceful gesture only." Lord Norton kept his hand loose at his side.

Martyn snorted, the loudest sound he could make past the gag. Sure, this was a peaceful mission. Please ignore the five hundred men sneaking through the prairie outside of town.

Martyn's snort hadn't been loud enough to pause Lord Norton. He raised his free hand, palm up, toward Westin. "Until the last few years, Kilm and Flayin Falls have always been allies. Together with Walden, we guard Acktar's northern frontier. I would like to re-establish the friendship our towns once had."

Lies, lies, and more lies. This was nothing but a diversion.

But why had Lord Norton taken Martyn and Owen along to see it? Having two bound men in tow wasn't the way to go about convincing Westin of peaceful intentions.

Westin glared, his hands fisted so tightly on the reins that his horse tossed its head and dug a deeper hole with its pawing hoof. "Why should we believe you? My brother is dead thanks to Respen's Blades."

"I never agreed with all of Respen's policies, and his use of assassins was deplorable."

Said the man with four disguised Blades guarding his back.

Lord Norton smiled and waved at the men behind him. "I know you don't believe me. That's why I've brought you and your town a gift."

A gift? What—Martyn stiffened as Daas and Offen dismounted and sliced through the ropes binding him to the horse. Daas grabbed his bound hands and dragged him from the saddle. Martyn fell onto his shoulder, his legs too stiff to move.

Daas and Offen yanked him up by his shoulders and marched him past Lord Norton into the open space. They shoved him down, and gravel bit into his knees through his buckskin trousers.

His stomach tightened. He was the gift. Delivered like a trussed up calf for a feast. That's why he'd been gagged. He couldn't explain that King Keevan had granted him clemency. He couldn't tell Westin that Lord Norton was protecting the five Blades that weren't supposed to be in Acktar.

Daas grabbed a handful of Martyn's hair and yanked his head back. He blinked at the pain tearing across his scalp. Something cold and sharp pressed against the vein in his neck. Daas grinned and said low enough for only Martyn to hear, "Don't move. I'd be more than happy to slit your throat."

"What's the meaning of this?" Westin's voice accompanied the clatter of his horse's hoofbeats trotting a few steps closer.

"This man is a Blade. My men caught him trying to sneak into Acktar with this young Rover. You can have them, along with their horses. Such fine animals will probably fetch a nice price at Nalgar."

Knees scuffed into the dirt next to Martyn, followed by a grunt. Out of the corner of his eye, Martyn caught sight of Tooley and Crossley pinning Owen on his knees next to Martyn.

Offen gripped Martyn's right sleeve, drew a knife, and sliced through the fabric near the shoulder, then slit the fabric down Martyn's arm to his wrist. When he let go, the two ends of the fabric flopped open.

Gasps tore through the people gathered on the boardwalks. A few of Westin's men muttered under their breath.

Martyn didn't have to look to know what they saw. The parallel lines of his marks marched down his right arm, now exposed for the entire town to see.

Even if he could speak, nothing he could say now would make a difference. People who were bitter enough to turn away an innocent, injured girl because she was distantly related to Respen would do far worse when presented with a not-so-innocent Blade. It didn't matter that Martyn hadn't been the one who'd killed Lord Westin and his wife. He was a Blade, and that was enough.

"I know it will not bring back your lord and lady, but I

believe the execution of a Blade would go a long way in procuring the justice the king denied you."

Martyn jerked, causing Daas's hand to tighten in his hair. That was Lord Norton's plan with all this. That's why he'd spared Martyn.

Shouting started along the boardwalks. Footsteps clattered.

Martyn closed his eyes, trying to block the sound of the various suggestions for his death. Lord Norton couldn't just kill King Keevan. The Resistance towns would revolt again.

But if he discredited King Keevan and gained the loyalty of several of the Resistance towns most hurt by the Blades?

He'd just secured the support of Flayin Falls and planted the first idea that King Keevan was, in fact, the one protecting the Blades. When Lord Norton revealed that King Keevan had kept not one, but four former Blades alive and pardoned in Acktar, the groundswell would build. When Lord Norton captured Stetterly, he probably planned to use Leith, Ranson, and Jamie as "gifts" to other Resistance towns. Perhaps Emilin or Ably would react like Flayin Falls was now.

Lord Norton wouldn't have to stop there. He could bring down Lord Alistair, Lady Lorraine, and Renna by their connection to Leith and their knowledge of his past. Whatever leadership role Lord Alistair had among the Resistance towns would be undone.

Martyn struggled, but Daas and Offen held him too tightly. Daas's knife pricked his neck, and something warm and wet drooled onto Martyn's collarbone.

He was helpless to stop it. Lord Norton didn't have to

torture or kill Martyn. All he had to do was turn him over to the furious townsfolk and let them tear him apart.

Feet pounded closer. Daas and Offen released him and tossed him to the ground. Martyn barely had time to curl into a ball, before a stampede of people surrounded him. Boots crashed into his arms, his stomach, his legs. A woman shrieked, and her pointed heel smashed into his ribs. A toe clipped his ear, and blood gushed warm and sticky down the side of his face and into his hair.

Was this how he was going to die? Beaten and kicked to death in the street like a dog? Martyn tried to suck in a breath, but dust choked what little air he could force into his lungs past the gag and vicious kicks.

Owen? Where was Owen? Were the townspeople giving him the same beating? He didn't deserve it. He wasn't a Blade. He hadn't hurt anybody, not like Martyn had.

And Kayleigh. Where was she? The mob might turn on her next if they spotted her. Had she found a place to hide until she could slip away?

Hoofbeats drummed the ground. The kicking stopped, and firm hands hauled Martyn to his feet. He cracked his eyes open and tried to focus past the swirling in his head. Westin's men gripped his arms, holding him upright.

A few yards away, Owen swayed between several more guards, one eye swollen and blood pouring from his nose. In the distance, Lord Norton, his guards, and the Blades rode freely from the town.

Westin's voice broke through the pounding in Martyn's ears. "...not like this...too quick. We should give this Blade justice! A proper execution!"

"Hang him! Hang him!"

"Chop off his head!"

One voice screeched above the others. "Burn him!"

More voices took up the cry until it became a chant. "Burn him! Burn him!"

Westin rode into Martyn's line of sight and held up his hands. "Very well, we'll burn him at the stake tomorrow morning. That will give him plenty of time to dread his death."

Burning? That's how he'd die? Martyn struggled against the hands holding him, but their grip wouldn't budge. One guard punched Martyn in the stomach. Pain flashed through his body, and he doubled over, retching against the gag still clogging his mouth and throat.

"Tie him to the post and take the Rover to the jailhouse. We'll decide what to do with him later. And take off their gags. We'll want to hear his screams tomorrow."

Martyn couldn't resist as the men dragged him to the lamppost and tied his hands above his head to a ring set just below the glass enclosed candle at the top.

He craned his neck to watch more men march Owen into the building a few yards beside and behind the lamppost. Based on the stone walls and barred windows, it had to be the jailhouse.

One of the men untied Martyn's gag and yanked the cloth free. Martyn spit the wad of fabric out of his mouth, barely missing one man's face. "You've got to listen to me. Lord Norton is going to attack the king. He has five Blades with him. He—"

The man backhanded Martyn's jaw. "Mangy cur. Like we'll believe any of your lies. You'd say anything to spare your own hide."

"Leave the dog be. He'll get what's coming to him tomorrow." The other man smirked at Martyn. "I'm sure he'll be begging for mercy by the time the flames lick his toes."

Martyn gritted his teeth. They weren't listening. Of course not. Why should they when he was so obviously a Blade and Lord Norton looked like such a hero for turning him over to them?

Some of Westin's guardsmen fanned out in a wide circle around Martyn and the jailhouse, walking back and forth in a steady patrol.

"Martyn?"

Martyn craned his neck to peer over his shoulder at the sound of Owen's voice. In one of the windows at the side of the jailhouse, a face peered between the bars. What could Martyn say? They had no escape. Maybe he could lie and tell Owen it would be all right, but Owen wouldn't believe him. "I'm sorry."

"No, I'm sorry." Owen gripped the bars. "I got you caught, didn't I? Without me, you would've gotten away."

"But I wouldn't have known I still had a brother." That was the one good thing that had come out of all this. Or was that a good thing? In the end, Owen would have to watch his brother burn to death in front of him. Perhaps it would've been better if they'd never seen each other again, the same way it would've been easier if Leith had never returned to Nalgar Castle.

Though if Leith had never returned, Respen might never have been defeated. And Martyn would still be loyally serving the man who lied to keep him from his parents.

A flash of green caught Martyn's eye. He faced forward again as Kayleigh crossed the square, her head held high.

What was she doing? She should get out of here before the dispersing mob turned its violence on her.

She strode straight to one of the men patrolling around Martyn and Owen. "I need to speak with the Blade."

The guard crossed his arms. "So you can set him free?"

"Of course not! My father was killed by a Blade." Kayleigh stabbed a finger at Martyn. "I have to know if this is the Blade that did it. Please. You served with my father. You knew him, and you used to know me. You know I'm not about to let this Blade go, especially not if he killed my father."

Martyn squeezed his eyes shut. He had thought he'd wanted her hatred, but this...it tore something deep inside him.

"Fine. But I'll have to search you." The guard's voice remained hard.

Martyn's heart thumped loud in his ears. When he forced his eyes open, Kayleigh had stopped within arms reach of him, close enough for him to see the lighter glints in her dark brown hair and the flashes of sunlight on the floral pattern of her shirt. How had he ever mistaken her for anything other than a beautiful girl?

"Owen Hill, how could you?" She slapped him across his uninjured cheek.

He flinched. How could he what? Lie to her? Be a Blade? Kill her father? She had so many reasons to slap him.

Martyn stilled. She'd *slapped* him. But Kayleigh wasn't the slapping type. If she'd truly hated him, she would've punched him hard enough to break his nose.

Had the slap been for show for the guard? Did that mean she didn't hate Martyn?

"It's Martyn, actually." He cleared his throat. Really? That's the first thing he could come up with right now? His name? But right now, it seemed important that she know his real name. As if she'd remember him or some such rot once he died. "My real name's Martyn Hamish."

She dropped her hand, something dying in her eyes. "Oh. I guess I should've realized that was a lie too."

Martyn winced. Yes, that's how she'd remember him. The man who'd lied to her about everything, including his name. Just the person she'd think about fondly after his terrible death-by-burning. "I'm sorry. I should've told you the truth."

"Yes, you should've. You should've stuck around long enough to tell me. Instead you ran." Her fingers clenched and unclenched at her sides, her gaze focused on the ground. "Were you the Blade who killed my father?"

"No. I was in Uster that night." And he couldn't be more thankful for that. "Fourth Blade Craven killed your father. And I really am a scout for King Keevan. He granted me clemency."

"Then what you shouted is true? About Lord Norton and the Blades?" She searched his face, her voice lowered.

Martyn glanced over her head at the guards. The guard who'd challenged her stood still, arms crossed, as he watched the two of them.

"Yes, he has five hundred men, including five Blades. He plans to take over Stetterly and ambush King Keevan when he arrives for his cousin's wedding." Martyn tugged on his bound hands. He had to warn Renna and Leith. Somehow.

When she looked up at him, new steel gleamed in her

eyes, and her voice lowered further. "I couldn't bring a knife this time, but I'll try to sneak back tonight."

For a moment, it was so tempting. Escape from this town and the death that waited for him. Martyn's chest ached to do anything to avoid the flames.

But Westin wouldn't relax his guard tonight. If Kayleigh was caught, she'd suffer at the hands of the townsfolk. Would they be angry enough to make her join him at the stake?

More than that, Martyn couldn't risk having her wait around for a mere chance she could save him. He had to get the information he knew into the right hands to save Leith and King Keevan. He couldn't jeopardize that even for escape.

With a warning, Leith would survive. He'd marry Renna, and they'd have a whole pack of children. One of them would probably be named Martyn, and Leith would tell him stories about how his namesake sacrificed his life to save Leith's.

Martyn could die for that.

"No, I need you to get out of here." Martyn opened his eyes and didn't continue until she met his gaze. "It's our only chance to warn King Keevan."

Where should he send her? Sierra was closest, but Lord Norton's army marched between Flayin Falls and Sierra on its way toward Mountainwood. If Kayleigh went to Nalgar, she'd have the same problem.

It had to be Walden. All Kayleigh would have to do was mention Leith's name, and Lord Alistair and Shadrach would trip over themselves in their haste to help.

"Ride to Walden. My horse should be in the town stables.

Fetch him and another horse that looks like it has stamina. Alternate walking and loping the horses, switching between them to give one a rest. Once you get to Walden, tell them Leith Torren is in trouble, and Martyn Hamish sent you. That'll get you brought to Lord Alistair right away. He will know what to do from there." He cleared his throat. "Lord Norton also caught my brother."

Kayleigh's stance stiffened once again. "Your brother? So all that about your parents and brother was a lie too?"

"No, I really thought he died. He finally managed to track me down a few days ago and got caught with me. Please ask Lord Alistair to send men here to get him. If they get here in time, they might be able to stop the townsfolk from doing anything to him." Whatever happened, Martyn had to keep Owen safe.

"All right." She squeezed her hands into fists. "They won't be able to get here in time to save you, will they?"

"No." The word tore through him. Sending her away was as good as giving himself to the coming fire.

What choice did he have? He had to save Leith. Maybe this was the reason he hadn't died in Nalgar Castle. He was supposed to die here so that his friend could live. Like that story of David and Jonathan that Brandi had told him all those months ago.

"There's nothing you can do to help me. You'll only be caught." Martyn shook his head. "Leith Torren is at Stetterly. He was like a brother to me, but I betrayed him. I let Respen torture him. I can't let it happen again. Please. I need you to go."

Her eyes wide and wet, Kayleigh reached out and rested trembling fingers against Martyn's cheek. He closed his eyes.

He'd been such a fool to run. To think that he could fight the warmth growing in his chest.

But it didn't matter. He'd lost whatever chance he'd had, and now it was too late for him to ever discover if he could've been more than a Blade.

"I'll go, but only if you make one last deal with me." Kayleigh's firm tone compelled him to look into her brown eyes.

He forced himself to grin. "I lost our last deal, you know. I didn't finish reading the Bible. I got stuck somewhere at the end of Hebrews. And I skipped Leviticus. And Nehemiah. And several other parts that got a little too boring. Guess I owe you a month of shed cleaning."

"Doesn't matter. I cleaned the shed the day you left while trying not to use every swear word I learned from you." She grinned back, but a tear still leaked from the corner of her eye and trickled along the base of her nose.

"I hope you kept the soap handy. I have." He glanced past her. The guard took a step toward them. They were out of time.

She cast a glance over her shoulder, another tear joining the first. "Promise me you'll consider everything I said about God and the Bible and faith. I don't want to leave knowing that you...you died hopeless."

The guard stalked closer. Martyn swallowed. "Deal. I'll think about it. Now I need you to go. The king's life depends on you."

She nodded but hesitated for another second. Standing on tiptoes, she leaned closer and for a moment, her lips brushed his jaw. Then she turned and marched away, swiping at her face.

Martyn leaned his head against the lamppost, aching both outside and in, and closed his eyes. She was going to leave. Hopefully she realized that, in the end, he was going to win one deal. She would have to move after she'd linked herself to him in front of the guard. That, and the town might consider her a horse thief.

Shadrach was too disgustingly chivalrous to allow her to return without an escort. He'd figure out what was going on and make sure she was taken care of properly. He'd do the same for Owen.

As would Leith. He and Renna would step in and make sure both Kayleigh and Owen never lacked for family and friends again, like David in Brandi's story adopting Jonathan's son into his own house. They'd all live long, happy lives. Perhaps they'd think about Martyn every once in a while. Like he had to his parents, he'd become better as a memory than he'd ever been in real life.

Hoofbeats clattered in the road's hard-packed dust. Martyn cracked his eyes open as Kayleigh galloped through the town square on Wanderer, a small black horse running on a leadrope behind her. The guards shouted, shaking their fists. Two dashed to the stables, but she would be long gone by the time they got horses saddled.

Martyn sagged against the lamppost. She was gone. And with her went his last chance of escape.

Tomorrow morning, he'd burn.

27

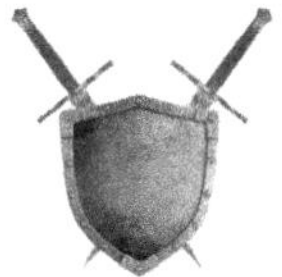

"You told her your name was Owen?"

Martyn sighed and turned his head so he could see the hazy shape of the jailhouse window out of the corner of his eye. "At the time, I thought you were dead, so it seemed like as good a name as any."

"So who is she?"

Even now, he wouldn't be able to avoid annoying, little brother questions. But, Martyn probably should tell someone about Kayleigh. When Owen was rescued—and he would be rescued, Martyn couldn't let himself believe anything else—Owen would tell Leith and Shad about Kayleigh, and Leith would figure out how much she'd meant to Martyn. "I stayed the winter in a cabin near hers. She's…"

Special. But there was no way Martyn would ever say that out loud.

A group of women walked past the guards, several of them carrying baskets. The guards grinned and turned to face his post. One of the women pulled a rock from her basket.

Martyn braced himself. Of course they wouldn't let him spend his last day alive in peace. He managed to dodge the first stone, but the second smashed into his ribs. A third glanced off his shoulder.

He grunted. Rocks peppered his body and his legs. Pain cracked through his skull. Insults hurled along with the rocks, but the ringing in his ears drowned them out.

Eventually, the women ran out of rocks, and insults that were acceptable for polite society. If Martyn's mouth wasn't so dry and his head aching, he would've snorted. He could've come up with much better insults, if he hadn't had swear words soaped off his tongue.

Martyn pressed his bleeding forehead against his arm. He raised his voice loud enough for Owen to hear. The guards would hear too, but Martyn didn't care. He only had these few hours left with his brother. "What was it like growing up in Surgis?"

Owen might've said he had nothing to tell, but now he shared story after story of the years he'd spent in Surgis. Mostly funny stories with Owen getting into trouble.

Martyn closed his eyes. He should've been there, getting into trouble with Owen. Seeing his father's disappointment and his pride. His mother's gentle hand stroking his hair.

He fought the lump gathering in his throat. All those years in the Blades, he'd pushed the memories so far into a hard, bitter corner of his chest that he'd nearly forgotten so much. His father would tell him and Owen stories each night before their mother tucked them into bed, singing them to sleep while stroking their hair. If Martyn concentrated hard enough, he could still feel the tingles along his scalp.

Somewhere during that day as the sun dragged into the afternoon, Martyn found himself telling Owen stories about the Blades. Some of the more mundane missions he and Leith did together, like scouting the Sheered Rock Hills. Training. Tracking down Rovers. Martyn spoke until his words scraped in his raw throat.

As the stars began to blink into view in the purple-blue sky, Martyn ran his tongue around his mouth. When was his last drink? He should've appreciated it more. He wouldn't get another one before he died. "You should get some sleep."

"Not a chance. Not tonight."

Martyn rested against the cold lamppost. His brother would stay with him until the end.

A cold breeze drifted through the town, trailing cold fingers along Martyn's bare right arm. He shivered. An early spring night like tonight would drop to near freezing. Tied to this lamppost as he was, his fingers already tingled.

Tortured by nearly freezing before he was burned to death in the morning.

How had Leith remained so calm while waiting a tortuous week for his death? Martyn swallowed and tried to still his shaking hands. Tension spiraled deeper into his chest until he struggled to breathe. How was Martyn going to face burning to death in the morning?

He couldn't. He'd scream. He'd sob. He'd break. And Owen would be forced to watch all of it. His last memory of his brother would be Martyn's broken agony.

Yet, Martyn had been positive Leith wouldn't be able to

face torture and death either. He'd counted on Leith's fear to keep him from returning to Nalgar Castle.

But Leith had returned. He'd faced Respen. He hadn't broken. Sure, there was that one time during the torture when Respen had forced him to confirm King Keevan's plan. But everyone in that room, Respen included, knew Leith's courage hadn't broken. And Leith didn't give them any information Respen didn't already know.

The cold, hard fact was, Martyn knew with absolute certainty that Leith hadn't had that much courage. If he'd had, then he never would've killed the first time. Or the second. Or the third.

And Renna. Martyn could've sworn she had even less courage than Leith. After all, he'd seen her break. But even broken, she'd only become stronger and had faced death like a victory rather than a defeat.

It all came down to the one thing Marytn had avoided considering. Faith.

But he'd promised Kayleigh. Even if it meant facing things about himself he'd ignored for over a decade.

Had he lied to Owen when he'd told him he'd never been convinced faith or God was real? Sometime back in his childhood, he had believed it, right? Before logic had taken over and told him it couldn't be real. He no longer knew.

Renna had once said that no child of God was ever lost. They might stray for a while, but God would always draw them back to Him. Did that mean Martyn had simply been running all these years or that he hadn't really been one in the first place? And if he'd never been a Christian, would he never be?

All of this could be an utter load of nonsense. There was that pretty convincing possibility.

Martyn shifted against the freezing iron post. His breath misted a cloud in front of his face. Someone in his situation might be tempted to make a last-minute conversion just to cover all the angles before he died. But Martyn wasn't about to give himself over to a delusion just to make himself feel better for a few hours before death.

No, if Martyn made that step, it would be because he genuinely believed it was all real, and he had every intention of living out that conviction for the rest of his days, however long or short that was.

He needed proof. That was the only logical way to go about this. And all the evidence he'd built up over and years pointed in the direction of foolishness.

What was that verse he'd just read in the Bible? Something about faith being the substance of things hoped for and the evidence of things not seen.

That was real helpful. Faith was the evidence of faith. Great argument there. Invisible thing the substance of more invisible things.

Over the years, he'd learned to trust only in things he could see and touch.

You can see faith in actions. Brandi had once told him, back when they'd argued on the trail to Nalgar Castle.

At the time, all the actions he'd ever seen had proved otherwise. His parents' abandonment. That minister kicking him out onto the streets. And right now, a town with the majority of its population calling themselves Christians was going to burn him to death in the morning.

Yet, Martyn's parents hadn't abandoned him, and that

minister was Respen's man more than anyone's. Everything Respen told him was a lie. Was he lying about faith too?

Had this always been about Martyn believing God abandoned him? If so, then what was Martyn running from? Running implied that something chased him.

The fool hath said in his heart there is no God.

Respen was a fool. Was Martyn also being a fool? Or were Leith, Renna, Brandi, and Kayleigh the fools as Martyn had always said?

No. Whatever else he'd done, Leith was no fool. Neither was Kayleigh.

If the actions of others had always been Martyn's proof against faith, then wouldn't that mean Leith's actions could be proof for it? Leith was Martyn's evidence. Renna. Kayleigh. Brandi. Owen. Even annoyingly perfect Shadrach Alistair. Their faith was his proof.

Even that wasn't enough. Kayleigh had said her faith was based on God's actions, not on something she or anyone else had done. Yet the only way to experience God's actions was through faith.

It all came back to faith. Again. And he'd only get his proof of faith after he'd already done it, not before.

He'd read that God's Word was like a two-edged sword. But could it be as firm and real as Martyn's knives? If he reached out and grabbed hold, would he find it solid or would it wisp through his fingers like everything else he'd ever trusted?

What else had Martyn trusted? Respen. Leith. His parents. Mere people. Any wonder they'd failed him?

Where was the logic in trusting people while expecting

them to fail? If he knew better than to trust anyone, then why keep hoping? Why keep trying?

If God was everything the Bible said, then He was the only one who could be trusted because He wouldn't fail. That was...*if* the Bible was true. *If* this wasn't all nonsense.

Martyn couldn't trust people. He couldn't trust himself. It was either trust God or trust nothing.

Only one way to truly find out.

Faith.

The most logical illogical thing he could do.

Martyn banged his head back against the lamppost hard enough to hurt. "Blistering soapsuds, you're right about everything, aren't you?"

"Right about what?" Owen sounded like he'd been nodding off. Not that Martyn could blame him. He'd been too busy having a debate in his head to bother keeping up a conversation.

"Faith. God. The truth. I'm the fool, aren't I?"

"Um, yes."

"But how can you be so sure? How can I be sure?" Why was it so hard for Martyn to trust like this? He and Owen had the same parents, the same upbringing up to a certain point, yet why did Owen trust God so unshakably when Martyn didn't dare?

"How can I be sure? Because God gives faith. He works faith. It's not dependent on me so I can't shake it with my own actions." Owen's voice lowered. "How can you be sure? Well, you've had all these nagging questions eating away at you no matter how hard you try to run from them. That's God working in you already. Keep on fighting or surrender, though either way, you're fighting a losing battle. You can't resist God."

That sounded like a foolish idea, put that way. Martyn flexed his fingers, trying to work some warmth into them, but no matter what he did he couldn't feel his fingertips.

Squeezing his eyes shut, he tried to remember his six-year-old self. The way he'd prayed. Short, childish prayers. But had they been sincere? Had he believed, once? If only he could remember what it was like to trust. To surrender.

Perhaps it felt like that moment in the Tower, holding his knife to Leith's neck, when he'd finally realized he couldn't kill Leith no matter how hard he tried to convince himself he could.

He'd fought. He'd deceived himself. And, in the end, he'd surrendered. Because it was the only thing left for him to do.

Martyn let out a long breath. Surrender. "I suppose I'm a Christian now."

"You're getting there, at least. Though, you sound like the most reluctant Christian I've ever heard." Based on the tone of his voice, Owen had to be smiling. "Well, maybe not the most reluctant. Do you remember the story about Paul? He had to have Jesus appear to him personally to give him a good shake before he finally stopped fighting."

Martyn huffed a laugh. And once he started laughing, he didn't try to swallow it back. When was the last time he'd truly laughed? Not since Leith returned from his winter mission in Stetterly and began acting strangely.

Owen laughed too, and for a moment, the stars far above seemed a bit brighter in the black sky.

But it was only a moment. The cold air burrowed deeper into Martyn's body until his bones ached with it. His toes, fingers, and nose barely had feeling, and what they did have throbbed. Perhaps by morning, Martyn would be so numb he wouldn't be able to feel the flames gnawing at his skin.

His laughter died. What time was it? How much longer did he have?

Far too little. Only a few short hours to be Owen's brother. He'd never have a chance to repair his friendship with Leith. Never admit to Kayleigh what she meant to him.

He cleared his dry throat. "Do you believe our parents are in Heaven?"

"Yes. We'll see them there. Both of us."

Martyn remembered Renna and Leith's conversation about Heaven. Martyn had paced outside the room, pretending not to listen. But he couldn't help but hear every word. Renna said relationships didn't exist in Heaven like they did now, but they would be closer, deeper.

Martyn hadn't known his parents all that well, nor had he seen the better side of them the way Owen had. But in Heaven, none of that past, nor Martyn's past would matter.

This was probably where he was supposed to pray. But it had been so long since the childhood prayers he'd recited before bedtime. He tried anyway.

To the east, a line of pink spread along the horizon.

Dawn.

28

Metal scraped against metal with the faintest of clicks.

Leith held himself still, keeping his breathing even. The only light in the dugout he shared with Ranson and Jamie filtered around the wooden door set in the hillside. At this time of night, even that remained nothing more than a lessening of the shadows in the faint outline of a door.

The sound grated again. A hint of starlight glimmered along the blades of two knives, above and below the sliding bolt holding the door closed.

The Blades. After months of waiting, they'd finally come for him.

Leith touched Ranson's shoulder. Ranson started, but his breathing eased after only a second's pause. A moment later, Jamie's breathing also caught before leveling out as Ranson nudged him.

Easing upright, Leith gathered his knives, strapping

them on by feel in the blackness. Movement, sensed more than seen or heard, told him Ranson and Jamie did the same.

Ranson bumped Leith's arm. They were ready.

The two knives scratched against the bolt again. Half a minute more, and the Blades would be inside.

Dirt cascaded. Starlight brightened the dugout as a hole appeared. Jamie's body blocked the view of stars and sky before he rolled clear.

Ranson followed, then Leith crawled through their escape tunnel at the rear of the dugout and rolled onto the damp prairie grass. No sooner had his toes cleared the opening than Jamie shoved the dirt-covered hatch back in place. Exactly as they'd practiced.

Leith wiggled on his stomach around the dugout while Jamie crept the other way. Leith reached the front as a black figure pulled the door open. Three more black figures followed him inside.

Springing to his feet, Leith slammed the door shut behind them, shoving a wooden bar into place to lock it from the outside. He leapt aside as Jamie shoved his whole weight into a stack of sod pieces next to the trench cut into the hill for the door. The sod tumbled, filling the trench and sealing the door shut. At the rear of the dugout, Ranson would be piling more sod across the escape hatch.

Voices shouted from inside. Something banged against the door.

Leith drew a knife, his stomach knotting. They'd only trapped four Blades. That meant one...

A scream, then a cry of pain, echoed into the still, night air.

He sprinted toward Renna and Brandi's dugout, knife in hand, ice in his fingers. As he turned into the trench and lunged for their door, a figure barreled into him, soft and shaking. Not the Blade. "Renna?"

A smaller figure dashed from the dugout and slammed the door, heaving the bar into place. "Got him. I think. That was close."

Leith let out a breath. Renna and Brandi were safe.

"Leith?" Renna sagged against him.

Something wet and warm drooled over Leith's hand. His stomach drained into his toes, leaving behind nothing but cold.

"Renna!" Leith dropped his knife and wrapped both arms around her, lowering her to the ground. "Where are you hurt?"

Brandi dropped to her knees beside them. "Renna!"

"What's going on?" Sheriff Allen's stocky form loomed from the darkness as he exited his dugout next door to Renna and Brandi's.

"Fetch a torch!" Leith eased a hand over Renna's back and down her side. Where was she hurt? How bad was she bleeding? She shook against him, her teeth chattering. Was she even now dying, and he couldn't even see her face in the darkness?

"Renna. I need you to focus. Where are you hurt?" As he gripped her arms, she cried out.

Her arm. Leith ran his hand up her right arm, his fingers growing slick with blood.

She cried out again.

Leith pressed his hand over her wound. How bad was it? Was she bleeding out even now?

Sheriff Allen returned with a torch. Leith lifted his hand and inspected Renna's wound. The gash ran for a couple of inches through the muscle of her upper arm. Painful, especially for someone who had never experienced a wound like this before. But not life threatening.

She wasn't dying. He held her tight, not sure if it was her or him shaking. Maybe both.

Renna tried to straighten against him. "I should be braver about this. You've had worse."

"I'm used to it. You aren't." Leith forced himself to breathe. Stop panicking and start helping.

Brandi sliced off the bottom of her skirt and held out the fabric. Like Renna, she'd taken his advice to sleep in her clothes in case of trouble. "Will this help?"

"Yes." Leith clamped the fabric over Renna's wound, took her left hand, and closed her fingers over the makeshift bandage. "Hold that there."

He didn't want to let Renna go, but he had to check on the Blade in Renna and Brandi's dugout to make sure he wouldn't cause any more trouble. "Brandi, can you help Renna? Where did you leave the Blade?"

Brandi eased behind Renna, placing her fingers over Renna's on the wound. "I whacked him with the cook pot. Not sure if I knocked him out or just winded him. We didn't stick around to find out."

"He ran into the table. That's what woke me up. I wasn't sure what it was at first. I thought it might be you, but you would know better than to stumble. I woke Brandi, but then the Blade was there and he was stabbing down and I rolled and..." Renna squeezed her eyes shut, shivering.

"That's when I kicked out his legs, and we ran. He started to follow, but I grabbed the cook pot and swung it at him."

The cast iron cook pot could do a lot of damage. Leith crept to the door and eased the bar off. "Bring the torch."

Sheriff Allen joined him, and Leith motioned for him to stay back as he opened the door and slipped inside. As Sheriff Allen stepped into the doorway, the torch cast orange light and shadows into the dugout's interior.

A young, blond-haired man dressed in black sprawled in front of the fireplace, groaning. Former Blade John Uldiney, the youngest and lowest ranked of the banished Blades.

Locating a sash from one of Renna's dresses, Leith tied Uldiney's hands behind his back, divested him of his weapons, and cinched his ankles together with his belt.

Sheriff Allen strode farther into the dugout. "All the Blades captured in one night. We can send a rider to the king tomorrow to send men to retrieve them."

Leith eyed Uldiney. Something wasn't right. Uldiney wore clean, good-quality black clothes, better than he could've gotten if he and the other Blades had been on their own this whole time. Why had they attacked now, before Leith and Renna's wedding? Why not wait and try to kill them after their wedding when they would be in one place instead of two? "I don't think it'll be that simple. Wake some of the men and have them help Jamie and Ranson guard the other Blades."

With Uldiney still only semi-conscious, Leith took the time to light a lamp and several candles and ducked back outside. Renna hunched where he'd left her, Brandi pressing the fabric over the wound. He knelt next to them. "How're you doing?"

Renna's teeth still chattered, but she was at least sitting up by herself. "Hurts."

"I know. Let's get you inside." Leith picked her up and carried her into the dugout, Brandi trotting next to him. As he set Renna on the bench by the table, he nodded toward Uldiney. "Brandi, can you watch him? Let me know once he starts waking up enough to start moving around."

Drawing her short sword, Brandi placed herself within an easy lunge of Uldiney, her stance wary. She stayed back far enough that Uldiney couldn't roll or grab her sword.

Renna peeled the fabric away from the wound, twisting her head and arm to inspect it. "You'll have to stitch it."

"Me? No, Renna..." Leith clenched his fists, his stomach already churning as blood dribbled down her arm.

"Michelle is still at Walden, and I can't stitch it myself. That leaves you."

Stitch Renna's wound? Pull a needle through her skin, watching her wince at the pain he was causing? "I can't."

"You've stitched wounds before." Her face remained white, but some of her trembling had steadied.

"It won't be very good. Or neat." She had to listen. Could he force himself to tend her wound as she had done so often for him?

A smile cracked across her face. "I know. I pulled out the stitches you put in Ranson."

But that had been different. Ranson was a fellow Blade. But Renna? Leith couldn't. Not Renna. "Surely one of the farmers' wives know how to put in a few stitches or someone else or..."

"I'd rather it be you." Renna's eyes, blue and bright with pain, met his. "I trust you."

He didn't have a choice. Stumbling to his feet, he found Renna's bag of medical supplies and brought it back to the table. While Renna laid out the supplies he'd need with her uninjured hand, he dragged Uldiney out of the way and started a pot of water boiling.

Brandi didn't take her eyes off Uldiney, though her mouth pressed into a hard, tight line.

Once he had everything gathered and the water had boiled, he straddled the bench next to Renna and sorted through the supplies. "You don't have any painkiller set out here."

Renna clenched her fists against her skirt. "No. Something's happening tonight, with the Blades showing up here now of all times. I'm the lady of Stetterly. I can't be passed out somewhere."

No, she couldn't. But could he stand to stitch her wound closed with her alert and shaking with pain?

He tucked her against him, and she wrapped her good arm around his waist and rested the hand of her injured arm against his chest, pressing her face against his shoulder. He lifted her elbow to give himself a better view of the gash. "You ready?"

She nodded, her fingers already fisted into his shirt.

After cutting her sleeve away from her wound, Leith sloshed alcohol into the bleeding gash. Renna stiffened, and her fingers turned into claws digging into him.

He mustn't think about it too much. Not the warmth of her blood as it covered his fingers or the feel of the needle sliding through her skin, and especially not her muffled whimpers and the damp spot that grew on his shirt.

Finally, he wrapped the bandage over her arm and tied it. "All done."

She straightened, scrubbing her face. "Thank you."

He wiped a tear off her chin. She didn't look like she should be thanking him, not with her eyes still too wide and her mouth trembling.

A surge of something both hot as midday and cold as the darkest winter night filled his chest with the familiarity of a knife in his hand and blood pouring from a victim's throat. Uldiney had hurt Renna. He'd tried to kill her. And now he lay across the room within easy reach.

"Leith. Just so you know, the Blade is starting to wake up." Even Brandi's voice didn't stop the heat curling into Leith's hands.

It would only take a moment, a slash of Leith's knife, to kill the Blade who'd hurt Renna.

Leith closed his eyes and forced himself to take deep breaths. Returning to killing like a Blade wasn't the answer. God had brought him beyond that.

But Leith didn't let go of the cold in his chest. Not entirely. Perhaps in the morning he'd regret what he was about to do, but with Renna's blood still warm on his fingertips, he embraced the ice of the Blade he'd once been.

"Renna, Brandi. Step outside." He slid to his feet and drew his knife.

"Leith?" Renna tottered upright and touched his arm. "What are you going to do?"

"Do you trust me?" Leith didn't look at her. If he did, he might not be able to control the cold filling him.

"Yes."

"Then leave."

Brandi's footsteps padded to Renna's side, then together they shuffled outside. The door clacked shut behind them.

Leith stalked around the table, grabbed the back of Uldiney's shirt, and yanked the Blade upright. He trailed his knife along the tender skin at the base of Uldiney's neck.

Uldiney's eyes went from blinking to wide in a heartbeat. "You...you wouldn't hurt me."

"You tried to kill the woman I love tonight. I've killed for far less than that." Leith lowered his voice, his knife tracing circles against Uldiney's skin.

Uldiney's eyes searched Leith's face, and a shudder traveled down his back.

29

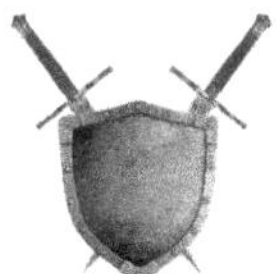

The town woke slowly. Even in their eagerness, the first townsfolk didn't gather in the square until the sun had fully risen above the horizon. Guardsmen approached Martyn with a rope, pinned him in place, and tied his legs at his knees so tightly he couldn't shift an inch from the post.

The guards brought kindling, arranged it next to his feet, and piled larger logs and dead branches around his legs. They didn't add any pitch or oil to the pile. Apparently, they intended this fire to build slowly and painfully.

Martyn's heart hammered in his throat. Despite the cool morning breeze swirling the dust, beads of sweat dribbled down his temples.

He couldn't do this. He couldn't face this. His fingers shook. His breaths pounded hard and sharp through his chest.

Westin and his entourage of guards rode into the square. Townsfolk packed into the space, some climbing onto rooftops or hanging out of second story windows. Jeers hurled Martyn's way.

Westin held up his hand. When the town quieted, he began making a speech about justice and evil men paying for their crimes.

Martyn concentrated on taking slow, even breaths and tried to still his trembling. He really needed a dose of that courage Leith had talked about in the Tower.

A guard strode forward, carrying a blazing torch. He shoved the torch between the stacks of logs.

The kindling popped and caught, threads of wood curling and blackening. So slow, so tiny, for something that would soon devour him.

This was it. His final mission. Die bravely.

Flames shot from the kindling, dancing around the edges of the larger logs. Heat built near Martyn's toes, but he couldn't move.

He couldn't move, and the fire was growing, growing. Hotter. Hotter. Smoke curled around Martyn's body and face. He coughed, turning his face away to find a gulp of cool, clear air.

Heat smoldered through his boots. He jerked and tugged at the ropes holding his legs and hands. He couldn't move. His heart pounded harder. He had to get out of here. Twisting, flailing, yanking, but the ropes held tight. The heat. The flames. And he couldn't move.

He was burning.

The buckskin cuff of his trousers flared into flames. Pain seared into his skin. He cried out, fighting, struggling, straining to free his hands.

"Martyn!" His brother. Screaming and sobbing.

Martyn turned his head, squinting through the haze, the smoke, the heat. Owen shook the bars of his cell like he intended to rip the iron from the stone.

Martyn clamped his teeth against a scream, but the flames clawed deeper into his skin until he couldn't...he couldn't... "Owen! Remember...Mama....how she...please..."

He coughed and gagged, his words ending in another half-smothered scream. He needed his brother's voice. He wasn't strong enough to die alone.

Owen's choked voice rose above the crackling, hissing fire. "The Lord is my shepherd; I shall not want."

The smoke swirled around Martyn's face, smothering him with ash and heat. He squeezed his stinging eyes shut. Sweat poured down his back and chest. The flames roared higher.

He was on fire. His boots, his trousers, his skin. Pain, deep and raw, scorching, tearing, clawing.

Burning.

Owen was shouting, barely audible over the flames. "...leave me not, neither forsake me, O God of my salvation. When my father and my mother forsake me...the LORD will take me up...Deliver me not over unto the will of mine enemies..."

Not abandoned. Not forsaken.

Martyn couldn't drag in enough air to even scream as agony raced up his right side all the way to his ribs.

Take me, please. I can't...please...

A pounding rumble clattered in his ears. Martyn cracked his eyes open. Beyond the shimmering heat and twisting spikes of flames, the black shapes of what looked like horses and riders thundered closer.

Was this what death looked like? Horses and riders coming to claim him?

One black shape dove from his horse and flung himself into the fire, stooping to reach into the flames to slice a knife through the burning strands holding Martyn's feet in place.

An angel?

The figure straightened. No, not an angel, not unless Martyn was hallucinating an angel with Shadrach Alistair's face.

Mouth twisted in pain, Shadrach pressed closer to Martyn and sawed his knife through the ropes holding Martyn's hands above his head.

Something snapped. Shadrach hurled them from the fire. Martyn's shoulder struck the ground. A blast of cool air hit his face. Hands beat at the flames still covering him, but he couldn't move. Couldn't breathe.

Something cold and wet landed across his legs and jolted his body, but his chest remained seized. He was slipping into blackness, his body nothing but fire and pain.

Small, soft hands gripped his face. Kayleigh's face appeared in the narrow tunnel in the consuming darkness. "Breathe, Martyn. Come on. Please breathe."

He couldn't.

Something pounded hard against his back.

Martyn gasped, choked on a breath, and broke into hard, wracking coughs. He managed to roll and turn his face to the side as his coughing turned into gagging. He heaved and vomited. Bile stung against his scorched throat.

Footsteps scuffed, and someone yanked him off the ground, squeezing tight.

"Martyn." His brother's tortured voice came from the shaking body gripping him.

A hug. That's what this was. Martyn rested his forehead on his brother's shoulder, coughing and choking too much to speak. He managed to find just enough strength to lift his arms and embrace Owen.

He wasn't dead. Somehow, he wasn't dead.

"Lord Shadrach?" Kayleigh's voice had a pinched, tight tone to it.

"I see them. I'll take care of it."

Martyn peeled his eyes open as Shadrach pushed himself to his feet, grimacing. Strips of his charred trousers hung around his blackened boots. Beyond him, a crowd of townsfolk faced a small knot of guardsmen. Based on the way the guardsmen glanced at Shadrach as if looking for orders, they had to be from Walden. A few men, lacking weapons and dressed in basic homespun, joined the guardsmen facing the mob. A few of the townsfolk also trying to stop this?

"I've seen some low-down, despicable things in the war, but this...this makes Respen Felix look honorable." Shadrach's voice cut across the town, sharp and cold. "Many of you call yourselves Christians, and today you have shamed the Name you carry."

"He probably needs a drink. Lay him back down." Kayleigh's voice came from somewhere close.

Martyn couldn't do more than cough as Owen laid him on the ground, and Kayleigh drew his head onto her lap. She pulled out a canteen, uncapped it, and pressed it to his mouth. "Try a few sips."

Water splashed into his mouth. Lukewarm, stale, and

metallic. Best thing he'd ever tasted. Martyn held his breath long enough to swallow once, twice, and the water trickled down his aching throat.

How had Kayleigh managed to get back here so quickly? And what was Shadrach doing here? He was supposed to be riding to Stetterly to save Leith.

Martyn coughed and rasped in a voice he didn't recognize as his own, "Leith?"

Kayleigh rested a hand on his chest, and Martyn realized he was covered from the waist down by a wet blanket. "Rest easy now. Lord Shadrach has it all handled."

Back straight, jaw tight, Shadrach still faced Westin and the mob of townsfolk, giving them a tongue-lashing lecture like only a lord's firstborn son could. The town deserved it.

Kayleigh brought the canteen back to Martyn's mouth, and he sputtered through a few more mouthfuls. A surge of pain crashed through him, and he couldn't stop his moan.

Martyn closed his eyes, trying to ignore the pain raging through his legs and feet. Kayleigh's hand still rested on his chest. He reached up and laid his hand on top of hers. A bold move, perhaps, for someone who'd once told Kayleigh he wasn't tempted by her.

She pulled her hand away. A new ache throbbed in Martyn's chest. She didn't care for him that way. Of course not.

Her fingers twined through his and squeezed. Maybe... he smiled and let his eyes close.

Somehow, the touch of her hand kept the pain bearable. He was vaguely aware of Owen fetching water and tending the burns. Shadrach shouted orders, arranging for more buckets of water and a wagon.

Still Kayleigh was there, holding his hand, giving him water, administering a large dose of laudanum. Even with the drug numbing some of the pain, Martyn couldn't stop a cry of pain as four of Shadrach's guards lifted him into the wagon and set him onto a straw mattress.

After she and Owen clambered into the wagon, Kayleigh settled down next to Martyn. "We're taking you to Sierra. I don't trust the healer here to so much as dab your burns with water."

"Me either." Martyn gritted his teeth but couldn't completely swallow his gasp of pain as the wagon rocked with Shadrach's weight. Shadrach collapsed next to Martyn's mattress. A damp rag covered his right hand.

He gave an order, and the wagon lurched forward. Shadrach pulled off his boots and socks, dragged a bucket closer, and plunged his feet into the water. "Owen, is it? You'd better keep wet cloths on his burns. That's the best we can do until we get to Sierra."

Kayleigh stifled a yawn and rested her head and free hand on the back of the wagon seat. "Anything I can do to help?"

"Rest. You rode nearly to Walden and back without stopping." Shadrach waved his hand, winced, and wedged his right hand into the bucket with his feet.

Martyn patted the space next to him. "Here. Sleep."

She raised her eyebrows. "That's hardly proper."

He snorted and winced when it tore at his seared throat. "Don't care. It's practical."

"You don't exactly lack chaperones. Get some sleep. Both of you." With his arched eyebrows and tightened square jaw, Shadrach somehow managed to look both concerned and dignified with two feet and a hand stuck in a bucket.

Kayleigh yawned again. She eased next to Martyn, leaving a few inches of space between them. Probably a good thing. Martyn wasn't sure if he could've held back his moan if she bumped his burned legs.

She rested her head on his shoulder. "Is this all right? It doesn't make it harder for you to breathe?"

He wouldn't have admitted it if it did. He slipped his arm around her shoulders. "It's fine. Sleep."

Her breathing slowed and deepened. Martyn should've let himself sleep. After staying up all night and with the amount of laudanum in his system, he should've been exhausted. Instead, he drifted on a warm haze, the pain a dull ache.

Not sleepy. Curious. That's what he was.

The wagon rattled over a bump, jarring Martyn. Agony flared through his skin, but it numbed after a moment.

Martyn squinted up at Shad. "You jumped into a fire for me."

Shad grimaced down at his hand and feet and shrugged. "It's what Leith would've done, if he was here."

"Leith's not the best example to follow if you want a long, pain-free life." Martyn tightened his grip around Kayleigh's shoulders as the wagon rocked back and forth. "Then again, you're probably immune to fire or something like that."

Shad raised an eyebrow. "How's that?"

"You're Shadrach. One of Daniel's three friends. Like the story in the Bible." Martyn suppressed a cough.

"If that were the case, then you should be immune to fire. You're also one of Daniel's friends." Shad grinned as well, though his grin also looked like it wanted to turn into a grimace.

Daniel. That was what Leith called himself these days. "Guess that makes me Meshach. Who gets to be Abednego?"

"Jamie."

Martyn would've laughed, but his lungs ached too much. Already, this much talking scraped his throat and turned his voice into a rough growl. Instead, he settled for another coughing fit.

When he caught his breath, Owen held a canteen to his mouth. Martyn tried to gulp in the water that sloshed into his mouth and onto his face whenever the wagon jounced. Finally, he pushed the canteen away with his free hand. "Thanks, but that's enough. I don't need to drown on top of burning."

Owen sat back on his heels. "You're supposed to be drinking lots of water. Your burns..."

"I know. I know." How often had he heard Renna give that same instruction to Leith after he'd been burned? "You're my brother. You don't have to be my mother."

Owen shook his head. "If I knew you were going to be this much trouble, I wouldn't have tracked you down."

"Too late. Stuck with me. You're supposed to be dragging me back to the straight and narrow and all that." Martyn found himself grinning. How he'd missed having a little brother to rile.

Shad eyed him. "Is it the laudanum making you talkative?"

Did it? Was he being talkative? "Maybe. I don't know. Puts Leith right to sleep." Leith. Renna. Lord Norton's army. Martyn fought to drag some thoughts through the cloud in his head. "How did you get here? Aren't you supposed to be racing to Stetterly?"

"When we hadn't heard anything from you since the snow melted, we began to get concerned. I took ten of Walden's guards and set out to find you."

Did he really think he would've found Martyn with ten men bumbling along behind him? "You got bored."

Shad grinned. "Yes, I was bored. There hasn't been much to do since the war ended. We were about half a day's ride west of Walden when we spotted her."

Kayleigh's hair tickled Martyn's neck and her soft breath wafted against his chest. Even with a half a day's ride cut out, Kayleigh had still ridden a two-day round trip in a day and a night. About twenty hours in the saddle with no time for breaks or rest.

And she'd done it for him. How had he ever thought he could hurt her and ride away that easily? He owed her, and when this was all over, he'd have to figure out how to go about repaying her.

"We intercepted her, and she nearly fought us until she learned who I was. When she explained, I sent one of my men to Walden with the two horses she'd ridden with a message for my father. We then went straight to Flayin Falls." Shad leaned against the wagon's side, lines of exhaustion etched into his face.

Kayleigh had probably caught them around sunset or just after, and Shad had ridden hard all through the night. He and his men hadn't gotten any more sleep than Kayleigh or Martyn had.

"Father should've left for Stetterly by now, and he'll send

a rider to Nalgar Castle. I expect to hear more news when we reach Sierra."

Martyn closed his eyes, trying to calculate the distances, the time, the head start Lord Norton had, but he couldn't concentrate. He was sinking deeper into the hazy weightlessness. "He won't get there in time, will he?"

Shad shook his head, his shoulders slumped. "No. Even if Father rode straight to Stetterly, Leith and Renna will have to hold out on their own for a day. It'll probably be longer since Father will stop at Uster to gather more men. He'll still be outnumbered when he reaches Stetterly."

Lord Norton had been planning this since last fall. He'd had months to gather his men and supplies. How many men could Lord Alistair and King Keevan assemble on such short notice? Would it be enough?

Either way, Leith would be on his own when Lord Norton, the Blades, and the five hundred riders attacked Stetterly.

30

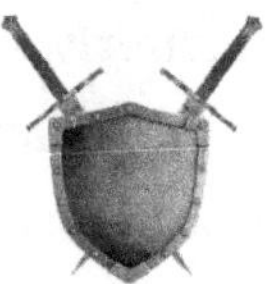

Renna cradled her injured arm and leaned against the church wall next to one of the high windows. The wooden walkway beneath her feet vibrated as Sheriff Allen directed his archers to man the other windows. She blinked, trying to stifle a yawn. She needed to be strong this morning, not sagging.

Boots scuffed, and Leith appeared at her side, steadying her elbow. "Everyone safely inside?"

She nodded and rested her head against the stone. "How bad is it?"

Leith pulled her against him. He smelled of prairie grass and nighttime dew after spending most of the night scouting. "Uldiney didn't lie, though I suspect he didn't tell me everything. They'll be here within the hour. Five hundred men."

Five hundred men. Renna squeezed her eyes shut. And Stetterly could scrape together a hundred men, maybe a hundred and fifty fighters if some of the younger women and older children joined in. None of them had much for fighting experience, even if Leith and Sheriff Allen had trained them in archery over the winter.

"Ranson got away safely. He'll bring help from Uster and Walden."

It wouldn't be enough. Even if Uster and Walden could scrape together five hundred men, the soonest any of them could get here was six days. Stetterly wouldn't hold out six days.

Leith pressed his cheek against her hair. "I wish you would've gone into hiding."

"I can't. Not this time. My duty is here with Stetterly." Renna rubbed her throbbing arm. She hadn't run in the Tower. She wouldn't run now.

Brandi joined them, her short sword in her hand, her mouth pressed into a firm line. "Jamie spotted them from the bell tower. We'll see them from here in a minute or two."

Renna clenched her fingers into Leith's shirt and swallowed. She had to be strong. They had to survive this until help could arrive. Somehow.

Trust. Courage. Wait on the Lord. No matter the outcome.

Leith pulled back and tensed. "They're here."

Renna straightened, smoothed her skirt, and faced the window. A line of men on horseback crested the far hill, flowing down toward the ring of dugouts she and the people of Stetterly had turned into barricades during the night. The rising sun cast long shadows to their left, staining the prairie black.

Two men rode between the dugouts. After a moment, they halted, and one of the men pointed to the dugout and waved a few more men forward. When the men converged on the dugout, the two riders continued past the dugouts into the space in front of the church. Above their heads, a white flag flew next to a black and green banner.

Renna narrowed her eyes and leaned forward. "I think that's Lord Norton's standard."

The warmth of Leith's body filled the space behind her, and his breath tickled her ear. She might've enjoyed being close to him, except for the army surrounding them and the cold edge to Leith's voice when he spoke. "He's riding with General Wentle. He commanded Respen's army."

Behind Lord Norton and General Wentle, four black figures dashed from the dugout.

Sheriff Allen halted next to her and crossed his arms. "I still think we should've kept the Blades prisoner."

"Guarding them would take men away from the windows." Leith shook his head. "Unless you planned to shoot them down in cold blood, there was nothing else we could do."

"That didn't stop you from interrogating that one Blade."

Behind Renna, Leith went rigid. "I didn't draw so much as a drop of blood when I questioned him. I didn't have to."

Renna scrunched her fingers into her skirt. She'd seen the Blade in Leith again that night. For a moment, it had scared her. Not that he'd hurt her. Never that. But that he'd do something he'd regret.

He hadn't had to. Peering through the crack between the door and the dirt wall, she'd watched the former Blade Uldiney crack under the coldness of Leith's voice and the reminder of what he'd once been.

Lord Norton eased his horse to a halt. "Lady Rennelda Faythe."

She shivered under the sneer in his words. Lord Norton expected her to crumble into a weak, simpering girl who'd beg for mercy.

But she'd survived King Respen. Lord Norton couldn't be worse than that.

Leith rested a hand on her shoulder. "None of his archers are in range. Go ahead and step into sight. I'll be right here to pull you out of the way if I spot trouble."

With a deep breath, Renna stepped in front of the window. This was her town, and Lord Norton wasn't welcome. "Get your men out of my town."

Even at this distance, Renna could see the hard lines of Lord Norton's angular face. "You are hardly in a position to make demands, Lady Faythe. I have five hundred riders with me. My quarrel isn't with you, but with your cousin Keevan. If you surrender now, you and your people will not be harmed. You and your people will necessarily be kept prisoner until after your cousin arrives. Can't have you warning him."

"Why are you doing this? To be king?" Renna had to keep him talking. As long as he was talking under that white flag of truce, he wasn't attacking.

"I wouldn't have a quarrel with Keevan either, except that he kept several Blades in his employ. I won't wait for him to turn them on my family. Or do you deny the former Blade Martyn Hamish has been snooping around Kilm?"

If Lord Norton knew where Martyn was, then Martyn had been spotted, at the very least. "What about him?"

"He won't be a problem now. I turned him over to Flayin Falls. Last I heard, they planned to burn him alive."

Martyn. She shuddered as tears pricked her eyes. Leith's grip tightened on her shoulders above the wound in her arm. Martyn couldn't be dead. Not after everything she and Leith had tried to do for him.

She glanced over her shoulder. Leith's face had hardened into cold lines. A Blade's face.

"Which reminds me of my other demand. Hand Leith Torren over to me."

So that Lord Norton could kill him? "There's no one by that name here."

"Don't play word games with me. He goes by a different name now, but he's still Leith Torren, First Blade of King Respen. And the man you are set to marry in less than two weeks."

Renna's blood iced in her fingers. Murmurs stirred through the gathered townsfolk along the parapet and below in the sanctuary. Lord Norton's voice carried far too well, echoing through the church building.

"You didn't tell them, did you?" Lord Norton's eyes burned across the space as if he could melt the stone walls around her. "He has the blood of your parents and your townsfolk on his hands. Yet you're going to marry the dog."

Renna sagged against Leith, her hands shaking. The whispers built behind them.

They knew. Everyone knew about Leith. All the secrets they'd tried so hard to hide. She'd known it would come out, but not like this.

Leith tugged her from the window, and Sheriff Allen stepped in her place. He planted his hands on the sill. "I don't care who you are. I won't stand for you to slander Lady Faythe."

She let Leith pull her into the dark stairwell and leaned against him. "I knew trouble would come. I knew it. I hoped it wouldn't be this soon. I hoped the town would get to know you before they learned about your past. I..."

"It'll be all right." Leith pressed a kiss into her hair. "I have to go."

"What?" Renna stumbled back. The cold was into her chest now. What was Leith talking about? "Why?"

His eyes—green and piercing—met hers. "I have to. The townsfolk won't stand to have me here, and you need the town united under your leadership if you're going to survive this."

"But..." How could she survive this without Leith? She needed him. She couldn't do this by herself. What did she know about war and sieges and fighting off the massive army gathered outside this building? She didn't.

He cupped her face with his warm, calloused hands. "You can handle this. You'll have Sheriff Allen, Jamie, and Brandi to help you. But I can help you more out there. I'm a Blade. I have to fight like a Blade."

Like a Blade? Surely he didn't mean...Renna would've dismissed the idea entirely, but the cold light in Leith's eyes chilled her. He looked like he could kill. After what Lord Norton had done to Martyn, she couldn't blame him. Not when she could too easily imagine Martyn screaming, flames covering him.

She shook. "I can't do this without you."

"Yes, you can." He kissed her forehead. "I won't go far

away. Together, we'll hold off this army until help comes. We'll survive this. God is with us as He was at Nalgar."

They could do this. Renna shoved all the cold into her spine until she could stand straighter. From the first, Leith always told her she was brave. She'd been brave at Nalgar Castle. She could be brave again, with God's help. "Go. Fight your way. I'll fight here."

He leaned closer and kissed her. She fisted her hands in his shirt, feeling the strength of his heartbeat and the steel of his muscles.

He pulled away, brushing her cheek with the back of his hand. "Stay safe."

Then he was gone, vanishing into the dim stairwell. Renna leaned against the cool stones of the wall and wrapped her arms around her stomach. Was this how it would always be? Leith having to leave for some reason or other and her waiting, always waiting?

The voices outside the stairwell rose. Brandi shouted above them, but Renna couldn't bring herself to concentrate on the words.

She had to go out there. This was her town, and it was her responsibility to restore order. But it would be so much easier if she could just curl up in this corner until someone else did it for her.

There was no one else. This duty belonged to her. No more shirking.

She raised her chin and marched onto the walkway. Brandi had her hands on her hips, face red. "Leith isn't a Blade anymore! He's my friend!"

Men and women gathered in the sanctuary below. Some raised their fists and yelled back. Renna rubbed at her temples. Was anyone even watching the windows anymore? Or had their personal mutiny driven all thoughts of the army outside from their heads?

Outside the window, Lord Norton still perched on his horse, close enough that he would be able to hear the raucous shouting.

This wasn't acceptable. Bad enough to argue among themselves, but they shouldn't give their enemy any satisfaction. If Renna could manage as much when facing Respen at Nalgar Castle, then surely her town could pull together long enough to fend off Lord Norton.

"Quiet, please." Not loud enough. Renna drew on the fire building in her chest. She stomped to a spot next to Brandi, drew in a deep breath, and shouted with all the breath in her. "Quiet!"

The townsfolk below cut off mid-shouts.

Renna pressed her fingernails into her palms to stop her smile. That actually worked. She filled her voice with sharp steel. "Yes, Daniel Grayce is Leith Torren, a former Blade, who has been pardoned by King Keevan. Yes, I've known who he was since the day I met him. No, I will not discuss it any further right now. Our current concerns must be directed to fending off the army intent on wiping out Stetterly again, an army led by Lord Norton, one of Respen's staunchest allies, and the five banished Blades. Or do you really think they are of less concern than Leith, who helped you build this refuge and trained you to fight off this attack?"

The townsfolk muttered in a low rumble. One of the farmers stepped forward, arms crossed. "Maybe so, but I refuse to fight under him."

Of all the prejudiced, intolerant...Renna ground her

teeth together. How had they forgotten everything Leith had done for them in the past six months? They would all be dead, killed out in the fields, if not for Leith's preparations.

Yet the mere mention of his past destroyed all of it.

"You won't have to. You will fight under me. Leith's gone. He left so he wouldn't be a distraction." Renna pointed at the window a few paces away. "The enemy is out there, not in here. Get back to your posts, all of you, before Lord Norton decides to storm the place and finish this siege here and now."

Grumbling, the people drifted away, most avoided looking at her. Most of the women remained clustered, whispering and shooting glances at her.

There went her reputation. Not that Renna cared a dead grass stalk for it.

She spun on her heel and faced Lord Norton once again. "We won't surrender. This is our home and Keevan is our king. You claim to fight for your wife and children, but what about the wives and children sheltered here? Are you willing to kill them? Because that's what it will take."

Lord Norton tightened his grip on his horse's reins. "You're willing to sacrifice every man, woman, and child in your town for Leith Torren?"

"He isn't here." Renna refused to turn away. She wouldn't let Lord Norton scare her. She'd faced down both First Blade Harrison Vane and King Respen.

"Lord Norton!"

Renna leaned farther out the window at Leith's shout. He stood on the far hill between Lord Norton's army and the Spires Canyon. Even that far away, the hilts of the knives strapped across his chest glinted dully.

And, for the first time since Respen died, Leith wore black.

"You want me? You'll have to hunt me. Ask your Blades. I'm no easy prey." Leith drew his knife, then seemed to disappear.

Lord Norton cursed and wheeled his horse around. "Fine. Don't surrender. But don't say I didn't give you a chance to spare yourselves."

He cantered his horse back to his men waiting on the far side of the dugouts.

Renna let out a long breath and sagged against the wall. The lives of everyone in this building rested on her shoulders. Had she done the right thing in refusing to surrender? Would it do any good to fight?

Yes, it would. Surely Keevan would have scouts ahead of him, even if he was riding to what he thought would be his cousin's wedding. They would see Stetterly under attack and turn back before it was too late.

And Ranson was out there, riding for Uster. Lord Segon or Lord Alistair might even get a message to Keevan to warn him before he left Nalgar.

After ordering a bench brought up to her, she took a seat next to the window where she could safely peek out. Thanks to her town's efforts during the night, Lord Norton had to order his men to clear the barricades before they could get the bulk of their horses and supplies closer to the church. Men rummaged through their dugouts, but they wouldn't find anything of value.

Renna was still there, sitting on the bench staring into the night, when Brandi plopped down beside her and held out a plate with cornbread and a slice of dried beef. "You'd better eat something. You can't go around starving yourself."

"I'm not…" Renna shook her head and took the plate. Her stomach rumbled, reminding her that she probably should've been thinking more about food and less about battle tactics, Blades, and Leith.

Brandi hugged her knees and peered out the window. "Leith will be all right. You'll see."

"I know." Renna picked up the cornbread and bit into it.

She shouldn't worry about Leith. This was the kind of thing he'd trained for as a Blade.

In Lord Norton's camp, something flared. Renna leaned forward as several fires spiraled into the night sky. The night was so clear and calm the panicked shouts of *fire* drifted to her. If she had her distances right, those were the tents Lord Norton's men had pitched on the freshly tilled fields beyond the town. The bare earth would prevent the fire from spreading.

Brandi grinned. "That would be Leith."

A thunder drummed into the night. More shouting. A herd of horses stampeded through the enemy camp and disappeared into the prairie.

"Yes." Renna felt her own grin tug at her mouth. Tonight, Lord Norton would find out exactly how much trouble he'd stepped into when he'd attacked a First Blade.

31

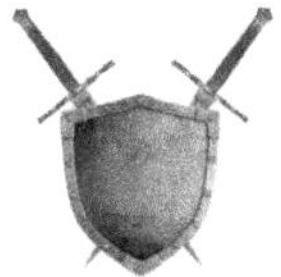

The fire devoured his feet, his legs, up and up his body, eating, tearing. He gasped. His breath tore down his throat into aching lungs. Coughing, Martyn snapped his eyes open.

"How do you feel? Do you need water?" Kayleigh's voice drew his gaze past the bare, light brown walls to her pale face framed with locks of shining, brown hair.

How did he feel? Like someone still held his feet in glowing coals. He tried to talk, but all that came out was more coughing.

She shoved a pewter cup against his mouth. He inhaled a mouthful of water, choked, and coughed it out before he managed to swallow properly.

When she set the cup aside, Martyn glanced around. What time was it? This room didn't have a window. Were they in Sierra? Had Shad already left for Stetterly?

Martyn had to go with him. No matter how badly his burns hurt, he had to get to Stetterly. He shoved himself onto his elbows and started to get up. "Where's Shad? Has he left yet?"

Kayleigh shoved him back down with a hand on his chest. "No, don't get up!"

Martyn looked down at himself. He seemed to be missing a shirt. He peeked under the blanket. Nope, that wasn't all that was missing. He wore nothing besides bandages and undershorts, and the undershorts weren't even his. Though, he was so covered in bandages he was pretty much decent. "Where are my clothes?"

"Mostly burned off." Kayleigh grimaced. "They weren't salvageable."

He raised an eyebrow. "Did you help? Because that *would* be improper."

Her cheeks and ears flushed as red as the burns visible above Martyn's bandages. "Owen—Martyn Hamish! I...of course not! I stood outside while Lord Shadrach and your brother helped the healer. I wouldn't..."

He smirked. Of course she wouldn't, but it was worth seeing her squirm. He let her squirm a few more minutes before he let his grin fade. "I'm sorry the clothes you made me got burned."

"I don't care about the clothes. I can always make another pair." Kayleigh twisted her hands in her lap. "I'm glad we got there in time. I was...really worried."

Something warmed in Martyn's chest. She cared something for him at least.

This was probably the moment for a heart-to-heart talk. A few apologies. Sappy stuff like that.

All stuff Martyn wasn't ready to face. Not yet.

He had a mission to finish first.

He propped himself on his elbows again. "I'm glad I lived too. Now, can you fetch Shad?"

"You need to rest. Lord Shadrach has it all taken care of." Kayleigh rested a hand on his shoulder.

Martyn gritted his teeth. Staying in bed would be so easy. Even shifting his legs a few inches sent stabs of agony through his whole body.

But he couldn't rest. Not while an army bore down on Stetterly. Not while Leith was in danger.

Martyn had turned his back on Leith once. He wouldn't do it again. He swung his legs over the edge of the bed, ignoring the pulsing pain eating at his skin. "I'm getting up, clothes or no clothes. So unless you want to help, I suggest you get Shad."

Kayleigh bolted to her feet and from the room. Martyn eased himself upright and rested his feet on the floor. Pain shot up his legs.

He gripped the edge of the bed, fighting the bile rising in his throat. How was he going to stand the ride to Stetterly if he couldn't even set his feet on the floor without nearly passing out?

Somehow, he'd have to tough it out.

Footsteps halted in the doorway. Martyn dragged his head up and faced Shad. "Get me some clothes."

Shad crossed his arms. "What do you think you're doing?"

"I have to go along." Martyn clenched his fingers tighter on the edge of the bed. Why was he so tired already? Even sitting up for a few minutes drained him.

"No, you don't. My mother-in-law is preparing her men

and we plan to meet King Keevan about a day's ride from here. We'll rescue Leith. You've already done enough."

Martyn sucked a breath into his aching lungs and fought the spasm of coughing. "No, I haven't. Not yet. I stood by and watched while Respen tortured Leith. I put my knife to his neck and told myself I could kill him. I have to prove that this time I have his back."

"And nearly getting burned at the stake isn't enough?"

"No." Martyn didn't let his voice waver. Leith had willingly walked into Respen's torture, prepared to die if necessary, to spare Martyn. To repair the brotherhood they'd once had, Martyn had to sacrifice just as much.

Besides, there was no way Martyn would let Shad get all the ride-in-at-the-last-moment glory for this rescue.

He met Shad's gaze. "You need me. You know how this will go. Leith will do his best to draw the Blades off on his own. To rescue him, you'll have to track them down."

"I can track."

"I know. And I know you've had some experience fighting Blades. But not like this. If you aren't careful, you'll track yourself right into a trap. I've already done it once and look at the mess it got me in. It'll take both of us."

For a long minute, Shad studied him. Martyn tried to sit straight and hide the fact that Shad was blurring in and out of focus.

Shad huffed something under his breath about stubborn Blades. "Fine, you can come. I'll scrounge something for you to wear."

By the time he and Owen returned with a bundle of clothes, Martyn had gotten out a good coughing fit and gathered his remaining strength.

Still, he was so annoyingly weak that Shad and Owen had to help him dress, an ordeal that nearly caused Martyn to black out several times.

Somehow he managed to totter outside with their help. Shad nodded toward the cluster of men. "I can arrange for a wagon for you."

Martyn shook his head, sending the world into swirls. Not a good sign. "I can ride. I don't want to slow you down."

Shad snorted. "You can't ride."

"Yes, I can." Martyn gritted his teeth and tried to stand straight.

"Fine." Shad released Martyn, and Martyn staggered on his charred feet.

Owen adjusted his grip. "You really should just take a wagon. You don't have to kill yourself."

"I can handle it." No, he couldn't. His vision faded in and out of black. But he wasn't going to say that out loud, or Shad and Owen would tie him to a cot and leave him behind.

A few minutes later, Shad returned leading a large, dark brown horse. "All right. Mount up."

Martyn gripped the saddlehorn. Was he shaking? Or was the horse tipping toward him? The soles of his feet screamed with blisters.

He could do this. He wasn't going to let Lord Norton win. He wasn't going to give in to weakness. He was tough. He was strong.

Martyn lifted his left foot. Pain tore through both legs, sharp and hard as knives.

He was on the ground, head and arms held in someone's

grasp. The sky swirled, white and blue mixing into hazy patterns.

Owen's voice. Kayleigh's. Asking if he was all right. Calling for someone to bring water.

And Shad, so calm he might as well have said *I told you so.* "Bring the wagon here."

He was coughing, shivering, sinking. Pain. Blackness.

Kayleigh was cradling him, his head on her shoulder, her hand stroking his hair. "Hang on. The wagon's nearly here. And Owen's fetching laudanum."

Her hand in his hair, the tingles across his scalp...just like his mama used to before bed each night. Stroke his hair, then kiss his forehead. Every night. Even that last night, when perhaps her voice had quavered, her fingers trembled.

Kayleigh's hand stilled.

"Don't stop...like Mama..."

"Sssh. The wagon's here. Drink this."

Something sloshed into his mouth. Bitter and strong, burning down his throat and into his stomach. He swallowed, coughed, and swallowed again.

As the numbness spread through his arms and down his legs, he managed to peel his eyes open. "Need soap. Orders."

Kayleigh's face was nothing but a blur of tanned skin and brown hair. "I know. I'm spouting off orders again. And I'm going to keep doing it until you start listening."

Martyn didn't have the strength to keep his eyes open any longer.

32

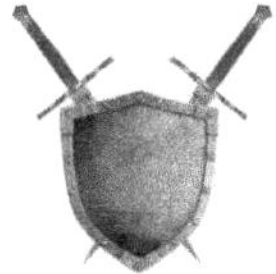

"Push them back! Keep them back from those windows!" Renna pointed as she dashed past, falling to her knees beside one of Stetterly's farmers with an arrow in his side. She pressed one hand over the wound and broke off the arrow shaft with the other. "Hold on. I'll wrap this up and get that arrow out tonight."

The farmer winced and managed a nod as she tied a wad of rags over the wound to staunch the bleeding.

She staggered to her feet. A man cried out across the church. Shouts. Screams. Men struggling at each of the windows.

They weren't going to survive the day. Actually, they weren't going to survive the hour.

She stumbled past the men fighting at the window, past a pair of women holding one window with nothing but a cook pot and a soup ladle, and reached the far end of the walkway.

She leaned against the wall, squeezing her eyes shut. She couldn't do this. She wasn't a war leader. She was a healer.

In the Blades' Tower at Nalgar Castle, God had provided her with enough courage for herself and for Leith. Now, she needed courage for her whole town, and surely God would provide it as He had then.

"Not so tough without that Blade to protect you."

Renna caught her breath and peeled her eyes open.

The burly Rover, Captain Loust, stood a few yards away from her. Behind him, two more men climbed over a windowsill.

No Leith to save her this time. Brandi and Jamie fought together at a window across the building. No one even saw her huddled in the shadows of this corner.

She was on her own. She reached into her pocket for the knife strapped to her thigh.

"Don't even think about drawing that knife." Captain Loust leveled his sword in her direction.

She withdrew her hand. He was right. One knife wasn't going to help her. Not against three men.

What could she do? She couldn't fight.

That's why she was the target. She was Stetterly's weakness. A lord like Lord Alistair could've led the town in its defense. A girl like Brandi could join the fighting.

But Renna? Renna was just a pawn in a Raiders game. Respen had used her to trap Leith. Lord Norton planned to use her to trap Keevan. And these Rovers could use her any way they wanted. She had no way to fight back.

She was tired of being the pawn. If she couldn't fight back, she'd have to think of something else she could do.

"What do you think you'll gain by fighting for Lord

Norton? If he succeeds, he'll want to set up a stable government. And stable governments don't allow Rovers to run wild." Renna inched along the wall. A few feet to her right, a door led into the bell tower. If she could only reach it... "Lord Norton will turn on you."

Captain Loust stalked closer. "He won't. He's giving a reward for anyone who can capture the Lady Faythe. I lost too much during the war. I should get something in return."

"You'll be arrested. Or killed." Renna fumbled behind her, found the door latch, and yanked the door open. Dashing inside, she slammed the door shut behind her and raced up the stairs.

Perhaps she should've gone down. She would've been able to escape on the main floor. But many of the women, children, and wounded were down there. She couldn't lead the Rovers to them.

The Rovers' footsteps pounded after her. She raced upward, gasping short, wheezing breaths. Her muscles burned. She staggered onto the platform on top, its sides ringed with a waist-high wall on one side, a railing on the inside next to the bell.

She had nowhere else to run. Nothing but sky and prairie rolled out from the church building. Lord Norton's army surged against the stone walls below her, men clinging to ladders and ropes as they tried to gain entry through the upper windows.

Captain Loust tromped up the last step. "You can't run. Might as well come easy now."

What else could she do? She wasn't going to surrender. Not like this.

But she was trapped. Helpless. Stetterly's weakness.

Movement to the north snagged her gaze. Was that—

Captain Loust lunged toward her. She darted away from him. She had to get away from him and down to the main floor quickly.

Scrambling onto the railing, she leaned forward and grabbed the thick bell rope. It swung in the deep shaft in the center of the bell tower, all the way to the main floor.

Once before she'd stood at the edge of a long drop, a pursuer after her. She'd hesitated then, but she couldn't let herself pause now.

She jumped.

The rope slid in her hands, the rough sisal fibers prickling, tearing, burning. The wound across her upper arm screamed. Her body swung against the rope, and she wrapped her legs around it.

Her weight dragged on the massive bell. It swung, and its edge caught Captain Loust in the stomach. He collapsed to the platform, arms wrapped around his middle. The bell clanged, and the rest of the Rovers froze, hands clamped over their ears.

As the bell swung back upright due to its huge weight, Renna was pulled upward even as she continued sliding down. The rope tore skin from her hands. She cried out but didn't let go.

A few feet from the ground, she tightened her grip with her legs, slowing herself until she could step off the rope onto the floor. She staggered, her head buzzing, her heart roaring in her ears.

There wasn't time to steady her senses. Knots of men and women fought by the storage rooms on either side of her. Children cried. Women screamed. Lord Norton's men poured through half the windows to Renna's left. Archers from the other side had turned, firing across the church to try to halt the enemy.

They were being overwhelmed.

"To the doors! Hurry!" Renna sprinted the length of the church. Could anyone even hear her over the clashing steel, grunting, shouting, screaming that pounded against her temples?

"Renna!" Brandi grabbed her arm, pulling her against the wall. Jamie held off an attacker long enough for Sheriff Allen to step forward and club him. A few yards away, the doors were shuddering, a booming sound echoing into the building. A battering ram?

Renna gripped Brandi's arm. "Stand by to open the doors."

"What? But there's a battering ram." Brandi waved her short sword in that direction.

Renna tried to ignore the blood dripping from its tip. "No time to explain. Wait for my signal and get those doors open, got it?"

Both Brandi and Jamie nodded and took off for the doors. Renna dashed for the narrow, spiral staircase leading to the parapet.

When she reached the top of the staircase, men crowded the parapet, pushed back into a knot by Lord Norton's men. She pointed at the windows above the doors. "Archers! I need men at these front windows! Now!"

A few archers were already there, trying to shoot down at the men battering at the doors. Several women had the hatch above the doors open and threw rocks from a dwindling supply down onto the attackers' heads.

Muted thunder drummed beneath the other sounds of battle. Some of the men around her stiffened, turning toward the windows. Renna curled her aching fingers into the fabric of her divided skirt. If she was right about what she'd thought she'd seen…

A wedge of galloping horses crested the far hill, banners for Walden, Uster, and Duelstone flying above the dust. At one side of his army, Lord Norton turned, pointing and shouting.

His men didn't have time to react. The riders slammed into the men clustered in front of Stetterly's church, driving deep into Lord Norton's army.

In front of the church, the riders dove from their horses and dashed for the doors. A slap on the rump sent the horses galloping, riderless, back through Lord Norton's army, causing more chaos as they bucked and swerved. More of the riders poured in, and a gap opened between Lord Norton's army and the church. The battering ram fell silent.

Renna leaned over the railing. "Brandi, Jamie, now."

Brandi and Jamie lifted the two beams holding the doors shut and heaved the doors open. Men sprinted inside, led by Lord Alistair, his limp, left arm strapped to his chest.

Lord Alistair nodded toward her, then placed himself next to the doors, directing his soldiers inside.

Renna leaned against the wall and finally gave in to the shudders that crept along her back and into her hands. She was still alive.

Reinforcements had arrived. How had they gotten here in two days instead of the twelve it should've taken Lord Alistair to receive Ranson's message and leave for Stetterly?

Didn't matter. They were here. Stetterly still stood.

Renna forced her spine to straighten. She had to get a hold of herself. On trembling legs, she stumbled down the staircase as the last of Lord Alistair's riders sprinted inside. Brandi and Jamie, with help from some of the townsfolk, slammed the doors shut and thunked the locking bars back into place. Several of Lord Alistair's soldiers dragged a large log, probably the battering ram, and rolled it also across the doors to hold them closed.

"Lady Faythe." Someone caught Renna's arm.

Renna turned. Ranson stood before her bracing a shield over Michelle Allen's head and back.

Michelle bobbed a small curtsy. "Stetterly's healer reporting for duty."

Had Renna once doubted Michelle had what it took to be Stetterly's healer? She shouldn't have. "I'm so glad you're here. There are too many wounded. I haven't been able to keep up. Clear out a space in the back. See if you can get some of the women and children to help."

Michelle frowned. "I think you need to be my first patient."

Renna glanced down at herself. Blood dampened her right sleeve above her wound. When she reached up to touch it, her hand spasmed. Forcing her fingers open, she inspected the raw and bleeding patches across her palm and the pads of her fingers. "There are others hurt worse than me. I'll soak my hands in warm water as soon as I can."

"If you say so." Michelle hurried past her, clutching a satchel that hopefully contained more medical supplies from Walden.

Ranson set the shield down, staring after Michelle as if he wanted to follow but didn't dare.

Renna nodded in Michelle's direction. "Go on. She could use help."

Ranson flashed a grin and dashed off after Michelle.

Flexing her aching fingers, Renna joined Lord Alistair by the doors. Before she could speak, he gave her a half-bow. "My men are at your command and await your orders, Lady Faythe."

"What?" Renna blinked and glanced around at the men patrolling the now enemy-free parapet. Wasn't Lord Alistair going to take over now? Leading wars and resistance movements, that's what he did.

"This is your town. You give the orders here." Lord Alistair's mouth twitched into a smile beneath his bushy, untrimmed beard. "Of course, I'll lend my expertise as needed."

"Thank you." Renna wrapped her arms around her stomach, trying to relieve the pain throbbing through her hands. Across the church, two of Lord Alistair's soldiers led Captain Loust, hunched and grimacing, from the bell tower. Renna swallowed and turned back to Lord Alistair. "How did you get here so quickly?"

"Martyn Hamish sent us word from Flayin Falls. I left immediately with whatever riders I could find, gathering more from Duelstone and Uster on our way south. I fear I've only brought a hundred and thirty men, not enough to end this siege." Lord Alistair scrubbed the gray-brown bristles of his beard. "But help is coming. The rest of my soldiers were following on foot, and they'll be joining King Keevan. I'm not sure when they'll arrive."

Help was on its way. Renna closed her eyes, her knees

close to buckling. Would Lord Alistair's men be enough to help them hold on for another day or two?

· She pressed her palms into her sides, tears pricking the corners of her eyes at the increasing ache. "Martyn? Is he alive?"

"Shad rode for Flayin Falls, but I don't know if he arrived in time." Lord Alistair glanced past her, then swept his gaze over the battlements. "Where's Leith?"

Where was Leith? Hopefully safe. Hopefully still alive. She pointed at the doors. "Out there, somewhere, being hunted."

LEITH HELD HIS BREATH AS THE FORMER BLADE DAAS PACED outside the command tent, his boots squeaking against the sand and his trousers whispering against the grass.

In Leith's hand, Lord Norton's dagger eased a fraction of an inch. Lord Norton slept, his breath whuffling in and out rhythmically. One hand rested only a few inches from the hilt of the dagger that Leith worked from under the pillow.

It would be so easy to kill this man now. He slept soundly. The Blades outside didn't realize Leith had slipped past them. All Leith would have to do was draw his knife and slide its edge across Lord Norton's throat.

Heat curled in Leith's chest, building and burning outward into his fingers. Lord Norton deserved death. Leith had watched—helpless to do anything but keep the Blades occupied—as Lord Norton's soldiers nearly overran Stetterly. If not for Lord Alistair's arrival, Renna might've died. Leith would've died trying to get to her before it was too late.

And Martyn. Leith's hand trembled. So much hurt and betrayal lay between them, and now Leith would never have the chance to repair their friendship.

Not since First Blade Vane had Leith been tempted this much to put a knife in someone's back. It would spare Stetterly. Save Renna.

And it would be wrong.

Leith forced down the heat in his chest, the cold in his blood, until his heart and hands steadied. He couldn't kill Lord Norton. It wasn't right and would prove Lord Norton had been right all along about Leith and Martyn.

Protector or assassin. A thin, thin line. Both sides of it held bloodshed, but an assassin killed in the dark of night, in the back, when he still had a choice to walk away. A protector killed in battle when pressed until there was no other option.

Then, and only then, would Leith kill again.

Right now, Leith had a choice. He had to trust God with the future. Trust that Lord Alistair, well-practiced in siege warfare against superior numbers, would help Renna and Stetterly hold. Trust that Shad hadn't come with Lord Alistair because he was fetching more soldiers for Stetterly's defense.

Protector, not assassin.

Leith edged the dagger out another inch. Last night and during the battle, Lord Norton had ordered only three of the Blades after Leith. The other two had remained with Lord Norton as his bodyguards.

Leith needed all five to chase him. He would draw them away from Stetterly. Keep them so busy Lord Norton wouldn't have a chance to use them to assassinate Renna, Lord Alistair, or anyone else.

He slid the dagger the last few inches from under the pillow. As quietly as possible, he stabbed the point into the ground a few inches from Lord Norton's nose. When Lord Norton woke, it would be the first thing he saw. He'd know Leith could've killed him in his sleep.

And, with fear and rage clouding his judgment, he'd order Leith tracked down at all costs.

When Daas' footsteps crunched on one side of the tent, Leith crept out the other. Once he was clear, he strolled through the shadows. What chaos should he create tonight? Last night, he'd caused so much trouble, they hadn't had time for a night attack. Tonight would be no different. Already, the guards were jumpy. All the better to start a panic.

Nearby, a guard rocked back and forth on his heels while he patrolled around a paddock with the horses Lord Norton's men had captured during the day.

Leith pressed a knife to the guard's neck. "Do exactly as I say, and you won't get hurt."

The man stiffened, swallowed, and slowly bobbed his head. The fear of a knife in the dark still reigned in Acktar, despite Respen being dead and buried.

"Release the horses." Leith accompanied the words with a prick from his knife.

The man scrambled to obey. Leith crept into the shadows while the man untied the ropes holding the horses in the makeshift pen and flapped his arms at the animals. Once one made a dash for the opening, the whole herd thundered through.

The man stood there, panting, and glanced around as if searching for Leith. Any moment now, the man would realize he was alone, and he'd raise the alarm.

It took the man almost a minute to gather his courage enough to grip his sword and shout for more guards. As guards scurried in all directions, Leith crept back the way he'd come, setting fire to two tents in a plowed section of field while he was at it.

Lord Norton charged from his tent, yelling and waving his dagger. Leith suppressed his grin. Exactly as planned.

He slipped into the nighttime prairie. Behind him, Lord Norton bellowed orders to the Blades.

The hunt had begun.

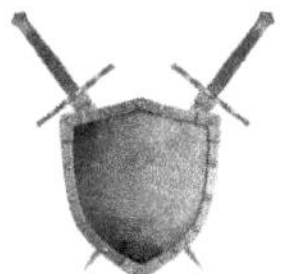

33

A low rumble. Voices. The thud of horse hooves.

Martyn blinked. Canvas stretched above his head. Where was he? Why was there a tent over him?

Daylight filtered through the gap near the doorway. Why were they stopped in the middle of the day? Shouldn't they be rushing toward Stetterly as quickly as possible?

He tried to sit up, and the blanket slid down his chest. He peered down at himself. What had happened to his clothes? Again?

This was getting a tad disconcerting.

"I told them you weren't going to die on us."

Martyn turned his head. A few yards away, Shad leaned back in a chair, his feet propped on a supply crate. He was binding goose feathers onto the end of a new arrow. Next to him, more unfletched arrows stabbed into the ground while a bundle of finished arrows rested on his other side.

"Where are my clothes?" Martyn searched either side of

the bed, but he couldn't see any bundles of discarded clothing.

"I'm not telling. You have to rest." Shad gave him one of those commanding, know-it-all lord's son looks. "You won't be of any use when we reach Stetterly if you push yourself now."

Shad was even more annoying when he was right. Martyn flopped back onto the pillow. "Fine. As long as you give my clothes back before we ride into battle."

"Actually, they're my clothes you're borrowing." Shad tied off the fletching and added the arrow to his pile.

A face, pale beneath a thatch of blond hair, peered through the opening in the canvas. Owen's eyes widened. "You're awake!"

As Shad gathered his arrows and strode from the tent, Owen bounded to Martyn's side. Unhooking a canteen from a tent pole, he shoved it at Martyn's face. "Here."

Martyn grimaced and drank. It wouldn't be so bad drinking all this water if people didn't keep insisting on watering him like he was some dying cornstalk. When Owen finally stopped dumping water into him, Martyn managed to gasp a decent breath. "How long has it been? Where are we?"

And where was Kayleigh? Why wasn't she here? Martyn tried to ignore the stabbing in his heart. She didn't have to spend every minute of her day with him, even if he had been dying or something like that. It wasn't like they were anything to each other. Not really.

"We're camped south of Aven. We've been here since last night while King Keevan rallies the lords. I think he plans to leave tomorrow at dawn if all goes well." Owen held out the canteen again. "More water?"

"No." Martyn knocked the canteen away. Any more water and he'd choke. "Tomorrow is too late. We should be heading for Stetterly, not sitting around here."

"What is it with you Blades? You believe you know best when it comes to military matters." A rasping voice came from the doorway to the tent. "When will you learn it does no good to rush into the battle until you have the means to make sure you win."

Martyn bolted upright, sucked in a breath of pain, and reached for the blanket that had fallen to his waist. "Sir... sire...Your Majesty..."

"Don't bother bowing." King Keevan strode across the tent and took the chair next to Martyn's cot as Owen vacated it. "I wish to speak with him alone."

Owen bowed and left the tent.

Martyn swallowed and eased down onto his pillow. What did King Keevan wish to speak to him about? "Sire?"

"I owe you my life." King Keevan leaned his elbows on his knees, his head bowed. "And the lives of my wife and son. If not for your warning, I would've ridden into a trap with them beside me. Thank you."

Martyn drew in a breath, pain flaring across his skin. Had Respen ever thanked him for completing a mission? Ever said he owed Martyn his life?

No, Martyn had taken lives and sold his soul for Respen. But King Keevan? He asked for lives to be saved, not destroyed. He was someone worthy of trusting and following.

And Martyn had spent too much of his life following a liar and a murderer.

Maybe that was where Martyn had gone wrong so often.

Choosing the wrong loyalties. Following the wrong men. Following men at all.

Tied to that lamppost, Martyn had changed loyalties. He wasn't sure what that would mean, yet. He wasn't sure how to go about following Christ and His commands. But if Christ was everything the Bible said He was, then He was the worthiest commander of all.

No more ifs. No more doubt. Trust.

"It was my mission." Martyn managed a shrug and sucked in a breath at a blast of pain. The breath caught in his throat, turning into a coughing fit.

His eyes watered with the force of his coughing. Had the smoke permanently damaged his lungs? He wouldn't know until his body healed. If it healed.

When Martyn caught his breath, blinking, King Keevan held out the canteen. Martyn fumbled to hold the canteen with shaking hands. With a sigh, King Keevan steadied the canteen while Martyn sipped at the water.

"When you're up to it, I'll have one of my men take your statement." King Keevan returned the canteen to its hook.

"My statement? You mean, what I saw at Kilm and the hidden valley?" Martyn resisted a yawn. His muscles felt as if he'd coughed out all his strength.

"That, and what happened with the mob at Flayin Falls. I already have Owen's account, but I'd like yours as well. Once I've settled with Lord Norton, I'll swing through Flayin Falls to arrest Dean Westin."

"You're going to arrest him? For what he did?" Martyn swallowed down another tickle in his raw throat. Wasn't Flayin Falls a Resistance town? "Why?"

"He incited mob violence, decreed an unlawful execution without a proper trial, and nearly burned a man at the stake, a manner of execution that has been illegal for decades." King Keevan's rasp turned the words into a growl. "Doesn't matter who breaks the law. It's my duty to see that justice is done."

Justice. Even for a former Blade like Martyn.

King Keevan's tall, dark-haired bodyguard stepped into the tent. "Lord Conree has arrived. Owen Hamish has gone to greet him."

"Show him in here."

Lord Conree of Surgis. Martyn tensed and tried to catch his breath. Lord Conree had known Martyn's parents. He respected Owen enough to give him leave to search for Martyn.

Minutes later, a thin man with dark blond hair and drooping mustache stepped into the tent, Owen at his heels. King Keevan stood. "Lord Conree. Thank you for your support and your men."

"My pleasure, sire." Lord Conree bowed.

"There's a meeting tonight to plan our strategy. Until then, rations will be distributed to your men and your horses cared for. Please let my general or captains know if you require anything else." With one last nod, King Keevan strode from the tent. Through the opening, Martyn caught a glimpse of his two bodyguards falling into step behind him before the canvas flapped closed once again.

Owen led Lord Conree across the tent and gestured at Martyn. "Sir, this is my brother Martyn. Martyn, this is Lord Conree of Surgis."

Martyn probably should try to get up again, just to be polite, but his body throbbed. His eyelids drooped. He'd been awake all of a few minutes, yet he was tired already. It was pitiful, really. Though, with all the people coming and going, his tent had to be the busiest one in the whole camp.

He managed a nod. "Thank you, sir, for looking after my brother and parents all those years."

"Owen has served me well." Lord Conree rested a hand on Owen's shoulder, and Owen squirmed as if embarrassed. "Both of you will have a place at Surgis, if you want it."

"Both of us?" Martyn couldn't have heard that right. No one invited a former Blade to their town.

"Yes. Both." Lord Conree studied Martyn and nodded as if he approved of what he saw. "Owen, we should let your brother rest. Would you show me where my men and I should camp?"

Owen nodded but turned back to Martyn. "Go back to sleep. I'll send someone in to check on you in a while."

As Owen and Lord Conree left, Martyn settled back under the blanket and closed his eyes. Middle of the day, and here he was napping. But his legs burned, his head was too heavy to lift, and perhaps he could go back to sleep for a few minutes.

Kayleigh's voice.

Martyn cracked his eyes open as she perched on the chair next to him. "Wondered where you were."

"I had breakfast with Lady Lorraine, then joined Lord Shadrach's sword drill." Kayleigh glared over her shoulder. "And someone neglected to inform me you were awake. Being distracted by a king and a lord was no excuse."

Martyn caught a glimpse of Owen ducking out of sight outside the tent. There was something about seeing Owen and Kayleigh acting like friends, or even family, that lurched through his chest. Especially considering they'd fought on the opposite sides of the war.

To distract himself, he checked the blanket, tugging it farther up his chest. He was getting better at the whole propriety thing.

"How do you feel?"

When Martyn glanced up, Kayleigh's gaze focused on him. Her eyebrows scrunched so tightly he had the sudden urge to touch her face and smooth them out. He clenched his fingers. Great. More impulses like that, and he'd get all lovestruck and moon-eyed like Leith.

He cleared his throat. "Fine. I'm...really fine. Can't feel the burns anymore, actually."

To be honest, it wasn't that he couldn't feel the pain. He'd just gotten used to it, as if pain had become as a part of him as his scars or breathing. As long as he didn't move, it wasn't too bad.

The wrinkles didn't smooth from Kayleigh's face. "You're hurt pretty badly."

"I'll heal." He grinned. "And I'll get a few good scars."

That got a smile out of her. She crossed her arms and huffed. "Scars? That's all you can think about? You nearly died."

He shrugged as much as he could while lying down. "It's not that unusual." He glanced down at his right arm, where his marks ranged down his arm. Did he dare bring it up? She'd been so nice to him since seeing him tied to the post in

Flayin Falls, but had she really forgiven him? "I was a Blade. It's what I do."

She stilled, her gaze dropping from his. "I'm sorry I reacted the way I did when you told me. I've always told myself I wasn't like the townsfolk in Flayin Falls, but then I pulled a sword on you and threw you out without giving you a chance to explain. I'm sorry."

Great. A heartfelt apology. Now what was he supposed to say? She probably expected something equally mushy back. "It wasn't your fault. I pushed you into it, knowing I was leaving and probably wouldn't come back."

"I hoped you would." Kayleigh plucked at her skirt. "I regretted what I'd said as soon as you left. I checked your cabin every day to see if you'd returned."

He'd tried to kill her hope, but all he'd done was make her hope even more.

But that was back when he'd had no hope.

Now he had Owen, a piece of his family restored to him. He was on his way to save Leith and Renna, and that made him oddly hopeful that, if they all survived, he and Leith might repair something of what they'd once had. Even if they couldn't, Martyn would have a place waiting for him at Surgis if he wanted it. Or King Keevan might ask him to continue scouting.

And he might be on his way to figuring out how to have the faith he'd once had as a child. "I managed to keep our deal this time. I thought about...a lot of things that night."

"And?" Kayleigh leaned forward, her fingers still fidgeting with the fabric of her skirt.

"I'm not good at trusting yet." Or believing. Or praying.

"Perhaps that's why you were spared. You're too deliberate and logical for quick belief and blind trust." She reached out and straightened the blanket, her gaze focused on her hands. "God has work to do with you yet. But then again, He had a lot of work to do with me too."

This was still too new and raw. Martyn let the silence lengthen until he could safely change the subject. "I'm, uh, glad I stumbled across you in the Sheered Rock Hills. You turned out to be less of a nuisance than I thought."

"And you turned out to be even more of a hassle." Her mouth turned up at the corners as if she was fighting a grin.

He grinned back. Being a hassle to her was strangely satisfying.

BLIZZARD'S SNORT ALERTED HIM.

Leith eased onto his elbows and peered over the boulder sheltering him. Blizzard and Valor stood in front of the cabin in the hidden crevice. Their heads were up, ears pricked, staring toward the entrance.

Voices. Leith slid into a crouch, thankful he'd changed back into his dust brown shirt and trousers after last night's raid.

The Blades had found him.

Two figures, dressed in black, broke through the stand of pine trees and stalked to the edge of the clearing. One motioned over his shoulder. "There are his horses. He's got to be here somewhere."

Leith suppressed a snort. Foolish mistake, shouting and standing in the open.

Six more men stepped from the trees. Leith tensed,

resisting the urge to reach for his knife. Three of the men carried strung bows, quivers filled with arrows resting across their backs.

Archers. The best defense against a Blade.

Two of the Blades stayed near the entrance while the other three Blades paired with the archers. The archers nocked arrows to their bows and stayed a few steps behind as the three Blades moved in different directions, searching each side and the center of the clearing.

Leith slowly lowered himself out of sight. If they caught him, they'd shoot him down as easily as Shad shot Vane a year ago.

He scrubbed dust through his hair since its dark color would stand out against the sun-dried rocks. For good measure, he rubbed dust over his knives, his face, his hands, and his boots. Anything that might stand out or glint.

Wiggling forward on his stomach, he peered around the boulder. The archer and the Blade, Franklin Tooley, stalked closer.

Leith was trapped.

34

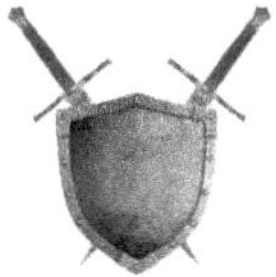

Martyn gripped the saddlehorn, dressed and armed for the first time in far too many days. His legs already hurt where they rubbed against the saddle. But he'd tough it out. He had to.

A few feet away, King Keevan sat astride a pale palomino. Fishing into his saddlebag, he pulled out a gold crown and settled it onto his hair. The setting sun behind them sent orange beams glinting off the gold.

One of his bodyguards, the shorter and stockier one, grinned and adjusted the large shield on his arm. "Planning to overwhelm them with your kingly majesty?"

"That, and thirteen hundred foot soldiers." King Keevan flashed a thin smile, the expression tightening the scar across his cheek. "Those are my people down there as much as here. I have to end this with as little bloodshed as possible."

He gestured at the ranks of men arrayed in battle formation in a sweeping curve at the base of the hill, out of sight from Lord Norton's army surrounding Stetterly.

Sierra, Dently, Clarbon, Keestone, Aven. All Resistance towns.

But also Blathe and Surgis. Towns who had fought for Respen, but now rallied behind their Eirdon king.

It was the most united Acktar had been in far too many years.

King Keevan's tall, dark-haired bodyguard unfurled the king's banner, a silver cross on a light green background. King Keevan gestured to Martyn. "He's going to carry it."

"Me?" Martyn pointed at his chest. "You want me to carry the king's banner into battle? Isn't that some sort of great honor?"

"Yes." King Keevan's shoulders rolled in what might have been a shrug. "Carrying the banner takes both hands. Since you're already wounded and can't fight effectively from horseback, I won't be down another soldier."

He was the practical choice. Martyn took the pole and braced the end against his saddle. The flag's long tails flapped in the breeze wafting down the hill toward them.

Kayleigh and Owen halted their horses on either side of him. Shad sat astride a bay horse a few yards away at the head of Walden's foot soldiers.

Kayleigh flexed her fingers on the hilt of her drawn sword. "Guess we'll have to guard your back."

"A girl and my little brother. I'm dead, aren't I?" Martyn huffed, but he couldn't stop a grin.

Kayleigh glared while Owen snorted. "The two of us managed to survive a war. Where were you? Oh, yes. Guarding a girl in a tower."

They had him there. Martyn didn't have time to come up with a proper comeback because King Keevan was giving the signal to move out.

As the command worked its way along the ranks, the men marched forward. Row upon row of solemn, tight-mouthed soldiers. Martyn tightened his grip on the flagpole and nudged his horse forward, wincing at the pressure on his bandaged legs.

Martyn reached the crest of the hill moments after King Keevan. On the next hill, an army surged around a large, stone building. The bell tower marked it as a church. Ladders leaned against the building as men fought at the narrow windows set into the upper story.

"Sound the bugle." King Keevan kicked his horse into a trot. The bugle's notes floated on the breeze, answered by each of the captains. All along the hill, the lines of soldiers marched double time.

Lord Norton's men started and wheeled to face the army now surrounding them.

When only a hundred yards separated the two armies, King Keevan ordered a halt. Even with its rasp, his raised voice held steady. "Lord Norton. Step forward."

Lord Norton's army stirred and parted. Lord Norton strode from his ranks of men. Blood splattered his ripped clothing and his mussed hair. His face appeared even more angular under a layer of dirt.

Martyn smirked. One small town holed up in a church had thwarted Lord Norton's plans. That had to be a bit galling.

"Lord Norton, I suggest you surrender." King Keevan sat straight in the saddle.

"You will guarantee my men safety. They can return home in peace." Lord Norton crossed his arms.

A power play. Even Martyn could see that. Lord Norton was trying to dictate the terms.

"I will make no guarantees. Either you surrender unconditionally or not at all." King Keevan motioned toward the half-circle of thirteen hundred men behind him. "Your choice."

Martyn suppressed a grin. King Keevan probably would allow Lord Norton's men to return home, but it had to be on his terms, not Lord Norton's. If Lord Norton wanted to surrender, then he would have to trust his life and the lives of his men in King Keevan's hands.

And in doing that, he would admit that King Keevan was an honorable, trustworthy king, not the sort of king who would use Blades as assassins.

Lord Norton's gaze latched on Martyn. His mouth tightened as his eyes narrowed. His hand twitched.

No, not just a twitch. A signal.

Martyn spotted two of Lord Norton's archers, deep within his army, raise their bows. Martyn drew in a breath, only to have it catch in his throat in a wracking cough. He couldn't give a warning.

King Keevan's bodyguards threw themselves sideways in front of the king, holding up their large shields. Two arrows thunked against the wood.

Shad stood in his stirrups, whipped out an arrow, and drew it back. But he didn't release.

King Keevan hadn't flinched. "What will it be? Surrender or death?"

Lord Norton drew in a deep breath. His shoulders

sagged. Kneeling, he set his sword on the ground. After a moment, the men behind him did the same, the movement spreading like a breeze waving tall grass.

And that was how to overwhelm with kingly majesty. Martyn struggled to hold a blank expression. It was rather satisfactory to see Lord Norton put in his place.

While King Keevan's men marched forward and herded Lord Norton's men away from the church, the church doors swung open.

Shad urged his horse forward, and Martyn turned his horse to follow, taking the time to pass the king's banner to one of the bodyguards. He nodded to Owen and Kayleigh. "Stay here."

Lord Alistair, his paralyzed hand tied across his chest, greeted Shad. Shad swung down from his horse as Renna hurried from the building and dashed down the front steps. Bandages wrapped around her upper arm and both her hands. "Shadrach! You have to—Martyn?" She skidded to a halt and stared. "Lord Norton said you were dead."

"Nope. Net yet." Martyn tightened his grip on the saddlehorn. It probably would've been polite to dismount and give her a proper greeting, but getting off his horse would involve a lot of falling and crying out in pain. "Where's Leith?"

Renna pointed in the direction of the Spires Canyon. "Somewhere out there."

Martyn scanned the knots of surrendering men. He didn't see the five Blades. "And the Blades? Have you seen them?"

Renna shook her head. "No."

"Then Leith's still alive." Martyn touched the hilt of the

knife strapped to his waist. "The Blades have to be chasing something."

But what shape was Leith in? Did the Blades have him cornered? Was he hiding in some hole, too hurt to even crawl to Stetterly for help?

Shad gripped Renna's shoulders. "We'll find him."

Ranson and Jamie approached. Jamie crossed his arms. "We're coming too."

Shad nodded. "Very well. Jamie, you can ride double with me, and, Ranson, you can double with Martyn until we get to the Canyon."

"You aren't leaving without me." Owen halted his horse next to Martyn.

Martyn shook his head. "No. Absolutely not. This is a Blades' fight, and you'd only get hurt in the middle of it. I need you to look after Kayleigh until I get back."

"I don't think she needs looking after." Owen crossed his arms and shot a glance toward Kayleigh. She had dismounted, her sword drawn, as she stood between the knot of Lord Norton's surrendering soldiers and Martyn.

"You know what I meant." Martyn dragged a hand through his hair. "Just...stay here, all right? I'll be back."

"Fine. But you aren't allowed to die on me, got it? As foolishly stubborn as you are, you're the only brother I got."

"I'll try not to." Martyn leaned forward to give Ranson space to swing up behind him. When Ranson was settled, Martyn trotted his horse past Renna and nodded.

She fixed her gaze on Martyn. "Bring him home."

Her words weighed on Martyn's shoulders. That was his mission. Bring Leith home, dead or alive, no matter what it took. "We will. I promise."

With one last salute, they set off at a canter.

At the rim of the canyon, everyone but Martyn dismounted. He had to save his strength until his skills, whether tracking or fighting, were needed.

Shad knelt and studied the scuffs in the trail leading down. "The tracks are muddled, but it looks like several men on horseback have gone up and down this trail frequently in the last few days."

"Probably the Blades chasing Leith." Jamie rested a hand on the hilt of his knife. His voice, a bit deeper than Martyn remembered, squeaked on a few of the words. Jamie swallowed, as if he'd hoped none of them had noticed.

Based on the twitch to Ranson's mouth and the way Shad turned away, they'd all noticed.

Leaving all but Martyn's horse at the canyon's rim, Shad led them down the trail. The sharp, jagged walls loomed on either side, broken only by slim spires of rock and the harsh spikes of pine trees. At the bottom, the Ondieda River gurgled over the boulders strewn in its path. With the sun sinking below the horizon, shadows deepened into darkness.

Shad scouted a few paces ahead before he beckoned them forward. Ranson's eyes darted back and forth, his mouth a thin line, while Jamie stalked in a half crouch.

"The tracks go that way toward the wall. They're too jumbled for me to tell. I think a herd of horses galloped through here as well." Shad pointed farther down the canyon and toward a cliff, his voice low.

Jamie's eyes widened. "I know where Leith is."

Martyn gaped down at the boy. How had he seen something that Martyn had missed?

Jamie pointed at the cliff. "There's a hidden crevice with

a meadow and cabin back that way. Renna and Brandi showed it to us."

Shad studied the prints in the ground again. "They must have him cornered inside."

"What's the layout like?" Martyn slid from the horse's back. His legs buckled, and he would've fallen if Ranson hadn't steadied him. Martyn nodded his thanks. Not that long ago, he'd been Ranson's First Blade. Ranson had little reason to show any sort of concern now.

"The opening is very narrow, barely big enough for a saddled horse to squeeze through. The walls are sheer, so it would be difficult for someone to ambush us from above. Once inside, the crevice opens into a meadow with a dense stand of pine trees at the entrance. There are fallen boulders around the edges that could provide cover." Jamie squeezed his eyes shut, as if to better picture his memories. "It'll be dark in there already"

Shad gave a sharp nod and straightened. "Do any of these Blades know how to throw knives?"

"No." Martyn limped forward a step. Pain sliced through the soles of his feet and tore all the way up to his thighs. His chest tightened, as if in preparation to begin panting for breath. How could he be tired already? "They'll have two or three stationed by the entrance. The others will be searching for Leith, trying to flush him out. Once they have him in the open, they'll try to take him out all together."

"Which means they'll be looking into the clearing, not watching the entrance." Shad nocked an arrow to his bowstring. "Stay close."

Martyn gave him a slow nod and drew his knives. A year ago, he never would've guessed he'd follow Shadrach Alistair, heir to Walden, into battle, much less that he'd do it willingly.

But this is what Martyn did best. Follow orders. At least Shad was a worthy commander to follow.

Shad stalked toward the crevice with Jamie at his elbow to point out the hidden entrance. Martyn fell in line behind them, his legs trembling with each step. Ranson took up the rear guard.

As they rounded a bend, the crevice opened into a gloom-filled clearing, the dark shapes of pines blocking most of Martyn's view. Shad kept his back to the cliff face, motioning them to do the same.

Martyn searched the gathering darkness for the Blades. Where would they be camped? Most likely in the pine trees where their black clothes would blend in. Tapping Shad's shoulder, Martyn motioned to their left, away from the pine trees. If they were going to sneak past the Blades, that's the direction they should go.

Shad nodded and crept to his left. Jamie, Ranson, and Martyn tiptoed behind him.

Something moved in the shadows of the clearing. Was it Leith? No, it was someone dressed in black and was that...

"Get down!" Shad dove behind a boulder as an arrow cracked against the rock.

Martyn stumbled a few steps and collapsed to his knees behind the boulder with Shad. "Archers. They weren't in the plan."

"No." Shad flexed his fingers against his bowstring. With a deep breath, he straightened, stretched his bow to full draw, and loosed the arrow. He dove back into cover as two more arrows tore the air.

"You didn't get him." Martyn grimaced and gasped at the pain wracking his legs.

"No. And there happen to be three archers out there." Shad nocked another arrow.

"Better and better." Martyn tugged at his hair. Some rescue this was turning out to be.

"Where do you think Leith is?" Shad leaned against the boulder and peered over.

Ducking around the boulder, Martyn scanned the meadow. Leith could be anywhere—holed up behind a boulder, tucked into a small cave in the cliff face.

"I don't know." Martyn adjusted his grip on his knives. What if Leith was too injured to find them? How would Martyn, Shad, Jamie, and Ranson fight off five Blades and three archers by themselves?

Boots thumped to the ground behind Martyn. "You're supposed to be dead."

35

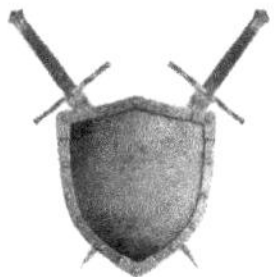

Martyn managed to swivel without falling over. Leith leaned against the cliff face behind them, arms crossed, the hint of a grin playing across his face. The fading light cast shadows in the lines around his mouth and the circles under his eyes.

"Turns out Shad thinks he's fireproof." Martyn shrugged.

Why had he been so worried? Leith had survived the Waste and a week of torture. Five lowly Blades would hardly be a challenge, even if they'd brought a few archers as back up.

Shad huffed. "I'm really getting tired of having to save the two of you all the time. It seems to be all I do lately."

Martyn sank against the boulder, his whole body aching, including his grin. But he couldn't think of anyone, except Leith, he'd rather have guarding his back than Shad.

LEITH'S GRIN FADED AS HE STUDIED MARTYN. SWEAT DRIBBLED from Martyn's hairline and across a pale, drawn face. He knelt on the ground, shivering, and leaned against the boulder to keep himself upright.

This wasn't the time to ask. Not while they still had five Blades and three archers between them and the crevice.

There was only one thing more Leith had to know. "Renna?"

"Safe. Both her and Brandi." Shad's gaze never wavered from the trees, though his stance shifted as if he stood on broken glass. "Lord Norton surrendered."

Martyn hauled himself to a crouch, his muscles straining and shaking. Yet his gaze was steady. "What are your orders, First Blade?"

Leith stilled. "I'm not the First Blade. If anything, you are. You were the last First Blade."

Martyn shook his head. "I was about the worst First Blade ever. All I did was guard a girl too injured to escape, a girl who shouldn't even have been there if I'd done the right thing in the first place. No, you were a First Blade like the First Blade always should've been. The kind of leader men can respect when they follow him because he does the right thing and protects those under him. So what are your orders?"

Leith glanced from Martyn to Ranson, who gave him a slow nod, and Jamie, who gripped his knives tighter.

When Leith turned to Shad, Shad grinned, though he never relaxed his ready stance with his bow and arrow. "You know I'd jump off a cliff if you gave the order. I've done it before."

Leith couldn't stop a grin. Of course, there had been a rope tied around Shad's waist back then.

Yet, that night on the cliff, Shad had been dressed as First Blade Vane. Shad. Martyn. Both fellow First Blades in some way.

And now they were Blades the way the Blades should've been. Not assassins, but something more. Something better.

This fight ended here and now. Whatever the Blades had been had to die in this meadow one way or another.

Leith drew his knives. "Jamie, you're with me. Ranson and Martyn, watch each other's back. Shad, you'll help us best by standing back and providing covering fire. I'm going to give them one chance to surrender. If they don't, we fight."

Grim faced, they all nodded.

Leith slid into place behind a boulder a few paces away from Shad and Martyn. Jamie knelt next to him, tense.

A cold weight settled into Leith's stomach. Fighting and killing these Blades wasn't what he wanted. It would've been better had they taken their chance of freedom and remained banished outside of Acktar's borders.

He would give them one last chance. But if they didn't take it, the fight to come would be to the death. There was no other option. No mercy left to give.

"Archers, Lord Norton has surrendered. You have no reason to stay here. Leave now and you'll not be harmed." Leith peered above the boulder. He could make out two Blades and their archers at the far side of the clearing. Two Blades moved among the trees. Where was the last Blade and archer?

Jamie tapped his arm and pointed. The other Blade and

archer crept through the boulders to their left, trying to get around behind Leith and the others.

"All of you." Leith fixed his gaze on the stand of trees. "If any of you wish to leave, do so now. Leave Acktar, and I'll not follow. But I promise you here and now that if any of you remain behind, I will hunt you down, and I will kill you."

The harsh words grated, even in his own ears. He didn't want to kill again. But the Blades had pushed far enough. Lord Norton, and through him these Blades, had hurt Renna. They'd hurt Martyn. This couldn't continue, and either the Blades died here in battle or, if Leith and Shad somehow managed to capture them, they died in Nalgar Castle's courtyard.

A Blade sauntered from the treeline. Quinten Daas based on his swagger. "I don't believe you'll kill us. You're too tame for that. How do you like being Lady Faythe's pet? I hear you'll do all sort of tricks just for one of her glances."

Did Daas really think such childish insults would rattle Leith? Especially not with Renna safe under King Keevan's protection. "Last chance. Leave."

"Do you think you scare us? You only have one other fighter who *might* be able to stand against one of us. The rest are either boys scared of their own blood or too injured to walk straight." Daas laughed a harsh, choking sort of sound. "Besides, between us and the archers Lord Norton lent us, we outnumber you. You're not going to survive this one."

That was it, then. Leith didn't feel the ice that had spurred him as a Blade, though the iron still remained.

All it took was a twitch of a hand, a nod of his head. Shad released an arrow, and Daas dodged behind a tree, the arrow missing him by inches.

Martyn and Ranson darted to the left, cutting off the Blade and archer circling that way.

Leith dashed forward, Jamie's footsteps crunching in time with his. They ducked into the trees. Leith crouched, holding his breath to listen.

Was that a faint crunching sound?

Daas kicked out from behind the tree. Leith spun to avoid the boot Daas had aimed at his knee and struck downward with his knife. Daas shoved his hand aside, his other hand carving his knife upward toward Leith's stomach. Leith blocked the strike and twisted Daas's hand away from him.

Steel clanged on steel somewhere behind him. Jamie, guarding Leith's back.

Stepping in closer, he got a boot behind Daas's foot, and he rammed an elbow into Daas's shoulder. Daas toppled to the ground.

"Leave. This isn't a fight you can win." Leith stepped back. Somewhere behind him, a body thunked to the ground, pine needles crackling. Jamie or the Blade he'd been fighting? Leith couldn't turn around to look.

Daas swore, jumped to his feet, and charged.

No more mercy. No more chances. Leith had to end this and help Jamie. He sidestepped, shoved Daas's arm away with a forearm, and plunged his knife into Daas's chest.

Daas's eyes widened. "You…" He collapsed to the ground.

Pine needles crackled. Leith spun, his knife raised. Crossley charged him, one knife aimed at Leith's chest, the other at his stomach.

An arrow buried itself in Crossley's throat. Crossley choked, grabbed at the arrow, and fell at Leith's feet.

Shad stood in the center of the clearing near the cabin, Blizzard and Valor snorting and prancing behind him.

"Shad!" Leith pointed. Off to Shad's left, the dark shape of a man, an arrow nocked to a drawn bow, stepped from behind a boulder.

Shad wheeled, sidestepped, and shot in nearly the same motion. The archer lurched and fell.

Jamie picked himself off the ground, a cut oozing blood along his hairline. He adjusted his grip on his knife and regained his position a few steps behind Leith.

Two Blades and an archer down.

The archer Shad shot should've had a Blade with him. Leith searched for movement in the rocks.

Blizzard snorted, his ears swiveling first toward the rocks to the left where Martyn and Ranson had gone, then back to the right.

There. Leith rested a hand on Jamie's shoulder and pointed at the boulder where the Blade had disappeared. "Head straight for that boulder. Keep his eyes on you."

"Got it." Jamie ran forward.

Leith crept into the darkness. Somewhere behind him, another arrow hissed and slammed into a body with a dull thunk.

He circled along the ledges in the cliff face. Rough rock grated against his fingers. Dust whispered beneath his boots. The darkness closed around him like a familiar cloak. This, he understood. Darkness. Prey.

He eased into position behind the Blade. Perhaps he could take this one alive.

The Blade sprang toward Jamie. Jamie deflected his knife, but the Blade's momentum took them to the ground.

Jamie struggled, but the Blade's bigger size pinned him to the ground.

Leith lunged and dragged the Blade off Jamie. The Blade whipped around, his knife aimed at Leith's stomach.

Former Blade Offen.

Leith grabbed Offen's wrist and stepped forward, planting a boot behind Offen's leg. Leith whipped his left elbow into Offen's face.

Offen reeled backwards and tripped over Leith's foot. He fell onto his back but rolled, coming to his feet with knives in both of his hands. Leith leapt backward, but the move put him off balance. Offen pivoted and kicked, catching Leith just above his left knee.

His weak leg. Leith crumpled to the ground. A rock struck his back, knocking the breath from his chest.

Offen pounced, pinning one of Leith's hands to the ground. Leith swept aside one of Offen's knives, but the other stabbed down at him. With his arm trapped, Leith couldn't stop it.

Jamie dove from the darkness, grabbed Offen's arm, and plunged his knife into Offen's back.

Offen gasped and collapsed to the ground, wracking with wet coughs. As Leith clambered to his feet, Offen's coughs grew weaker and stilled.

Leith gripped Jamie's shoulder. "You all right?"

Jamie nodded and swallowed, though his shoulder shuddered beneath Leith's hand. If only Leith hadn't had to ask Jamie to fight this battle. Hopefully, it would be the last. Maybe this time, they would have peace.

Straightening, Jamie turned toward the clearing. "Do you think that's all of them?"

Across the way, two shapes tottered from the rocks, one leaning on the other. Martyn and Ranson.

Shad still stood in the center, an arrow aimed at a black-clad figure with his hands in the air.

"Please, don't shoot! I surrender! Please, don't!" John Uldiney, the youngest of the banished Blades, knelt on the ground, knives glinting in a pile.

"Yes. I think that's all of them." Leith strode toward Uldiney, careful not to get in Shad's way. When he halted a few feet away, Uldiney didn't move.

There had been enough bloodshed. Leith wasn't ready for yet another execution in a courtyard. Even if this was the Blade that had hurt Renna. "If I let you leave, will you promise never to return to Acktar?"

Uldiney bobbed his head. "Yes. Just please don't kill me. I didn't really want to return. Honest. But Daas said we had to. That it was the only way."

Leith wasn't sure he believed him, but Uldiney wasn't much of a threat by himself. Nor would he return after seeing the rest of the Blades killed within a few minutes. "I pray whatever life you find outside of Acktar is better than the one you've had here. Now, go."

Uldiney hesitated. "I...might need my knives. And I don't have a horse. You drove mine away."

"There's a horse outside the entrance." Shad used his bow and arrow to gesture in that direction. "You may have that one, as well as the provisions in the saddlebag."

Uldiney nodded and glanced at his knives again.

Leith tensed, his knives held ready. "Pick them up slowly. Wherever you go, don't turn back to killing. You'll just end up dead sooner or later."

Uldiney bent, scooped his knives from the ground, and fled as if he feared Leith would change his mind. Leith didn't relax until Uldiney disappeared in the darkness of the crevice.

It was truly over this time. The Blades were gone.

"Leith!"

Leith whirled. Ranson grasped Martyn under the arms, staggering under his weight. Martyn's head slumped forward.

Leith dropped his knife and dashed to them. He helped lower Martyn to the ground and swept a glance over him looking for wounds. In the darkness, he couldn't make anything out. "Was he injured?"

Ranson shook his head. "I didn't think so. But maybe. I didn't see. I..."

Shad knelt beside Leith and shook his head. "He was badly burned in Flayin Falls. I'm surprised it took this long before the pain got to him."

Lord Norton told the truth when he said he'd left Martyn behind to die by burning. Yet, even after being badly burned, Martyn had still come to rescue Leith.

Whatever betrayal Leith had done to Martyn, whatever torture Martyn had done to Leith, it had all been repaid, blood for blood, torture for torture.

Would it be enough? Had enough blood been spilled and enough pain shared?

Shad rested a hand on Leith's shoulder. "Let's load Martyn on a horse and get you home."

36

Renna eyed the man laid on the stretcher between two bearers. A bad cut slashed across his leg, but the blood was only drooling, not spurting. She pointed to her right. "Set him over there."

The bearers nodded and carried the man past her, laying him down at the end of a long row of wounded.

Behind and beside Renna, the wounded, mostly from Lord Norton's men and some from Stetterly, rested in rows on the hill beyond the town. Those with medical experience among King Keevan's soldiers assisted Michelle while more of King Keevan's men fetched blankets and water to make the wounded comfortable. Other soldiers stood guard.

With her hands raw and bandaged, Renna couldn't help the healers as she had after the battle at Nalgar. Instead, she had forced herself to sort through the chaos. Organize the wounded. Make sure torches and fires were lit. Set the townsfolk to cleaning up the mess of battle.

She searched the horizon yet again. No movement. No

sign of Leith and the others. How long would it take to rescue Leith? Surely it shouldn't take this long, should it?

What if something had gone wrong? What if Leith had been hurt or killed?

No, she mustn't think about that. She couldn't give in to her worst fears. Not now.

Especially not when she wasn't the only one worried. A few yards away, the girl Kayleigh sat cross-legged on the ground and scrubbed at her already-beyond-clean sword. Next to her, Brandi chattered with barely a pause for breath. Apparently Brandi and Kayleigh knew each other from the war, or something like that.

A few yards away, Martyn's brother paced, muttering about how he was never going to let Martyn out of his sight again.

Renna wrapped her arms over her stomach while she waited for the next pair of stretcher bearers. What would she do if she lost Leith now? Who would sit up with Brandi on nights when the nightmares of war became too much? Who would Jamie look up to as an older brother or who would understand Ranson when the guilt plagued him?

Owen stilled. Renna followed his gaze. Four figures crested the far hill, leading two horses. One of the horses had a bundle draped over its back.

Leith. Renna grasped her skirts, hiked them to her knees, and ran. The whole town, Lord Alistair's men, and King Keevan's army would see her act undignified. But they didn't matter. Not if the body draped over that horse was Leith's.

One of the figures handed the horse's reins to someone else and broke into a run of his own, a hitch in a stride.

When they met, there wasn't laughter or tears or spinning

hugs. She tucked her head against his shoulder, and he simply held her, pressing his face into her hair. It was a long moment, filled with warmth and a steady heartbeat, the kind of moment Renna would face any battle just to savor once again.

She pulled away and began patting his shirt. "Where are you hurt?"

"I'm not."

"Of course you are. You always get hurt." She eyed his dust-colored clothing. In the half-light cast from the torches of Stetterly behind her, she couldn't see any darker splotches of blood. At least, none that looked like they belonged to him.

"Not this time. I—" Leith grabbed her hands and held them up, inspecting the bandages. "What happened?"

"Rope burn." Renna tugged her hands free from his grip. If Leith wasn't the one hurt, then who was draped over the horse?

She glanced past Leith to the body slung over Valor's back. Martyn's head hung limply. Shad reached a hand to stop Kayleigh and Owen, forcing them to skid to a halt.

Renna curled her fingers into Leith's shirt. "Martyn?"

"He's alive, just unconscious." Leith rested his hands over hers. "The Blades are gone."

"Good." She wouldn't ask how. Not yet, anyway.

"Leith. Renna." Shad's voice had a tight, low tone to it. When Renna stepped back from Leith, Shad tipped his head at something behind her.

Renna turned. Stetterly's townsfolk gathered before the church building, the crowd growing with each passing second. A chill settled into her chest.

She slid her hand into Leith's, and he squeezed her fingers so gently her rope burns didn't even hurt. Together, they strode down the hill toward the line of men waiting at the edge of town, their arms crossed. Behind the men, the women gripped their children and scowled.

One farmer stepped forward. "He isn't welcome here. He's a Blade."

"A Blade killed my wife!"

"And my brother!"

"My father!"

The shouts came harder and faster, thrown like stones, battering her. How had she ever thought she and Leith could simply settle down into a happy life? Leith's past wouldn't let them.

"Blades killed your parents! How could you think about marrying him?"

The yells escalated. Fists pounded at the sky, a thunder building before the storm broke in all its fury.

Beyond the town, Lord Alistair and King Keevan moved toward the shouting with groups of men at their back. But would more men calm the storm or infuriate it?

Beside her, Leith drew in a breath. Renna clamped a hand on his arm. Something told her words from Leith would only stir the crowd.

No, this was her moment to speak. She was Lady Faythe. This was her town, and if a riot started now, it would be because she failed to stand when it mattered.

She forced herself to let go of Leith's arm and step away from him. To make her words count, she couldn't lean on Leith while she said them. She squeezed her aching fingers into fists, lifted her chin, and prayed for courage and a steady voice. "Silence, everyone!"

For some reason, the townsfolk listened to her. Her knees shook. What was she going to say now that she had their attention? She swept her gaze over the mass of people. Standing off to one side, Brandi met her gaze and nodded.

Renna could do this. She had to. She had faced Respen in his own castle. Surely she could face her own townsfolk, no matter how angry. "We have all lost much to Respen and his Blades. Blades killed my father, my mother, my uncles, aunts, and cousins. I have lost just as much as any of you."

That got a few of the townsfolk shifting. How could they forget what she had lost too? Her parents. Uncle Abel. Aunt Mara.

She swallowed and drew in a deep breath. Her head buzzed with the weight of so many eyes on her. She focused on a patch of star-filled sky above their heads. "Last winter, a wounded Blade stumbled into the kitchen at Stetterly Manor. As a healer, I made the decision to tend his wound. That Blade was Third Blade Leith Torren, and at the time, he'd never failed King Respen."

She heard the murmurs in the crowd and saw the stir, but she couldn't concentrate on that. Couldn't stop this story now that it was being told. The truth had to come out this time, once and for all. Then she'd deal with the consequences.

Half-turning to see both the townsfolk and Leith where he stood a few yards away, she forced her voice to remain calm. "Leith, show them your marks."

Not looking at her, Leith grasped the end of his right sleeve and rolled it to his shoulder. In the torchlight, the rows of scars shone against his skin, the newer ones near his elbow more visible than the faint ones at his shoulder.

Thirty-seven marks, and Renna knew the tale behind all of them. Leith had been right. The knowledge did stiffen her spine in this moment.

The murmuring grew louder. A few shouts tore from the back of the crowd. Some of the men clenched their fists, as if preparing to charge Leith and pound their revenge into him.

Not if she could help it. She sent them the best glare she could manage. Perhaps it wasn't as stern as Lady Lorraine's, but it quieted most of the unrest. "God used what little kindness I gave and Brandi's stories to touch Leith's heart. Leith turned against King Respen and joined the Resistance. He risked his own life again and again for me and for Acktar."

The crowd facing her didn't budge.

How could the townsfolk remain stone-faced at hearing this? Why wasn't it changing their opinion?

If she closed her eyes, she could see Vane's knife plunging into Leith's shoulder, Respen's knife into his leg. Hear the crack of the whip, the rattle of chains, and the screams echoing off dark, stone walls. Feel the anguish in Leith's eyes as he fought his best friend.

But the townsfolk couldn't see and hear the past. They hadn't witnessed what she had.

But perhaps they still could.

"Leith, show them the rest of your scars." Her words had a bite, a cold, she hadn't intended.

His eyes still focused on the ground by his feet, Leith pulled his shirt over his head and let it drop to the ground. The ridged scars from the burns blazed across his torso from his chest down to his stomach, patches of white and pink. A splotch at his shoulder marked the knife wound. Jagged welts and scars twisted across his back.

"Look at his scars. That was his reward for his actions. Torture." Renna pointed. Surely the townsfolk would see how hard he'd fought, how much he'd given. His heart, his courage, etched into his skin.

Silence had fallen across the crowd. Even the breeze held its breath.

Leith remained as still as the crowd, hands at his sides, head bowed as if he couldn't face their accusations.

But he should be able to face them. He had no reason to hang his head. Not now.

"Those scars are proof that God has changed him. Whatever Leith did as a Blade, it has been paid for with Christ's blood." As she spoke, Renna approached Leith. He probably sensed her, but he still didn't look up. She rested her hands on either side of his face and tipped his head up. "For that reason, he should hang his head in shame to no one."

Their eyes met, and the tiniest of smiles tipped one corner of Leith's mouth. He rested his hands on her waist but didn't pull her closer. Probably a small concession to propriety, considering he still lacked a shirt. Something she was working hard not to notice.

"Thank you." He murmured as he kissed her forehead. "But I think it's my turn to speak now."

She barely kept her knees from giving out. A tremble worked its way down her spine and into her fingers. Whatever anger or courage or determination that had kept her speaking coherently for the past few minutes was fading. "Good. Because I reached my limit of pretending to be confident for the day."

When he turned to face the crowd of townsfolk, tucking her hand in his as if to hide her shaking from all the watching eyes, Renna let part of her relax. Whatever the future held, they would survive it.

Together.

RENNA'S FINGERS TREMBLED IN LEITH'S. SHE'D GIVEN THE LAST measure of her courage to make that speech to the townsfolk. Leith couldn't mess up what she'd done now.

Too bad he couldn't grab his shirt and pull it back over his head to hide his marks. His skin prickled with the eyes counting his marks, cataloging his scars. All his secrets bared for them to judge and find him lacking.

But, as Renna said, he didn't have to hang his head in shame. There in the Tower, he'd been worthy. Wasn't he just as worthy now?

He straightened his shoulders. "I understand why you don't want me here. The Blades did terrible things to Acktar. I did terrible things. If you wish, I will tell you the whole truth and answer all your questions."

Perhaps in the truth, they would find healing. He had, when he'd learned the truth about his mother's death.

The townsfolk remained silent. Still. That was probably better than yelling.

He had one last thing that might sway them. "Knowing you wouldn't accept my past, Renna and I decided long ago that when we marry, I won't become the lord of Stetterly. Rule over this town will remain with Renna."

That started the murmuring and shifting again. One of the men glanced at Renna. "Is this true?"

Squeezing Leith's hand tightly, Renna nodded. "Leith is the one who suggested it. I will retain the full duties and title as lady of Stetterly."

The townsfolk muttered among themselves.

Sheriff Allen stepped forward, planted his feet next to Renna, and faced the crowd. "I once tried to kill this Blade. But over these past few months, I have come to respect him. His preparations for this latest attack saved this town. For that reason, I stand with him now."

Leith raised his eyebrows. A year ago, he never would've guessed the sheriff of Stetterly would stand at his side.

Michelle Allen joined her father, sending Ranson a smile as she did.

The rustle of footsteps sounded behind him. Shad and Lord Alistair joined him. For a moment, Lord Alistair rested his good hand on Leith's shoulder. "A year ago, Leith Torren became my spy in the Blades. Now, he is like another son to me. I would trust him with my life and the lives of my family."

A son. Leith sucked in a breath. Something deep inside him—something that had been broken his entire life— stopped aching.

King Keevan stepped past Lord Alistair and Shad. Leith's stomach clenched with a blizzard's ice. King Keevan's words would carry the most weight of anyone's, and he had no reason to speak for Leith.

The torch light glinted down the length of King Keevan's scar, from his cheek and down his neck. Evidence of Leith's knife.

When King Keevan spoke, his voice rasped, another reminder of that night and all the reasons King Keevan had for clinging to his anger. "Five years ago, I lost my entire family to Blades. I nearly lost my life because of Leith Torren."

Leith swallowed. If not for Renna's tight grip on his hand, he would've hung his head again.

"But," King Keevan turned to face Leith, "I have seen the courage in him. For his actions at Nalgar Castle, I pardoned him, and for that, he has the full rights of any citizen here. More than that, I have forgiven him."

Really? Leith studied King Keevan's bright blue eyes. Did he mean it?

King Keevan stuck out his hand. "And I welcome him into my family."

Slowly, Leith took it. King Keevan's hand was firm, the grip of someone who trained with his sword relentlessly.

Before Leith could react, King Keevan pulled him in for a guy hug, their hands clasped between their bodies. Leith stiffened. This had to be the most awkward hug ever. But that wasn't the point. All it was meant to be was a symbol.

"Let's never do this again." King Keevan hissed.

"Agreed." Leith muttered. As soon as he could, he stepped back.

Renna had her hands fisted in her skirt as she faced the crowd. When she spoke, her voice was fierce. So beautifully fierce. "Do you trust your sheriff? How about your king? Or me? You trusted me during battle. So trust me now. I am going to marry Leith Torren. You can either accept him or both of us will leave Stetterly. The choice is yours."

Leith was never going to deserve a girl like Renna. Not if he fought a hundred battles and carried a thousand scars.

Brandi marched forward, rolling her eyes. "And don't think you're going to plant the lady of Stetterly title on my head as a replacement. I'm sticking with Renna and Leith."

That widened the eyes of the men in the crowd, as if Brandi and Renna had just threatened their livelihood or something. Leith got the feeling he was missing something.

Shad leaned over and whispered, "They'd lose their representation in the Gathering."

Leith nodded. Now he understood. The Gathering of Nobles voted on things like taxes and land distribution. Without representation, King Keevan could do whatever he wanted to Stetterly without anyone standing in his way. And if they'd just kicked out Renna, he wasn't about to be kind.

One of the men strode forward. "Seems we don't have a choice, do we?"

"No, you don't." Renna slipped her hand into Leith's once again.

"Stop and think for a moment. Seriously." Brandi huffed, crossed her arms, and planted her feet in front of Leith. "Leith has been living here for six months. If he was going to go all Blade and kill everything in sight, you'd think he would've done it long before now. What did he do? Hmm... built a church. Harvested the crops. Protected you from Blades. Seems to me you should be the ones thanking him for staying here."

Leith rested his free hand on her shoulder. Only Brandi. He couldn't ask for a better sister.

One of the women stepped forward and swatted her husband's arm. "Stop being bull-headed. Have you forgotten how Daniel Grayce spent hours helping you rebuild our dugout after it collapsed under all the snow?"

"And shoveled the snow from my door every day." Another woman, one of the war widows, straightened her shoulders, her hands resting on the shoulders of her two young daughters.

A young man crossed his arms and grinned. "And chased away those Rovers during the Corn Festival. Without killing any of them."

Among the crowd, shoulders relaxed. The frowns faded, and in some cases, smiles returned.

"Now that this is settled, please return to your tasks." Renna waved her hand toward the town, the dugouts and church dark against the brilliance of all the torches. "We have a lot of work to do to set our town to rights."

As the crowd dispersed, Leith breathed out a long breath. After months of dreading this moment, he'd survived, and Stetterly now knew the truth. Maybe he wasn't considered one of them yet, but maybe someday.

Shad stooped, picked up Leith's shirt, and tossed it to him. "You Blades have no sense of propriety."

Leith grinned as he tugged his shirt on. Finally. "The bossy lord's son is back. And here I thought I was the leader."

King Keevan glanced between him and Shad. A twitch to his mouth might've been a smile. "You might be *a* leader, but you will never be *the* Leader. And don't forget it."

Leith's grin widened, and he saluted King Keevan. Perhaps not all of the hurt was gone, but this was a start at least.

37

Martyn was seriously tired of waking up in some random bed, in pain and missing his clothes.

At least this time, the bed was warm and comfortable, not the cot in the tent or a jolting one in the back of a wagon. Was Kayleigh there, waiting for him to wake up? He let himself picture her face, framed with her gleaming, brown hair and lit with her soft smile. There was something nice thinking about her sitting there, caring about what happened to him.

Well, it probably was time to get around to opening his eyes and finding out. Martyn pried his eyelids open, blinking at the brilliance stabbing through his eyelashes.

Once he could see, he turned his head. Someone sat in the chair a few feet away, but it wasn't Kayleigh. Martyn couldn't help the disappointed frown that crossed his face.

Leith grinned and stood. Turning the chair around, he sat and leaned his arms on its back. "I know I'm not the first person you wanted to see when you woke."

"No, I was hoping for someone a bit prettier and female." Martyn struggled to hold a scowl in place.

Leith's smirk grew. "She'll be here soon. She's at church with Renna and your brother. It's been months since she was able to attend a church service, so I volunteered to stay behind with you."

"You could've gone. I would've been fine."

Leith shrugged. "I think the townspeople need a bit more time to get used to having a Blade in church with them."

Martyn nodded. As he'd suspected, Lord Norton had wasted no time in informing Stetterly about Leith's past.

"I heard from Owen that you might be joining us in church eventually."

"Eventually. It takes a bit of getting used to." How many years had it been since Martyn had gone to a church service with his parents? Too long.

Martyn pushed himself onto his elbows and tried to scoot himself higher on the bed with his feet. Agony raced up his skin, needling into his toes. He flopped back onto the pillow, fighting a cry of pain. "Blistering soapsuds, that hurts."

Leith raised an eyebrow. "Soapsuds? No swearing?"

"If you'd ever washed your mouth out with soap, you'd know what I meant. Not that the taste is horrible, it just never goes away." Martyn grimaced and forced himself to take deep breaths to steady the pain thundering through his body. "I really don't understand your fascination with heroics. Next time, you can keep them. They hurt too much."

Leith's smirk crossed his face again. "When Kayleigh returns, you might understand the appeal."

"Maybe." Martyn adjusted the pillow behind his head.

Leith was right about one thing. Thanks to Kayleigh, Martyn understood a lot of things. If Martyn had to choose between saving Kayleigh and betraying Leith, what would he have done?

Martyn would never have that choice. If their roles had been reversed, Leith would've acted much like Owen. Follow with barely a question until he could get an explanation.

Instead, Martyn had been so scared to lose Leith as he'd once lost Owen that he'd nearly done just that.

Leith sobered and eyed Martyn. "Renna, Michelle, and Sierra's healer all agree you need to rest. Looks like you'll be stuck in Stetterly for a few months to recover."

Martyn folded his hands behind his head, matching Leith's casual tone. "I don't know. It's a nice place you got here. I don't think I'll mind sticking around a while."

Perhaps they couldn't start over. Too much had happened. But they could move on.

Because that was what brothers did.

Footsteps padded on the floorboards outside the room a moment before Kayleigh peeked inside. She wore the green shirt with a black skirt Martyn didn't recognize. Probably something she borrowed, considering the hem fell only midway down her shins. Her hair curled in glinting brown waves over her shoulder, and Martyn got a strange urge to run his fingers through it to see if it was as sleek and soft as it looked.

He had it bad. Any worse, and he'd start spouting some of the romantic nonsense he'd heard Leith tell Renna in the Tower.

Leith grinned and stood. "I'll see if Renna needs anything."

In other words, *I'm giving you time alone with her. Don't bungle it up.*

Kayleigh turned the chair the right way, scooted it closer to the bed, and took a seat. She stared at her lap, fidgeting with the fabric of her skirt.

Don't bungle this up. Yeah, right. As if Leith hadn't tripped all over his words trying to talk to Renna. Martyn would rather face Respen's knives again. It was safer.

He cleared his throat. "Uh, how was church?"

"Nice. I'd forgotten how much I missed it." Kayleigh's head remained bent.

Martyn fought a scowl. Talking was hard enough even when he could read her expression. How was he going to say the right thing if he couldn't see her reaction?

"I..." Kayleigh trailed off, and Martyn bit his tongue. Good thing he hadn't started talking. She hadn't finished yet. She smoothed her skirt over her knees. "I told Lady Faythe who I was. She gave me a hug."

Martyn owed Renna for that. "That's Renna for you. She cried over Respen's death, if you could believe it."

"She told me about him, and what he'd told her about Aunt Clarisse. Doesn't change things, but it helps." Kayleigh's fingers kept curling and uncurling until all Martyn wanted to do was grab them to hold her still. She hunched forward. "She also told me I could stay at Stetterly if I wanted."

Martyn's heart spooked into his throat. Did Kayleigh want to stay at Stetterly? And would she like him to stay as well? "Do you want to?"

"I don't know. I mean, it kind of depends on if you...well, you can do what you want, but I'd..." She shook her head and hunched further. "I guess you won our deal after all. After what happened in Flayin Falls, I can't go back there. But I don't know…"

Even Martyn recognized a *must make some kind of commitment* moment.

Was this what he wanted? What did he want, anyway? A home and a wife and a pack of screaming children? Or did he want to go back to wandering?

No, he didn't want the wandering and loneliness. And Kayleigh was…well, she was Kayleigh. Strong. Tough. Besides, he didn't know what she wanted. She might just want to be friends, and wasn't thinking anything beyond that at all.

Best just to get it all out, and deal with the consequences. "I'm stuck here for a while. But when I can, I'll take you wherever you want to go, whether that is Nalgar Castle or Walden or the farthest reaches of the Sheered Rock Hills. But if it's all the same to you, I'd like to stay here. Or Surgis and visit here often."

"Your family is here."

"Yes, it is." It was good to say that. Leith and Renna, they were his family. Martyn didn't know where Owen would end up. Probably Surgis. Or maybe he'd go wherever Martyn did. Little brothers could be worse than burrs.

She finally looked up. She smiled, but something in her eyes remained hesitant. "I hope you were planning on a chaperone for all that traveling. We were barely proper with the whole separate cabin thing. Traveling together would be beyond what even I would consider proper."

Why did his tongue have to feel so thick and sticky in his

mouth? He swallowed. "Well, in a couple of years, maybe we won't need a chaperone anymore."

Her smile bloomed all the way into her eyes. "That sounds all right by me. If you're saying what I think you're saying. And, if you are—and you had better be, because I'd owe you a punch in the jaw if you were implying anything else—I expect a better proposal than that when the time comes."

He couldn't help the grin that tugged at his mouth, even though it probably looked just as lovesick and loopy as Leith's did when he looked at Renna. "Don't worry. I'll get Leith's advice. Obviously he did something right because Renna actually agreed to marry him."

Martyn gave in to the temptation to take her hand in his and still its nervous fidgeting. Her fingers fit in his, warm and rough with callouses.

She slid off the chair and knelt on the floor beside the bed, putting their faces level. This close, he could see the faint sprinkling of freckles on her nose and the varying shades of brown in her eyes. He stretched his free hand and gently ran his fingers through one lock of hair. Yep, just as soft as he'd imagined.

All right, *now* he understood Leith's thing with heroics. If Kayleigh kept looking at him like this, he might be tempted to go out and do something brave and foolish just to keep that look on her face.

"I guess it's a deal then. I'll get around to asking that certain question one of these years if you can manage to put up with me." Martyn trailed his fingers from her hair to her cheek. "Though I think this is the kind of deal that needs to be sealed with a kiss."

"It might be. The kiss might even be a dealbreaker." She leaned in closer, so close he caught a hint of that floral something scent in her hair. It smelled like the soap had tasted, and for some reason, he was starting to like it.

And when he kissed her, he finally understood why Leith didn't care who saw him kissing Renna. Because nothing else mattered at that moment.

When they pulled back, Martyn glanced over her shoulder. The doorway remained empty. "Bother. I was hoping Leith would stumble in. I owe him a few awkward moments."

Kayleigh sat back on her heels and rested her hands on her hips. "Really? *That's* what you were thinking about while we were kissing?"

"Well, I had to distract myself somehow. There are temptations, you know. We have to have some propriety." Martyn fought his grin. He was going to enjoy bantering with her for the rest of their lives. Especially when all he could think about was planting a kiss at the end of that reddening nose.

"Martyn Hamish! You—You—"

"What has my brother done now?" Owen leaned a shoulder against the doorjamb.

"He's being a nuisance." Kayleigh hauled herself to her feet and flopped into the chair.

Martyn didn't try to deny it.

This was where he belonged. With Leith, Owen, and especially Kayleigh.

With his family.

EPILOGUE

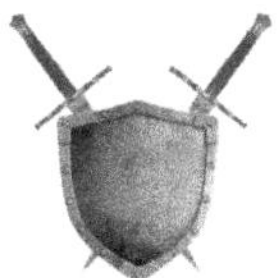

Leith paced back and forth across the kitchen of the cabin he would soon share with Renna. Two steps one way, three steps another.

"Seriously, Leith. Sit down. You're going to be on your feet enough once the wedding starts." Shad sat on a bench leaning against the wall, his legs propped up on the table.

Martyn huffed from his own seat near the fireplace. "It's not like Renna won't show up. What do you have to be nervous about?"

Nothing. That didn't help the tension curling in Leith's stomach. So many things could go wrong. Rovers could attack. Some of the townsfolk might have second thoughts about their lady marrying a former Blade. King Keevan could change his mind about welcoming Leith into the family. Thanks to Lord Norton's attack, the wedding had already been delayed three weeks so Lord Alistair and King Keevan could escort the prisoners to Nalgar Castle and arrest Dean Westin.

When a knock thumped on the door, Leith spun on his heels. It creaked open, and King Keevan stepped inside. He eyed Leith. "I might change my mind about having you for a cousin if you keep drawing knives on me."

"Sorry." Leith forced himself to relax and slide the knife he'd drawn back into its sheath.

Shad dropped his feet to the floor. "Martyn and I will be outside." He crossed the room and helped Martyn stagger upright. "Come on. We can sit on the porch."

Martyn grimaced. "Good. Because I have to save all my standing for the ceremony."

Leith crossed his arms and watched them go. Something was up. Shad and Martyn were acting like they knew why King Keevan was showing up here two hours before the wedding was to start.

King Keevan sank onto one of the benches by the table, set a saddlebag on the floor, and waved at the seat across from him. "Sit."

Leith slid onto the bench, his back cramping with tension. "What's this about?"

Something thumped from the bedroom off the kitchen. Voices echoed from the room along with more hollow thunks.

Leith reached for his knife, tensing. "What was that?"

"A few of my men are hauling Renna's wedding gift through the back door. Ignore them." King Keevan rested his elbows on the tabletop. His tight-lipped expression pulled his scar taut across his cheek. "You know I have little reason to admire the Blades. But Acktar was the safest it had ever been under them, and since they've been gone, Rovers have once again caused trouble."

King Keevan called the Blades *them*, not *you*. Did that mean he didn't see Leith only as one of the Blades? Leith flexed his fingers on his knife as more shuffling and voices came from the other room. What were King Keevan's men doing over there?

"There's little I can do with how things are now. The town sheriffs can gather a posse to track down Rovers, but they usually lose the trail. I can send the army, but the country has had enough of raiding armies. What Acktar needs is a group who can patrol the long stretches of prairie between towns. They need the Blades."

"What?" Leith sat bolt upright. Was King Keevan really suggesting that? Had Lord Norton been right that King Keevan planned to have his own assassins?

A ghost of a smile played across King Keevan's face. "Thought that'd get your attention. No, I don't want assassins. I don't want the Blades as they were. I want the Blades as they should've—could've—been had they been under a different king with a different First Blade."

The Blades as they should've been. Martyn had said something similar down in the Spires Canyon. "What does this have to do with me?"

"I want you to lead it." King Keevan's jaw worked, as if he had to fight to say those words.

"Me?" Leith wasn't so sure about that. "Shad's a more natural leader."

"I already asked him." King Keevan shifted on his bench. "But he said no. He has other duties as the heir of Walden. He can't dedicate his life to it as you can. But, he would be willing to join. He was getting bored."

"And Martyn? He was doing something similar for you these past few months."

King Keevan heaved a sigh. "Asked him too. But he said he'd only join if you were First Blade."

Leith resisted the urge to get up and pace once again. This felt...right. More right than sitting at Stetterly farming. The beat of the fight, the burn of the chase, still pumped in his blood.

Was this what God was calling him to do? To use the skills he'd gained in the Blades to be a protector?

"Still, why me? You don't like me." Leith leaned his elbows on the table. He didn't dare hope. Not yet.

King Keevan traced his scar with a finger. "No, I don't. But I don't have to. I only have to respect you. You're the same age as my youngest brother-in-law, yet I would never ask him to do what you've done. You're good at what you do. And politically, once you marry Renna, you'll be in the rather unique position of being neither a lord nor under the authority of one. In other words, you're the best man for the job."

If it was only up to him, Leith would've said yes right then. But he had more than himself to consider now. "I'll have to talk to Renna."

"If you keep saying stuff like that, you'll have a long, happy marriage." King Keevan's face split into something that could've been a smirk. He hauled two massive books from the saddlebag and thunked them onto the table. "If you agree, I'd like you to begin reading these books right away. One is a history of Acktar, and the other is Acktar's laws."

Leith stared at the books. King Keevan expected him to

read all that? "You do realize I'm getting married in a couple of hours?"

"Yes, of course." King Keevan's smirk widened, and his eyes twinkled. "I realized something the other day. Yes, you're joining the family, and I'm stuck with you. But, you're also stuck with me. That means no matter how much I torment you, you have no choice but to take it. Ask Renna. I'm very good at tormenting cousins."

Leith eyed him. Was King Keevan joking or serious? He was grinning but that didn't mean anything. "I...will start reading them right away."

"While Lord Alistair, Shadrach, Martyn, you, and I are all in the same place, I would like to discuss how to implement this idea, especially the measures we can take to prevent this from turning into the king's personal assassins." King Keevan touched his scar again. "I would like to put together a thorough proposal I can present to the Gathering of Nobles next month. I'd like you to be there."

"Do you think they'll accept a Blade leading this?" Leith's back stiffened at the thought of facing the Gathering of Nobles. Half of them would be out for his blood when the truth was known.

"Doesn't matter if they like it or not. We'll talk them around. Like I said, you're the best we have." King Keevan shrugged, his thumb still absently tracing his scar. "Besides, we can't hide the truth of your past any longer. When Lord Norton is placed on trial, the first thing he'll do is point out I pardoned three Blades in hopes of turning the Gathering's favor toward him. I plan to head him off by presenting the truth about you before he has a chance."

Leith released a long breath. He didn't have a choice.

One way or another, the truth would come out. He had faced it in Stetterly. He could handle facing it before all of Acktar as well.

A twitch of King Keevan's smile returned. "Besides, one might think you had the Gathering rigged. By the time it's called, you'll be married to the king's cousin. Your wife sits on the Gathering. Two of the most influential lords and ladies will back you. No, I don't think the Gathering and your appointment will be as tough as you think."

"Maybe. All depends on if I accept this job." Leith smoothed his palms over his dark gray trousers. In the other room, the back door banged shut, and the noises stopped.

King Keevan nodded. "Of course."

Leith stared at a spot over King Keevan's head. Was this the future he was meant to have? Upholding Acktar's laws. Tracking down Rovers. "Do you think these new Blades—or whatever you call them—will work?"

"Yes. I'm counting on you to pick and train men of integrity who love this country and its laws more than their loyalty to their king. Men who will defy me if I ever give an order unworthy of them." King Keevan leaned forward. His eyes burned in a way Leith had never seen before. "I want you to create heroes."

"That's impossible." Leith crossed his arms.

"Then I want you to do the impossible. I hear you're good at that." King Keevan stared back. "This country will never be united by a religion or a king. But they will unite behind a band of heroes."

"You sure about that?"

"If a country can no longer unite behind its heroes, it

won't unite over anything." King Keevan smiled. "I don't think we're that far gone yet."

A band of heroes. Leith shook his head. King Keevan had high expectations.

And for some odd reason, Leith found himself sharing them.

SHE WAS GETTING MARRIED TODAY.

Finally.

Renna peered at herself in the cracked sliver of a mirror she and Brandi had salvaged from the ruins of Stetterly Manor and propped along the wall in Sheriff Allen's unfinished cabin. Her light blue dress fell in soft waves from her hips with a short train flowing behind her. After the wedding, she'd take off the train and wear this dress as her Sunday dress.

When she swished her skirt, her hair fell over her shoulder, straight as always, though Brandi and Jolene had helped her weave flowers into a crown and into her hair.

She smiled at the mirror. She didn't look like a princess. Or a queen. She looked like herself.

"Your parents would be proud of you." Lady Alistair straightened one of the flowers in Renna's hair.

Renna turned and hugged her. Lady Alistair had spent the morning telling stories about Renna's parents, keeping them close on today of all days. "Thank you. Can you do one more favor for me? Can you make sure Leith..." Renna wasn't sure how to word her question.

Lady Alistair kissed her cheek and swept toward the

door. "Henry already asked. Don't worry. Neither of you will lack for parents today."

Renna smiled as she turned back to the mirror and touched her silver cross necklace. Yes, she missed her parents and Uncle Abel and Aunt Mara. But she and Leith were still blessed today with an abundance of family and friends.

Only a few minutes after Lady Alistair left, a knock rattled the door. Renna turned. It wasn't time yet, was it? "Come in."

When the door opened, Martyn tottered inside, wincing at each step. He sank onto a bench. "Just making sure you hadn't come to your senses and bolted. I've seen you do it before."

Renna crossed her arms, trying to look severe. "No last minute, life-changing remarks?"

Martyn grinned. "No, and I won't drag you down the aisle either."

She shuddered at the memory of that almost wedding to Respen. So many things had been wrong with that day. "You're where you are supposed to be this time."

At Leith's side, guarding his back.

Martyn's shoulders rose and fell with a deep breath. "You too."

Renna couldn't help her smile. "Yes, I am."

Brandi stuck her head in. "You'd better be ready, Renna. Because ready or not, this thing is about to start."

Martyn's grin didn't waver. "It's time."

She stuck her hand out and pulled him to his feet. "Then you'd better get back there to Leith's side and make sure he gets down the aisle. Drag him if you have to."

"Don't think that will be necessary." Martyn staggered past Brandi, nearly running into Keevan.

Keevan dodged out of the way and made it to Renna's side. "All set?"

Renna took his arm. "Of course."

"Last chance to change your mind."

She shook her head at him. "You know I won't."

He shrugged, but his grin remained. "It was worth a try."

Brandi held the door open for them. On the porch, Lydia and Jolene waited, dressed in sweeping, royal blue dresses. They both gave Renna hugs before they strolled up the hill to the stone church building.

Brandi helped Renna hold up her skirt and train to keep it free of the spring mud puddles. At the doors of the church, Lydia peeked inside and nodded. She and Jolene swept inside. With a smirk, Brandi followed a moment later.

The music swelled, and it was Renna's turn. Keevan held the door for her, and the two of them strode into the long aisle. Bluebells scattered on the floor. People filled the benches on either side. Townsfolk from Stetterly. Soldiers from Walden. Somewhere near the front sat Kayleigh, Lady Lorraine, Lady Alistair, the rest of the Alistair siblings, and Queen Addie holding Prince Duncan.

At the front of the church, the circuit-riding minister stood with his hands clasped around his Bible. Behind him, Martyn leaned against Shad while Jamie and Ranson planted their feet like soldiers, their eyes darting back and forth as they scanned the crowd for trouble. Off to the side, Jolene, Lydia, and Brandi held bouquets of flowers.

But none of them really mattered. Not to Renna.

Three quarters of the way down the aisle, Leith clasped

his hands behind his back. His white shirt contrasted with his dark gray trousers and the black knife sheaths strapped across his chest. More knives glinted at his sides and tucked into his black boots. She had expected nothing less.

Lord Alistair stood at Leith's side, taking the place of the father Leith never had. Warmth filled Renna's chest.

When she and Keevan halted in front of Lord Alistair and Leith, Leith held out his hands, and Renna clasped them tightly. She fought a grin when she realized Leith's hands were just as clammy and shaky as her own.

Keevan rested his right hand on her and Leith's linked hands. "On behalf of Lady Faythe's deceased family and as the king of Acktar, I bless this union."

Lord Alistair also laid his right hand on theirs. "And on behalf of my friends Laurence and Annita Faythe, and on behalf of Lena Torren, I am honored to give my blessing to this marriage."

Lord Alistair and Keevan stepped away and claimed their seats. Renna managed not to trip as she and Leith walked the last few feet to stand in front of the minister. Somehow she made it through the ceremony and remembered to respond when asked to take Leith Torren, also known as Daniel Grayce, as her husband.

Leith squeezed her hands, and she smiled. Yes, this was exactly where she belonged.

NEXT THING LEITH KNEW, HE WAS LEADING RENNA FROM THE church sanctuary into the dazzle of the setting sun. The blaze of orange and pink arched above the rolling waves of the green, springtime prairie.

They emerged into a circle of groomsmen and bridesmaids. Jolene and Lydia pounced on Renna and gave her hugs. Leith barely stopped himself from drawing his knife when they also hugged him.

Shad hugged Renna and tugged on the end of her hair. "I still remember you in short skirts and mussed hair."

Renna ducked her head. "Not my best summer."

Shad slapped Leith on the shoulder. "I'm glad I didn't accidentally kill you when you first showed up in Walden. I like having another little brother."

Leith laughed, but he didn't have time to respond because Martyn had finished hugging Renna, and now slapped Leith on the back. Leith clasped Martyn's hand and pulled him into a hug. Nothing could've been more right than this. Leith's oldest friend and his new friends together as one family. All brothers.

Ranson and Jamie both claimed hugs from Renna and back-slapping hugs from Leith. More brothers. More family.

Then Brandi was there. She squeezed Renna so tightly Renna winced. After whispering something that turned Renna's nose and ears red, Brandi bounced to Leith, wrapped her arms around his waist, and squeezed. "I never told anyone, but I always wanted a brother even more than I wanted a horse."

Leith hugged her. Her head now reached his shoulder, a reminder that she wasn't the little girl he'd met over a year ago. She'd grown, both in height and in the things she'd seen and done. "I'm glad to be your brother."

Brandi stepped back and grinned. "No offense to Keevan,

but someday when I get married, I want you to walk with me down the aisle."

Leith's hands stilled on Brandi's shoulders. Something cold settled into his chest. Brandi wasn't a child anymore. She'd turn fifteen this summer. If she got married at the same age as Renna, then they had only three more years. Three short years.

Brandi didn't seem to notice. She spun from him, grabbed Jamie's arm, and dragged him off somewhere.

Renna leaned in closer. "Relax. Anyone Brandi ends up marrying is going to have to go through you first."

He touched the hilt of one of his knives. Whoever that boy was, he was going to have it rough. Leith almost pitied him.

Almost.

The doors of the church opened, and the rest of the guests poured out. Leith barely had time to think, much less talk to Renna, as everyone and his neighbor shook his hand, including people that had been calling for his blood a month ago. Strange how charitable weddings made people. Tomorrow they'd probably go back to shooting him dagger-filled looks, but today they were all smiles.

No one seemed to know what to call Renna. Some called her Lady Torren. Others Lady Grayce. Renna responded to either name just as graciously. Perhaps because she was now both the same way Leith was both. His past. His present. And now their future together with whatever name someone wanted to use.

After surviving the feast and rounds of toasts and generally being the center of attention, Leith finally slipped outside, Renna's hand still gripped in his. A dome of stars had replaced the sunset.

With a rustle, Martyn appeared out of the darkness. "I scouted the area. No sign of trouble."

Leith rested a hand on Martyn's shoulder and could feel him swaying. "Thanks. Now you should get some rest. You've already been up longer than the healers advised."

Martyn shook his head. "I'm fine. Don't worry, I'll close my eyes for a few minutes during Shad's watch."

The sound of hoofbeats broke the stillness, and Shad approached, leading Blizzard. "We'll be fine. There won't be any trouble tonight, and if there is, we can handle it."

Leith nodded. When Shad and Martyn melted back into the darkness to keep watch tonight, Leith turned to Renna and lifted her onto Blizzard's saddle.

She gripped the saddlehorn, sitting sideways because of her long skirt. "Are you sure we can't just walk?"

"The cabin is far enough that you wouldn't want to hike the distance in that dress." Leith patted Blizzard's neck. "I'll lead Blizzard. Brandi loaned him to me tonight to act as guard horse."

When Leith tugged Blizzard forward, Renna's knuckles went white on the saddlehorn, her legs tucking against Blizzard's side. The prairie rolled into darkness in the distance, filled with the chirping of thousands of crickets. A faint breeze rustled the grass into a night murmur. When they crested the far hill, Stetterly's lights faded into a glow on the horizon, plunging them into the gray haze of night.

As he neared the cabin he'd built at the edge of the Spires Canyon, Leith's heart hammered harder and harder in his chest. Yes, he was thinking about spending his first night with Renna as man and wife. But right now, his first worry was showing Renna her new home. She'd been raised in a manor, in luxury. Yes, she'd gotten used to a lot in the past few years, and she'd spent last winter in a hole in the ground. After that, anything would be an improvement.

But he didn't want her to like this cabin simply because it was better than a dugout. She had to love it. She had to feel like this was home. She'd been robbed of so much this past year, and this was his one chance to give her back a piece of it.

When they stopped beside the wide porch, a lantern already glowed inside, casting warm patches of orange against the dark grass outside.

He swung Renna down from Blizzard's back. "Um, well, this is it. Let me unsaddle Blizzard, then I'll show you inside."

Renna stepped onto the front porch, her eyes wide as she grazed her fingers along the railing. But she didn't say anything. Was that a good sign or a bad one?

Leith unsaddled and hobbled Blizzard as quickly as possible, setting the saddle on the far end of the railing and draping the bridle over it.

With a deep breath, he opened the cabin door. Renna took one step inside and gasped. "Leith, you...I can't believe..."

He closed the door and joined her next to the kitchen table. He'd done his best to recreate the kitchen from his memories of Stetterly Manor. A wooden table sat in the center of the room, two benches on either side of it. A wooden countertop stretched the length of the far wall with cabinets above and below. Bricks covered the floor, a few still bearing black scorch marks.

The one major change he'd done was move the fireplace to the middle of the cabin instead of against one wall. He'd been told that would heat the cabin more efficiently in the winter, and it allowed him to use the solid stone column of the chimney as a support post for the rest of the cabin around it.

Renna knelt and touched the floor. "From the manor?"

He nodded. He'd spent hours prying them up by hand to prevent damaging them. "I was able to save most of the floor and the fireplace hearth to use here."

She stood and inspected the fireplace. "And an oven built into the side. Perfect."

Brandi had assured him that feature would make it easier for Renna to bake more of those maple sugar cookies. "I started on a matching one outside to avoid heating the cabin in the summer."

She moved from the fireplace to the white railing that separated the kitchen from the small parlor taking up the other half of the front of the cabin. It was one step up onto the wooden floor of this room, and the other rooms in the cabin. "This is also from Stetterly Manor."

They'd managed to salvage just enough of the railing that had once surrounded the upper gallery overlooking Stetterly Manor's ballroom. He cleared his throat. "There's a gate that can be closed over the steps."

One of the farmer's wives had given him that idea. She'd told him, with a rather knowing look, that it would make it easier for Renna to have children playing in the parlor without worrying about them crawling into the fireplace.

Leith pointed at the doorway leading off the parlor.

"Jamie and Ranson can have that room, at least until we can build a stable with a spare room above it. They'll want their own space before too long. Brandi already claimed the loft bedroom."

Renna craned her neck, and Leith followed her gaze up the small, steep staircase he'd built curving around the fireplace, to the space above the two bedrooms. A wall separated most of the loft from view, though a narrow ledge with a railing ran along its length. The ceiling over the kitchen and parlor remained open all the way to the roof, exposing the beams.

Leith took Renna's hand again and led her up the step into the bedroom leading off the kitchen. This room was stark, a few pegs on the wall holding clothes and a straw tick on the floor. When a strange look crossed Renna's face, Leith winced. He'd known this wouldn't be what Renna was used to.

Renna turned and gasped. "Where did that come from?"

Leith turned and eyed the large, oak wardrobe taking up the entire wall next to the door. Ornate carving covered both the moulding and the base. "I assume that's King Keevan's wedding gift. Now I understand why he said it was for you."

Renna patted his arm and pointed at the four small drawers below the wardrobe's large, double doors. "All your clothes fit in a saddlebag. One drawer should be more than enough for you."

True. He probably would have room to spare.

"I have one last thing to show you." He tugged her out another door leading back outside. Here, the porch wrapped around the side of the cabin facing the Spires Canyon only a few yards away from them. Deep in the canyon, treefrogs sang alongside the Ondieda River. The breeze purred through the stands of pine trees. At the far end of the porch, he'd built a bench swing with tightly braided ropes holding it to the roof beams.

His heart had clawed its way into his throat. Why didn't she say something? Was she that disappointed with it? All she did was stare at the Spires Canyon. "What do you think? Do you like it?"

She spun on her heels, and Leith caught the glimmer of tears in her eyes. That couldn't be good.

But she wrapped her arms around his neck. "Leith, it's beautiful. I was expecting a rough, one-room cabin. Not…not this. This—the loft and the oven and the pieces of Stetterly Manor—it's so much more than I dared dream. Thank you."

He held her for a moment, savoring the feel of her in his arms. But something she said distracted him. "Wait, you were expecting a one-room cabin, yet you knew Brandi, Jamie, and Ranson are planning on bunking with us?"

She gave a small shudder. "Yes. Believe me, I wasn't looking forward to it. Even with all the spare rooms, we aren't going to have a whole lot of privacy, are we? Not once they move in at the end of the week."

"The walls in the cabin are extra thick and sturdy. No chance of eavesdroppers." Or intruders, but he wasn't going to mention the cabin's defenses tonight. Leith kissed her forehead. "And I was thinking, after the Gathering this summer, we should travel to the Sheered Rock Hills, just the two of us. I can show you Eagle Heights and what Brandi calls the sparkling cave and a few waterfalls even Brandi hasn't seen. If that sounds like something you'd like to do. I know you don't enjoy riding."

"As long as I can ride double with you, I'll be fine." Renna leaned her head against his shoulder. She shivered and tucked her hands against his chest. "Though you don't have to come to the Gathering. Won't it be dangerous if someone recognizes you?"

Leith exhaled, and his breath misted into the night air. He stepped back from Renna. "You're cold. Here." He picked up the blanket he'd left on the swing and wrapped it around her shoulders. When she was warmly bundled up, he perched on the swing, pulling her against him. Renna leaned against his chest, and he wrapped his arms around her.

If he could, he'd remain silent and soak up the moment. But Renna had asked a question, and he had to give her the answer he'd discussed with King Keevan earlier that day, even if he wasn't sure how Renna would react.

"Actually, I do have to be there. Lord Norton will bring up my name at his trial, and Keevan believes the best way to outmaneuver him is to present the truth of my past to the Gathering before Lord Norton does."

Renna stiffened and tipped her head up to look at him. "Are you all right with that?"

"Yes. It's time." After a whole morning to get used to the idea, Leith had to admit it was the best option. The truth might have its consequences, but it also healed. So many families had questions about how their loved ones were killed and why. Even if Leith hadn't done the deed himself, he'd know which Blade did. He could provide those families with the closure they needed. Leith swallowed. "There's more. Keevan also offered me a job."

"What?" Renna swiveled in his arms. "Really? What is it

with men and making last-minute announcements on wedding days? He couldn't have just waited until tomorrow?"

"His way of exacting a bit of revenge, I guess." Leith shrugged.

"So what's this job? What does he want you to do?"

Leith's heart was doing its hammering thing again. Why was he so nervous telling her about this? "He wants to start a band of men to patrol the stretches of prairie between the towns to catch Rovers. It'd be like the Blades, just without the killing part. Keevan wants me to lead it."

She stilled and stared off into the Spires Canyon, her muscles stiff beneath Leith's hands.

Leith cleared his throat. "It would be dangerous, and I would probably have to be gone a lot, especially at first when there won't be enough men trained to cover the entire country."

"Are you trying to convince me or talk yourself out of it?" Renna turned back to him, lines wrinkling her forehead.

"I'm just pointing out the dangers. I told Keevan I'd have to ask you, and I don't want you to make a decision without knowing the dangers." Now he was starting to babble. He snapped his mouth shut.

"Will Martyn join?"

"Yes, if I do. So will Shad." Leith struggled not to clench his fists. He didn't want this job. Not really.

Renna sighed and leaned against him once again. "Then you'd better tell Keevan yes."

"What? You want me to say yes?"

She looked up at him and touched his cheek. "I always knew, deep down, that you'd end up with something like this. As much as you might enjoy spending a couple of weeks planting a few rows of corn, you aren't cut out to be a farmer your whole life. I firmly believe you'll do great things for Acktar, and someday you'll be remembered more for the things you have yet to do than your past."

Leith grinned, a heady warmth filling his chest. There was nothing quite as fulfilling to a man's ego as hearing his wife say she was proud of him, even if Renna's dream of the future was so grandiose it was almost embarrassing. Though not enough that Leith would stop her from saying it. "You think so?"

"Of course." Her nod scrubbed a few of the flowers from her hair onto his shoulder. "I know Martyn and Shad will always do their best to bring you home to me. And if worse comes to worst, I will survive it." She turned her face into his shoulder. "Though, I pray it never happens."

"Me too." Leith kissed her hair. "If it ever gets too much... I promise you right now, all you'll have to do is ask, and I'll quit."

Renna tensed, and she hugged his arms tighter. When she spoke, her voice had the same fierce quality she'd had when she'd thrown herself between Respen and Leith. "And I promise you, I'll never ask. Never."

"You don't—"

She twisted and clamped a hand over his mouth. "No, don't say it. I'll keep my promise as surely as you'll keep yours, Leith Daniel Grayce Torren. This is what you're meant to do, and you'll be good at it, and, God willing, you'll always come home to me. Got it?"

He nodded and tucked her against him.

They sat in silence for a few minutes, Leith rocking the swing slowly with his foot.

"Leith?"

"Hmm?"

"I know you like to be prepared and all, but this would be a lot more comfortable without your knives poking me in the back."

"Oh, sorry." Leith straightened and wiggled out of the crossed leather straps holding his knives across his chest. He dropped it onto the porch floor next to him, then unbuckled his knife belt and placed it aside as well. With Martyn and Shad on guard tonight, he wouldn't need his knives.

Though, he left his boot sheaths in place. Just in case.

Renna reclaimed her spot. "So much better."

And there, with the tree frogs chorusing in harmony with the breeze in the pines and Renna cradled in his arms, Leith knew.

He was home.

of Acktar. Will they be able to arrest their quarry before they are caught themselves?

From the story of how Leith and Martyn met to Ranson's search for a life outside of the Blades, these stories will answer plaguing questions and expand the world of Acktar.

Buy Now

FREE STORY!

Deal
A Blades of Acktar Short Story

Once there was a nine-year-old boy Leith Torren who only wanted to bring food home to his mother...and was noticed by Lord Respen Felix of Blathe.

Free for newsletter subscribers. Sign up at https://triciamingerink.com/my-newsletter/

ALSO BY TRICIA MINGERINK

DAGGER'S SLEEP

A prince cursed to sleep.
A princess destined to wake him.
A kingdom determined to stop them.

High Prince Alexander has been cursed to a sleep like unto death, a curse that will end the line of the high kings and send the Seven Kingdoms of Tallahatchia into chaos. With his manservant to carry his luggage and his own superior intelligence to aid him, Alex sets off to find one of the Fae and end his curse one way or another.

A hundred years later, Princess Rosanna learns she is the princess destined by the Highest King to wake the legendary sleeping prince. With the help of the mysterious Daemyn Rand, can she find the courage to finish the quest as Tallahatchia wavers on the edge of war?

One curse connects them. A hundred years separate them. From the rushing rivers of Tallahatchia's mountains to the hall of the Highest King himself, their quests will demand greater sacrifice than either of them could imagine.

For readers of adventure, fairy tales, and stirring allegories comes this fresh imagining of the classic Sleeping Beauty tale, the first book in a new YA fantasy series from Tricia Mingerink

Buy Now!

BOOKS BY TRICIA MINGERINK

The Blades of Acktar

Dare

Deny

Defy

Destroy: A novella

Deliver

Decree

Beyond the Tales

Dagger's Sleep

Midnight's Curse

Poison's Dance

ACKNOWLEDGMENTS

After four books, I'm running out of ways to say thank you to the same amazing people who started this journey with me and have stuck with it for two years now.

I don't know what I'd do without the support of my family. They keep things running even when I'm abandoning all my responsibilities to finish this book. Thanks to my parents for being supportive, my brothers for being brothers in the best sort of way, and my sister-in-laws for being the sisters I never had growing up.

A special thanks to my friends (especially Jill, Bri, and Paula) for sticking with me even when I cut out my personal social life to finish this book. I'm glad I can always know you'll be there for me when I come up for air.

Thanks to Nadine, Katie, and Ashley for being the best roomies ever, talking me through the tough parts of this draft when I needed it, and giving me the boost to finish it last summer.

Sierra, the best critique partner in the world, for reading this book nearly as many times as I did and helping me figure out what needed to go to the chopping block to make it a manageable book.

A huge thank you to Wanda Bruinsma, Mindy Bergman, and all the early readers who helped proofread!

All my other writer friends who encourage and support me. Your prayers and chats are much appreciated.

But most of all, to my Heavenly Father, my Captain and King.

www.ingramcontent.com/pod-product-compliance
Lightning Source LLC
Chambersburg PA
CBHW071428190726
48292CB00001B/157